# THE FORBIDDEN FAE KING

DYING LANDS
BOOK ONE

ROSA HEART

# ALSO BY

## ROSA HEART

DYING LANDS SERIES

The Forbidden Fae King
A War of Three Kings

A Heart of Two Realms (FREE Prequel)
Download at www.rosaheart.com

# CONTENT GUIDANCE

**Tropes:** Strong FMC. Huntress. Enemies-to-lovers. Forbidden love. Secret identity. Parallel magical realms. Elemental magic. Emotional scars. He falls first. Dangerous love interest. Forced proximity. Found family. Magical creatures.

**Content Warning:** Explicit sex (M/F). On-page battles and killing. Gore. Past loss of loved ones. Mild emotional and physical abuse (not MMC, no SA). Kidnapping. Pregnancy (side character). Misogynistic behavior.

～

*Those who were seen dancing*
*were thought to be insane*
*by those who could not hear the music*

— Anonymous

～

.

# CHAPTER I
# KEIRA

My body moves in time with my mare, her galloping hoofbeats in sync with my racing heart. The wind rushes at my face, throwing my hair back and offsetting the hot steam that rises from the horse's body in her exertion. The thick trees of the ancient woods fly past, a blur of brown and evergreen. My soul soars with the thrill of the chase.

It is the only time I feel free. Alive.

Another horse rushes in beside me, its hooves pounding on the narrow path, carrying the lean form of my sister. Caitlin flashes a quick smile at me as she darts past, a bow tucked under one arm and a sword strapped to her back. Her bright auburn hair flicks up and down in a cloud of thin braids behind her.

A great horn bellows in the forest nearby and we both turn our horses sharply in its direction, their legs prancing. The shouts of men and women calling to each other follows.

The hunt has begun.

Electricity runs through my veins as I scan the hills above the narrow, craggy valley I pause in. Horses barrel past us through the trees of the rise, their riders threatening to take our prize. I grit my teeth and will my mare forward.

We cannot lose to Gwyneth. I could handle the taunts that would go on for weeks, but Caitlin? Her prickly pride would not allow it.

My sister spurs to action, galloping her mount up the slope in quick bounds. A light spray of mud splatters my face as I follow close behind and I wipe it away with the back of a hand. The air is rich with an earthy scent, combined with bruised pine needles.

My mare struggles with her footing up the incline, sliding after each jolt forward. I crest the rise to a natural clearing, and the forms of the Protector Guard ahead of us are silhouettes to the west, falling into the treeline again.

A second horn bellows, the call long and low.

There are two packs of low fae to hunt? Far too many have crept through the gaps in the barriers between realms to threaten our lands.

"Keira. To the west," Caitlin snaps, then looks over my shoulder with disgust. "This is going to be a glorious hunt, if our guards can keep up."

I glance back at the men riding on our heels, in their bronze leather pants and quilted emerald surcoats sown in with iron discs, the emblem of our house embroidered on the left breast. Caitlin wears the same uniform.

"They weren't raised in these woods like us." When I turn back, my sister is already speeding away, a lone figure darting across the opening.

She is too headstrong and reckless.

There is danger in being caught in the woods alone. Especially during a hunt. We don't know which kind of fae is trespassing on our lands. It could be any kind of monstrosity. Fae do not belong here. This realm is for humans alone.

I take off at a full gallop, fighting to keep up. Blood crashes through me, and every muscle is taut with anticipation. My gaze flicks around, scanning for threats. For the beasts unfortunate enough to be our prey.

The nearby horn bellows again, three short blasts indicating the number of fae spotted here. The forms of the trackers and their small, spotted foxhounds are visible just beyond the trees as they chase our quarry, rounding it up then skirting away, staying at a safe distance.

I grab an iron-tipped ash arrow from the quiver at my back and nock it to my bow, squeezing my mount with my thighs and hardly slowing her pace. The creatures of the Otherworld release a high-pitched, earsplitting howl, both vicious and sorrowful.

Goosebumps raise on my arms and my stomach turns with the fear that is inevitable before the fight.

Our party slows marginally as we crash into the thicket, scanning between the wide, lichen-covered trunks of trees hundreds of years old.

A Cú Sídhe stalks through the forest. Time slows. It almost stops. The fae hound is as large as a horse and the cavities of its eye sockets stare back at me with ethereal green lights. Its entire skull is nothing but exposed bone, housing sharp teeth each the length of a finger.

The creature's body is covered in thick, furry moss, intertwined with prickly branches and twigs, and its feet are exposed bone. It snarls and bites the air.

Potent relief cascades through me. My prey is a monster indeed. It could have been a brownie, or a nymph, or any less sinister fae to unwittingly step into my realm. A creature that would beg for mercy, and I would have to kill it anyway, despite how my heart broke.

The beast gallops toward me, its powerful legs leaping over fallen trees and rocks.

I stand in my stirrups as my horse races in an arc around the beast. Twisting my body to the side, I nock an arrow to the bow, breathe in, breathe out, and let it fly. It cuts through the air, and I weave threads of magic around the whistling shaft, directing its path and pushing force into it to create an even deadlier missile.

The Cú Sídhe lunges into the air, completely unaware of its doom. The leafy strands of its pelt flutter like a majestic mane. It bounces off a fallen log, using the hurdle to lunge higher in the air.

My magic pulls the arrow into its new trajectory, piercing the creature through its gaping maw.

I weave a dozen more strands of air into that arrow shaft as it collides with the beast, throwing the entirety of its bulk backward. The magic radiates out from the initial point of contact with the strength of a typhoon, breaking its bones and crushing the fae from within.

I could shatter it into a thousand pulpy pieces, but we need the body.

The Cú Sídhe curls in on itself and its spine hits the broad trunk of a tree with a sickening crunch, then it falls to the ground in a limp heap.

The poor thing never stood a chance.

Not against an enemy that can kill it from a distance. A deep sadness rolls through me at the thought. I am a terrible executioner.

The sound of another beast crashing through the woods has me swinging in my saddle.

Three arrows glide through the air in fast succession, also fueled by magic, piercing the creature in a neat row. The sheer impact has its huge form jerking violently. It skids through the leaf litter and mud with velocity, leaving a long furrow of disturbed soil and vegetation around it.

There is only one other person in our band capable of such weaves of air.

Caitlin breaks through the foliage after her prey, a huge grin across her face. I swear the hunt is the only time she looks truly happy. A fire burns within her small emerald eyes and specks of mud accompany her dusting of freckles.

"No other fae gives the same thrill as hunting Cú Sídhe." My sister laughs.

Chittering echoes nearby, followed by the warning shouts of men. Worry flares through me. It is a rare day that we lose one of our people on the hunt, but my heart could not bear it if a guard died on my watch.

I sharply bank my mare toward the fight. My horse leaps over stony outcrops and I am forced to duck under low branches that fly past, but I do not slow my pace.

I nock an arrow as the trees fall away to a shore of polished, colorful stones and ride into the shallow stream at its center. Icy droplets of water splash onto the exposed skin of my ankles, sending a shock through my skin.

On the opposite bank, three men approach the third fae, cornering it. This Cú Sídhe is far smaller than its recently dead brethren, and the dark browns of its mossy fur are akin to dead and rotting leaf litter. Its snarl exposes yellow teeth, with many missing. A scent of decay rolls off the creature, and even at this distance, my stomach rolls.

Another abomination.

The three mounted Protector Guards shout orders at each other as they coordinate their attack, surrounding the beast. I wait while my horse prances on the spot.

This is their kill.

Brandan fires arrows into the fae's flank, but without a mastery of elemental magic, they are mere inconveniences to the beast. The two other guards, brothers, throw spears tipped in flames, but their quarry moves with lightning speed, evading the missiles then snapping at their horses, causing them to rear.

Both brothers lose their seats and roll from their horses' back to the ground.

My heart rate accelerates, but I continue to hold back.

Liam leaps to his feet first, all golden hair and pale skin where the Cú Sídhe is shadows and darkness. He pulls his sword from its scabbard and engulfs the blade in tongues of blue flame, then charges. The hound chitters and yelps, backing away from those flames.

Cú Sídhe fear fire, as creatures of leaves and moss.

Aiden, the younger brother, sneaks behind the beast that is focused on Liam's attack and his matching sword of fire prevents the fae's retreat. In multiple fluid motions, both brothers skewer the beast again and again, their quick footwork slipping them in and away before the Cú Sídhe's claws catch them.

The invader swipes frantically from side to side, as it cannot decide which man to gut. It becomes clumsy as blood seeps from it and smoke rolls from the wounds, then it thunders to the ground, almost crushing Liam beneath its weight.

I smile at my guards as pride fills me, but it falters as the Cú Sídhe's pelt immediately whooshes up in flames.

"The gods damn it!" Liam spits as he attempts to throw handfuls of water onto the fire.

With a gentle twist of the wrist, I guide a volley of air into the stream, and a wave crashes down on the fire and the men fanning it alike. I bite back a smile as three sets of eyes narrow on me, rivulets of water running down the men's faces.

"Thank you, Lady Keira. Could you not send enough water to drown us next time?" There is a hint of humor in Liam's voice.

I lead my mare to the shore and dismount. "If I had left it up to you, there would be only ashes for the druids to inspect. I bet they will pay you a decent price for a Twisted One."

"There will be no eating this fae bastard," Brandan adds. "Excuse the language, Lady."

Aiden spits on the ground in reply.

Some would frown at my familiarity with the Protector Guard, but my father, the lord protector, is not one of those people.

I lift my parted riding skirts as I approach so the jade wool doesn't drag in mud and toss the flame-red curls of my hair over my shoulder, then crouch before the Cú Sídhe.

There are black clumps of mushrooms in its grassy fur, and mushy leaves fall from its form. They are rotting and covered in a spotted blight. The blood that clots its fur is black as tar, unlike the crimson that spills from healthy beasts.

There is a sickness in the Otherworld of the fae. The idea of it spreading here sends a shiver down my spine. It is just another threat from which we defend our kingdom of Strathia.

The entire North of this land is the domain of the Appleshield Protectorate; my father the lord protector and his Protector Guard are the shield held against the fae. The first line of defense when the worlds align and creatures slip through the cracks from their realm into ours.

If there is another fae invasion, we of the North will meet them in battle first. It is here where the veil between worlds is thinnest, and it is here where they always seem to trespass.

The lords of the south, east and west have become soft and indulgent because the fae threats never slip through our protectorate into their lands.

A high-pitched horn blows two fast blasts from behind me, marking both Caitlin's and my kill. Liam pulls a brass horn from his saddlebag and matches the call with a beat of his own.

A crash of galloping hooves vibrates the ground and shakes the trees on the far bank of the creek. Branches swish as a creature charges through their depths. I leap to my feet, feeling at my back for the bow I left on my horse. The Protector Guards form a wall in front of me, weapons at the ready.

There were only three horn blasts at the beginning of our hunt, marking three beasts. The trackers could have missed a fae. Another could have just entered through a rift in the barrier between worlds.

My heart skips a beat.

Caitlin bursts through the tree cover with a handful of guards on her tail, circling us as she slows her mount. Not another fae beast.

"A Twisted One." Caitlin's lips press into a thin line as she examines it. We are always fearful of finding a Twisted One. It is an infection that can take any kind of fae, and we are terrified that we humans might catch it too. Caitlin's emerald gaze flicks to me. "Your kill or theirs?"

I tip my head toward Liam, Aiden and Brandan. Their backs straighten and their chests puff out under her scrutiny.

"You men made enough noise killing it. I heard so much snarling and yelling from a league away, I thought there was a whole damned army of men and fae at battle." Caitlin huffs a breath, then double takes. "There are only three of you. You did well. You have my invitation to the feast tonight." She nods to them, then turns away, not seeing the way their faces light up as they turn to each other in amazement.

"Thank you, Commander Appleshield," they say.

I suppress a smile. Caitlin has no idea of the imposing figure she cuts, despite being slim in build. She is the leader of our troops and heir to the lord protector, outranking the Captain of the Protector Guard. Her approval and invitation to the feast is an immense honor to these guards.

The healthy fae beasts slaughtered on today's hunt will be roasted over a spitfire and served with delicacies tonight. Their meat tastes like venison, bursting with earthy flavors.

Any who dine on it will have the creature's raw magic infused into their blood. It is the only way we can recapture their magic. It is almost gone from our human bloodlines, seeping away more and more with each generation.

This opportunity is so great that the king and his entourage travel to our lands during these festivals, sometimes staying for weeks to consume as much power as possible.

My head spins at the thought of the prince's arrival. His handsome face flashes within my mind's eye. The blue-black curl that hangs over his pale face. The dimpled smile he saves just for me.

I startle from my daydream as Caitlin leans down from her saddle and says something to me.

She frowns at my blank expression. "I asked, do you feel sorry for these creatures too, when you kill them?" Her words are soft, so only I can hear them.

I glance at the rapidly decaying Cú Sídhe. The areas of extensive rot blow away like ash on a breeze, revealing healthier flesh beneath. We still wouldn't risk eating it.

"Not that one. It seems a mercy to kill a Twisted One and end its suffering. The others?" I lick my lips, my throat suddenly dry. "No. Not predators like the Cú Sídhe."

Caitlin leaps down from her horse in a single, graceful motion and pulls me to the side, out of earshot. "You need to harden that heart of yours, Keira. Especially if you are going to lead a kingdom one day. How can you put down a rebellion if you struggle to kill a fae invader on our lands?"

I drag in a sharp breath, but I know she is right.

Caitlin continues her tirade. "All fae are dangerous in our lands. Predators like the Cú Sídhe have attacked the villages before and will destroy our natural ecosystem. The fae that can manipulate and beg for their lives are as capable of doing the same. Imagine if an entire tribe of pixies crossed over and carved out a little kingdom for themselves in our woods.

"Going to war with them would be a nightmare. Fighting an army of them would be like standing in the path of a hundred arrows and attempting to cut them out of the sky. And if the pixies take a kingdom here, then why not the sprites and nymphs and goblins? How long until they go back to their old ways and start hurting humans? Or, the gods forbid, the high fae cross too."

"I know. Gods, I know," I half whisper. "But they seem so vulnerable and lost in a foreign land."

"Perhaps it is a strength that you see the good in all creatures, but don't let their glamour blind you to their true nature. The same applies to people." Caitlin's gaze pierces mine, and it seems she will say more, but the sound of multiple footfalls crunching on leaf litter turns her away.

A handful of druids step out of the woods. Their simply cut robes of rough brown cotton billow around them. I find their youngest and tallest member, my brother Diarmuid.

His shoulder-length, mousy brown hair is ruffled as usual and his hazel eyes, which match my own, dart around the scene. Diarmuid is Caitlin's opposite, all dashing smiles and mischievous charm, despite being her younger twin.

Diarmuid nods to Caitlin and winks at me, a half-smile playing across his lips, but he follows his graying mentors as they lift their robes and walk through the stream.

I cringe at the sight of a few walking barefoot through that icy water and over the pebble bank. A lifetime of living as one with nature has probably hardened the soles of their feet.

The druids congregate around the Twisted One, muttering between each other. One dons the thick leather gloves of a blacksmith as she examines the beast, turning it over and lifting its legs. Another scrapes at the decay, securing samples in glass jars. Mushrooms, rotting leaves, black fur, they are all plucked from the Cú Sídhe.

I watch with rapt fascination. The customs of the highly secretive druids are fascinating. They form a circle and start chanting in soft murmurs, the tone low in pitch and slowly rising. Their language is foreign and their many voices overlap with different notes.

At the crescendo, a near shout, they raise their hands high above their heads, then drop them sharply. Air rushes around them, blowing leaf litter in spirals, circling in closer and closer to the fae.

The chant repeats until a bubble of moving air constricts around the Twisted One. Their strange magic lifts the creature off the ground in a storm-like torrent that has the hems of their robes drifting in toward that containment of magic.

The druid masters suddenly cut off their chanting and disappear into the forest with their quarry, immediately melting into their surroundings. They leave behind their apprentice, my brother.

Diarmuid strides to the three Protector Guards, who have their heads bowed in respect. I should have looked away during their cere-mony, but I couldn't help myself.

My brother pulls a coin purse from deep within his robe and places a few gold coins in each man's hands, purchasing the beast from its hunters. The druids will examine it, then turn it into potions.

Liam looks as though he will cry at the amount, enough to match his fiancée's dowry and pay for their wedding, while Aiden actually laughs. Brandan wipes a tear from his cheek.

I give Caitlin a sidelong glance, noting the tension coiled in her shoulders and the foot she taps. She will be the custodian of these lands and people after our father. If this disease among the fae gets worse, if it spreads to our realm, it will be her problem to solve.

The boundaries between realms are thinnest here in the North. If there is a natural disaster brewing in the fae world, it will bleed through to us first.

"It's getting worse," Diarmuid calls out as he passes over pebbles that tumble and slide beneath his footfalls. He wears good, stout boots, and his robes are of better cut and fabric than his masters'.

There's no taking the nobility out of Diarmuid, despite his years training with the druids. "There is something plaguing the lower fae in the Otherworld. My mentor doesn't believe it will spread to the inhabitants of our world, but—"

I don't let him finish before I barrel into him with a hug, wrapping my arms around his bony body. He gives me a lopsided smile and squeezes me with one arm.

"I rarely see you anymore and this is how you say hello?" I laugh.

Caitlin gives him a quick embrace. "When do you become a full druid, Diarmuid? You are twenty-six and as smart as any of them."

"You know the training takes decades, Caitlin," Diarmuid replies.

"Perhaps *you* don't need decades. You were well schooled before you were initiated."

"Perhaps the order is the one thing in these lands that neither you nor Father get a say in." Diarmuid's smile grows wider as Caitlin huffs, but the corners of her mouth also lift.

My eyes dart between them. "How many fae crossed into our realm today?"

"Two packs." Diarmuid frowns. "Five healthy Cú Sídhe, and three Twisted Ones in total."

"A pack of five? Taken down by Gwyneth's hunting band?" Caitlin asks. "The damn woman will never let me live that down!"

"There will be more hunts between now and Beltane," I chime in happily.

"More hunts and more feasts. I could drink to that!" Caitlin places an arm around Diarmuid's shoulders and leads him away from the clearing. "And you said this plague won't infect our realm? Our people and animals are safe from it?"

"Potentially. We believe it might be a matter of breeding that causes it." Diarmuid's voice is almost lost to me over the gurgling of the shallow stream as we cross it.

The tension drops from Caitlin's shoulders and she talks excitedly about the feasts and hunts to come. A lump forms in my throat.

My sister won't be here for all those events.

When the realms reach full alignment this spring equinox, the portals will open and humans will cross into the fae realm. It happens every seven years. We do not send armies or male warriors. Only our women step through the portals into the vicious fae lands, alone and almost completely unarmed, to bring fae magic back to our kingdom.

This year, Caitlin will make the pilgrimage into the fae realm.

# CHAPTER 2

# KEIRA

We take the descent through the woods at a leisurely pace, a procession of the Protector Guard and Trackers of the Hunt, led by Caitlin. I follow directly behind her, and Diarmuid walks beside my horse, refusing a mount of his own.

Thin mists hug the edges of the path that cuts through stone bluffs and between hills covered in pines, birches and twisted oaks. Intermittent drizzles fall in the lightest kiss, stealing the heat from my skin

An ecstatic high still rolls through me from the freedom of galloping through the forest and the empowerment of using my magic to protect my people.

The hunt is the only time I feel such purpose.

I hum a low song as my mare's footfalls clop on the road and slide on the slick moss that coats everything like a natural carpet. The entire valley seems to sing with me, birdsong, the trickle of tiny waterfalls and the many echoing hooves ringing on stone from our party.

My mind drifts between cozy daydreams. Taking a hot bath. Reading a romance novel while curled up beneath furs. The bright blue eyes of my prince shining at the sight of me, then becoming hooded, as we reunite after months. His fingers running through my hair, unbuttoning the front of my dress, slipping inside the neckline —

"What will you do with your kill?" Diarmuid absolutely shatters my fantasy.

"Sorry?" My mind returns to the present begrudgingly. "Oh, the Cú Sídhe? I haven't thought about it. The meat will go to the feast, the blood and organs I will give to the druids for their potions, and the fur I will sell. It is good for a woman to have a little money that doesn't come from her father or husband."

Diarmuid's brows knit. "You don't have a husband yet. Nor do you have a fiancé. And I know it is as good as promised, but—" Diarmuid holds up his hands as I glare at him. "But I wouldn't count on it until vows are made. Kings act on a whim. They do what is best for their people. And princes — well, they do what their king and duty demand of them."

My entire expression falls. "Have you heard something?"

"I want to protect my little sister. You give your heart away too freely. And not just to him. You were devastated the last time a guard did not come home from a hunt. A guard."

"I don't know how to be any other way." I leave so much unsaid.

How could I not know every one of the guards' names and faces? Not listen to their stories about their loved ones? Our Protector Guards devote their lives to defending our family.

Caring is the least I could do.

What is the point of having a person in my life, a sibling, a friend, a lover, if I don't give my all to them? By giving out our hearts, piece by piece, we gain so much more. Not only vulnerability.

I trust Prince Finan. He has given his promise of love and a future together, and that is all I need.

The road twists around a bend, then opens into a grassy bowl surrounded by walls of slate, where the other hunting party waits for us. The Captain of the Protector Guard vaults down from her horse, the intricate layers of braids in her long, jet-black hair flying in the air with the motion.

She starts slow-clapping as she nears Caitlin.

"Well, look who finally made it. I hear your party killed three Cú Sídhe. Isn't that cute." Gwyneth's voice bounces around the valley.

Caitlin dismounts and meets her. "Had the two packs combined, I could have killed all the beasts with just Keira. You got lucky."

"Oh, is that right?" Gwyneth puts an arm around Caitlin's shoulders, pulling her into her side. "That's something I'd pay to see. The mighty Caitlin, heir to the seat of Lord Protector of Appleshield, destroying a horde of fae beasts with her willpower alone. You know, I think if anyone could do it, it might be you. Of course, if I'm not there with my sword and spear first."

Caitlin wipes a splattering of mud and blood from Gwyneth's high cheekbone, and a look of utter devotion flashes across the captain's face. It matches Caitlin's own expression.

The moment is too intimate, and I turn away.

No one has ever looked at me that way, not even my prince. A stab of pain slices through my chest, but I shove it away. Not everyone shows their heart across their face for all to see.

My horse prances on the spot, picking up on my agitation, and I dismount.

Men and women of the guard lounge on the damp grass or tumbled slabs of stone, sharing a light lunch in groups. Voices high with excitement echo around me.

I pass the corpses of the Cú Sídhe, trussed up on a long pole of pine for transport. Their forms are immense, in varying shades of green.

My feet take me to the ring of stones encircling a grassy meadow large enough to fit a hundred people. The ancient slabs are hacked into rough rectangular shapes, taller and wider than any man, and piled on top of each other to form arches.

I run my fingers across the slick surface of granite that shimmers with a hundred shades of gray, broken up by the rough texture of yellow lichen.

Within the center, the Tower stands as tall as any castle's turret. The narrow building is completely hollow, with a grand external staircase wrapping around its outer wall, spiraling up to a flat roof.

Great arches follow the curve of the steps. I can see right through the Tower, no matter how I circle around it.

The stonework has corroded over the years, and surfaces that were once engraved with runes and decorations are now heavily pitted.

The Tower pulls me toward it and I wonder if it is imbued with some ancient, dark fae magic. We used to race to its top as children, Caitlin, Diarmuid and I. Never Brianna; she was always considered too small.

There is a single plinth of pure jade at its peak with thousands of fae runes cut into it. I used to trace it with parchment and thought that I would translate their language as an adult. That I would march straight into the Otherworld and demand they teach me their runes.

I had such ambitious, frivolous dreams as a child.

On the day of the spring equinox, the priestesses and druids will come together at the Tower and feed their magic into the jade plinth to open the portals to the Otherworld. It is only when our two worlds align every seven years that our magic is enough to open the paths between them.

Once, we had infinitely more magic, when the fae still walked our realm and contributed to our bloodlines, and the portals were always open, regardless of the year. Back then, even minor mages had enough power to activate a portal at will.

But we were at the fae's mercy, little more than slaves, and their atrocities piled up until we purged them from our lands.

I stride beneath the Tower, and look straight up.

The jade stone at its apex is visible through slits in the ceiling. In the center of the ground before me is a small jade altar, directly beneath the plinth. Its basin is filled with murky water and dried leaves, with four channels in a cross section that catch liquid magic and split it.

Each has a rune for a season: a spiral sun, a leaf, a snowflake and a flower. A directory of sorts to the portals that lead to the Summer, Autumn, Winter and Spring courts that surround the Tower in a full ring.

My feet follow the path of the flower bud, out of the Tower and across uneven grass, to another magic-splitting altar at the boundary of the ancient ring of stones. Beyond are ten portals that lead to the Spring Court, all lying dormant.

Each portal is a ring of cloudy moonstone, its colors muted by the dust that has collected on it, inserted straight into the stone of the mountain. A thin path winds through the jagged face of the bluff at a sharp incline to allow passage to each portal, some at the height of a small building.

In their dormant state, each doorway only leads a few paces into the mountain.

I inspect them for a long while, and only turn as the scuff of boots approaches from behind.

"Have you decided which one to take?" I glance over my shoulder at Caitlin.

We have spent years poring over every ancient book and scroll we can find on the fae to plan her journey to the Otherworld. The wilds of the Spring Court best suit her skill set and experience.

"That one." She points at a portal. "I will make my crossing through that one."

I glance at the doorway. It looks exactly like all the others. The knowledge of exactly where in the Spring Court it will lead was lost a long time ago.

"You don't *have* to go," I say gently. "You can back out at any time."

"And be forced to take a husband so I can produce an heir?" Caitlin spits her fury. "I will not marry. I will not take a man to my bed. Imagine the power I will hold if I walk through that portal and return pregnant to the magic. The independence. The reverence. I would be a mother saint, and the king himself would be hard pressed to force me to his will. I could—" She stops herself short.

"You could rule the Appleshield Protectorate as you wish, with Gwyneth at your side. Officially. Not as a lover."

"Yes, but my pilgrimage isn't just for personal gain." Caitlin bites her lip. "I need to understand the enemy. To visit the lands of the fae. How can I be the lord protector one day if I do not intimately know the threat our family shields this realm from? I must learn about the fae who would flood our world through these gates and set themselves up as our overlords if we allow them. This will not happen on my watch."

The gods know I don't want my sister to walk through one of those portals, to take such a risk, but I would never hold her back.

We have seen firsthand how terrifying the low fae beasts are when they trespass here, but to be surrounded by those vicious creatures in their own world? My heart stutters painfully at the fear that flares within me.

All low fae are feral predators that hunt humans, wanting nothing more than to sink their teeth into us.

I have heard stories from my grandmother's youth of the aftermath of goblins crossing over from the Otherworld and slaughtering entire villages until they were stopped. They killed anything living, people, horses, cats, and smeared their own bodies with the blood of their victims.

The Cú Sídhe hunt in packs like wolves and are just as deadly. The nymphs are brutal, with long-clawed hands and a thirst for blood to be drunk straight from the source.

It feels like we send our women into the middle of a battlefield, utterly alone and with only a dagger to protect themselves. Caitlin will literally walk into enemy territory where every creature will recognize her as a human and mark her for destruction.

And then there are the high fae. A shiver runs down my spine just at the thought of them.

There have been accounts through the centuries of war bands of high fae men arriving through the portals and attacking small establishments, killing, pillaging, raping, and then stealing the human women they find to be their slaves and consorts back in their realm.

There are so many ways a pilgrim can be murdered or abused in the Otherworld.

This is why it is the highest honor for a woman to travel to the Otherworld and to return with a relic infused with their power. It helps us replenish the magic of our world, when it has been slipping away with each generation.

But falling pregnant to the magic itself? The child would be born immensely powerful, and that magic would last for generations of their lineage. The pregnant mother would have magic infused through her from the fetus, increasing her abilities for the rest of her life and utterly changing her destiny.

Peasant girls have become queens and their unborn babes the heirs to the kingdom.

I shudder at the idea of being impregnated by such a foreign source. By pure magic in an immaculate conception. They say it can happen during the crossing, when a woman steps into the zone between realms.

My family has been gifted with great magic. It is our blessing to live close to the boundary and consume the magic that bleeds from the portals and gaps in the barriers. In these highlands, there are streams of water that have their source in the fae world.

There have been many magical pregnancies in our ancestral line. My grandmother took the pilgrimage and conceived my father by the magic. His power is the strongest by far in our entire kingdom.

We walk back to the meadow and Caitlin barks orders until the Protector Guard is back on the road. She sets a fast pace through the last passes of wooded valleys and mountains of slate, as though she is eager to get away from this place.

The lands open out to meadows, which give way to sprawling farms that smell of freshly churned soil. I scan the horizon as Appleshield Castle comes into view, my breath catching at the sight of my home on top of a great rise.

Golden towers jut high above the immense outer wall that encircles the entire hill, enclosing both the castle and the orchards that our family's wealth depends on.

The outer wall defends against human armies or thieves, but the castle itself is a fortress designed against a siege from the fae. It is a massive rectangular structure that has tall turrets and high walls, with a few courtyards.

The windows are either slit or heavily barred. The entire building is purely of a military design, to defend against an enemy who can fly and wield great amounts of destructive magic.

Haloed by the high sun, my home cuts a formidable figure against the blue sky.

I examine the path that snakes from the outer wall to the entrance of the keep, trying to make out the procession of black-clad bodies there. My mind hits a blank as I try to remember which house of the lesser nobility of the North has those colors.

"Shit. Shit. Shit," Caitlin snaps ahead of me, then holds up a hand. "Halt!" The entire hunting party stops abruptly. Caitlin vaults off her mount and stalks right up to me. "Get off your horse."

"Sorry?" I stumble as I realize that entourage is in dark purple, not black.

"The king arrived early. Get down now."

I don't argue. I slide down in shock.

Caitlin takes out her handkerchief and pours water from a canteen over it, then attacks me with the wet cloth, wiping my face and scrubbing at my clothes. "I would have brought a damn maid had I known this would happen. Gwyneth! Can you do something with her hair?"

I glance between both of them. "Caitlin? Do you really think the prince is going to lose interest in me if I present a little disheveled?" I can't hide my disbelief. He has seen me unraveled so many times when we've snuck away to the old gardens.

"He is a prince. They expect refinement in a woman. We're meant to be dainty, helpless blossoms, remember?"

Gwyneth picks leaves and twigs from my hair before braiding it in a crown, tugging with such force that I wonder if Caitlin's statement was triggering for her.

I grit my teeth to stop myself from yelping.

She leaves a third of my curls free to trail down my back to my waist. Caitlin stalks the line of guards until she commandeers two clean surcoats from female trackers.

"This will have to do." She looks me up and down. "Diarmuid!" she yells as Gwyneth gets to work on her hair.

Diarmuid appears at my side, pulling a vial from a sleeve and patting the liquid onto my neck. "Rose oil," he mutters. "So you don't smell like death."

"Not you too?" I groan. "Why do you even have that on you?"

"It's useful for wound healing." He shrugs, then dabs some on Caitlin.

I consider the king's entourage again and can't help the smile that creeps onto my face. I haven't seen Prince Finan in months.

"There is nothing more we can do with you." Caitlin's lips press into a thin line. "With either of us. I would have preferred to present to the king as the proper ladies he expects. It makes life easier. No matter that he wouldn't bat an eyelid if he caught Father dirty after a hunt."

I'm jittery with nervous anticipation as we pass under the outer wall. Only the teeth of the rolled-up iron gate are visible and the four guards salute us as we pass.

I pick at the dirt beneath my nails as doubts niggle at me.

The broad road winds up the incline, between the glasshouses of orchards, already blooming unnaturally this early in the season. An abundance of white apple blossoms are visible through the glass, covering the otherwise skeletal branches in clouds of petals.

My heart rate ramps up as we cross the bridge that spans over a deep ravine between the hilltop of the orchards and Appleshield Castle itself. The foundations of the fortress are built into a bluff of pure stone.

Most of the castles in the south of Strathia are sprawling amalgamations of freestanding towers and buildings, with beautiful courtyard gardens and huge balconies, but not ours. The entire North was built to defend so the rest of Strathia could indulge in safety.

The king's entourage fills the castle's main courtyard just beyond the bridge and gatehouse. The ring of our horses' hooves on the flagstones echoes in the space and turns all heads our way. I scan the crowd of dozens, swallowing as my mouth suddenly turns dry.

Most in the courtyard are royal guards in deep purple uniforms, holding spears and with swords or bows at their backs. The king's heavyset frame stands out from the rest, in a vibrant purple doublet seeded with pearls and ridiculous pants cut at the knee, ballooning out to the hips in ruffles of white velvet.

There is not a speck of dust from the road on him. I doubt he has ridden a horse since his youth.

A frown occupies King Willard's fleshy face as his gaze narrows on me and Caitlin. It flicks to the five Cú Sídhe trophies accompanying our hunting party, then back.

My father stands next to the king, witnessing the same sight but with a smile on his face that lights up his green eyes. With one look at him, all the tension melts from me.

A slight breeze blows his chin-length fiery red hair, which is permanently disheveled because he can't help running a hand through its length to pull it away from his face.

We dismount, our entire guard kneeling before our king. Caitlin leads Diarmuid and me right before him, and while we ladies curtsy deeply, Diarmuid bows.

"King Willard, it is an honor to host you at our keep," Caitlin says as she rises.

He examines us both with exaggerated motions, head to toe, over our kill and bows, then turns to my father. "Edmund, it is quite unladylike for your daughters to partake in a hunt like wildlings. Do you struggle to keep a rein on the willful creatures?"

My mouth hangs open until Caitlin kicks me. I don't understand how she tolerates the dismissal. I have met the king numerous times, and still his personality hits me like the shock of a thunderbolt.

My father laughs, raising a single eyebrow. "No wise man would hold back the women of Appleshield. This fortress would fall to lower fae without them. We do not have ladies here. We have warriors and priestesses."

"You are far too indulgent, old man." The king's lips quirk quickly upwards.

"You have a daughter, Willard, sixteen like my youngest. We'll see how indulgent you become."

The king slaps my father's back. "Ah! But I have already married

22

mine off. She is no longer my problem. Women become so willful at that age. Better to let another man deal with it."

I jolt at the harshness of those words. He speaks as though he sold off a brood mare. The king turns to Caitlin and me, nodding to us *wildlings* in a manner that is not unfriendly. He completely misses the expression that flashes across my father's face, anger that bleeds into sadness.

King Willard smiles when he notices my brother. "Ah, Diarmuid, my good boy. Why would a strapping young man like you have your sisters out leading a hunt of those horrible creatures?" He puts an arm around Diarmuid's shoulders and leads him away. "Yes, I know the druids do not kill." I cannot hear Diarmuid's reply, only the king's bellowing again. "You are always welcome to finish your training in my court, with my druid adviser."

As they drift away, I contemplate who has it worse whenever the king visits: myself and Caitlin, or Diarmuid, who always gets roped into spending hours entertaining him.

A roar of voices rises within the courtyard as the guards and nobles talk among themselves. They had fallen silent for the king's humiliation of us. My cheeks and neck heat with embarrassment.

"I can never quite work out if the king is joking or if he insults us," Caitlin mutters with a pleasant, courtly smile forced onto her face.

"Both, I think." I scan the crowd.

"Definitely both," our father chimes in behind us, placing a hand on each of our shoulders. "Because he sees our strength in unity. We will give him no other reason to feel threatened while here, right? Not even a threat to his masculinity. Wars have been fought over less."

Men. Typical men.

Affronted because we ride and hunt and thrive, because we have the prowess they value. As women, we are better hunters than most men, and *that* threatens their masculinity. It is so much easier to drag another person down than to put in the effort to improve oneself.

"I know what you two are thinking," my father half whispers to us, scratching his neatly trimmed, red beard. "And I agree with you. Any other chauvinistic bastard and I would love for you to put him and his insecurities in his place, but not the king. We all swallow our pride for royalty."

Our father pats our shoulders, then disappears into the crowd as soon as he catches the attention of the king's druid adviser.

"Keira." That musical voice calls my name, dragging out the syllables, and I turn to it like it is a spell.

Hidden behind chatting courtiers, Prince Finan leans against the wall, one leg bent and his foot pressed to the stone. I drink in the image of him like a woman dying of thirst. The blue-black curls of his hair are pulled back by a gold circlet, with a single ringlet flopping forward over his ice-blue eyes. He casts a simmering gaze at me, beckoning with a hand, and I jut forward like an eager puppy.

The crowd parts as I move to him, but I hardly notice them.

Prince Finan takes my hand and brings it to his lips, brushing the lightest kiss on its back. The fluttering sensation sends warmth up my arm.

I should curtsy to him, but our familiarity has far outgrown that.

"You do indeed look like a wildling." He pulls a leaf from my hair and caresses my cheek as he rubs something from it.

"You heard what your father said to me?" I raise my eyebrows. "And you said nothing? You chose not to defend your lady's honor?"

His laughter rings out. "One does not question a king. Not even a prince."

I examine his face as his head tips to one side. There isn't a hint of annoyance or protectiveness. Maybe I overreacted to the king's words.

"Besides." Finan drags out the word as he twirls a loose lock of my hair around his finger. "What made you think you could go on a hunt? It's far too dangerous for a lady. Better to leave that sort of distasteful business to the soldiers."

"Finan, aside from my sister, I am the greatest hunter in the Appleshield Protectorate. I join *every* hunt." It's like he doesn't even know me.

He spreads one of my curls across his palm, so each individual strand is visible against the contrast of his pale skin. "I love the beauty of your hair," he murmurs. "The way every strand is a different color. Gold, orange, red, burgundy and brown. It is like every shade of autumn leaf is captured within them."

His intensity steals my breath away and the capacity for thought escapes me.

The prince gives me a pat on the hip. "Go. Bathe and change. I want you looking pretty on my arm." With that command, he straightens to his full height, a hand's width above mine, and walks away from me, joining the conversation the younger Prince Niall is embroiled in with an ambassador.

I am left standing alone in a crowd of people. It feels like the sun has disappeared.

# CHAPTER 3

# KEIRA

I don't get to relax in the steaming hot water of my bath. The roots of my hair hurt as a maid untangles its snarls. Another maid scrubs my skin with a brush until it turns pink and the water is tinged brown. A third meticulously cleans and files my fingernails, then my toenails.

I am being pulled in multiple directions at once, with hardly enough time to get ready for the king's welcome reception. His entire entourage is currently cleaning up after their long journey, though I don't expect any of them to have worked up a sweat, arriving in a convoy of slow carriages.

Fatigue crashes down on me as I stand completely naked before the bath, rivulets running down my still-flushed skin, as the maids remove my body hair by guiding sharp blades across my flesh, in the southern fashion. The tension seeps from me as soon as they are done and my bathrobe is thrown around my shoulders.

I hate this. I only do it for Finan.

I am always so afraid they will cut me. It has happened before.

When I sit at my vanity table with its large bifold mirrors, a cup of coffee already waits for me, and I take hurried sips of it between being fussed over by maids.

They apply oils to my hair until it shines gold and red in the sunlight that enters through the large window. It is coiled into loops on top of my head, with long tresses left free to cascade down my shoulders. Combs with green jewels are inserted into my hair, matching the emeralds of my necklace and the mint velvet dress that clings to my ample curves.

I feel less like a wilding, clean and manicured after the hunt.

My footfalls echo through the long corridors of the keep, clicking on polished stone tiles and landing in muted thuds on tapestry rugs.

Burning orbs of fire hang suspended along the ceiling, illuminating the spaces where other castles would have torches on brackets. The orbs create no smoke and a little heat, the combustion producing light in a completely isolated bubble, until the fuel of magic is consumed and they wink out.

The orbs are another of our magical exports.

We have retainers who are strong wielders of fire, making such technology possible for us, but the process is slow and limited. Further out in the kingdom it is rare to find someone with so much power.

I could almost laugh bitterly at the thought.

Creating a fire orb was once such a basic thing that anyone could do it. I have read so many books in our personal library detailing the immense magic our ancestors once wielded.

Today, lighting a candle is the limit for most people's fire magic. It is one of the reasons why Liam and Aiden are so heavily prized as Protector Guards with their ability to light their swords on fire. Anyone with that amount of magic is usually consumed by more important work than creating fire orbs.

I reach the antechamber of the small ballroom, and am greeted by the eruption of voices that leaks out of it. Pausing a moment, I take a deep breath to steady my nerves.

The wrestle of wits and assault of false niceties at these sorts of events sets my anxiety on edge. I don't understand the need for all the twisted words that are petty insults dressed as compliments. Court intrigue will never be my strength.

The ballroom is filled with royal courtiers and minor nobles of our protectorate, clad in silks and brocades and jewels, moving around the room and buzzing with chatter like a hive of bees. There is enough gold to support the comparison, embroidered on cloth, fashioned into jewelry and adorning trimmings on the floral stucco artwork of the walls and ceiling.

I hardly take more than a handful of steps into the room before my mother grabs me by the elbow and pulls me away.

"I heard the prince intercepted you as you returned from the hunt. That you had leaves in your hair and mud on your face." She nods to courtiers as they pass by with a disingenuous smile on her face. The few loose blond curls at the top of her high hairdo bob as she moves.

"It wasn't *that* bad," I reply. "We were caught by surprise."

My mother waves to someone at my back, mouthing a few words to them. Sharp intelligence fills her dark eyes as they turn back to me. "We will discuss the details tonight, after the feast. Assume we are in damage control and lay on him every charm you have today." I nod and she raises her eyebrows. "Keira, I mean *every charm.*"

"I know what you mean, Mother." I can't help glancing at Finan.

She pats my shoulder. "Good. This family needs this marriage as much as you want it. You are twenty-four. I'm sure you're eager for marriage after all this wait."

Despite her cheerful mask, the strain is clear in her features. The pinched and tight expression. The way her smile is held too wide and her attention darts around the room then back to me.

I open my mouth to tell her not to worry, but she grabs my hands.

"Do not tell a mother not to worry — I know you were thinking it — a mother can never stop. I would sleep better if you were betrothed. I will still worry when you are married, and when you are queen. Both are difficult things to navigate, especially with that family," she says softly.

"Maeve, my dear." The Appleshield ambassador to the royal court appears at our side. "If I may have a discreet word with you?" He turns an apologetic glance to me, and they both move to a corner of the room.

I am a naive girl. I don't belong with a prince, or in this room, for that matter. If I could not see the repercussions of presenting slightly disheveled before the royal court when both Caitlin and Diarmuid did, how can I navigate the politics of the palace well enough to survive?

*Breathe in. Breathe out. Smile. You have this. You will learn.*

I square my shoulders and find Finan. He has a silver chalice in his hand, standing among people but somehow apart from them, taking in the room with a pout on his lips. Maybe he feels the same way I do. Courtiers talk around him, but he doesn't pay them notice, not like his younger brother Niall, who works the room.

Finan's eyes slide to mine and his thick lips curl into a slow smile. He takes my arm with a bejeweled hand and wraps it through his, the soft silk of his blue doublet brushing against my skin. There is lace at his neck and wrists and I wonder if it is the latest fashion in Sunbright City. Things seems to move so quickly in the capital.

"Keira, you look exquisite." Finan's breath carries the scent of mulled wine.

"Father is not impressed." Prince Niall joins us, addressing Finan.

It is uncanny how similar the two men look, the blue-black curls of their hair, the short, lean build of their stature, but where Finan is all charming stares and lazy grins, Niall has a sternness to him. The younger prince wears his hair short-cropped and doesn't follow his court's fashions, opting for a style that is minimalistic and practical. No jewelry. No frills. Even his doublet is entirely black, with a discreet decoration of purple swirls in the brocade.

"Father is never impressed. What has set him off this time?" Finan waves a hand as though it is all very unimportant.

"It is the fruit here. All of the food, actually. The harvest is losing its magic." Niall's expression is stone cold as he replies to his brother, but his gaze quickly flicks to me, assessing my reaction.

I raise my eyebrows and force a half-smile on my lips, despite how my heart thunders with painful palpitations. I half expect Niall to hear its crashing beat.

"I am sorry our food is not to his standard. Perhaps your chefs in the capital are more skilled than our own." My tone is coy, playful. "What gave him the idea that our harvest is losing its magic? I assure you ours is imbued with the highest amount of magic in the kingdom."

I stare at Niall, hoping my sweet words will be enough for him. I hardly notice Finan, who inspects his fingernails. We cannot afford for the royal family to discover our greatest secret. The one that could be our downfall. For a decade, we have done everything in our power to hide it from the rest of the kingdom.

"Yes, your lands will always have the highest magic in Strathia." Niall speaks as though he is explaining it to a child. "But that doesn't mean they aren't losing their magic along with every other province. That your harvest isn't imbued with the amount of magic it once was. If my suspicions are correct, if the rest of the kingdom can no longer receive a top-up on their magic by eating the fruit from your orchards, then the consequences would be dire. Many people would lose their meager magic entirely."

Niall's blue eyes lock on to mine and seem to unpack me, to see the lying fraud beneath. My mind reels, trying and failing to find the right words to distract him, to make him back down on his conviction. My family's survival depends on it.

"Don't be so dramatic, Niall." Finan's low tone cuts the tension. "The fruit is fine. I can see it glowing with magic from here."

I use the excuse to scan the room for my parents, starting at the table of cakes, pastries and fruit platters. There is an iridescence radiating from the apples, oranges, grapes and strawberries, each letting out their own colored light across the table. Of course, our best samples were presented to the king.

Both of my parents are engaged in a conversation with the king, whose mouth moves rapidly, a red flush creeping up his neck. My father runs a hand through his hair, glancing multiple times at the same banquet table. My mother's schooled face is the image of serenity, but her shoulders are held tight.

There is no need for me to inform them of the king's dissatisfaction.

Ice settles within my stomach.

Niall's razor-sharp attention is still honed on me. He pulls an apple out of his pocket and holds it. "The flesh of your apples doesn't glow like it used to. When I was a child, Appleshield fruit was luminous. It shimmered like a jewel in sunlight. Now it shines like dull metal."

The apple in his hand is indeed lackluster, its skin almost white, with pale washes of green and red. Worse, it is marred with small brown dints. Dread grows within me.

"So you found a bad piece of fruit. So what?" Finan seems about to lose his temper at his brother, and I realize that from his perspective, Niall is being quite rude.

"It hasn't been unnaturally ripened by magic over the winter and it has signs of a slight blight, like a regular apple. This tells me Appleshield doesn't have enough labor with skilled magic to tend all their orchards and crops. That not enough power is being put into some of the harvest."

"Those are big observations from a single piece of fruit." I shoot Finan a glance and laugh, hoping he will step in again. "Where did you get it from?"

"A servant picked it directly from the keep's orchard. I had to know if something was happening to the fruit we receive in Sunbright City while in transit, or if the problem is here."

Damn. Damn. Damn. Not good.

My hands become clammy, but I can't wipe them on my dress. I don't dare let Niall see my nervousness. "It has been seven years since portals to the Otherworld have opened. Magic waxes and wanes. If there are minor issues, they will be corrected when the magical relics are brought back into our lands. We have had a particularly severe winter this year, so the magical needs for our orchards have doubled."

These excuses were well planned and practiced by our family, only to be brought out in the most dire of situations. They are only a fraction of the truth.

Niall frowns deeply as he processes my excuses.

"Not to mention, we are only starting the season of feasts," I say with a joyful tone. "Did you see the five Cú Sídhe we brought in from the hunt this morning? There will be many more."

At the mention of the hunt, of my participation, Finan cringes, and I regret it immediately.

Niall gives me a searching stare, and I fear my lies and evasions will be undone beneath it. He takes a bite from the apple. "It doesn't taste as sweet and crisp as it did when I was a kid."

"Niall!" Finan rolls his eyes. "You are boring us with this talk of apples. So they aren't as pretty. Who cares? Keira said they will be more to your liking next year."

I laugh as though Finan told a clever joke.

Niall's lips compress into a thin line. "Nevertheless, Father has requested a tour of the orchards. We are going now, and I think you should come, if you believe it would be interesting enough." He turns and leaves, the muscles of his shoulders coiled tight.

Finan chuckles. "He is far too easy to goad. We'll do an inventory of the orchards and test the magic of the staff. It's not like there is anything more we can do about it."

I nod, and it takes all of my energy to keep that pleasant expression on my face.

# CHAPTER 4

# KEIRA

Gray clouds move across the sun as our party leaves the castle grounds and passes under the main gate of the inner wall. My father leads us, repeatedly running a hand through the length of his hair as the wind blows it in his face.

Caitlin is at his left and the king to his right, with Finan and me taking up the rear. Between us, Niall is in deep conversation with the king's druid adviser, Murdoc. A handful of king's guards move with us at such a distance that it's easy to forget they are there.

The intensity of the elements increases as we cross the wide bridge that spans from the rise of the castle across a deep, wooded valley and connects with the orchards. My velvet cloak billows around me. The king's white beard whips into his face.

"This blasted cold and wind," the king bellows. "By the gods, it never gets this cool down south."

My father turns to me and raises a single finger, motioning it in a circle. I nod, unlacing my arm from Finan's grip.

I focus my attention on the wicked breeze. On the particles of air all around us. I place my hands together, then spread them wide, weaving a thick shield of solid air around us, imbuing my magic into what was already there to make it perform to my will. I mold the structure into a dome that moves at the speed of our footfalls.

I call on my fire magic, bunching my hands into a fist, then slowly uncurl my fingers.

The air warms around us and I hold a small sphere of fire dancing in my palm. The two acts of magic are not related, the second purely for show, to impress king and prince alike. Another reason for both men to choose me as Finan's wife and future queen.

The wind still whips around, shaking the tops of the pine trees below the bridge and sending leaves spinning at our feet, but it no longer reaches us. Our hair and clothes remain motionless.

King Willard's eyes turn wide as he looks around himself, then they land on me. "You?"

"A small act of air and fire magic to make us more comfortable." I shrug, hiding the strain.

My awareness is pulled in multiple directions. I monitor the movement of the dome, constantly checking the edges so the king doesn't walk straight into the wall. I adjust the fire magic, fighting against any flares, so the air doesn't suddenly become suffocatingly hot.

My senses tingle as Caitlin's magic discreetly weaves into mine, taking some of the strain.

Our destination is the series of immense glasshouses positioned by the bridge. Their combined footprint is the size of a small village, and each one is as spacious as a cathedral, made purely of great panels of glass and metal. Rows of fruit trees are perfectly visible within, the panels enchanted to repel dirt to ensure the maximum penetration of light.

There is no way we could replicate such engineering to replace them. The metal beams were imported from the Winter Court smiths of the Otherworld. The glass panels were enchanted with immense magic to make it near impossible to break them. These glasshouses were built by the fae.

Appleshield once had a different name, and it was ruled by a fae overlord, before our family liberated it. The orchards and the outer wall are guarded day and night to protect against fruit thieves, or enemies who would sabotage us. Within these greenhouses are the last hopes of Strathia.

My father leads us to our top-performing orchard and the guards at the doors hurry to drag them open for us. The strain of using so much magic pulls on me, like treading water for far too long. I drop the weaves as soon as we enter and let out a long breath as deep relief fills me.

The broad glass doors in metal frames are pushed shut behind us and the change in atmosphere is immediately obvious. The air is hot and heavy with moisture, making it far more difficult to suck in compared to the crisp day outside.

Finan lets out a long, low whistle at the sight. It brings a smile of pride to my face.

Neat rows of trees spread out before us. All are heavy with an impossible amount of fruit, especially in late winter. Vibrant red apples glow with brilliance, black plums sparkle like gems and cherries like rubies. The fruits have an aura of light surrounding them and the colors are so bright they are unnatural.

Large, fuzzy bees fill the air with buzzing, their forms glowing with white light and the stripes of their backs a stunning indigo. Their breed was perfected in these orchards for hundreds of years, alongside the fruit.

"Right, Edmund. Do your best to impress me," the king says, bolstering himself up as he looks around.

"He has already impressed me," Prince Finan murmurs into my ear, wrapping an arm around my waist. I savor the press of his body against my side.

"We induce artificial seasons in these glasshouses. Spring, summer, an artificial cold snap to convince the trees they have gone through winter, then spring again." My father's voice carries as we walk down the rows.

"We control all aspects of the environment. Additional heat and sunlight are created as needed and maintained by our fire wielders."

He holds out a hand and a jet of fire whooshes from it, congealing into an orb, then rising up above the treeline to join many others.

The king and princes gawk like peasants at all those orbs and Caitlin shoots me a smirk.

"Deep beneath our feet, there is an underground stream that flows straight from the Otherworld, through cracks in the boundaries. It is imbued with magic, and our water wielders draw it to the surface." Father turns his palm to the ground, fingers splayed, then jerks his arm upward. A jet of brilliant blue water shoots from the ground, glowing intensely. "This water is life itself. It is the main source of magic for our produce."

"Well. That — that is more than I was expecting, but where are your laborers?" The king's tone is accusatory. "Surely you do not tend these orchards yourself!"

"Follow." My father takes off again.

The path between trees becomes narrow, and we move in single file, avoiding snagging branches. Finan places his hands on my hips from behind and I toss an inviting smile back at him.

"I am not sure what I want to ravish more, this fruit or this body," he whispers into my ear, nipping the side of my neck.

"Not with so many people around," I chide, but I don't move his hands.

"Hmmm," he murmurs, and I rest my cheek against his for a moment before pulling away.

"Those of us behind you would prefer to not witness a spectacle," Caitlin half growls.

"My dear lady, I didn't mean to upset your delicate sensibilities." Finan mock bows to her, grinning wide enough that his cheeks dimple.

Caitlin pushes past both of us. Finan shrugs at me.

Years ago, Caitlin and I put together a double-pronged attack on Prince Finan to make sure he became attached to the right Appleshield sister. I was sweet and kind to him, and Caitlin was abrupt and almost insulting. The personas matched our temperaments nicely, if somewhat exaggerated, and the tactic worked, but Caitlin never dropped her end of it.

At times, I have wondered if she despises him in truth.

The way opens to a cross section, and we turn down a wider path. There are retainers spread among the trees. Some move their hands in an elaborate dance, conjuring fire and air magic to create heat volleys and spread them through the glasshouse. Others crouch at the bases of the trees, small trickles of water running over their fingers as they call up the stream.

We stop before a row populated with many workers.

"Over here, the harvest is taking place," my father says, hand gesturing upward, where clouds of fruit float gently down from the trees and into waiting carts. "Our air wielders pluck the fruit with their magic. It takes a fraction of the time compared to manual labor, and none of the risk that comes with people climbing ladders or trees."

"Well. Everything looks in order here." The king nods curtly. "I was worried that even *your* lands were losing their magic. This kingdom would be plunged into the dark ages if it came to that."

My stomach twists. We hardly have the skeleton staff to operate our glasshouses, and we scour our county for more wielders each year. Too much of our lifestyle and technology is fueled by magic.

The sole reason my match was made with Finan when we were both barely more than children was because his family needed the magic in my pedigree to replenish their bloodline, and mine needed political connections and new opportunities. We cannot rely on our magic alone for much longer.

"I can definitely confirm that the fruit is delicious," Finan says while biting into a plum, drawing everyone's attention. "But, of course, I need to sample your cider and wine facilities as well."

My father laughs, the sound forced to my ears, and puts a hand on Finan's shoulder. "I like the way you think. I believe we should sample them immediately. Reward ourselves for a little hard work."

I let out a breath I didn't realize I was holding.

"Hold up there, Edmund. I'd like to see your other glasshouses,"

Niall commands. The undercurrent is clear. He believes we have shown him only our best face, and it is true.

My father glances at Finan regretfully, the opportunity for distraction lost. "As you wish, Niall. We have nothing to hide."

We visit another glasshouse orchard, this one set in spring. The trees are filled with clouds of blossoms: dainty white flowers on the apple trees, dark pink ruffles on the peach trees and wiry yellow sprigs on the avocado trees.

Fallen petals cover the ground like a fine dusting of colorful snow. Here there is a large team of earth wielders at work, using invisible tendrils of magic to churn the soil with compost.

When we leave, the world outside seems colorless and cold in comparison.

"I can show you more, King Willard, but the others will be no different," my father says.

"I would like to pick the next glasshouse we visit," Prince Niall cuts in.

"Of course." My father spreads out his arm toward the expanse of buildings.

My heart thuds so hard it hurts. Perhaps the king and princes won't know enough about farming to pick up on signs of neglect.

Niall takes the lead, inspecting each glasshouse we pass, as the druid Murdoc takes up whispering in the king's ear. The prince picks out a building that is dark and dank, with trees completely devoid of leaves.

I almost sigh with relief.

He has selected an orchard that has been forced into a winter snap. To the untrained eye, it would seem dead and neglected. There are no guards at this glasshouse, and my father pulls open the door of glass and metal framing himself.

A deep chill passes over us as we step inside. The lightest covering of frost crunches beneath our feet.

"Is it dead?" A deep scowl crosses Finan's face. I know that look. It twists his sweet face whenever he thinks he has been cheated at cards.

"Not dead. Dormant," I reply. "The trees won't flower unless they have undergone a chill first."

Finan pats my hand tucked into his elbow absentmindedly, but stares at my father. "Edmund? What is this?"

"As Keira said, this is winter. The orchard needs a time of rest before we can bring spring on again. Come." Father leads us down one face of the glasshouse, peering down every row, pointing out the sparse workers. "These fire wielders are drawing heat out of the atmosphere to further cool the orchard. If there were more moisture in the air, we would have snow."

The king, Niall and their druid adviser pick over every part of the glasshouse, demanding explanations. Then we visit another orchard, with the same interrogation.

"Why are you not drilling my father with them?" I murmur to Finan.

He plays with the rings on one hand. "Because farming should be left to farmers. Managing an estate should be left to the lord. I am not arrogant enough to believe I know more about a person's profession than they do. But mostly, because I trust you. And this is very bloody boring."

"There is truth in that," I venture.

A sickness rolls within me, knowing we betray his trust.

Our wielders work long, hard hours, and are able to get the bare necessities done, but there are signs of neglect everywhere that only an experienced eye can catch. In a few years, when our oldest and most powerful wielders are forced to retire, we will have to close multiple greenhouses.

Finan's eyes become hooded as he traces a finger down my cheek, my throat to my exposed cleavage. The heat in that gaze sends shivers down my spine.

He leans in, murmuring in my ear, "How about we slip away from this pointless inspection? Maybe go to that spot we like?"

"And which spot is that?" I place a hand on his chest. Our breaths mingle in the closeness. The party we came here with turns down a distant corner.

His lips quirk up, and I could kiss him here and now. "You know what I am talking about. I want you to myself. I want to make you moan and beg for more."

"Is that right? I don't believe it would be very becoming of a lady," I tease, pressing myself against his chest as his arms wrap around my waist.

"I want to bring you back to the castle as disheveled as you were this morning, with leaves in your hair. I liked that wildling."

I grab his hand and tug him out of the glasshouse before he combusts.

We run and stumble through the orchards to the ancient gardens of wildflowers and twisted rose bushes as tall as trees, which once belonged to the fae lord who ruled this land.

Now, they are untended and deserted.

The paths have missing cobbles filled in with weeds and the wire-frame arches that loop over it are either completely engulfed by creeping rose bush vines and impassable, or mere bare bones.

In the center of the Old Fae Garden is an immense tree that looks like a weeping willow, but the colors are wrong. Its foliage forms immense curtains of cascading red and yellow blooms. We laugh as we run through them, pushing layers of soft branches out of our way. When they close behind us, the entire world is blocked out.

Finan wraps his hands around my waist and lifts me off my feet. I throw my arms around his neck and my thighs encircle his hips, my skirts falling away to expose the bare skin of my legs. His hand runs up my calf, across my thigh and lands on my ass, my flesh tingling and heating beneath his touch.

His perfumed scent of citrus, bergamot and sandalwood fills my nose as the warmth of him pressed against me sends tingles throughout my body. I kiss his generous lips, then part mine for him and our tongues meet, gliding together ever so gently, building with urgency until our mouths bruise against each other. I bite his lower lip and he groans.

Finan's hand finds its way down the neckline of my dress, taking the fullness of my breast into his grip and squeezing. He flicks his thumb over my nipple and I gasp, throwing my head back.

Those lips find their way to my neck, starting behind my ear and kissing down to my chest, to my breasts, pulling my neckline as far as the fabric will allow.

Finan stumbles toward the twisted trunk of the tree, still bearing my weight, then deposits my body against it. The bark at my back is smooth. It generates its own heat and glows a soft white, being an ancient gift straight from the fae Summer Court. The entire space around us is a bubble of warmth and of fiery foliage.

He presses his body against mine and every inch where we touch feels divine. His hardened length presses against my hip, making my heart leap in anticipation.

I unfasten Finan's cloak and sprawl the fabric across the ground.

"Sit," I command.

Finan does so without question, leaning his back against the tree and pulling me into his lap. I straddle his hips, my skirts pushed up around my waist, and he snakes his hands under the fabric and up my body. I untie the laces on his britches, so the thin fabric of our under-garments is all that separates us.

I watch his expression as I stroke the hard length of him, his eyes heated and hungry, his lips parted and gasping. I press my core over his erection, the fabric of my undergarments already wet, and I thrust myself against him, again and again, reveling in the delicious friction.

Heat builds between my legs as sensation shoots through me in sharp thrills with each grind of my hips. I let out a moan as the pure pleasure rises and the tension builds within me. My breaths become short and sharp.

"Stop fucking teasing me and put it in already." Finan's growl shatters the moment. Pangs of guilt run through me hot and fast. I have only been thinking about my pleasure.

With a swift motion, I free him from his undergarments, then try to do an awkward shuffle to get out of mine. Finan tears them off me before I have a chance.

Our hands collide as we both try to grab his shaft, but I quickly whip mine away and allow him to guide it while I ease his cock into me. I hold on to his shoulders as his hips thrust upward and he drives his hardness into me in a brutal motion.

I try to ride him with the same enthusiasm as before, my hips bouncing upon his as his length pulls in and out of me. The tension starts to build again and I arch my back, trying to hit that spot within my depths that makes pleasure quake through me. Finan's body shudders before I can find it, unraveling beneath me while I am still unsated.

He pants and a slow smile grows on his face, then he gently pushes me off him.

Finan gets up and laces up his britches. "The feast is starting soon. I don't want to be late."

I stare at him as the arousal falls from me like a bucket of cold water has been tipped over my head.

He is right. We really shouldn't be late.

I clean myself up, but there aren't leaves in my hair like he promised. It has hardly been disturbed. My undergarments are tossed on the floor, a ruined heap of lace, and I am annoyed by it.

Finan pulls me by the hand out of the privacy of the willow tree, and out of my own thoughts. The late-afternoon sun has made an appearance, warming our backs as we make the trek to the castle. Finan talks about something, on and on without caring to see if I am listening.

A single thought keeps flittering through my mind. I don't know how I feel about the intimacy we just had. It was pleasant, I guess.

# CHAPTER 5
# KEIRA

A roaring of voices combined with the fast-paced music of a multi-piece band crashes through the great hall. It is alive with almost a hundred guests, dressed brightly in their finery and jewels, contrasting against the pale marble mosaic floors and mahogany-paneled walls.

My father spared no cost for this feast.

Professional dancers move with fluid motions before us. Their vibrant skirts swish with each sway of their hips and strings of tiny bells chime, worn as belts, bracelets and anklets.

The movements of their arms and hips and legs are in perfect synchrony with the racy tune of the music, bolstered with flutes and trumpets. My heart rate quickens in time with that beat.

There are bouquets of flowers in immense vases on each table and garlands hang alongside the ribbons and banners that adorn the ceiling and walls. Expenses were not cut by using winter blooms; there are roses and lilies and peonies, everything out of season and cut from a glasshouse.

We can't afford this show of wealth, but we also can't afford to show weakness.

The thought drags down my mood. It reminds me how much is at stake. Something else pulls at me. An intuition that something is off, and I am filled with apprehension. I can't quite put my finger on what I am missing.

"Aren't they beautiful?" Brianna asks, gesturing at the performers.

A smile lights up my baby sister's face, framed by ringlets of spun gold. I swear it was only months ago that she still looked like a skinny child, all elbows and legs, but she filled out around her fifteenth birthday. Now, she is the most beautiful woman in the room.

Brianna sighs and plops her cheek into her hand, elbow braced on the table. "I hope Prince Niall asks me to dance. He doesn't normally notice me."

"I am sure there will be plenty of men wanting to dance with you," I say.

The music cuts off with a bang of cymbals. The dancers bow to the applause of the crowd, then clear off the dance floor. The voices of our guests halt with the music and their attention becomes focused on our table, raised upon a dais and seating the king, the royal family and my family as hosts.

Father stands, raising his goblet of wine and surveying our guests, courtiers of both the royal household and ours. Minor lords of the North who owe their allegiance to my family have ridden in from the countryside to honor the king. Guards who distinguished themselves during the hunt join us.

I find Liam, Aiden and Brandan in the crowd, all beaming with excitement to be here. My favorite guards almost look strange out of their uniforms.

My father clears his throat. "May our wine and harvest ever be blessed with magic. To those brave women who take the pilgrimage and bring magic into our realm from the Otherworld, we thank you. To our mighty warriors who slay the fae that invade our land so we can feast on the magic of their flesh, we thank you." He takes a long swig of his wine, and everyone follows. "Let the feast begin!"

A resounding cheer erupts. I can't help the brimming smile that forms on my lips and the pride of my people that fills my heart.

On cue, servants file into the hall carrying trays of steaming spit-roasted meat with gravies and mint jelly. Dishes of root vegetables in butter and herbs, spiced eggs wrapped in thin layers of meat and a selection of preserves and pickles. My mouth waters at the aroma and I heap food onto my plate.

It is divine, the meat juicy and tender, and the vegetables creamy and bursting with flavor. I lean forward to take a second helping, but cool fingers grasp my hand.

"Unfortunately, we women have our waistlines to think about," my mother says from behind me as she passes by to mingle among our guests.

I hate this. I really do.

Nobody cares if a man puts on weight, but I am expected to fit a rigid mold of beauty.

I am not the skinny slip of a girl that our society prizes, like my sister Brianna. I have curves. Large breasts that I am proud of and rounded hips so Finan has something to take hold of. My waist may not be perfectly narrow, but he has never complained.

I have caught men's eyes following my figure hungrily regardless. It makes me wonder who exactly writes these rules.

The platters of the main meal are ravished until they are empty, then cleared and replaced with trays of pastries filled with glowing fruit. People pair up on the dance floor and begin a waltz.

Niall stands, and poor Brianna's faces lights up beside me, but he places a hand out to his mother, the queen, and takes her to the dance floor instead.

The king's voice booms loudly over the garbled noise of the crowd, but I am thankfully seated too far away from him to hear what is being said. Caitlin has taken my mother's position at the table, and the slight scowl on her face as she follows the conversation is enough for me.

"Would my lady care for a dance?" Finan smiles wickedly down at me, his arm cocked for me to take.

I glance at the dance floor, where people are in two columns, dancing in fast, swirling motions, constantly changing partners to the beat of rowdy music.

"I'm not in the mood for dancing," I sigh.

Finan raises his eyebrows. "You? Not in the mood to dance with me? There's not some other man here you'd prefer to dance with, is there?" A self-assured smile grows on his face, as though the joke were both hilarious and ridiculous.

I huff out a breath of air and deflate a little more.

Finan grabs me by my hand and pulls me up from my chair. "At least come sit next to me. I can hardly see your pretty face over here."

I turn to ask Brianna if she will be lonely on her own, but she stares up at Niall, who takes her hand and leads her to the dance floor in time for the next song to start. The expression of pure wonderment on her young face brings a smile to mine.

Finan deposits me in the queen's seat, right next to the king. For a moment, I wonder if he did it to put a buffer between himself and his abrasive father.

"Ah, Keira. We were just talking about you," King Willard announces with flakes of pastry falling out of his white beard. "One would expect you are keenly awaiting Finan's announcement on who his bride will be. It will be made after the Beltane Festival. Better play your cards right, girl, to make sure his eyes don't rove before then, to a sister perhaps."

King Willard bellows a laugh, but I don't take his bait. It would give him too much enjoyment if I stammered or cried.

Finan stiffens beside me. His hand squeezes my thigh, hidden under the tablecloth, but he doesn't say anything.

"No betrothal period?" I ask.

"No need." The king sucks sugar off his fingers as he eats another sweet. "The wedding will take place in Sunbright City after the pilgrims return from the Otherworld."

"I do not see why we need to wait, Father." Finan bristles. "Why not have the wedding now? Why not years ago? I know who I want to marry. I always have."

"We've had this conversation, boy," he growls.

"I — I would like to know too." The words are out of my mouth before I can stop myself.

The king laughs again and turns to my father. "Ah, the passion of youth, eh. Don't you remember those days, Edmund? And then their tits sag and their bellies go round and they don't dote on your every word anymore."

The king stares straight at his wife across the room as he speaks. She is dancing with her brother, missing the twisted look of disgust on my father's face.

King Willard speaks over my head to Finan. "It is uncustomary to marry a woman before the first crossing of her youth. It is the right of every woman to take part in the pilgrimage to the Otherworld if she chooses it." Those watery blue eyes beneath bushy white eyebrows land on me. "Tell me, Keira, do you want to take this insane pilgrimage?"

The breath catches in my chest and for a crazy moment, I don't know what I want.

"No!" Finan stands behind me, putting his hands on my shoulders. "No. She doesn't want to go."

I don't say anything. When I glance at my father, there is a deep sadness in him. He searches my face for any hint that I want to take the pilgrimage, because he would fight with everything he had to give me that chance.

The pilgrimage had once been my dream, but that was a child's folly, not the desire of a future queen.

"Good," the king says. "The danger is too great, with all the vicious monsters in that realm, especially when Caitlin is already putting herself at risk. My own cousin came back disfigured from her pilgrimage. Shame. She was pretty before that."

He turns to my father. "Perhaps your oldest will return carrying a child to the magic and will do a great service to our realm." The smile that creeps onto his face is sinister. Loaded, but I don't understand the ammunition.

Father stiffens at the suggestion. "Caitlin will make her own choice in life, *especially* if she returns with a magical pregnancy."

There are undercurrents here that I don't understand. I hardly hear the rest of their exchange.

Finan's shoulders slump as he returns to his seat and frowns deeply. He becomes lost in a sight across the great hall, and his dark mood slowly clears. Those eyes light up again in an expression he usually reserves for me, as though he is appraising a fine work of art.

I double take when I realize the subject of his attention.

Caitlin dances a fast-paced gig with the Captain of the Guard. The curls of her bright auburn hair bounce with each leap and her cheeks are flushed prettily. I turn to Finan as he leans back in his chair, a half-smile on his face.

I need to lure him back with sweet nothings or dirty promises. To grasp his attention by dragging him out of the ballroom to a dark, private part of the keep and taking him again. To blow his mind so that when he leaves for the capital, I will be the only woman he will think about.

But I just don't want to.

I shouldn't have to work so hard. To remind him it is me he wants every few hours. It is exhausting. Maybe it is different because he is a prince and his options are vast. Maybe it is my own insecurities at play and there is nothing abnormal about a man enjoying a glance at another woman.

My head spins, thoughts and convictions slamming from one direction to another.

It's okay. It's very much not okay.

The room closes in on me. I struggle to draw in each breath. The voices around me are indistinct roars, so loud they bounce around inside my head, but I cannot make out a single word over the rushing of blood in my ears.

I need to get out.

Finan and King Willard talk over the top of my head.

I stand so fast my chair clatters to the ground, and it draws the attention of everyone at the table.

"Keira, sit down, sweetheart. Have more wine." Finan gives me his most dazzling smile, but it doesn't work on me, not tonight.

"I have a headache," I say. "I'm going to retire early."

He nods, patting me on the arm, then returns to his conversation on racing horses with his father.

I take a single wobbly step away from the table, and then another, before a strong arm wraps around my waist. "A migraine?" my father whispers in my ear as he leads me out of the room.

"Yes. I feel overwhelmed," I mutter.

He leads me through the foyer of the ballroom and into an empty sitting room. A fire whooshes to life in the fireplace and multiple orbs materialize and rise to the ceiling, all without my father taking his attention off me. He guides me to a couch.

I take a long breath in, hold it, then release it in a whoosh. Each breath is slower than the last. I focus my attention on them, on easing the pounding of my heart. Bit by bit, I release the tension in my muscles. Caitlin taught me how to take control of my body and release anxiety. It is a battlefield technique, but also an essential one for life.

"How are you feeling?" Concern etches my father's features. There are furrows on his forehead and subtle crow's feet around his eyes, but he hardly looks old enough to be my father, more like he is in his mid-thirties rather than past sixty. The magic in his veins will extend his life beyond a common person's. He has always said it is why he married late in life.

"How can I be queen if I cannot manage a simple feast?" I hold back my tears, but not because I am afraid to cry in front of him.

He sighs. "You will not go to that court alone. Diarmuid will be your druid adviser and he will always be at your side. It is what he has been training for. You will learn, I have complete faith in it. You have a large, open heart and a tremendous capacity for empathy. It means you are more vulnerable to getting hurt, especially in a royal court, but it will make you an excellent queen who will protect her people."

A laugh escapes me. "How do you always know the right thing to say to make me feel better?"

"It's my job. I'm your father." He tips his head at me. "Besides, King Willard is callous enough to make a grown man cry." He gives me a searching stare. "You just say the word, Keira, and you won't have to marry him. It will always be your choice."

Calls suddenly erupt from down the corridor, with gasps and shouts and loud applause.

"The firelight show has started." My father looks over his shoulder to the doorway. "I better go. They need my contribution to get the colors intense enough. Will you be okay, or should I send in your mother?"

"I'm okay, thanks. I might spend a couple of hours in the library to unwind."

I walk through the dimly lit, winding corridors until I leave the chaos of voices and music far behind. The familiar calm and quiet of the library is a balm to my soul. The orange glow of the firelight is like a waiting embrace.

I am immediately wrapped up by the scent of old leather and aged paper, making my heart rise.

Mahogany bookshelves reach from floor to high ceiling, occupying every wall, with sliding ladders that allow access to the highest books. A rich assortment of colors pops on the shelves, and many leather spines have gold titles embossed on them that glitter in light.

Orbs hover at the top of each bookshelf and there are multiple fireplaces still lit and roaring.

My footfalls click on the mosaic floor as I leave the first room and come out into the main body of the library. In its center, there are couches for lounging and broad desks for research. There are currently a druid and two scholars reading tomes instead of remaining at the feast. I nod to each as I pass.

More rooms branch off this one. There is an entire section for fiction, collected by generations of my family. Another completely dedicated to war, with a tactile table in the middle with maps of both the human realm and the Otherworld. It is in this room that fae history books are kept, but we have precious few, and many are contradictory, especially around the Great War.

I sit down at my regular table and take in my surroundings. This place is full of opportunities; escapes to different fictional worlds and an immense amount of knowledge.

The answer to any question must be in these books.

Except...I can't seem to find the greatest answers I need.

Something doesn't feel right. It curls within my gut. Something *big* that I am not piecing together. My mind keeps replaying that look Prince Finan gave to Caitlin. The smug smile on King Willard's lips.

Maybe it's nothing.

What is there in a single look? A smile?

I have a tendency to overreact.

But why are we not betrothed? Unless he wants to keep his options open.

No. It is the king who is being fickle.

I glance down at my table, in desperate need of a distraction. There are stacks of books piled high all around me, and more spread open at different pages. All are on the fae, and what our historians knew of their world when travel between realms was common in both directions, and people of both races migrated across the veil.

None are original volumes, and that has always bothered me. Information can get lost or twisted when paraphrased.

It is pure insanity that a human would have *chosen* to live in the fae realm, among those cruel people. What could their lives have been like, to live as an underclass to the high fae?

But maybe they spent their lives hidden away in the wild parts of that world, where magic flows through the water like tiny bright lights and mists in the air. Where the low fae live their lives bonded to trees and flowers and lakes, and every day is a celebration of nature and a festival without limitations or formalities.

The fae realm has been described as a place where a person can be whoever they want to be, with absolute freedom. So long as they do not end up in the clutches of the wicked and possessive high fae.

A deep longing rolls through me.

Absolute freedom to make my own choices is so incredibly enticing, but I would need to make too many sacrifices.

My vision blurs as I stare off at nothing. I rub the fatigue from my eyes and study the maps propped open on my desk.

There are four of them, one for each of the fae courts. They are copies of maps almost five hundred years old, and I am painfully aware of how out of date the data is.

In the very center of my desk sits a book bound in crimson leather and embossed with silver flowers and leaves and hearts. It is a romance between a human woman and a high fae lord.

The idea seems preposterous.

Completely implausible that a high fae could love anything, especially a human, but something keeps drawing me into picking it up. Curiosity perhaps.

It must be a complete fantasy.

The utter passion and devotion between the pair, it couldn't be real, and the world-shaking sex…it doesn't sound possible. But I can't stop reading it.

I tap my fingers on the cover of the romance. It is another relic from before the war. I cast it aside for a history tome. The pages crinkle beneath my touch, and I hold my breath as I turn each one, afraid of tearing them.

If Caitlin will take this pilgrimage to the Otherworld, I will ensure she is as informed as possible.

I read the same line again and again.

It is a passage about a powerful fae overlord who once controlled the lands of an entire province in our kingdom, then began harboring soldiers from the Summer Court of the fae realm. He accrued an army, began attacking human merchants to weaken our trade, before he brought his threats upon the king himself. It is one of the many instances that brought about the Great War.

I rub at my temples.

Finan's expression as he leers at Caitlin flashes in my mind. I'm sure he has done it before, on previous visits. A glance too long here, a touch too intimate there. I grind my teeth and push the tome away.

I am driving myself insane.

Footfalls echo through the library, and I glance up at my

approaching mother. Her blond hair has been pulled out of its updo, and the glossy waves reach her waist. She carries a tray with three cups on it and I make some space on the desk for her to put it down.

She hands me a small ceramic cup. "Am I right to presume this tea is required?"

I scrunch my nose at the foulness of the steaming liquid as I take it. "Yes. I was going to take it tomorrow." The contraceptive tea is so bitter I almost gag, but I finish it.

"Tell me what is wrong," she says, sitting opposite me and moving a pile of books. Research on the politics and history of our realm. The things a queen should know.

"I, um—" I shake my head. "I don't really know. Sometimes, I fear that Finan only sees me as a pretty thing to hang off his arm, and the king a potential brood mare. That neither will ever take me seriously."

Mother exhales a long, tired breath. "Every time the prince visits, you fret and worry and pick out all the things that are wrong with him. When he is gone for long enough for you to miss him, you forget your insecurities and pine over the idea of him. You remember him differently from the way he is, and when he doesn't measure up to those standards, you get upset."

My breath catches in my chest.

She continues mercilessly, "Most men are fools, and they find it hard to take the intelligence of a young, beautiful woman seriously. It takes subtlety and years of work to become such a man's ruling partner. First, simple suggestions that slowly nudge him in the right direction, convincing him that your idea was his. Then advice in private, until he becomes so dependent on it, he asks for your opinion in front of others. After months or years of gentle manipulation, a woman might rule at his side. It is a very gradual process, but extremely effective."

I nod vigorously.

"Should I worry he might pick another as his bride?" I ask.

"Yes."

That single word drives home with the force of a battering ram.

"Yes?" I repeat dumbly.

"The marriage has never been guaranteed. We must do everything we can to sway the prince and the king." Mother gives me a long look, and it softens as she grabs my hand and holds it in hers. "But it also means you are not trapped in this relationship."

"But we need the political alliance!"

"We do," my mother answers, patting my hand before releasing it. "But we will manage without it. There are other alliances that can be made. I will not sacrifice my daughter's happiness for riches."

"This is what I want."

Mother leans across the table, stroking back the loose strands of my hair and pinning them down. Her eyes glow as she takes me in.

"I am incredibly proud of the woman you have become. Know that I love you, and everything I do is with your best interests in my heart." She takes in a deep breath and lets it out slowly. "Your father is in his study, and he requires you to join him."

It comes as a surprise. The night is deep, past midnight. Mother ushers me out of the library, then makes her excuses to retire.

As I walk through the empty corridors, an ominous feeling settles upon me. It is almost palpable.

Disembodied voices float toward me as I near my father's personal library. They come from his study beyond. King Willard's words boom as I step into the library, hardly absorbed by the columns of books.

"If Caitlin returns from her pilgrimage pregnant to the magic, *she* will marry Finan. If not, then he can marry Keira. One daughter can be risked in the Otherworld, but the other must remain here as a surety. Keira will not be allowed on the pilgrimage. This is non-negotiable!"

I freeze at his cruelty, halfway to the study. The room spins around me, a blur of bronze and mahogany and leather spines. My chest constricts painfully, making it a struggle to breathe. Something claws within me, tightening around my windpipe.

"Caitlin will not marry Prince Finan. I cannot make that clear enough. No child of mine will be forced into a marriage. And you cannot forbid Keira from making the crossing!" my father roars, and it spurs me on toward that room.

I should run away and cry. Never let them know what I overheard. Gaslight myself into believing that surely I misunderstood.

But I will not be that girl.

Everything fades from my vision except the open doorway of the study and the glow of light that seeps from it. Anger burns red-hot within me, crackling and consuming until no rational thought is left.

"Your girls will do as their king demands!" the king bellows.

I reach the threshold of the study, and the light and heat of multiple blazing fireplaces almost blind me, but I still see enough. Father stands before his chair and leans over his desk, his weight poised on two muscular arms and his face flushed with rage. The imposing figure of the king sits in an armchair opposite, but my father stares at the prince, slumped in the other couch.

"And what do you say, Finan? Have you not told my Keira that you love her? Have you not promised for years that you will marry her?" My father tosses those barbs at him and makes him flinch.

Prince Finan looks to his father, then shrinks into himself. "I will do my duty. I will marry Caitlin if my kingdom requires it," he mumbles.

Mumbles! His betraying words break my heart, and he doesn't even bother to articulate their treachery.

The pain that twists within my chest, that curls out its tentacles and poisons my blood, it immediately fuels the fire that burns within me.

Fury is all I can see. It is all I can taste.

Wind howls through the room, knocking pages to the ground and whipping at clothes. It spins around me as its source, and sheets splinter and form a small whirlwind filled with debris.

My hair surges upward, carried by all that magic, forming a red crown dancing in the air. Sparks crack in the storm around me.

All eyes turn to me, but it is Finan's gaze that I seek. Fear blooms on his face. He stands and staggers away from me, but slips on a book and lands on his ass.

"Keira! I didn't m-mean..." he stammers, hand raised and arm outstretched toward me.

My temper flares at his words and the scraps of paper encircling me combust into swirling embers. How many lies has he fed me over the years?

"I will make the pilgrimage to the Otherworld." My voice echoes throughout the room, intensified by my air wield. I turn and point a finger at the king. "And when I return, *I* will decide if I want to marry Prince Finan."

# CHAPTER 6
# KEIRA

M y teeth are bared as I stare at Finan, at the king, towering over both of them. My power still assaults the room, wave after wave of it crashing down on them like a physical force. It brings out the animal in me.

"I will not be threatened by this wisp of a girl!" The king stands and his heavy couch is pushed backyard, groaning against the floor.

"No one is threatening anyone," my father growls, then looks at me pointedly.

I drop the instinctual magic and my hair crashes down onto my shoulders. Bits of it are smoldering, but the strands remain undamaged by the fire, like it is a part of me. The beast within still simmers, ready to bring out the teeth and claws again.

So much for not making the king feel as weak and pathetic as he is. For being sweet and desirable to lure the prince in with honey.

I am done with that.

"I make my own choices," I snarl through gritted teeth. "This realm does not tolerate kings who force women into marriage — who deny them their right of a pilgrimage."

The king shoots a furious stare at my father.

"Whoa. Okay. Everyone is in shock and angry." My father holds both hands up. "Let's calm things down and talk it through. Keira? Sweetheart? Please, take a seat."

A couch flies across the room and scoops me up into it as I am pushed with a fist of air from the other direction.

"I don't think there is anything else we need to say to each other," I bite out, turning to the man I thought loved me. "Unless, *Prince Finan*, you have something to tell me? Maybe more promises about how you will only ever want to marry me? How I am your soulmate? Already your queen?" I flutter my lashes at him in a sickly-sweet manner.

"I — ah…" Finan glances at his father and swallows. "I want to marry *you*. And I do love *you*, Keira. I tried to fight for you, but—"

"That is true enough. Damn fool of a boy," King Willard chimes in and Finan flinches as though he expects to be struck.

Finan tentatively places himself on his couch again. "But I have my duty to consider."

"Your duty?" I ask. "Your *duty*? Is my power not enough to satisfy *your duty*?"

Beads of sweat form on his forehead and he opens his mouth.

"You know what?" I get up in a flurry of skirts. "I've heard enough of your lies for one night." I turn and leave the study.

"Perhaps the youngest sister would be better for you, Finan. This one has too much fire in her soul." The king's barb follows me as I stalk out of the library.

My father retorts, but I am too far away to hear it. He will have his hands full to repair the damage I have done tonight.

I run blindly through the corridors as I hold the pieces of myself together. A blade twists in my chest, but I won't give any from the royal party the chance of seeing me undone.

By the time I enter the sanctuary of my rooms, I am a sobbing mess. My chest heaves with my sobs. Hot tears stream down my face. I run my hands through my hair, then pull it with such force that the pain kills all thought for a precious moment.

Stupid. Stupid. STUPID.

How could I have been such a naive little girl? Every single red flag I dismissed comes crashing down on me. The lingering glances at other women. The fact that we aren't already married. Sex that is only focused on Finan's pleasure and never mine. Every warning from a family member to guard my heart.

I curl up on my bed like a child, cradling my head in my hands. The wetness of my tears runs down my hands and arms. Each breath comes out in a gasping, choking scream that bounces around the room. My self-control has turned to dust.

What happened to that girl who had dreams? Who had ideas of her own? I have become nothing more than Finan's lover. Being his future queen became my whole identity, and now that those foundations have crumbled, I don't know what is left. Who I am anymore. I am utterly lost and it terrifies me.

I don't register when my father enters my room, but I cry with complete abandon with my head in his lap while he strokes my hair. My mother speaks as she restlessly stalks the room, but I don't know what she says.

The sobs end and much of the pain ebbs away with them. My eyes burn from the salt of all the shed tears, and are so swollen I can hardly see.

Gentle hands remove my ballgown and coax me into my night-shirt, and it isn't until they tuck me into bed that I realize they belong to my mother. She could have called a servant, but she took care of me herself.

My last thought as I drift to sleep is that I will always have my family to protect me.

～

I spend a day locked in my chambers, mourning my old life and the blissful ignorance I lived in, then I return to my duties. Finan came to my door multiple times, probably to fill my head with more empty promises. The first time my mother dismissed him, the second my maid sent him away, and the third time I didn't bother to answer the door and he left. His attempts were pathetic.

My maid laces up the front of my riding dress of navy wool, then pulls leather gloves onto my hands. "I can use powders and pigments to correct the rings under your eyes, m'lady. It is best not to show any weakness to the king...or that prince," Anya says.

"Later." I wave a hand. "Neither will be up for hours, and I'll need a bath when I return. I'd hate to look like a *wildling* before them."

It is time I take back the reins of my life.

The keep is still asleep as I make my way through it, the corridors faintly illuminated by a watery light as dawn arrives. The guards at the gatehouse of the inner wall are the only people I see as I step out into the courtyard.

They look frozen, and rub their hands over a fire in a small brazier that struggles to pick up. They greet me as I pass, and I smile and use my magic to give life to their fire, the coals suddenly flaring bright.

A thin layer of frost crunches under my boots as I cross over meadows surrounding the orchards and make my way to the Protector Guard's training fields.

Shouts and the clacking of wood on wood fill the air as a circular arena comes into view. It has compacted grass, with archery targets and mannequins of fabric and sand for hand combat techniques.

In the ring, Caitlin trains with the Captain of the Protector Guard. Both wear tight dark pants and long emerald overcoats, split at the sides. It is the uniform of the female guards.

Gwyneth holds a thick pad braced on her chest and Caitlin lands high kicks into its center.

I stop to watch them.

"High. Right," Gwyneth yells, and Caitlin's leg swings out and meets the pad as it moves to the captain's side, three times in fast succession. The force of those blows is substantial enough that Gwyneth's body jolts each time she takes one.

"Center!" Gwyneth calls, pulling the pad to her front, and Caitlin brings her leg up, bends it at the knee and thrusts it forward in a powerful move that is lightning-fast. Gwyneth staggers backward. "Again!"

Both women pant with sweat rolling down their faces as I finally approach the training field.

"You can't train in that," Caitlin says immediately, eyeing the narrow skirts of my riding dress.

"I need to learn to fight in dresses. They are what I wear."

My sister takes a long drink from a canteen. "Have the seamstress make you dresses with detachable skirts, like mine. You are right, we need to be trained to protect ourselves at all times, even at a feast. Maybe especially at a feast."

"That is…ingenious," I say.

Caitlin grunts. "Tomorrow you will come here in pants. You will train every day until the spring equinox when we make the crossing."

My stomach rolls and the fire of anxiety rushes through all of my extremities.

"Did I make the wrong choice? I've hardly trained for the pilgrimage." I run a hand across my face. "Gods, I told Finan I don't know if I want to marry him. In front of the king!"

Caitlin takes my face in her hands and her small green eyes narrow. "You made the right choice and you know it. You have been preparing for this crossing your entire life. Late-night reading in the library to help *me* out. Hunting fae in these woods to bring magic home. Honing your magic when you could have spent your days reading fiction and no one would have lifted an eyebrow."

She lets out a long breath. "You have been suppressing how badly you want to travel to the Otherworld for years. Remember your dream of exploring and cataloguing their world? Of becoming a priestess and visiting every time our realms aligned? You lost that dream when Finan came into your life and you decided to live for his cause instead. You will find yourself on the pilgrimage. Work out the rest when you return."

I nod, desperately trying to suppress the tears that threaten to spill.

"I'm glad you're making Finan sweat." Caitlin barks out a laugh. "Men like that pine harder for what they think they can't have."

"Thanks, Caitlin. This feels right, down to my bones, but I needed to hear it from you." I take in a steadying breath, but my voice still trembles. "How long have you known? That they were considering you as well for Finan's bride?"

I feel dirty saying it, like it is my shame.

"Officially, I found out when you did. But I had a feeling. We all since this last year, since my pilgrimage announcement. They have been far too interested in it."

Tears roll down my face and I scrub them away angrily. "I'm sorry." It is not enough. How it must have felt to have her sister's lover encroaching on her. Somehow, Finan's actions always seem to be my responsibility to manage.

"Finan doesn't deserve you. He doesn't deserve to be king. He is too stupid," Caitlin spits.

"I know," I half whisper. "That is why I feel this crushing responsibility to become queen. They need a woman from our family, not only for our magic. We are educated, strong-willed and outspoken. Someone needs to stop him from becoming a disaster as king. He doesn't know how to rule a kingdom or lead an army."

Caitlin nods. "The entire kingdom is not your responsibility. Strathia *will* survive without you. Anyway, there is nothing we can do about that right now." She tosses me some padded gloves. "We are going to spar, and you are going to see how difficult hand-to-hand combat is in a dress, even if those skirts are split."

Gwyneth calls us out on our technique as we land light kicks and punches on each other's bodies. We pull any force from them, but each strike still smarts. Caitlin taps me on the jaw with a fist, then kicks the back of my knees, making them buckle.

"Keira, you'd be on the ground in a real fight," Gwyneth bellows. "You need to work on that defense!"

We circle each other. I feint forward with a low blow to the ribs, then connect the other fist to her chin with enough strength to knock it up, then raise a knee to her stomach.

"Good, Keira. Caitlin, you'd be missing some teeth," Gwyneth calls.

We spar until both of us are heaving messes, hair slick with sweat and plastered to our faces. I smile stupidly at Caitlin and she returns the expression.

"Tomorrow." Caitlin holds up a hand as she sucks in more air. "Tomorrow we will meet at the indoor gymnasium. So…" She focuses on breathing again. "So we can do some proper flipping techniques on the mats."

Gwyneth has me practice various kicks on a dummy of sand and fabric until I can hardly lift my legs, while she continues to train Caitlin with the pads. We both cool down with stretches to make sure we don't pull a muscle, and by the time we finish, the rest of the Protector Guard arrives at the training grounds.

Exhilaration from the exercise flows through me. For the first time in years, I have a dream, and it is for me alone.

# CHAPTER 7
# KEIRA

T he entrance courtyard is bursting with people. The royal court, those of my house and the minor nobles. It is almost suffocating, with far too many bodies packed in between the main gate and the castle doors. I stand at the front of the crowd, where an empty column runs through our center. Voices bounce off the stone of the building, the wall and the pavers beneath our feet.

Nervous anticipation rolls through me, making my stomach churn.

I have watched the Mothers of Magic make their grand entrance through Appleshield Castle countless times before, but today it is different. This time, I have a role to play.

Music fills the air, bleeding in from the band positioned where the orchards meet the bridge that leads to the guardhouse. Slow and harmonious, as instruments are plucked, strummed and blown, with wields of air amplifying the melody to reach my ears. The scent of roasting, sugared nuts hangs in the air, hinting at the festivities to come. It fills my heart with the warmth of fond memories, with excitement and hope.

I duck my head into the clearing, and an excellent view opens before me through the gates. I can see the entire length of the road that winds up from the outer wall and through the orchards to Appleshield Castle. Crowds of villagers wait on either side of the road to pay their respects and offer their daughters to the pilgrimage.

A brooding presence materializes at my side, and I glance at the slender form of Prince Niall, then away, not acknowledging him.

"I heard what happened," he murmurs.

"And what was that, exactly?" I don't look at him.

Niall doesn't take my bait. "Our father is a vicious man, and a bully. He can tear down those with the strongest of wills, and we both know that is not one of Finan's characteristics. My brother does fight for you, in his own way. He tries."

I turn on the prince and whisper harshly, "It is beneath you to make excuses for their bad behavior."

Niall's lips press into a thin line, and a muscle feathers in his jaw. "We had an arrangement, Keira. We were going to work together to make sure Finan's reign isn't a complete disaster. This kingdom needs you. Is that nothing to you?"

"Don't speak to me of duty. Speak to your brother," I hiss, but the heat has fizzled out of me. Damn. Prince Niall knows exactly how to tap into my guilt.

There is a desperation in his eyes. "You know I try every single day."

"Give me time to cool off, Niall," I snap. "Let me go on my pilgrimage. You and the rest of the kingdom will have your answer when I return." I can no longer look him in the eye, but from my periphery, I register his long, scrutinizing stare, then he nods and leaves.

Twin brass horns sound from the top of the watchtowers, causing me to startle. At the far end of the road, a long column of women in white robes becomes visible before the outer gate, trailing off down the countryside as far as the eye can see. Mothers of Magic.

I will become one of them, if no one stops my pilgrimage.

Any woman who crosses into the Otherworld returns as a priestess. A Mother of Magic. She is entitled to all of their privileges, no matter what she does with the rest of her life. The order does not require a woman to dedicate herself to the temple. She could be a mother and a wife. A queen. A warrior. Or she could live in one of the Priestesses' Sanctuaries and work as a teacher of magic, a specialized wielder or healer.

The breath leaves me at the sight of those powerful women parading into our fortress. I am filled with awe at their presence, even at this distance. These Mothers of Magic are truly independent women.

There is a disturbance in the crowd to my left. A shuffling of bodies as someone pushes through. I stiffen at the familiar perfume of sandalwood and citrus.

"Keira. Please talk to me." Finan doesn't even bother to whisper.

"Have you no respect?" I hiss.

"This is important. You are important," he retorts. "And you haven't let me come near you in days. Not since…"

I whip around to him. "Not since you betrayed my trust, Finan. Not since you made it clear you don't care which sister you marry, as long as you get a bit of magic in your heir." My fists clench tight at my sides. He visibly flinches. I am so tired of letting this man walk all over me.

"No. No. I never meant it. I've only ever wanted you, Keira. You have no idea what my father is like. The consequences of saying no to him. So, I tell him things I don't mean, and fight the battles on the day they matter. Can you really hold a single moment of weakness against me?" He looks so vulnerable I almost believe him.

"Yes," I snap. "I can hold it against you. A husband should fight for me *every day*. I'll need you to have my back if I move to the palace."

Finan places his hands on either side of my face, caressing my cheek with his thumb. "We will make it work, Keira, I am sure of it. You will see that in time."

I struggle to breathe. To think. "I need to work out what I want, Finan."

"By going on this pilgrimage?" He drops his hands.

"Yes."

"Please, Keira, don't go. I couldn't stand not knowing if you are safe that whole time. You *know* what high fae do to our women if they get their hands on them. It would crush me if you never came back. Please. I will give you anything else. I will announce right here, to all these people, that I choose you as my bride. *Just don't go.*" His voice breaks.

"I am taking the pilgrimage, Finan," I grind out.

"Why?"

"Because it is *my* choice."

He stares at me with huge puppy-dog eyes, hurt rippling across his features.

I shake my head. This isn't about him.

"Enjoy the festival, Finan." I slip away from him, positioning myself between my father and Caitlin. Both had been staring daggers at our exchange and keep that heated gaze on the prince. Finan doesn't even try to follow me.

The trumpets sound again in a long, brassy note, signaling the approach of the procession of priestesses to the gates of the inner wall.

There must be fifty women in that stretched-out column, each as striking as the next. Ceremonial robes of white silk drape around their bodies in dozens of styles. Long, billowing sleeves extending past hands, short sleeves in puffs of fabric, or no sleeves at all with fur shawls. Loose bodices, tightly laced fabric corsets, gaping necklines or high necklines right up to a throat.

Some women wear veils over their faces or draping down their hair. Others are adorned with crowns of white flowers, long feathers or animal horns protruding from headdresses, simple and curved. All wear furs.

I soak in the individuality and sameness in wonderment. No woman needs to lose her identity to become a priestess.

Flows of magic are woven discreetly around them. The hair of the priestesses floats gently in the air, perfect locks drifting upward. The skin of many glows with the luminance of fire magic like body paint splattered across their skin in bright colors.

Halos of roaring flames surround some, and thin streams of rapidly flowing water encase others. Flowers the size of fists sprout in the grasses along the road in their wake, the many bright petals blocking out the green of the meadow.

The high priestess leads the procession, riding on a saddled elk that has fine gold chains draping from its highly branched antlers. Her wizened hands hold its reins loosely.

Pride soars in me at the sight of her and a wide grin forms on my lips.

A mask of gold engraved with deep, swirling runes covers the top half of her face, and a stag's antlers crown her head. A cascade of white feathers explodes from the sides of the mask, reaching out in great wings, making the entire headdress wider than her slim shoulders. I wonder how she stays upright at all with it on.

My father steps out into the center of the courtyard as the procession enters. "High Priestess Naomi. Mother. Welcome." He helps her down from the elk, though she hardly looks like she needs it.

The high priestess, my grandmother, scans her sharp, gray gaze across the people amassed, not even blinking at the presence of the king.

"I bring the blessing of magic to enrich these lands." Her voice carries upon the wind to all the people. "I open the sacred rite of the pilgrimage to all women and beckon forth the next generation of priestesses."

The courtyard and the people beyond have fallen utterly silent in reverence for their high priestess. Even the musical instruments of the band have halted.

"Candidates for the pilgrimage, join us now," the high priestess calls, then turns on her heel and continues the procession into the castle.

Caitlin leaves the crowd of the audience and joins the column of priestesses, walking among them with her chin held high. Other women follow her lead, bolstering their ranks of white robes.

I take a step toward that line of priestesses, and then another.

It feels like I move within another woman's body. This surely cannot be my life. The hope and exhilaration of my old dream blooming to life makes my heart swell, and I join the procession without remorse or fear.

~

I can hardly contain my excitement as I practically bounce in my seat. Caitlin throws glances my way while we wait, then finally claps a hand down on my knee to stop my tapping leg.

The small ballroom has been converted into a classroom, the banquet tables removed and rows of seating placed in the middle instead. The dais is set up with massive chalkboards borrowed from the war rooms for the use of the priestess educators.

I have heard of the universities in the capital of Sunbright City, but never imagined I'd attend a lecture. That I would have people to study with me.

"I can't express how happy I am right now," I say to Caitlin.

"I know. A lecture on the fae and their world." She spreads out her arms. "It's a dream come true for you."

I beam a smile at her.

We are the first in the classroom, seated in the center of the front row. I don't want to miss a single thing. Three women take a step into the room, then stop abruptly and hover in the doorway. Their gazes dart around the room, from the marble mosaic floor to the gold trimmings on the stucco walls.

I wave the women over. I met them yesterday, at a high tea for the pilgrims and priestesses. I rack my brain for their names. Alice, Nora and Erin.

All three are huntresses from the same small village, clearly uncomfortable in their lord's castle. I urge them to sit beside me and make small talk with them until the unease melts from their shoulders, while Caitlin analyzes the rest of the pilgrims who gingerly enter the class.

"Gods, I hope there aren't exams," she mutters, and the woman beside her giggles.

The room fills with hopeful women from across the Appleshield Protectorate.

Footsteps ring out on the dais and the entire space falls silent. I turn toward the high priestess, my grandmother, as she surveys her prey with a narrow gaze. There is no other way to describe her severe look. I almost smile. There is vast warmth beneath her stern exterior, for any who care to look for it.

A simple white wool dress drapes her sinewy figure, with a gold belt and ermine-fur shawl. Her white hair is worn loose in soft curls, with a few braided bands holding it back, and her skin is a maze of wrinkles. Thick cords stick out along her neck and collarbones as she presses her lips into a thin line.

It is strange to see my grandmother in this role, the gentleness she reserves for her family completely gone. These women around me cowering before her would have no idea of the countless times I cried into her chest as a child, while she stroked my hair and kissed away my worries. She has always been a pillar of support in my life.

"Welcome, pilgrims, and congratulations. You are braver than any warrior," the high priestess declares. "Before we begin, you will give a blood oath to never share the secrets of our order, unless I release the spell."

Her eyes find and lock down on each woman, only moving on after her victim has cringed beneath the weight of her stare.

"You will learn harsh truths that could cripple the kingdom if weak minds discover them. I will not bind you in any other way. If you change your mind before the crossing, you are free to walk away. This is not for the fainthearted."

I glance around at the other women in the room. We volunteer for a deadly pilgrimage that we are painfully ignorant about.

My grandmother steps off the dais and takes the hand of the first woman in the front row of seats. She murmurs softly while the candidate nods, then pulls a tiny blade from her belt and slashes across the woman's palm.

The high priestess curls the pilgrim's hand into a fist and places her own over it, forcing blood to drip. Both women speak and thin wisps of the palest smoke rise from the blood as the oath is made. I watch with an academic's fascination.

When my grandmother reaches me and takes my hands in her icy grasp, pride brims across her features. "I did not expect you to volunteer for the pilgrimage, Keira, though I had hoped," she murmurs. "Good to see you have stopped following every order of that princeling and will take up your own destiny. Hold out your palm for me, child."

I offer my hand and she slashes the fine blade across it. I suck in a sharp breath at the sudden pain, which is only worse when she curls my hand and encases it in her bony fingers.

"Repeat after me. 'I swear an oath to never speak a word of the lessons taught in preparation of the pilgrimage to any other than a priestess. I swear an oath not to speak a word of my experiences in the Otherworld to any other than a priestess.'"

I make the pledge as my blood drips onto the floor. A deep chill runs up the skin of my left middle finger and my palm. A silvery pattern of swirls and loops appears as a thick banded ring, so faint it's only visible as I move my hand in the light. The gash in my palm is completely healed.

Within little time, we are all bound.

The high priestess returns to the dais. "I implore you to listen *very* closely. We will have a week of classes. In this time, you must learn everything you need to know about the fae, their world and their magic. You cannot take notes, so you *must* memorize everything. This knowledge could be the difference between life and death. Once these classes are done, you will have training sessions to fine-tune your magic wielding abilities and hand-to-hand combat. The crossing at the spring equinox is fast approaching."

My heart pounds with anticipation and fear.

The high priestess turns and scrawls on the blackboard. "Lesson one: the fae world is brutal and cruel, and you will need to be the same to survive it. You must understand that we are stealing their magic. Taking things they need to survive. It is a drop in a fae ocean compared to the magic in their realm, but it will likely destroy the fae you take it from. They will fight you to the death to keep it. Now, can anyone tell me what sorts of objects you should aim to steal?"

I glance at the other women. Their expressions range from confusion to complete terror of my grandmother.

"Go on," Caitlin mutters to me. "You might as well answer it."

"Magic-imbued relics, heart-stones or a pregnancy to the magic," I say with confidence. I have read so many books, I probably know most of this lesson.

The high priestess taps a nail against the podium. "Relics. Stones. Pregnancy. As easy as that, right?"

An audible sigh floats through the room.

"Wrong. Have any of you wondered why we do not send men to the Otherworld? Trained warriors in armor? Why not an army?" the high priestess spits. Tension runs up my spine at the sheer anticipation of her next words.

My grandmother leaves a pregnant pause before continuing. "Because they would immediately be seen as a threat and the fae would swarm on them. But a woman? A pretty young girl or a priestess? Surely, she is as harmless as she looks. Perhaps she got lost and wandered into their lands. Maybe she is there to worship the narcissistic beasts they are. Big, strong men and powerful fae are alike: they are too stupid to see a human woman as the threat we can be.

"Our entire culture is built around the needs and convenience of men. For women to survive and thrive, we must be subtle and manipulative and use our wits to earn what they take for granted. We become masters of deception and persuasion. In this, women have been training for the crossing their entire lives."

A silence falls on the room, and many women nod. Anger clenches Caitlin's jaw. We both have our struggles in being taken seriously as leaders by anyone outside our court.

My grandmother claps her hands twice. "Now, let's discuss fae relics imbued with magic." She scrawls again on the chalkboard. "While being incredibly powerful objects, most are hidden within temples and protected by magic, or in the palaces of the high fae. There are lower relics in ancient ruins that could be targeted."

The lesson on relics consumes most of the morning, and I swear I hardly blink as I take in every detail. There are so many different types. Jewelry, blades or armor, all imbued with specialized magic that is either protective or gives the bearer special abilities. Objects passed down to the fae by their gods, or created by the strongest among them, bestowing blessings upon the wearer.

Midday arrives and servants enter with platters of thinly sliced cold meats, aged cheese, dried fruits, chutneys and steaming-hot bread. A comfortable silence falls over the room as we eat. I mechanically shove food into my mouth, my mind a thousand miles away, until I notice how the women from the villages stare at the food and take second helpings, like it is a feast of delicacies. I suppose it is for them, especially at the end of winter.

I nudge Caitlin and make sure she notices, then make a mental note to speak to my father on the state of the villages. If our crops are failing, theirs must be worse, and we cannot have anyone starving.

My grandmother claps her hands, the sound echoing down the corridor, and servants immediately remove the food.

"Heart-stones," the high priestess begins without preamble, chalk scratching against the board. My stomach tumbles, because I already know this is going to be heart-wrenching. "They are taken from the nymphs of the fae realm, who are spiritually connected to the land. Tree nymphs bind to a grove, body, spirit and soul, and within its center there will be a great mother tree that holds their heart-stone. It is a fist-sized piece of amber that carries the source of their power."

She pauses a moment to survey the class. "This is where our mission becomes absolutely brutal. If you steal the heart-stone, the trees will die and the nymph will die, unless another tree nymph gives it shelter, but it will be forever maimed without its power and heart. So expect it to fight you to the bloody death. For it to beg for mercy. You must use your wits. There are a thousand ways to lure the nymph away from its grove before you take its heart. Can anyone suggest any other types of heart-stones?"

I try to swallow down the horror that rises within me, but bile burns my throat anyway.

My heart races at the acknowledgment of my people doing that to any creature, vicious fae or not.

It's not easy to accept that sometimes we are the villains. I only calm myself with the conviction that *I* will not be stealing any heart-stones. Surely there is another way to get what I need.

I lift my hand despite my inner struggle, to answer my grandmother's question.

"Anyone other than Keira?" My grandmother raises her eyes to the ceiling in silent prayer as the room remains silent. "By the gods, do they not teach you anything in the villages about the fae?"

"Flower nymphs, my high priestess," a timid voice calls out from behind me.

"Good. Please, call me Naomi. No need for titles here. Anyone else?"

"Lake Maidens," Caitlin volunteers. "They have multiple heart-stones and seed-stones. A woman could gain a seed-stone with the promise of planting it within another lake and nurturing the new spirit that is born. To help spread its offspring."

"Yes. In theory," my grandmother replies, considering. "But that woman would need to be a very convincing liar. No Lake Maiden would agree to having her seed-stone brought to the human realm, because without the magic of the fae world, her offspring would not be intelligent or self-aware. It would be no better than a sea monster guarding its waters, and could not take solid shape or leave its lake."

The high priestess turns away, dismissing the subject.

"Perhaps if a woman were to make a bargain with the Lake Maiden." Caitlin says.

The room seems to bristle with tension. I swallow nervously. I know where she is going with this.

"Dangerous words, Caitlin. You should never make a bargain with a fae. They are devious by nature and they will try to trick or cheat you. If you are cornered into it, you must be incredibly careful in setting out your terms, and still they will find a way to take advantage of you. Take it from me, you do not want to be at the mercy of a fae. They don't understand the meaning of the word."

A muscle bulges in Caitlin's jaw. I kick her under the table, but that look tells me she won't back down. "The pilgrim could offer to spread many of the seed-stones to other bodies of water in the fae lands, for the payment of one heart-stone. From my understanding, the Lake Maidens can generate more heart-stones. Losing one would be only a temporary loss of their power. What they cannot do is travel more than a mile from their lake, and therefore they rely on other creatures to spread their seeds."

A huge, proud smile fills my face. I found that chapter on water spirits in an incredibly old tome in our library, and excitedly recited my notes on it to Caitlin while she practiced archery. She said nothing at the time, but clearly listened.

"An interesting theory. It could work, but has its risks. This could be one way to avoid cruelty, for the gentle-hearted." My grandmother's eyes slide to mine.

A chill runs down my spine. Caitlin should be planning her own pilgrimage, but it sounds like she has put more thought into mine. "It could work for you," she whispers.

I nod, forcing down the brimming emotion.

As confidence builds within the classroom, more women put forth their suggestions on how to bring fae magic back to our home.

One mentions the dwarves' mines, where they dig magic from the ground as glowing ores and glittering gems, and smith them into enchanted blades and jewelry.

Another, the goblin mechanics of the winter realm, who use the same raw metals and imbue them with magic to and create amazing technologies. The fuel cells of such a device could gift our realm with immense magic.

No one mentions the fact that dwarves and goblins have a taste for human flesh and must be avoided at all costs. Stealing from them would have to be a very covert operation.

The pros and cons and risks of every option are scrutinized until even my head swims. The classroom is abuzz with low, excited voices by the time the orange rays of the setting sun illuminate thick stripes across the marble floor.

There is a wicked twist to my grandmother's lips as she takes in her audience.

She claps her hands twice, and the room falls silent immediately. "There is one very important way to bring magic back to our realm that we haven't discussed yet. The most powerful, the most cherished, that grants us priestesses our name of Mothers of Magic, and gives immense magic to generations of people. Achieving it could give you the honors of royalty and the freedoms of the wealthy. The contribution *I* made from *my* pilgrimage."

"Magical pregnancy," Caitlin whispers. It was how our father was conceived.

"Magical pregnancy," the high priestess barks. "Everyone who plans on a magical pregnancy, please stand up."

Multiple women in the group rise gingerly, including Caitlin.

"Come on, don't be shy. Anyone who has even daydreamed about it. The slightest interest in becoming pregnant to the magic. Stand."

Almost half the room is on their feet now, but I remain firmly seated, because a pregnancy is the last thing I need. There is a sick feeling in my stomach. A sense of anticipation. I know my grandmother well enough to pick up when she is being cruel.

"There is no such thing as falling pregnant to the magic. As pure, untainted magic quickening a womb." Her words ring out. "There is only one way to get pregnant, and it is the same in the Otherworld as it is here."

# CHAPTER 8

# KEIRA

Caitlin's face drops, turning deathly pale, and her eyes become glassy. Her hands visibly shake. I want to pull her into a hug, to take away that pain and bitter disappointment. To allow her to cry into my shoulder, but she would never show that kind of emotion, not even to me. For her, all vulnerability is weakness. To me, there is strength in being able to express it.

I settle for taking her hand and squeezing it, then pulling her back into her seat. My heart breaks looking at her.

"You heard me right," the high priestess continues. "There is no such thing as a *magical* pregnancy."

Caitlin isn't the only one who looks visibly sick. My own stomach twists with revulsion at the thought of bedding a fae. They were once our greatest abusers when they ruled this realm. Rapists. Murderers. Kidnappers. Surely such an experience would be horrible. Traumatic beyond belief.

"But how?" one woman cries out. A lord's daughter who probably saw her way out of a marriage. "Can we even bear their children? Must we lie with a fae beast? Surely, they would be cruel. They would hurt us."

My grandmother lets out a long breath, and her tone softens. "It is true that the high fae kidnapped our women for hundreds of years to be their consorts and carry their offspring, because we humans are far more fertile than their females. Sometimes we hear of incidents of it happening in current times."

I cringe. Those words really do not help.

My grandmother continues on her warpath. "Humans had no magic until ancient Tuatha Dé Danann of the Otherworld opened the portals and visited these lands. Those old gods combined their bloodline with humans to create the fae. Once, when the portals between realms were open and fae lords ruled these lands, our people had great magical abilities due to the interbreeding, but we were not free until we banished the fae from these lands.

"Now the only way to bring real magic back to our people is to mix our blood with the fae, as we once did. Magic does not truly belong to humans, despite how we have built our technology around it. The greatest secret of this realm hides the fact that a magical pregnancy comes from lying with a fae. That our most blessed offspring are half fae. There is no immaculate conception where the magic itself is imbued in a womb, as we would have this realm believe. If this secret were known, this kingdom could erupt into civil war. Those with great prejudice would attempt to slaughter the children of the fae and their descendants."

I am stunned by the revelation. We all are.

Women have been lying with the fae for generations. *My grandmother* did it. The people who enslaved us and took all the wealth of these lands for themselves. Who oppressed us.

I have read brutal accounts of their deeds, copied by scribes to preserve knowledge hundreds of years old where original works didn't survive. So much of the truth has been lost over time. We know nothing of the fae who used to rule from Appleshield Castle, other than his gravestone.

A woman puts up her hand, but it wavers and she lowers it again.

The high priestess' gaze focuses on her. "Speak, child."

"Naomi, was—was it horrible? Was he abusive?"

A high-pitched laugh erupts from my grandmother. "Horrible? No, child. It was thrilling and exciting and incredibly delightful. I almost didn't want to return home. The fae are not like us. There is no stigma around sex. Sometimes, it seems there are no rules at all in their world. They are incredibly free, and every moment in a lover's embrace is celebrated and cherished, unlike many human men who only focus on their own gratification. They are incredibly beautiful and very proficient lovers.

"I suggest you treat this pilgrimage as you would any festival day. Have fun, explore what the place has to offer, and if a low fae takes your fancy, then indulge yourself. The fae definitely know how to celebrate, and there are constant forest parties you can slip into. A single low fae can take many forms, so if a wild form doesn't take your fancy, they can become human-like. They usually do, to entice one of us. Keep away from the high fae *at all costs.*"

Have fun?

She says it as though it is the simplest thing while roaming enemy lands. Falling into the clutches of a fae man is meant to be the worst possible thing to happen to a human woman. How could I ever trust one enough to allow him to touch me? I look around the classroom and notice I am not the only one who isn't convinced. We all wear varying degrees of scowls and sick expressions.

Despite my conviction, my treacherous heart soars at the idea of dancing among the fae. At not only observing their culture, but actually participating in it. Of living, rather than reading life through books.

"Won't we stand out? As humans?" a minor lord's daughter asks.

"Won't they try to kill us immediately?" a villager says at the same time.

My grandmother lets out a long breath as she takes us all in. "One hidden truth is that there are entire villages of humans who still live in the fae world. The druids constantly cross over when we open the portals every seven years. Some unwitting humans accidentally step through the places where there are unmarked rifts between the worlds. Pilgrims decide not to return home. While humans are rare in the Otherworld, they are not completely out of place."

"Why would any pilgrim choose to live among our enemy when their responsibility is here?" Caitlin spits.

"The Otherworld is said to be enchanting, and able to steal a naive woman's heart," I say without thinking, my mind full of that fae romance novel sitting on my desk in the library. "It is said that high fae are especially charming when they want to be."

"Do not become attached to any fae." My grandmother's eyes stare straight at me. "And stay away from the high fae at all costs. Those stories you hear of rape and pillage? The high fae are responsible for those. They are masters of manipulation and they *will* trap you. If any fae discovers a pilgrim is pregnant, whether it is their child or not, they will lock you up and never let you return home. They will use and abuse you as a brood mare. They can smell the hormones and it sends them into a crazed, animalistic state. Remember, it is your duty to bring magic back to this realm. *You must return.*"

A woman raises her hand. "Are you saying that the low fae nymphs and spirits will party with us and make us their lovers, show us kindness, until the moment we fall pregnant, and then they become our villains and captors?"

"Yes, child," my grandmother says softly. "It is exactly what happened to me and I almost didn't make it home. When it is your time to leave, you must run."

The surrounding women nod vigorously. The idea of choosing to stay in the fae realm, of leaving behind my family and people, seems absurd. It is a betrayal of our kingdom.

The classroom erupts in excited chatter once more before the high priestess reins us in again. "We must discuss the different types of fae you may encounter. There are four courts, Spring, Summer, Autumn and Winter, each specializing in different elemental magic and with its own kinds of low fae. Sprites, elementals, nymphs and beasts. They live in the wild parts and are more interested in the pleasures of the flesh than plotting and scheming.

"The vicious high fae live in the cities and palaces, and can easily be avoided." She pauses for dramatic effect. "We will discuss the fae courts in greater detail in tomorrow's class, where we will study maps. You are dismissed for today." She turns and wipes the chalk from the board.

The other women shuffle out of the room, pale from the sheer onslaught of information, but I feel strangely frozen in place.

I turn to Caitlin, who hasn't moved either. "Are you okay?"

"It's a lot of information." Her tone is flat.

"The magical pregnancy?"

She looks at me with distant eyes, then nods. It had been her lifeline. Her way to get an heir without having to endure a man, and it has been taken away from her.

Footsteps click toward us and our grandmother suddenly looms over our position, the facade of our high priestess and educator gone.

"None of that, girl." She slams a hand down on the table in front of Caitlin. "You haven't even crossed into the Otherworld and you're already disheartened? Toughen up. Select a different task and take a niece or nephew as an heir. But if you are set on a pregnancy, listen to me closely."

She leans over the desk to stare at Caitlin. "Many fae are shapeshifters. Some are neither male nor female, and some are both. A Lake Maiden can reproduce asexually to create her seed-stones. They are pure water and spirit, and take the shape of their choosing on land. A Lake Maiden can create a seed-stone through union with a man, or create a pregnancy through union with a woman. The child grown within a womb would be as human as your father is. The Maiden would need to be impressed indeed by a human to make that choice, but of all the fae, they may be the most likely to let that child go to another realm."

There is still a heavy weight upon Caitlin's shoulders, and it is clear she needs to have a conversation with Gwyneth without being able to fully explain what she is asking permission for from her partner, but that deadness within her is gone.

That pure dread of having to touch a man.

"And you, child?" My grandmother places a gentle hand on my shoulder.

"I think Caitlin already has a plan for me." I send my sister an affectionate smile.

"We will stay together when we make the crossing," Caitlin declares. "We will approach the same Lake Maiden."

"Good," my grandmother says. "Walk with me to my chambers. We will discuss this plan for you both."

We stay up for half the night, and I can't stop yawning in the lecture the next morning. The rest of the classes fly by, taught by different priestesses.

My mind explodes with the new horizons that are being opened before me. At the sheer wealth of knowledge their order has collected and kept secret over the years.

After the classes each day, I sit with Caitlin in the library and we talk for hours about tactics and plans, even our childhood. Whenever we speak of subjects revealed in our classes and someone who hasn't taken the oath nears, the silvery tattoos around our fingers shine and the words die on our lips.

A closeness grows between Caitlin and me that had diminished since our childhood. After Caitlin took up the many responsibilities of being the heir to the Appleshield Protectorate, and I became idle, waiting on my prince and my future.

The classroom lessons end, replaced by physical training. I wait with the other pilgrims in the main courtyard of the keep for our teachers to arrive and take us to our first session. We huddle together, shivering in the cool morning. Alice, Nora and Erin cling to me, asking a hundred nervous questions about the training to come. I answer absentmindedly, noticing other women listening in.

Within the space of minutes, I am surrounded by a circle of pilgrim candidates, their buzzing voices reverberating off the stone of the walled courtyard. My attention is pulled in multiple directions as they talk over each other. I rub at my temples.

Gwyneth and Caitlin burst out of the castle's entrance in a show of swinging doors and with a tail of guards behind them.

"Listen up, everyone!" Gwyneth shouts, causing squawking birds to launch off the parapets. "You will learn hand-to-hand combat with me for the next week." She looks around the group appraisingly. "Form a circle around me. Yes, that's good. Now, has anyone here had formal combat training? Swordcraft, archery, wrestling or anything of the like? Step backward out of the circle if you have."

I step out of the group, along with all the other daughters of lords and women who have trained as guards.

"Great. I want you to form the first group," Gwyneth continues. "Any women who are proficient hunters or who are at least semi-proficient in wrestling or boxing or another fighting sport, step out of the circle and form another group." Another sizeable chunk of the pilgrims moves at her command.

Only four women are left, and Gwyneth probes them intently while Caitlin stands at her side, arms crossed. One woman has five older brothers and constantly brawled with them growing up. The next two are professional dancers and women of the night, with enough street smarts to survive. The fourth is an acrobat from the circus.

"This is a good group. Everyone has enough experience to hold their own," Caitlin mutters to Gwyneth, not bothering to lower her voice.

The Captain of the Guard nods. "The women who are drawn to the pilgrimage are almost always fighters."

Gwyneth leads us out of the inner walls and toward the outdoor training field, with a group of Protector Guards flanking us. They will be our trainers for the week.

My boots squelch in mud. The air is fresh but not icy, and instead of frost glittering across the grass, small early flowers jewel the way. Winter has truly passed, and we are creeping toward the spring equinox. I bite my lip at the thought of that deadline. Of the crossing.

"You haven't mentioned Prince Finan in a week. Do you know that?" Caitlin murmurs.

I have hardly thought of him since the priestesses arrived, except to brush him off whenever our paths crossed. How strange, when he was once the center of my universe.

The daily physical training is intense. We spar against each other, perfecting kicks and punches, how to defend or roll out of a grasp.

Each of us learns to fight against a male guard, as tall and broad as the male fae are said to be. How to find his weaknesses, to disarm him and use those weapons against him, how to run and hide. I am paired with Liam and give him a good run for his money.

"Use everything you have in a fight against a fae," Gwyneth announces during one session. "Anything can become a weapon. Snapped branches. Large stones. A handful of sand. If it comes to a fight, assume it will be to the death. But do everything in your power in a head-on confrontation. Forget your pride. One does not take on a bear with their hands alone."

An entire afternoon is dedicated to throwing knives at bodies made of cloth and sand, and another to wrestling huge guards with blunt knives, learning about the best places to cut.

"When are we going to practice archery?" Erin, a huntress, asks.

"We won't," Gwyneth says curtly. "Unless anyone wants a brief, private lesson outside of the class." Eyes turn to her in shock, and she wipes her hands on her tunic, then claps them three times loudly. "Okay, everyone, listen here. There is one thing we must get straight. You are crossing into the Otherworld and masquerading as sweet, lost human girls looking to experience the fae world. Not as soldiers. Not as obvious assassins, though that is what some of you may be.

"The fae must see you as harmless fun. A passing curiosity. At the slightest perceived threat, they will destroy you. You will not engage in a direct attack and you will not have swords or a bow and arrows on you. A knife or two may be passable, perhaps even a staff, but no obvious weapons. That is why we will focus on hand-to-hand techniques."

An icy shiver runs down my spine, and from the many pale faces around me, I know I am not the only one who is unnerved.

My entire body aches by the end of each day, and I return to the castle limping with smarting muscles and blistered feet. I cannot help the permanent smile on my face. I am working toward something that is just for me, a bolster to *my* identity and *my* achievements, and it feels great.

The final week is spent tutoring the pilgrims on their magical ability, and I take on a teaching role rather than that of a student. My father runs the classes, as the most powerful mage in our protectorate, accompanied by the strongest of the priestesses.

The powers of almost all the women are minimal, because any substantial wielder is scoured from the lands and given a high-paying position of prestige in our orchards or guard.

The weeks of training disappear in a flash, and I lose myself in them. Then the ceremony of the crossing is suddenly upon us.

## CHAPTER 9
# KEIRA

I hardly sleep all night, tossing and turning under my blankets. I gasp awake, drenched in sweat and heart hammering, with no recollection of the dream that caused the night terror. The shadows of the room choke me. I create a fire orb to chase them away, watching as it slowly makes a meandering path up to the ceiling.

What if I made a mistake? What if the risks of the pilgrimage are too high?

I must be insane for choosing to trespass into the lands of our greatest enemy, like a lamb to the slaughter.

I slip out of bed and pad to the barred windows, pulling back the velvet curtains and sliding open the small glass pane. Cool air rushes over my face, causing a shiver to run down my spine, but relaxing the knots of my mind.

I can do this.

The world outside is bathed in the silvery light of a full moon. I soak in the entire sight, committing every single detail to mind. There is a sharp drop from my chambers to multiple levels of red-tiled roofs slanted against the main body of the castle.

A full view stretches before me, from the snaking inner wall with guards prowling its top to the expanse of the meadows and orchards beyond the bridge and ravine. There are more protectors making their rounds in the shadows, especially with the king in attendance.

It seems hard to believe that my grandmother was once one of those guards. That she met my grandfather and fell so deeply in love with the heir to the lord protector that she took the pilgrimage to fall pregnant to the magic, so she could throw off the shackles of her low class and marry him.

How far she rose in her lifetime, born as a peasant, to become Lady Appleshield, then high priestess when my mother took over the role of matriarch of our house.

There is fighters' blood in my veins.

I remain there, a silent sentinel, as the sun rises above the horizon, bleeding light across the sky in streaks of orange and red, and the Appleshield grounds wake up.

Teams of people and oxen erect marquee tents along the road that leads through the orchards, huge ones where performers and musicians will entertain crowds, and rows of smaller ones for market stalls. They tie thousands of ribbons to the branches of trees and large garlands of colorful blooms are brought into the courtyard and tied along the bridge.

The celebrations will not begin until the portals open and we pilgrims leave this realm. My legs turn to jelly at the thought.

*You are braver than any warrior.* My grandmother's words return to me, and I know the truth of them.

The bell of the clock tower chimes eight times, marking the hour, and servants flood into my rooms. Sick anticipation rolls through me as my hair is brushed, pulled and fixed, and my face is painted. A mirror is brought before me so I can appreciate my maids' handiwork.

The top half of my hair is braided into a simple crown with fresh white flowers woven into it, and the rest of my fiery curls drape down my back. My full lips are painted in a shade of crushed berries. Colored powders make my already huge hazel eyes look wide and innocent, and a hint of rouge covers some of my freckles and adds to the image.

A sweet, harmless human girl, hiding a killer of fae beneath.

The servants then help me into a simple gown of pale sage-green wool. It laces at my bust, and the skirts are very narrow, parted discreetly for riding, like wide, flowy pants. Leather boots lace up my shins, with discreet blades tucked into each one.

A maid approaches from behind to drape an olive cloak over my shoulders and fasten it at my neck, while another holds out a leather satchel to me. It is my only accessory, containing everything I need to take with me. A change of clothes, a needle and thread, contraceptive herbs that will stop my cycle while I travel, a spare blade and so much more.

I leave my chambers in a daze and follow the sounds of revelry to the small ballroom, where the other pilgrims gather nervously.

We are arranged into a procession by rank, the priestesses at our head, followed by Caitlin, then me, with the lower nobility behind us, then the women of the villages. We appear drab and plain compared to the glory of the priestesses in their showy white gowns, like we are a shadow cast by their brilliant light. They are dressed to inspire awe, and we for travel.

I can't help smiling at Caitlin's outfit. She wears a dark blue variation of her guard's uniform. A light woolen dress that reaches just past her knees instead of her overcoat, but split at the sides to reveal tight leather pants and knee-high boots. Her cloak is a deep navy, with slits in the sides for her arms to reach through.

I am surprised they managed to stop her from wearing a sword at her side. There are flowers braided into her hair, and they are at complete odds with the scowl on her face.

My heart twists as the procession begins.

The cool morning air bites my skin as we step outside, moving in our long column through the main courtyard. The usually drab space has a rainbow of petals scattered across the gray pavers and my house banners drape from the inner wall and gatehouse. They billow slightly in the breeze, their flapping the only sound other than our feet clicking on stone.

The line moves across the broad bridge that spans the gap between the castle and the orchards beyond, its entire parapet colonized by freshly picked flowers bound to it with string. A thick mist hides the valley below, with only the treetops visible.

Slow, winding music reaches my ears, and a cheer rises as the high priestess rides her elk onto the road that winds down the hill of the keep. Our people line it on either side, forming a thick tunnel of bodies. The sight of support is uplifting from the bridge, but when I reach the midst of that crowd, it becomes utterly over-whelming.

People throw petals at us, reaching out to touch our arms as we pass, and so many smiling citizens compete for my attention, waving and calling out my name.

Their joyful voices are incredibly loud.

I am being crushed under all those well-wishers, under those eyes expecting something from me. The world constricts to a sea of faces and moving bodies that all become alike.

My breaths come hard and fast as I try to acknowledge every single person who sacrificed their morning for this show of support, but it is too much. I glance at Caitlin. She stares straight ahead, and I use her tall, slim form as an anchor point. I plaster a smile on my face and wave absently instead of trying to hold each person's eye.

My feet continue on that path of crushed petals as the amalgamation of voices and wind instruments jumbles around in my head, causing it to spin, but I keep my spine straight.

The moment I step through the outer gate and leave Appleshield Castle, it is like a bubble pops. There is not a single person flanking the road through the countryside and the stillness and quiet are incredibly peaceful. A bright blue sky soars above us and the calls of birds are the only songs we need.

Our steps on the paved road take us through rolling meadows with sleepy villages in the distance, past farms and orchards, toward the Mystic Mountains covered in dense forest. The great, open expanses of green end at the foot of the woods. My second home.

The stone road leads through a tunnel of gnarled, ancient trees. Their trunks are wider than a man, covered in spongy moss. Their twisted branches reach up to the heavens and white blossoms cover much of the canopy, alongside green sprays of new growth. Rocky outcrops occupy the spaces between the great snaking roots.

The trek gets much harder in the forest, on a path that has dips and divots, corroded in places, all at a steady incline. I am short of breath as we near our destination.

Not a single woman breaks the formation, not to utter a word or lag behind. This procession is part of the ceremony, symbolizing the journey we are to take. While we cannot speak to each other, we take this pilgrimage together. There is a strange comfort in that. I am a part of something larger than myself.

Every so often, Caitlin reaches behind and squeezes my arm, as if to reassure herself that I am still there. That she isn't doing this alone.

The broad path cuts through a narrow valley between two sharp, rocky hills. All those stones and boulders on either side of us seem to be held in place by roots thicker than my arms. Ropey vines hang high over our heads and small ferns grow out of hollows.

The damp coolness of the forest seeps into my skin, as though spring has not quite arrived here. I pull my cloak tighter, convincing myself it is the air that makes me shiver and not my nervousness.

We pass under the first stone arch spanning over the road. It has three mermaids chiseled into it, with shells, seawater and fae runes all around them. An ornamental gateway that once honored the Summer Court of the fae.

I hungrily examine every detail as I step under it, despite the chill of foreboding that ripples over my skin.

The next arch represents the Autumn Court, with engraved leaves scattered around fae with butterfly wings. Winter has a single beautiful woman, completely naked and removing a seal-skin from her body, with another selky still in its seal form beside her, snowflakes drifting around them.

A tremor runs through me at the last arch. The Spring Court of the fae, my destination. Something draws me there. Something I cannot quite put my finger on. A massive Cú Sídhe is chiseled in mid-leap across the top of the gate, its skeletal maw wide open and its mossy fur appearing to ripple. Flowers bloom all around it.

The path opens to the Moonstone Labyrinth.

Our procession of priestesses and pilgrims funnels into the huge grassy bowl cut straight into the surrounding hills of slate, and into the circle of stones. Each set of arches and pillars in the circle is cut from immense rectangular slabs. The granite sparkles in every shade of gray, with much of its surface covered in yellow lichen.

Druids and priestesses line the inside of that stone circle, white robes intermingled with brown, facing the Tower.

My heart skips as the high priestess takes pride of place at the foot of the Tower. I drag my eyes up and up to the top of it.

An ancient staircase wraps around its outside, and the strongest magic wielders of the druids and priestesses climb its height.

The Tower is completely hollow; its exterior walls are rows upon rows of arches, and those mages on the stairs are visible through them even when they are on the opposite side of the building. Already figures wait on the platform roof, circling the jade plinth sparkling in the sunlight.

I gather before the high priestess with the other pilgrims, every step made as though through water.

It is then that I hear the music. It is wild and free.

Voices sing in a language I do not recognize, accompanied by the sorrowful sound of flutes. It comes from the druids that encircle us. Beyond them, outside of the circle of stone arches, are our spectators and supporters. Our loved ones, the court of the Appleshield Protectorate and the royal court.

"Blessing upon you who dare make this pilgrimage to the Otherworld," the high priestess' voice echoes through the valley, her words projecting through an air wield. "Your sacrifices, your strength and bravery, will save our kingdom. All of you gathered here will enrich our realm with precious magic. May the grace of the old gods protect you and speed your steps back to us. When you return, you shall be initiated into the order of the priestesses."

Caitlin takes my hand and squeezes it. The other pilgrims around me sigh.

"Let the opening ceremony begin!" The high priestess raises her arms directly above her shoulders and tips her head back, ivory and pearl bracelets jingling. My grandmother shoots dual shafts of lightning into the air, dancing and crackling with intense light, then gone a moment later.

Our family never puzzled out where her rare magic originated from.

The fae of the Autumn Court where my father descends from have magic of fire and destructive earth. Winter court fae wield ice and water. Spring Court fae specialize in creation earth magic and spring rains. The Summer Court fae wield wildfires and sandstorms. All have varying dominion over air magic. None I have read about wield lightning.

All human magic comes from mixing our blood with the fae's, and there must be more courts that we do not know of.

My gaze travels to the apex of the Tower. The jade plinth glows softly, building in intensity. Magic wielders surround it, mere silhouettes that fuel jets of raw magic into the plinth.

Thick white beams whip out from their forms, glittering with the colors of the rainbow. The light around them intensifies, blinding in its radiance, until the people are no longer visible.

I force my eyes away, and black auras dance across my visual field. A knot forms in my throat and a vise clenches my chest.

The melody of the druids' incantation increases in speed and intensity, those voices growing louder until they reach a deafening note.

The jade plinth explodes green light across the valley.

The power is captured in a great stream of magic like liquid diamonds that shoots down the hollow center of the Tower.

It hits the jade altar beneath and splits in four directions, one for each fae court, quartering the original beam. Those fluid bodies bubble and boil as they hurl into a second set of altars beneath the immense granite arches, and the rainbow flow of raw magic splits again into at least fifty paths, each one slamming into the portals themselves.

Those Otherworld gateways transform immediately, from dirty, dull, unpolished moonstone that was almost indistinguishable from the slate around it, to a rainbow iridescence that could rival diamonds. A light glows from within the moonstone, revealing a swirling mosaic pattern, where before the portals appeared as haphazard pilings of rocks.

Thick white mists now curl within the entrance of each, rather than the shallow alcoves I had become so accustomed to.

I turn in a full circle, taking in the sight of all those activated portals to the Otherworld. They will be guarded day and night, because now it is just as easy for fae to slip into our realm through them as it is for us to sneak into theirs.

The portals pull at me. That open connection to the fae lands makes my magic swell beneath my skin. I was born to make this crossing.

A priestess approaches each pilgrim, ready to usher us to our destinations. One comes for me, and another for Caitlin.

"We are going together." Caitlin grips my arm with fingers of bruising strength.

"It is not wise to travel in a group," a priestess with a silk hood covering her hair and part of her face says.

"Not a group. Just the two of us," Caitlin cuts in.

"Then please make sure no others take the same portal as us," I chime in at the same time.

"As you wish. Where are you going?" the priestess replies.

"The Spring Court," Caitlin says.

The priestess simply walks off, and it takes a moment for us to recover and follow her. She strolls under one archway of the stone circle and stops at the altar before the spring portals.

"The portal you take is yours to choose," she says in a most unhelpful manner.

She takes two moonstone bracelets from a pouch at her side and places them on our wrists. I immediately feel a gentle tug from the glowing portals before me.

"Can you sense the pull of the spring portals on the bracelet?"

We both nod.

"Good," the priestess purrs. "It contains one stone from each portal. Hold a single bead between your fingers, and it will guide you to the active portal. If you do not feel the call, it means the portals have closed. Do remember that you have until the festival of Beltane to return. It is little over a month in our human realm, but closer to three months in the fae world. Their time moves differently from ours, slower. You may cross now."

I stare at her, rooted to the spot. Caitlin is so still next to me I wonder if she even breathes. It is our time to cross. There is nothing holding us back. No ceremony left. Our entire bodies have frozen in place.

The priestess moves an outstretched arm toward the portals. "Your loved ones are waiting to send you off—or to take you home if you cannot make the crossing." There is no judgment at all on her face.

My gaze follows her pointing finger.

A tunnel, formed by bodies, arms outstretched and holding branches of orange blossom. My father and mother opposite each other at the front, Brianna and Diarmuid beside them. High-ranking members of the guard who are close friends with Caitlin, including Gwyneth. My childhood friends from our court. And at the very end stands Finan. My heart twists to see him there, looking so out of place. Guilt rolls through me at the way I have ignored him these past weeks.

The priestesses never revealed this surprise show of support we would receive at our crossing.

I approach my loved ones on shaking legs, the world spinning around me. I tug Caitlin behind me, our hands interlocked. A tear rolls down my father's cheek and is lost in his beard, but a huge, proud smile beams across his face. He pulls me into a bear hug, his cheek pressed against mine, then releases me just as quickly.

He holds me before him, examining my face intently, his large green eyes full of emotion and his fiery hair in disarray. I pick petals out of his short-cropped beard. "Keira. He may be hunting for you in the Otherworld." His words die on his lips.

"What? Who?" Panic rears within me.

"Never mind. Keep hidden from the high fae and you will be safe. Remember what they did to your grandmother." His hands shake slightly where he grips me, then he pulls me into another crushing embrace. Before I can question him, I am passed to my mother.

She gives me a quick squeeze, then brushes my hair with her fingers. "Stay together. You will do well."

As I pass my brother and sister, I squeeze each of their hands, then offer smiles to the rest of the people. A warmth fills me, lending me the confidence to conquer the world.

I finally reach Finan and crumble into his arms. He holds me so tight, kissing my cheek, then my hair, and I almost don't want to leave. In this moment of fear and vulnerability, I nearly forgive him and want to stay in his safe arms instead of crossing into the unknown.

He pulls back. "There is no convincing you to stay?" Tears form at the corners of his eyes as I shake my head. "The temptation to hold you here and never let you go is incredibly strong, but your father will throttle me. I won't leave Appleshield until you return. I don't care how long it takes."

I nod, then peel his hands from me. Caitlin's grip finds mine and tugs me along those crucial steps toward our portal. She scrubs tears from her face with a single angry swipe of her sleeve.

The moonstone gate vibrates with magic. It is a sweet song that beckons us to the Otherworld, daring us to take the leap. I become entranced by its beauty and there is no doubt in my mind of what I need to do.

Mists curl from its depths, obscuring what lies beyond the veil.

Caitlin's hand wrapped around mine is an anchor point as we step through the portal. Brilliant white light burns my eyes and the high-pitched melody of magic overrides all other sounds. The mist curls in thick tendrils around us, blocking my sight of my own feet, moving sluggishly across our path as I breathe it in, damp, heavy and scented with flowers.

We take one sturdy step after another on even ground that doesn't feel completely solid. An ethereal calm settles over me. Our slow march seems to last a lifetime as we cross realms and universes, stretching on and on, but is also over within no time at all.

The mist thins, swirling quickly and parting to reveal a circle of light at the end of the tunnel, one that grows to show the trees beyond. The music dims until Caitin's panting breaths are audible again...and other sounds from the Otherworld beyond.

I strain to understand what my senses are detecting. Shouts, the whinnying of horses and the grunts of beasts. A high-pitched snicker-ing. The scent of trampled earth hits me, along with the iron tang of blood. Sporadic clangs of metal hitting metal scream out and I grab Caitlin's arm as panic flashes through me.

I know those sounds. They are not dissimilar to the thick of a fight on a hunt.

We are walking into a battle.

I try to scurry backward in the portal, but the ground gives no purchase. It only pushes us forward. The wall of mist continues to clear.

At the center of that parting, a man stands on top of a massive, crumbling tree stump. The long sword gripped in his hand drips with black blood as he surveys his surroundings.

Dark brown hair flows down to his shoulders, framing a severe face that is all sharp angles. Thick bands of black war paint accentuate the hard planes of his high cheekbones, sharp jaw and straight nose. His intense gaze is mostly hidden in shadows. Narrow, branching horns adorn either side of his head, like a crown of twigs.

I forget to breathe. Every single rational thought escapes me. He is the most beautiful man I have ever seen. I cannot drag my gaze away, soaking up every inch of him.

It doesn't matter that he wears battle armor of brown leather and bronzed metal plate, that each segment of the shoulder guards ends in spikes and is adorned with fae runes. My scrutiny dips down to where the leather is unlaced over his deeply tanned chest, revealing rippling muscles beneath. The blood splattered across him doesn't even register.

I want to reach out and touch him.

Caitlin tugs me to the side and I stumble, but I can't drag my gaze away. I am completely transfixed.

His amber eyes flick up to me and narrow, holding my gaze with simmering intensity as broad eyebrows crease over them. His stare does not lift from me, even as his sword slices through the air and cleaves a treelike beast in front of him, spraying more black blood. A spriggan. Those beasts are spriggan.

I know without a doubt that this brutal, beautiful man is *high fae*.

And we are to avoid high fae at all costs.

Our misty shroud disappears completely, and we step into a high fae battle almost completely unarmed.

# CHAPTER 10

# ALDRIN

I pull my blade from the dead spriggan and face another. Black rot drips down the woody branches of its body. This one walks on four legs like a beast, each limb a different shape, with the joints set at sharp angles. Short, leafy branches jut out all over it and the thing's head hangs low on its body, with red eyes glowing back at me with fire. Sickly sap jewels its flesh.

With a sweep of my sword, its head falls to the ground and thick, black blood spurts out. The thing's body lumbers and lands on its side, its shoulder splitting open from the slow impact, revealing the depth of the rot.

The stink of decay fills my nostrils as its flesh dissipates to ash floating away on the wind.

The sight boils my anger. It breaks my fucking heart.

These are peaceful lower fae, and I have to put them down like pox-infected goblins.

"Aldrin!"

I turn at my name being called.

"Cyprien is here!" Hawthorne shouts, pointing his sword to the treeline.

A dozen warriors stand there, wearing the royal uniform, silent sentinels watching us do the dirty work for this realm. We are outnumbered and I do not care.

My impotent frustration runs fire through my entire body, down to the tips of my extremities.

"Do you not see?" I jump onto a tree stump and roar at them, amplified by magic. I raise my sword straight up into the air. "Do you not see the rot on these creatures? The way they fall apart the moment they die, because the magic cannot sustain them? Are you still blind?"

Cyprien shifts on his feet. The elaborate gold trim on his brown leather armor throws the light, along with the gold beads woven into the many braids of his black hair, pulled into a thong and shaved on the sides.

"What I see is snow on the spring side of the border," he throws back, voice booming as loud as a clap of thunder. "No wonder the tulips have died here when winter encroaches on our lands. No wonder the flower nymphs suffer."

I want to shake the man who should have my back. Who should trust me after all these years, but supports my enemy instead. He has always been blind to what is right before him and cursed by his own inaction.

A sharp movement catches my attention and I slice clean through the middle of another spriggan, one that is humanoid in form but has lost most of its arms to the rot. It falls with a disgusting squelch.

These poor creatures are decaying as they live. I cannot imagine the pain they must be in.

Killing them is a mercy.

That much is clear from their high-pitched wails. From the sluggishness of this pack's movements. Their magic can be sown back into these borderlands. The gods know we need every last drop of it.

"Come here and see these spriggan for yourself!" I yell across the space.

All around me, my band of high fae warriors efficiently slaughter the beasts. The ten still loyal to me, doing the work of an entire kingdom. We are not enough.

"I have seen," Cyprien calls back after a long pause, stiff but yielding.

Shock reverberates through me, and I turn to stare at him. There is gravity behind this admission.

I dare to hope for a single heartbeat.

Perhaps I can convince Cyprien of the truth. That *he* could bring others to our cause. That maybe we can save our kingdom, our entire realm, in the short time we have left.

Within a flash, his expression twists from humbleness to something dark and cruel as his gaze flicks over my shoulder. That olive branch dissipates immediately.

An ethereal song whispers in my ear and I swing around to the source of that power behind me. The old portal in the middle of the clearing hums to life, the moonstone arch glowing brightly through the growth of vines draping across it. Mists bellow out.

"No," I whisper to myself. "No. It cannot be."

The portals to the human realm have been locked since the Dividing War. Fae are forbidden from activating them without the approval of the leaders of every single court, or at least their own king.

It is for our protection.

To stop the slaughter humans inflicted on our kind when they still allowed us in their lands. To stop those from both realms dragging back victims.

"I should have known!" A viciousness tears from Cyprien. "I should have damn well known! I almost fell for your lies, Aldrin. Your convenient stories. So we are back to this, are we? You would go against your council? Your people? This idea of yours was the reason you were exiled."

"No, Cyprien! I didn't open the portals." My words fall on deaf ears as he swiftly turns and addresses his soldiers. My weaves of air drag back his commands not meant for me.

"Arrest him. Arrest all of them," Cyprien snaps.

The squeal of metal on metal fills my head as they pull their swords from their scabbards in unison.

The ground vibrates around me as something huge charges and I turn to the alpha male spriggan just in time. I cut it down without a second thought, despite the healthiness of the creature. I have killed too many of its diseased kin. We all have our breaking point when we betray our nature and turn violent.

I fixate on that portal as two human women walk through.

Such insubstantial, slight things, to be my utter undoing.

Pretty, with white flowers in their hair and scatterings of faint freckles over milky white skin, one with red-gold locks and the other auburn. Sisters, perhaps, the first with fire in her emerald eyes and stern angles to her face, the other with big doe eyes and parted rosebud lips. Both have rounded ears.

They look like lambs led to a slaughter, startled by the butcher's blade.

My attention lingers and lingers on them. On the one with a curvaceous body, a generous swell of breasts and the sweetest curve of hips hidden beneath a green dress. She has a magnetism that pulls at me.

I drag my attention back to Cyprien's warriors charging down the slope, double taking.

Men and women pour from the hilltop, double the amount he initially revealed. The sun glints off the metal of their swords and the plates in their armor. The air rumbles with the crashing of their boots and the yells of their attack.

"To me!" I yell at my loyal band of exiles. "Forget the spriggan. Do not let them take the human women." I point my sword at the humans stepping out of that damned portal.

My people rally to either side of me, and we form a wall of bodies. The few kelpies of my band transform to their half humanoid and half horse shape, pulling free the weapons strapped to their sides. They stride eagerly back and forth across our line, without the discipline to hold position.

"Do not kill Cyprien's guard," I growl. "I will not have any deaths from the Spring Court on my conscience."

"Makes our job a hell of a lot harder," Silvan grunts at my side, pulling throwing knives from the sheaths strapped to his thighs.

"I didn't say you can't maim." I ignore the smirk that forms on his face.

The enemy streams down the hill. I wait for them to enter the reach of my magic, calculating the speed of each body and their position in the next moment. The first boots land within my domain and I allow them to trek through it, allow more to enter before I spring my trap.

I thrust my power down into the earth and pull up the roots beneath their feet, belonging to the surrounding ancient trees. The thick lengths elongate into spikes that crush up through the ground, forming a woody wall between Cyprien's people and mine.

Soldiers crash into that sudden barrier at full speed and the crack of their bones reaches my ears. The second wave of warriors hacks at the roots, slicing through them with swords. I pull more roots out of the ground, plucking up soldiers and wrapping them within woody binds.

None would even attempt to rival my magic to wrest control of the roots from me.

Cyprien conjures a localized wind volley that picks up dust and branches alike, forcing me to shield my eyes from the dirt that flicks in my face. With that tempest, he snaps multiple sections of my wall and walks straight through it.

A ripple of anticipation runs through my band as the enemy falls upon us. Sweat drips down my back and my muscles tighten in preparation.

In a great crash of their air shields against ours, bodies against bodies, a clap of thunder rises from us. My teeth jar as the impact runs through my bones and my feet slide back in the dirt, but I hold my stance.

The enemy soldier before me bares his teeth. It is all I can see of his face beneath a helmet with a nose and cheek guards. His sword swings at me and I evade the strike, catching it on the spiked armor of my forearm, reinforced by a shield of air. Sparks fly as the blade slides away and the metal against metal releases a high screech.

I kick the man in the center of his torso and propel him away with a blast of air, his body arcing through the air and colliding with a tree trunk. With a flick of my hand, I have the branches wrap around him, pinning him in place, but he uses the same vein of magic to part the flesh of the entire trunk in two and slip through the back of it, healing the tree as he retreats.

Kai bolts before me, the hooves of his powerful equine legs beating against the ground, and shoots an enemy rushing toward our line with a jet of water. The kelpie rears on his hind legs, kicking another in the chest, then speeds away. There is a huge smile on his humanoid face.

These lower fae are absolute chaos on a battlefield.

An arrow whistles past me, nicking the bare flesh of my shoulder. The wound is shallow, but it hurts like hell. The sting radiates throughout my muscle.

Iron arrows with ash shafts. It takes longer than it should to heal.

"Gods damn you, Cyprien! You're going to kill someone!" I scream, looking for him on the battlefield.

Hawthorne has a shaft through his thigh and two of Cyprien's warriors are binding his arms in iron where he kneels.

A rage runs hot through me, powering my every muscle and focusing my attention on Cyprien. That fool would have saved us both a lot of heartache over our lifetimes if he listened to me.

I stalk straight to him, parting the battlefield around me with a huge gust of wind that picks up all the fae in my path, tossing the enemy force like rag dolls and wrapping them in roots on the ground, and gently placing my own people back on their feet. It expends far too much of my power.

I swing my sword in loops as I approach Cyprien, pooling all of my menace into my words. "Call your people off. Let us have a rational conversation. I don't want to hurt you," I say through gritted teeth.

He sends the sword out of my hand with a sharp slap of wind, then has roots grab my ankles from under the earth.

"Well, now you're really pissing me off," I snap.

Cyprien laughs, but there is no mirth in it. "We can talk when I have you in iron chains."

I unsheathe my daggers and throw them at him, toward his arms and legs, and run into my attack, snapping the twigs wrapped around my feet. A battle of whirlwinds erupts around us as my magic tries to guide the blades and his to throw them off course. Every single one slices into his flesh, leaving gashes too shallow for my liking.

The blood that drips from him is satisfying. How did we come to this?

I barrel my shoulder into Cyprien's chest and my weight throws us both to the ground, rolling in the dirt.

"I. Didn't. Open. The. Fucking. Portal," I growl, landing on top and punching him in his stupid face.

He spits blood. "Then who did? The humans? *Please.*"

"Maybe," I say.

Somehow, in the havoc my attention is stolen for a split second by those human women, as they run through the edge of the battle toward the forest.

We could lose them in there, and I am not about to track humans with an enemy force at my heels. I need them, as witnesses to my innocence and as my glimpse into their Otherworld.

I throw out a hand in their direction, my power taking hold of those vines wrapped around the portal and making them whip out to catch the women in their ropey lengths. I bundle up the two humans in vines and move them slowly, delicately, back to the moonstone portal.

It is a callous, desperate move, but they will have to forgive me.

In that single moment of distraction, with my air shield down, an unnoticed arrow flies through the battlefield and pierces my right shoulder.

The impact throws me off Cyprien.

My head rebounds off stone and the entire world turns black for an instant. Pain rushes in, exploding within my skull and chest, and all I can do is breathe.

I cannot get up, my mind too jarred from the brute force. The iron tang of blood fills my mouth.

The sounds of the battle crash around me, the panicked voices of my soldiers as Silvan calls out to form an overlapping tortoise formation of their bodies and shields.

The whistle of arrows flying through the air registers in my mind, then dozens of thwacks, as they puncture the ground all around me. I shudder as the sensation of arrows slicing into my magic shield reverberates through me. Not all of my people have my immense ability to form them.

We are losing, I can feel it.

I am only senseless for a few seconds, but it is enough to turn the tide of the battle. I scramble to get up and find Silvan pulling me to my feet. An enemy charges at his back and he whips around to defend. Both Drake and Klara materialize behind me, protecting my flank from three of Cyprien's warriors.

I scan the high ground and find the bastards with the bows and arrows, four of them standing at the top of the hill. Rage thunders through my veins as I send roots through the ground to whip out and crush their bows and bones alike.

They will heal in time.

Another volley of arrows whistles through the air and I swing around to see a second group of archers hiding in more trees. I make quick work of trapping the soldiers in the wood, feet, bodies, hands, whatever I can grab at in a fraction of a moment.

But there are more archers. Cyprien must have another dozen people out there, taking us down from the shadows. This show of force means he is desperate.

I whip around in a full circle, trying to find Cyprien within the madness of fighting bodies, throwing away any who rush me with a volley of air. A crazed spriggan bolts past, notched with arrows and screaming.

My energy is sapping away with each drop of blood that flows from my wound. My magic is disappearing just as rapidly. The iron and ash are preventing me from healing.

"Retreat!" I roar. "Retreat to the delta site!"

I use the last of my power to throw up an air shield over the entire battlefield to stop those damned arrows, unable to distinguish between friend and foe who tangle so closely in their wrestling and clashing blades. Arrows hit the surface and sink in. I feel each one like a slap to the back.

"Silvan! With me!" I yell at the man and he follows immediately.

We run toward the human women, so vulnerable in the bonds of vines I put them in.

Their eyes grow wide and their faces pale at the sight of me. I can imagine why. I must look a brute. Blood smeared across my skin and armor, both black and red. Sweat and dirt and stubble across my face. The horns and war markings of my warrior power.

A pang of guilt fills me at the sight of what I did to them: hands, arms, legs, all bound into a spindle like flies captured by a spider. Even their mouths are covered, like my subconscious couldn't bear to hear them scream.

In the heat of the battle, I didn't put the proper care into their treatment. I wouldn't want to be that helpless with so much fighting around me.

My lost sword flies up into my hand as I run past it, thrown to me by my thrust of air. I swing it to cut the vines tethering the women to the portal. It is far quicker than unraveling all that magic. Before I make contact with the bindings, my weary mind tries to think up something heroic to say to them, about how I will save and protect them.

As my blade swings to meet vines, something snaps in those huge doe eyes of the prettier woman. Her red hair turns into pure firelight, red, orange and yellow tongues of flame licking the air. This close, the heat of it sears my face.

A blast of wind and earth magic radiates from her, cracking in a loud boom, then shattering the vines into a hundred darts that hurtle from the two women.

I am thrown to the ground by the sheer force of the power, with multiple projectiles needling my body. Silvan lands next to me moments later, spikes in his body as well. My flesh heals slowly with that ash shaft still through my shoulder, but I try to crawl as the woody spines fall out of me one by one.

Those women run from me.

All I can do is watch as I try to pull myself up, terror mounting within me. Silvan chases them, but he is slow, battle-fatigued and injured. I *need* those two humans. They could be my salvation, my ticket out of exile. And right now, as they head for the dangers in our forest, they need me.

The humans run, holding hands with their arms outstretched as one woman practically pulls the other, who is drained from using too much magic. They crash straight into Cyprien's hidden archers.

I reach out my left arm and the branches of the trees swipe at those archers. I pull at the roots, trying to grab the women so Silvan can catch them, but the other sister destroys them with her autumn earth magic.

"Stay still, Aldrin." Klara is suddenly at my side and her knee presses into my back. "You're going to bleed out if we don't get this ash shaft out of you. Damn, it's close to your heart."

She snaps it and sends fire through the wound. I muffle a scream as the shaft is pulled from my shoulder, then collapse into the dirt, splattered with blood.

Probably my blood.

The pain builds to a boiling point as Klara thrusts healing magic into my open flesh to cauterize it, and I am left panting. Blackness rushes across the edges of my vision, threatening to steal my consciousness, but my sight returns. There is pure chaos around me.

Arrows land in the dirt, penetrating through cracks forming in the shield I still struggle to hold over the entire battlefield. Cyprien himself is dragging my man Hawthorne by the neck of his armor to his ranks.

An enemy archer grapples one of the humans around the waist, dragging her backward. She uses the embrace to lift herself up and kick another fae in the chest with both her legs, a powerful blow that sends him sprawling.

Kai's hooves pound the ground as he gallops toward the edge of the trees, zigzagging through the volley of arrows that flies at him. The earth explodes beneath his feet as Cyprien tries to catch him with whipping tendrils of roots.

More and more enemy warriors rush to cluster around the humans, but one sister kicks the other's captor in the head, forcing him to release the pretty woman. She runs wildly from Cyprien's force that converges on her, but Kai gallops past and collects her in his arms, then thunders away.

Thank the Tuatha Dé Danann themselves for creating those beautiful, utterly insane creatures of human, horse and fae.

The human's screams trail behind Kai as he breaks into the woods, and I swear it is a name that leaves her lips. That she cries for Caitlin.

Klara pulls me from the ground and drags me along in our retreat.

Waves of hot guilt crash through me at leaving Hawthorne to be carried away by the enemy as their prisoner. Ideally, I would want to take the other human woman from Cyprien as well. We have lost this battle and my hand has been forced.

My head spins and black marks the edges of my vision as my energy goes into the healing of that arrow wound. I am damn lucky it didn't take my heart out. My blood still dribbles down my chest, causing my leather armor to chafe across my skin.

The adrenaline of the fight is wearing off, fatigue is setting in, but we are not safe yet.

It is a struggle to get past the dead forms of the spriggan, their woody bodies littered across the battlefield and the branches scraping the bare skin along my shoulders. Some of the low fae crouch over their fallen, wailing in long, low-pitched notes. It is heartbreaking.

There are no dead high fae on this field. Keeping it so was my greatest weakness in this battle. Plenty of wounded limp away.

Cyprien took as much damage as we did, and a quick glance over my shoulder tells me he retreats in the opposite direction.

My air shield over the site drops completely as I slip and crash down on my knees, but there is no pursuit. Silvan pulls me up and both he and Klara support my weight with an arm around me each.

Iris thunders toward me, the kelpie transforming from half mare to her full horse form, skidding to a stop long enough for me to be deposited onto her back.

Agony shoots through my arm as I grip onto her, each jolt from her galloping tearing more of my shredded flesh, but I grit my teeth through the pain. She slows at my command. Somewhat.

The woods fly past at high speed and I put all my energy into not falling off Iris' back or into unconsciousness.

## CHAPTER II

# KEIRA

I am the prisoner of the high fae. Terror squeezes my heart in an iron fist.

They have tied me to a kelpie as it gallops through the woods and I bounce around on its back. My legs straddle its horse half, and vines are looped around both our torsos, pinning my stomach and chest against its bare human back.

The position is too intimate. The creature too human.

I grip my arms tightly around its waist anyway, too afraid to let go. I have never ridden without a saddle or stirrups and have no idea how to remain on otherwise.

Tree trunks whip past at an impossible speed and the woods are a blur of deep green and brown. Branches narrowly miss my arms, and every so often the insane kelpie makes a massive leap over depressions in the landscape, flying through the air and scrambling for purchase on the opposite side, but never slowing its galloping pace.

I cannot breathe for fear. My throat is so tight that dragging in each gulp is a struggle.

I lost Caitlin.

We hardly made it two steps into the Otherworld and I lost her. Our greatest enemy surrounds us, has us each captured, and I don't know how to find my way back to her. I don't care what these fae have planned for me — I will not be their slave or consort.

The kelpie skids to a stop in a large clearing between immense trees. The high fae crash through the woods and join us.

Those restricting vines fall from me and I slide from the kelpie's body, landing on my feet then staggering on the spongy grass. I take three wobbly steps away from it and throw up bile in the bushes. My stomach keeps heaving and heaving until there is nothing left and my throat burns with acid.

"By the gods, Kai! Did you have to make the poor girl sick? You were galloping like you had the wild hunt on your tail," a female yells out.

I jolt, even though I shouldn't be surprised that I understand their language. It is the same one that the Tuatha Dé Danann brought to my realm when they collected humans to breed with and create the fae. Somewhere over the centuries we humans lost ours.

"The spirits overtook me. I could not resist their call," a low, lisping voice replies, one that sounds like it's not meant for this language.

"Kelpie spirits," the woman curses.

"I am not surprised she is throwing up," a man cuts in. "Considering how much magic she used. I would have thought our magic lost from the human realm after all these years of separation between our races."

I heave again, despite every inch of my soul screaming at me to run. To get away from these high fae who bound me and could kill me with hardly a look over their shoulder.

My arms shake as they support me on my hands and knees. A bone-deep fatigue washes over me. Twigs crunch as footsteps approach from behind and I swing rapidly around, landing on my bottom.

That huge fae man approaches me, the one I was enchanted by as I came through the portal. He is as terrifying as he is beautiful, as though every hard plane of his face was sculpted by an artist. High cheekbones, sharp jaw, perfectly straight nose and amber eyes with a simmering intensity.

His russet armor is splattered with gore and a deep wound in his shoulder has a stream of dried blood soaking his leather. He is tall, so impossibly tall, and his shoulders are made even broader by the spikes at the tips of his plate armor. At least the horns and war paint seem to be gone.

A deep frown occupies his face, pinching his dark eyebrows, but that gaze softens as it meets mine.

A wave of intense fear ripples through me at the sight of my hulking captor. I scurry in the dirt, kicking my feet out and finding purchase to push myself backward, away from him. The blood freezes in my veins as my eyes dart across all the swords and daggers strapped to different parts of his body.

He holds up his large hands. I bet he could crush my windpipe with a single one. "No one is going to hurt you." He crouches a few strides away.

"Let me go!" I gasp. "I have to find my sister."

"No one is holding you against your will." He sighs. "And I apologize for Kai's treatment of you. Kelpies are not known for politeness…or great intelligence."

"I heard that," the strange, gravelly voice snickers. "I got her away from the battle, did I not?"

I stare at the high fae before me. There is even blood in his dark brown hair, tied in a knot but with loose strands escaping to hang over his face. Through the gaping neckline of his undershirt, defined pectorals are visible and the muscles of his arms bulge.

I saw him throw multiple fae in the air with a flick of the wrist.

Everything about him screams death and slaughter and power.

I'm too scared senseless to move, to run from this enemy.

"What are you doing here? In this realm?" He doesn't take that intense gaze from me.

"I — we just wandered in. We were picking wild berries growing around a gate, and then we reached through and—were transported." I stumble over my thoughts.

"Liar," he says simply. "It takes great magic to open a portal. Not every fae has enough power to do it. I suspect a dozen human druids at least would be needed. I will ask again. How did you get here?"

I glare at him. He is insane if he thinks that I'm going to give him any information on my realm. That I would betray my people to the enemy.

"Why are you here? Who sent you?" His tone has become more urgent.

"Why do you care?" I bite out the words.

"Why do I care?" he echoes. "These are my lands. If the humans plan to return to them, I want to know."

"I can assure you, humans do not want to return to slavery at high fae hands," I spit.

My entire body trembles, with fear for Caitlin, with terror for myself. I did not travel all this way, I did not fight Finan, to become another man's plaything.

"And yet, you are here! Prejudice and all." Frustration pitches his voice higher as he spreads out an arm. "Did they force you through the portal? You look like a virgin sacrifice, with flowers in your hair."

My hand trails up to my hair before I realize it, touching the bruised ruins of those flowers.

A man in the camp laughs, drawing my attention. He sits on a large stone a few paces away from us, leaning forward in his seat as though he is watching a show.

A woman with lilac hair cleans a bloody wound on his arm.

He is a peculiar-looking man, with skin so bronze it is almost red in tone and hair shaved almost to the scalp, but it is the tattoo of an immense tree across his face that captures my attention. The faint silvery lines start as roots reaching across his chin, the trunk a thin line up his lips and nose, the branches of the canopy expanding over his forehead and under his eyes. It all accentuates the sharpness of his pointed fae ears.

I stare at him, wide-eyed.

"Oh, those were the days!" he says.

"Not helping, Drake." My captor throws a glance over his shoulder.

"What? The virgins were willing. They chose to migrate to our realm," the man called Drake retorts.

"I don't think humans remember that part of their history," the woman at Drake's side mutters.

"I am NOT a virgin sacrifice!" I stand. Boiling rage simmers through me. I have endured too much over the last few hours.

"Did you hear that, Aldrin? Not a virgin." Drake raises an eyebrow, then laughs again.

"Will you shut up!" we both roar at Drake at the same time. The man shrugs.

The warrior before me, the one called Aldrin, gives me an examining look. "I will make you a bargain, human girl: I will free your sister from Cyprien and give her back to you. Both of you will answer all of my questions and then return home immediately through the portal."

A cocky half-smile curls on his face and he holds out a hand to me, bridging the distance, as though he offers an olive branch and not a curse.

I will not fall for this trickery. A bargain is how they bind humans.

"You expect me to trust a high fae with secrets from my land? To be used against my people? I know better than to make a bargain with your kind." I cannot help the venom that spews from me. This anger is the only thing keeping me together.

"Fine." He drops his hand. "But I *will* toss you and your sister back through that portal. Maybe I will send a message with you to your rulers. These are harsh, dangerous lands. I will not have naive girls wandering freely through the forest and getting themselves killed, then having the humans blame us high fae for it."

Aldrin stomps away, but glances back. "And for the record, we do not take humans as slaves."

I have no words.

*Be wary of the high fae. They will outmaneuver you at every turn*, my grandmother's voice rings through my head.

He might not call me a slave, but I am his prisoner, and there is an invisible line between the two.

"Klara, heal her wounds next. Humans bleed out stupidly quick," Aldrin bites out before leaving.

As soon as he disappears, I become a shaking mess, all the fight draining out of me. Bile rises in my throat, but I manage to keep it down. Bone-deep fatigue rushes through me and I sway on my feet.

I finally notice blood smeared across my skin, and the abundance of cuts crisscrossing my arms. Most are shallow, but some are deep gashes, still seeping blood. When I shattered those vines, the fragments cut me too. I hardly felt the pain.

What if I hurt Caitlin? Injured her badly? A sickness rolls through my stomach at the thought. I didn't know I had power like that.

I look at the fae woman. What was her name again? Klara. My vision doubles and her form becomes a lavender blur.

I am taken over by a sinking feeling, and even though my body is still upright, it is like my mind is toppling head over heels, falling and falling down a rabbit hole. My steps falter, but strong hands catch me under the arms and I am lowered slowly to a thick moss carpet.

"Damn, they are fragile." Drake's voice cuts across my senses.

Breathe, I tell myself. Just breathe.

"She is wounded. And used more magic than any human should have a claim to. The girl is drained. And you and Aldrin terrified her," Klara says as she approaches me.

"Me?" Drake's voice is high-pitched. "I was being friendly."

"Well. Go be friendly somewhere else." Klara rolls her eyes at me. They are the most vibrant shade of violet.

I blink, then really look at her. Lilac hair elaborately styled in many thin braids, pinned and pulled back from her face into a large knot, but long tresses erupt from it and drape down her back. Small feathers and gold bands are woven into it. There is a scatter of the palest pink freckles over the tanned skin of her sharp cheekbones.

Her ears have those pointed tips that make dread roll within my stomach.

Despite the prettiness of her features, there is no softness within them.

"I'm going to heal your cuts," Klara murmurs. "It will sting as the flesh mends, especially the deeper gashes."

I nod, completely lost for words, as she grabs hold of my shoulders.

I am not prepared for the searing pain that bites all over my body, like being attacked by a hundred gnats. A gasp flies from my lips and I try to pull away, but she holds me tight. The burning sensation intensifies to a crescendo, before quickly ebbing away.

Slick sweat covers me and panted breaths escape my mouth. I don't know what I was expecting, but it was not this.

"See. Not so bad." She pulls away from me.

I blink at her, gingerly sitting up.

"Hungry?" she asks.

"Yeah." It is all I can manage. I hardly ate before the crossing and now only the silvery light of dusk penetrates the canopy of the trees.

Klara helps me to my feet and leads me through the small clearing between huge ancient trees. She keeps those strange eyes focused on me, and I don't know if she expects me to run or collapse or perhaps both.

The spongy moss carpet is dotted with flowers and completely undisturbed. There is no sign of a military camp here, or other fae. Something is not right, but I cannot put my finger on it.

"How far away is the camp?" I ask.

Klara smiles at me and reaches a hand forward, touching an invisible barrier that ripples and distorts the air. The whole forest in front of us bucks unnaturally beneath her touch. I take a step back as a primal horror fills me, but she grabs my wrist and forces me forward with her.

We step through an illusion and out the other side of the barrier. The world transforms from a tranquil and undisturbed space to a loud and chaotic camp, filled with people and voices. It is like swimming to the bottom of a still lake, then breaking the surface for air and suddenly being bombarded with sound. Behind me, the same sight of the peaceful forest is laid out again.

A ward hides this camp and restricts who can pass through. These are the bars of my prison.

A fire pit roars in the middle of the space and multiple fae sit around it on stumps of wood. A couple of cauldrons hang over the flames with steam billowing off them and a frypan sits in the coals, flatbread baking within it. My mouth waters at the foreign aromas of spices.

My eyes are dragged to Aldrin where he sits around a spread-out map with a handful of other warriors. He points a finger at a location on it, shoving flatbread into his mouth while deep in conversation. Behind him, a pair of female soldiers play a board game with colored stones while one of them is being treated with a herb poultice by a healer.

It is such a normal scene. One I have been a part of many times when we have taken extended hunts. None of the high fae even take notice of me where I stand awkwardly. They don't taunt me or hurt me or even try to throw me in a cell.

I jump violently as the kelpies thunder past. They gallop randomly around the camp, wrestling when they catch each other, hooves flying in the air and bodies that are half humanoid and half horse rolling on the ground.

I take it all in, scanning from one cozy scene to another, trying to find the threat I am not seeing.

At first I look for tents, then I notice the trees. I stare in awe, my arm falling out of Klara's grasp.

Houses are built into those impossibly huge trees, where the trunks' interior are hollowed out close to the ground. Narrow door-ways are built between the grooves of ancient roots taller than any man and small leadlight windows dot the bark of the trunks. Chimneys breach the woody surface at odd angles and the glowing orbs of lanterns hang from the lowest branches of the trees.

These homes are like the apartment buildings of the cities of my realm.

Boxy huts with peaked roofs jut out of the sides of one tree, the structures climbing up its height, supported on top of immense branches. Many have platform balconies that ring the entire trunk, with railings of thick vines in bloom with giant bluebells.

I turn in a full circle to take it all in.

All of the trees have living rope bridges connecting them. The platforms and jutting huts have external staircases and pathways between them. There are four ancient trees converted to fae homes, but within them there are enough buildings to support a small village.

"*This* is your military camp?" I cannot hide my wonder.

"It is one of many abandoned places we visit," Klara states.

"What happened to this place?" My head spins at the idea of this beautiful, peaceful town completely deserted.

The signs of neglect are clear, like a garden that was once sculpted but has since been forgotten and allowed to grow wild.

Lengths of untamed vines hang chaotically from many of the structures. A couple of thatched roofs have partially fallen away and heavy pockets of decaying leaf litter threaten to damage others. A few windows are cracked and all are splattered with dirt, and sparse curtains of foliage hang over some. Slick moss grows on many of the staircases and ladders.

"The same thing that happened to many of the villages in the woods and wilds. High fae abandoned their duties to the land in these parts, in favor of the comforts and thrills of the cities." She spits on the ground, then walks past me, beckoning with a hand toward those cooking pots.

I stare at the apartment buildings grown into trees for a few more seconds, wondering if I could draw them. If my oath to the order of the priestesses would allow me to document them.

The scent of flatbread sizzling in butter drags me to the present and forces me to follow Klara numbly.

My eyes trail again over the amassed band of fae warriors, rippling with muscle and strapped with countless weapons, their hidden magic the most dangerous aspect of them. I should be terrified. I should run as far and fast as I can. My legs should buckle under me and my mind turn to a racing mess, but I am far too spent. None of this feels real as dissociation takes me hard and fast.

I find myself standing before the fire with a metal plate of food in my hands, and I have no idea how I got to this moment. To one side, Klara sits on one of the many logs, back to me and facing another fae woman, deep in conversation. She uses the flatbread to collect the yellow and red curries from her plate and spoons them into her mouth. I deposit myself onto a smoothed stone and follow suit.

My entire existence narrows down to that plate of food, my brain unable to process everything else around me. Perhaps the heat of the bread burns my fingers. Maybe the curry is aromatic, an explosion of flavors on my tongue that is warmth and comfort all in one. I don't know if even a small part of me registers these things, or if my mind expects this. My senses no longer belong to me.

There is a yelling inside my head, drowning out all of my thoughts. A clawing that rips through me with talons of fire, my stomach, my chest, right to my extremities.

I am a prisoner of the fae.

Caitlin is a prisoner of the fae.

We are slaves to their whims and I don't know if we will ever get out.

I stare into that fire, the orange and yellow tongues dancing and flickering, drying out my eyes, and still I cannot blink. My limbs are leaden. My head is groggy and the world swims around me.

I shudder with a start. The people around me have changed and full dark has fallen. Klara is nowhere to be seen, or Aldrin, but that fae with the wicked humor now sits next to me, feet up and sipping from a goblet. He must be my sentinel. I rack my mind for his name. Drake. He notices me staring at him wide-eyed, and tips his head at me.

"Aldrin is a good lord. You will see that." Drake half smiles. "He is fair, and cares about all people; high and low fae. Humans too, despite what they think of us."

So, he is a lord. I tuck that bit of information away, even if I'm not capable of responding.

"I don't think she can hear you. Still too drained from the magic she used, but I am flattered you think of me in that way." A familiar masculine voice floats to me, but I can't quite put a finger on who it belongs to. "She must be in shock. I wasn't expecting her to crash like this."

I sway in my seat, blackness encroaching at the edges of my vision.

"What do we know of humans?" that man I had been staring at says. What was his name? Drake.

Someone curses. It is followed by sharp orders I can't grasp.

That handsome tanned face with those serious amber eyes appears right in front of me, frowning. "Can you walk?"

I stand as if commanded, but the world tilts. Did they drug my food? Enchant me? Make me vulnerable and incapacitated, so I cannot escape, so I am dependent on my captors?

More low curses follow, something about a fragile human, but that cannot be me. I have always been a fighter. Independent. One of the strongest.

I have always stood on my own two feet.

Except for right now, because two arms thick with muscle carry me through the darkness that encloses on all sides.

# CHAPTER 12

# KEIRA

A deep, all-consuming sleep engulfs me. There are no dreams, only endless stretches of nothingness.

When I wake, thick beams of sunlight pierce through the window, and I don't know if it is dawn, midday or dusk. The light is colored by leadlight windows. Their patterns of tulips and daffodils are cast upon the dusty wooden floors.

I am alone in this room, tucked neatly into a bed piled with blankets and furs and pillows, as though I might shatter at the slightest bump.

I glance around wildly, with no recollection of how I arrived here.

Then the memories rush in hard and fast and I hyperventilate.

I snatch up my satchel in a panic and hold it to my chest as though it is armor against any high fae who might burst in and force their will on me.

But they could have done that already if they wanted to.

The groaning of wood and voices outside my hut catch my attention. There is no door in this room, but a curtain of vines hangs over the entrance to give me privacy. But there are also no bars to lock me in.

I move to the window and peer through. This room is perched dizzyingly high, tucked between the trunk of the tree and multiple huge branches. The doorway leads to a balcony and a meandering staircase, which joins with another hut below, and then into the tree itself.

No wonder there are no guards or prison cells locking me in. I'd have to saunter past the entire war band before I could escape, and that is assuming I can penetrate their ward around the camp.

A knock on the doorframe has me turning sharply to it. "I'm coming in," a deep rumble informs me, followed by a pause, as though he expects a response.

I freeze at the rustling of foliage, which permits a tall figure. My heart stops completely at the sight of the fae standing in the doorway. He is a silhouette, the sun behind him blinding me to any details, but the form is tall, with broad shoulders and muscular arms.

Those peaked ears are all too clear, reminding me I am not safe.

He steps into the room and I register those beautiful, brutal features. Aldrin.

I want to back away. To run. There is nowhere to go. He blocks the only exit. The muscles of his shoulders ripple. He could overpower me easily and take the one thing fae men really want from human women.

Aldrin takes another step toward me and I press myself into the wall, reaching for my magic. His eyes look me up and down, drifting across the bare skin of my neckline and arms beneath my rolled-up sleeves.

I will not let him abuse my body without a fight, even if he could take both my wrists in one of those large hands and pin me easily.

I watch his every movement with huge eyes.

Aldrin sighs and leans against the wall casually. "Don't look at me like that. I have come to check on your wounds, not devour you. Humans don't believe *that* of fae now, do they?"

I move to the other side of the room as he tries to approach again. "Klara already looked at them."

"Klara was depleted yesterday, and couldn't completely heal you. I had my own wounds and couldn't do any healing." He stretches out a hand toward me. "I can still see deep cuts half healed."

I let him take my hand in his. It is warm, with skin calloused from regular sword use. He trails fingers across my palm and up the tender flesh of my wrist to my elbow, examining each gash.

Shivers run over my skin, starting from his touch and spreading down my spine.

I peer at his face as he concentrates, that almost constant frown gone, softening his dark features. I want to reach out and trace the sharp angles of his face. To touch those pointed ears. I don't know where the urge comes from.

His fingers slide back down my exposed skin and the desire for him to touch more of me hits my blood.

I snatch my arm back. "I don't need any more healing." The lie rolls off my tongue while my heart thunders.

Aldrin straightens to his full height, over a head taller than me. "Your people do us a disservice. We do not deserve our reputation since the Dividing War. It suited your ancestors to manipulate your histories and cast us as monsters to justify their actions, which made your lands lose its magic. I would have liked to have known your story."

He considers me with deep sadness, turns and walks away, toward the vine curtain of the door.

"You never even asked my name," I call out.

"It's Keira." He glances over his shoulder with an ironic half-smile on his face. "Your sister Caitlin called it out."

I stare at him with nothing left to say.

"Klara will take you to the healing waters to bathe your wounds, since you seem more comfortable with her." Aldrin walks out the door.

I let out a long breath and slide down the wall, falling into a heap on the ground. My chest constricts and sobs threaten to bubble to the surface, but I push them down.

I don't understand Aldrin or what he wants from me, but I am a jittery mess from hypervigilance. From trying to anticipate each threat, his every move, and coming up wrong each time.

Disembodied voices drift to me, most likely from the staircase below.

"Why don't you take her there yourself?" Klara retorts.

"Because she's terrified of me," Aldrin replies.

"You've wanted to meet and understand humans and their realm for years, and now you're keeping your distance from one? Try looking like less of a brute." She laughs. "It doesn't help that you're always dressed in armor, have a thousand blades strapped to you *and* constantly frown. Try smiling." Her laughter amplifies and the sound is jarring to my ears. "Not like that. You definitely need more practice."

His reply is an unintelligible rumble. He must be walking away.

A chill claws through my body. Aldrin is looking for a human pet, and insight into our world. Anything a fae lord would be planning for us must be horrendous.

Footsteps creak on the stairs and then the leafy curtain pulls away and another fae invades my space.

"Come on, I'm taking you to the Living Waters Lagoon." Klara's tone is brisk. "Trust me, you'll like it. The waters are enchanted. They close up wounds, remove knots in muscles and rejuvenate the mind. We go there even when we haven't just fought a battle. You've had a bloody intense couple of days, mind the pun."

I can't help the interest that's piqued within me. "Is there a Lake Maiden or water nymph there?"

How I would love to meet one. Perhaps a lower fae could help whisk me away from these people.

"The waters once belonged to an extremely powerful Lake Maiden, but the magic faltered there a long time ago and she disintegrated. Her essence still lives in the waters, fragmented into a million pieces. This entire area has been abandoned for too long." There is such emotion in her at the loss, I don't dare ask questions.

Klara looks me up and down. "You'll need to wash your clothes as well."

I glance down at myself, noticing for the first time the speckles of blood and dirt that mark my clothes, bits of leaves clinging to the fabric. There is a long gash in a sleeve and another in the bodice that I need to sew.

Embarrassment fills me at sleeping in this. In someone else's bed.

Klara leads me out through the ward again, its mirrored surface bubbling and the sounds of the camp abruptly cutting off.

Ancient, broad trees and mossy open spaces immediately give way to dense woods. We follow a path, a narrow, earthy furrow that could be a dried-up river bed. It cuts between natural stone walls and ends at a winding series of steps chiseled into slate.

A deep cavern opens up before us, with an immense pool encircled by stone walls that extend high above us, open to the sky. Great ropes of leafy vines hang down those walls, covering them in green curtains that almost reach the water below.

I stare at the colors of the lagoon. Great regions of blue, green and purple slowly intermingle and expand across its surface, as though it is coated in oil, but the depths are completely visible through it. The shades are vibrant where the sun hits the water and it sparkles like liquid diamonds.

The stairs lead me to a rocky shore within the sinkhole. Ferns grow across much of the surface and I glance around for the ideal spot to take off my clothes.

"Are you getting in the water or not?" Klara asks in a flat tone. She probably has other places to be and doesn't want to play nursemaid to a human.

I quickly undress, scrub my clothes in the water in such a fluster I hardly watch what I am doing, then lay them out on rocks to bake under the sun.

I approach one of many caverns pocketing the stone wall of the main pool. The entrance is almost completely obscured by curtains of foliage, but it shares the same water as the rest of the lagoon. I consider that it is right next to the bank.

"Why don't you swim in the main lagoon? It is nice under the sun." Klara folds her arms over her chest.

"Are the other fae going to swim in these transparent waters while I am here? I would prefer my privacy, without a bathing suit and all." I am already far too vulnerable to these people. No need to tempt them.

Klara glances at me, clearly suppressing her amusement. "I forgot how you humans value your modesty."

"Have you — are you old enough to have—" I stumble over my words. "Did you visit our realm before the separation?"

"I'm not *that* old." She turns away from me. "If you want privacy in the water, you better get in now while no one else can see you. They'll be here soon. I cannot join you — it's my turn to guard the pass."

Klara leaves as I dip a foot into the pool, testing the temperature. It is warmer than I expected. The water illuminates around my touch like a fire orb was born in its depths. It turns every shade of the rainbow, with white shimmering motes rushing away from me in a ripple. Spheres of lights peel off the surface of the pool, thousands of them floating above the water and bobbing in the air.

Slowly, I lower my entire body in, and those glittering particles flee in droves. As I push myself away from the ledge and swim to the nearest cave, settling in, the microscopic diamonds inch toward me, climbing across my body until they cover every bit of my skin. I glance at my hand, turning it around to watch it refract the light and send shards of rainbows across the cave's walls.

This display of foreign magic should terrify me, but my flesh tingles and the pain of all those cuts and half-healed gashes disappears. It is like my mind floats in a sea of calm alongside my body.

The water is even warmer in my little private pocket, and I wonder if there is a thermal vent beneath me. I breathe in steamy air and listen to the tranquility of water dripping from the ceiling.

I dive under to wash my hair. The water is crystal clear, and despite my privacy above the surface allowed by the cave, underneath I can see all the way to the far side of the lagoon.

It is impossibly deep, its bottom lost in shadows.

I return to the surface and recline on my back, idly floating in the water, a sense of peace and bliss filling me. The bits of white glitter dancing within the water crowd onto my bare body in my stillness, like a blanket of starlight.

The Lake Maiden's magic.

I have heard something similar occurs when the heart-stone of the nymph is taken to my realm and infused in water.

The deep, all-consuming blanket of fatigue upon my mind lifts. The pure panic and fear at my situation dissolves in the water. I can finally think clearly. Rationally.

I need to escape and find Caitlin.

These high fae clearly underestimate my abilities. I am not chained, put behind bars or kept under constant guard.

I finger the moonstone bracelet around my wrist, touching each stone until I find the greatest pull of the nearest portal; the one we entered through. If I get back to it, I can track the other high fae party by all the prints they left in their retreat, but I'll need to do it soon. Before the trail is lost.

Tonight. When they are eating and drinking around their fire.

The beginnings of plans swirl in my head, and I follow each tendril of thought.

Voices catch my attention.

I tread water as a group of fae arrives at the pool. Aldrin leads them down the steps and into the sinkhole. The other faces are familiar, but Drake's is the only other one I can put a name to.

I float closer to the curtain of vines and peer through, thanking the gods for my hidden position.

Their conversation doesn't pause while they peel off their clothes on that narrow shore, the men and women alike, without even turning their backs to each other. The very idea of stripping off in front of any man in my court horrifies me.

I was warned about the liberal ways of the fae, but I am still shocked at the extent of it.

These people are known for dancing naked in flower fields en masse, and for wild forest orgies. Why would bathing together faze them?

Their bodies are beautiful.

They all unfasten buttons and clips, undo laces and pull leather and fabric over flesh, but I can't take my eyes off Aldrin. He wears a simple tunic tucked into leather pants, with a light cloak over the top, and is slowly unbuckling armguards that protect his wrists while talking.

He tosses them to the ground, followed by his cloak, then grips his tunic and pulls it over his head.

My mouth goes dry.

His chest is a sculptured work of art, every muscle bulging and gleaming with sweat like polished stone. I want to reach out and touch it. To run my finger down each hard abdominal muscle.

His pants hug his hips so low that the lines of his legs show above them. His tapered torso drags the eye down lower and lower. A thin trail of hair runs from that center point up to his navel.

He reaches up, hooking one elbow behind his head and stretching it with the other arm, biceps enlarging and raising more of that torso above his pant line in an agonizing sight.

I should look away. Give him the privacy I value for myself. Then his fingers dip down to the laces at his crotch. He undoes them painfully slowly.

My breath catches in my throat, but I finally force myself to turn away. I need to think about escaping, not how exquisite my captor looks without his clothes on.

Those voices on the rocky shore become louder, and I turn back in a panic.

Aldrin is completely naked, stepping into the blue waters of the lagoon, but his body twists at an angle so I get a view of his perfect ass, tight and curved, with thick thighs of ropey muscle. Even his back is defined.

Heat flushes through my entire body, but disappointment spikes within me that I didn't see all of him.

He dives into the water and the spell over me is broken.

I must be insane.

Aldrin swiftly rises to the surface with sparkling water dripping from his long brown hair like some sort of god. The rainbow sheen across the water's surface goes wild around the high fae, and its rippling show is utterly magnificent.

Aldrin runs a hand through his hair and his voice floats to me. "It's not enough to tell Cyprien what we know. He won't believe it. None of them will, especially not from us. We need to show them evidence of what is happening at the borders. To bring the Council of the Spring Court there so they can see it for themselves."

"And how exactly do we do that?" Grumbles a man, with half his head shaved and tight strawberry blond curls draping to his shoulder on the other side. His hair is paler than his tanned skin.

"That is the question, Silvan," Aldrin retorts.

"Can we bring a corrupted spriggan to court? Find one that isn't so far gone it would turn to ash and float away on the journey?" Drake cuts in.

"If the fools would even believe their eyes," says a woman with midnight-black hair and the strangest yellow eyes, like those of a snake.

"No. That would make life too bloody easy," Drake spits.

I float closer to the curtains of vines that hide me, intent on their conversation. These fae are speaking of the Twisted Ones.

Aldrin shakes his head. "It pains me how the lower fae suffer with the corruption. The pain of enduring flesh that rots and breaks away while they live, all because we have abandoned them and these lands."

That same woman turns sharply to him. "*We* did not abandon these lands. *They* did. The council would prefer to remain blind, and the people care for comfort and entertainment only." Anger radiates from her.

Aldrin turns to consider her. "Zinnia, we too were blind for long enough."

Zinnia mutters something I cannot hear, but I swear Aldrin's gaze lands over her shoulder and straight on me instead. It lingers, his expression deepening.

I stay completely still.

Surely he cannot see me, not with the shadows and foliage covering me.

Too much of my body would be visible through the clear water. I can make out the entirety of his bare chest. Aldrin drags his eyes away.

"We need to make an alliance with the humans. Open these lands up to them and allow trade and travel. Our people need each other; they always have. But first we need information on how they would receive us. We need an ambassador," Aldrin says.

"If that girl's reaction is anything to go by, they'll be equal parts terrified and enraged," Drake retorts.

"If history is anything to go by," the man called Silvan, snaps and the rest mumble an agreement.

My stomach tightens.

"You can't waltz into their world and petition their king." Silvan's words are slow, thoughtful.

"No." A slow half-smile grows on Aldrin's lips. "But we have two human women in this forest. So if we are very kind to them, and they understand our good intentions, that we want to improve relations to the benefit of both realms, then maybe they might decide to speak with us. If their king sends us a party for negotiation, then no one will need to waltz into their realm."

My head spins. Aldrin definitely saw all too much of me. I wonder if he realizes how obvious his manipulations are.

Drake actually laughs. "Yeah, you make it sound like getting the cooperation of the human woman is the greatest challenge here. Have you forgotten about why we were exiled? Hell, Cyprien took one look at us standing near two humans and accused us of treachery."

"It is a significant obstacle to get beyond," Silvan states.

Galloping hoofbeats echo throughout the cavern, and the kelpies race into view at the entrance to the lagoon in a cloud of dust particles. Shock shatters through me. My heart leaps and thunders wildly in my chest.

Are we under attack?

What could spook all three kelpies like that?

They leap impossibly high into the air, their back legs shifting into fishes' tails. I stare, mesmerized, as scales flip up over fur, legs shrink into small fins and tails expand and widen rapidly.

When they hit the vibrant water of the lagoon in mer-horse forms, the surface explodes in shudders of rainbow light and huge waves curl out from the site of their impact.

I scream.

They land almost in front of me.

Then I scream again as the billowing water completely opens my curtain of vines and I wrap my arms over my chest in a panic.

It gets worse. They swim below the surface, where they can see the entirety of my nudity.

The kelpies can transform into a full humanoid form. They can speak our language. I have no idea how they feel about our flesh, but the consideration makes my skin crawl.

All the high fae turn and stare at me. I flush from head to toe, wanting to die.

"Someone is in there—" Drake squints in my direction, trying to see around the bulky forms of the others, who clearly block me from his view.

"Give her some privacy. You know how humans value their delicate sensibilities," Aldrin says, and they all laugh, but he has to drag his own gaze away from me. The look on his face for that split second is hungry, almost feral.

They turn away, everyone except Drake, who is still trying to get a good look into the cave with an expression of confusion. Aldrin shoots out a burst of magic and dumps a wave of water over his head.

I scramble up the ledge to the sounds of more laughter. It isn't directed at me, but it might as well be for the way it makes me feel.

As soon as my feet are on land, I create a thick curtain of vapor around myself, picking up water from the lake with a frantic air wield and turning it to mist with a hint of fire, so no one can see through it.

As I stumble over the stony ground, stubbing my toes, I hardly question being able to handle so much power at once.

I find my clothes, shove them over my half-damp skin and run. I hurdle past Klara, who is still on sentry.

"Hey. Hey! What happened?" she yells after me. "Is there a threat?"

Klara swears, but I keep running and she doesn't chase after me.

The gravel path slips beneath my feet, making it hard to pick up speed, and overhanging branches whip past me. The narrow dried-up creek bed gives way to the dense forest of newer growth and I stop in my tracks.

I could easily escape right now, but I don't have my satchel with my basic supplies.

And they would look for me almost immediately.

But I can't go back to the camp, either. The ward has completely hidden it, and for a moment I wonder if its purpose is purely to hide the base. If maybe there isn't any magic locking me in. I thought Klara was my guard for this morning, but she let me run straight past her.

Footsteps thunder up the path and I turn and stare like a frightened doe, gripping one of the hidden knives in my belt. Panic grips me and I shiver with the adrenaline that pumps through me, preparing for fight or flight, but I have nowhere to run.

Aldrin crashes around the bend and into my sight. He is wearing only his leather pants and boots, and rivulets of water still run down his bare chest.

He holds up his hands as he approaches. "Look, I'm sorry if we upset you. The kelpies are literally half-wild beasts. There is no keeping them to social niceties, and I…well, I thought if I joked about it, you'd feel less embarrassed."

I stare at him.

"We have gotten off to a bad start," he mutters.

"I can't imagine why. Our first meeting was completely pleasant." The look I give him is deadpan.

Aldrin holds out a hand and slowly reaches toward mine, as though approaching a wild animal. Part of me screams to back away, but the greater part wants him to touch me.

He takes my wrist gently and turns my arm from side to side, but I still gaze at his face, not concentrating on what he is doing. I do not understand this man, or his small acts of kindness.

Aldrin gives me a lazy smile. "The waters healed your wounds without a scar."

My eyes dart across his glorious bare chest, to where the arrow ripped right through him and left a gash so large their magic couldn't heal it completely.

Any evidence of the damage is gone. Gods, I don't understand this entire realm.

# CHAPTER 13
# KEIRA

I sit in a nook between the tall roots of the trees that hold the village, next to the barrier of the shimmering ward. Shadows swim around me and keep me apart from the fae. I hope they forget me, even for an hour.

The warriors sit around the bonfire, eating and drinking for another night. Aldrin reclines with his people, and snippets of their conversation float to me—contemplating whether to send a messenger to Cyprien or to plan an ambush on his forces. The discussion goes around and around in circles.

I need to escape here. To infiltrate the other fae camp and free Caitlin before Aldrin makes his move, so we can be far away from these parts when their two forces clash and we have double the number of fae captors to contend with.

I grip my satchel so tightly my knuckles turn white and my fingers ache. It's packed full of flatbreads and a canteen of water. The ward ripples beside me. My entire plan depends on being able to trick the magic here and pass through it.

On the far side of the camp, the next sentry approaches the ward. My heart pounds against my ribcage as I scramble to my feet. I don't know what kind of magic he uses to peel it open, but I hope that it makes the entire barrier penetrable in that moment. That as the sentries swap shifts and exchange a few words, they won't notice a small human slipping away.

I am relying on it.

The sentry puts a foot through the ward, making the entire thing vibrate and distort, and I plunge through it. Part of me expects to hit a solid wall, but I pass with a complete lack of resistance from the magical barrier.

My mind roars with anticipation of discovery, every sense heightened as the calm voices of the guards float to me. I spare them a single glance as they change shifts, then I make for the thick forest cover nearby.

Every slight crunch of twigs under my careful footfalls makes me cringe. My instincts scream at me to run, but I can't draw attention to myself. I jolt at every sound, mistaking the breeze moving branches for be a sentry coming for me. The cries of animals for the raising of the alarm.

I creep with painstaking caution through the shadows from the camp to the thick woods, darting between trunks and stones, and constantly checking the position of the sentries to ensure they won't notice my movement.

Minutes last a lifetime, and though I have mastered the patience of a huntress, I have never been the prey.

I reach the dense foliage of the ancient woods, out of earshot and sight of the sentries, and I run like the wild hunt itself is on my tail. I thrust out my wind magic to ruffle behind me and hide the tracks I leave.

Branches whip by, and I duck and leap as I move to avoid their lashing needles. My chest heaves and my muscles burn with the exertion, and still I don't stop running. The fear that rushes through me chases away all thought but the need to escape. To be free.

The darkness of the night is so thick I stumble and trip, landing face first in the leaf litter and mud, throwing out my hands to catch myself at the last moment. I am forced to light an orb to illuminate my way, or to slow my pace right down. I choose the orb, uncaring of what I might disturb.

The landscape all looks the same to me, and I don't know if I have been running for minutes or hours. All I can hear is my heavy breaths, the swishing of foliage and my boots hitting the ground. I pray to the gods that there are no predators nearby.

The pull of the moonstone bracelet becomes stronger as I move in the right direction.

I could be at the portal before Aldrin knows I have left his little war party. I hope he has too much to drink and stumbles to bed half blind. That he wakes up in the morning bleary-eyed, and doesn't notice until noon that his pet, his intended plaything, has disappeared. Maybe he'll be too hungover to think I am worth the effort of a chase.

Unfortunately, he doesn't seem the type.

Fatigue builds in my muscles until pain laces through them and I can hardly breathe. I stop and brace my arms on my knees, almost doubled over, and pant.

The space between trees has widened, and the underbrush is minimal. This is probably the way we fled from the battlefield, not that I could think straight strapped to the back of that insane kelpie.

I jog at a steady pace. When I get home, I am going to kiss Gwyneth for all the endurance training she drilled into me.

Two moons hang in the sky above me, one full and the other waning, casting the world in shades of indigo and deep green. Tree trunks resolve out of the gloom into shadowy pillars covered in spongy moss, and their girth could almost be mistaken for the silhouette of men, if not for the broad branches heavily laden with foliage. My pace quickens to a run as I regain some of my energy.

That portal is enticingly close now, maybe a third of the distance I have already covered.

A chittering sound rushes above me from the branch tops. It turns my blood to ice. I stop and swivel, looking for the source, but see nothing. It's the wind. Nothing to be afraid of.

But I *know* that sound.

I flee with all the power I have left.

Pairs of glowing emerald lights blink at me from the darkness, then disappear. The short blades at my belt are in my hands in an instant, and I grasp my magic at the ready. I will not be undone by wild beasts, not when I have come this far.

I skid to a stop as a huge Cú Sídhe lands a handful of paces in front of me. The beast is majestic, with rippling mossy fur and vines trailing away from a skeletal face that is stark white in the dark night. It snarls, saliva dripping from sharp fangs.

Another runs along the branches above my head, chittering again. A scratching in the canopy on the opposite side alerts me to a third beast. The Cú Sídhe in front of me howls, then snaps its jaws, feigning an attack toward me, then curving away.

I know this game. They hunt in a pack.

Both Cú Sídhe in the trees lunge down at me, their graceful bodies outstretched as they arc through the air with those huge, clawed paws aimed at me. I throw out my arms, a hand pointed at each creature, and thrust blades propelled by air magic into their chests. Each Cú Sídhe flies away from me, curled up and spinning through the air, until their backs strike tree trunks.

I am left shaking by the sheer amount of magic I burned through, but my fight isn't done yet.

The beasts slide to the ground, shake their heads, then slowly approach me. In my realm, such a blow would have killed them, but the fae are so much more powerful in their own lands. My blades were too short to do enough damage. If I had a bow and quiver full of arrows, all three would be dead by now.

The third leaps to the ground, and they surround me on all sides.

The Cú Sídhe circle around me slowly, yowling and toying with me. I form a lasso of air around each of their throats, then pull it taut. The beasts whip backward by the neck and claw desperately at my tethers of magic, scratching rents into their own flesh. They gasp and pant for air that isn't coming.

My heart breaks at the sound, at the brutality of what I have to do. Silent tears run down my face. I don't want them to die, but I need to live.

A blast of magic smashes into my chest. Air propels me up and over. The entire world tips on its side and the ground rushes up to hit my face. I instinctually drop my grip on my attack and use my magic to catch my fall instead. To my surprise, I land on a soft bed of moss that I swear wasn't there a moment ago.

I am going to die.

Those Cú Sídhe will rip me apart the second they escape. But the attack doesn't come.

A narrow stream of fireballs erupts above my head, right through where I had been standing. The high-pitched yelps of the Cú Sídhe pierce the night, so close and loud, I clamp my hands down over my ears. The ground vibrates with the galloping of their retreat.

The expected scent of burnt fur or foliage is absent. The beasts don't wail in pain, so they aren't injured. I have no idea what happened.

I roll over, then freeze as Aldrin stands over me.

I collapse my head back onto the moss. The fight flees my body as bitter disappointment floods me.

I am slowly lifted to my feet, not by his arms, but by the roots of the trees surrounding us.

A dozen tendrils smoothly wrap around my body until I am completely bound by him again, arms pinned to my side. I try to pull free and fail. I could try destroying them, but I would probably pass out.

I glare at Aldrin. A distance behind him, a few other high fae wait in the shadows, but they are too far away for me to make out their faces.

"I had this!" I growl at him. "Don't think you have come in as a big hero and saved me!"

I never wanted to see him again.

"Saved you?" Aldrin barks a harsh laugh. "Keira, I saved *them*." He points in the direction the Cú Sídhe fled in. "There was no need for you to kill such healthy creatures. Not when this world is dying because there aren't enough fae in it. A simple fireball scares off Cú

Sídhe. If you don't know something as basic as that, you shouldn't be running off into the night in these lands."

I glare my hatred at him. At the injustice of those words, when I was fighting for my life.

"This is typical of humans, to kill a fae needlessly," he dares to throw at me.

"You are the one who has taken me as your slave. You have stolen my freedom, and you dare to chastise me for defending myself? Those Cú Sídhe tried to make me their meal. I did not hunt them!" I spit venom at him, but I don't show how close I am to breaking. My whole body trembles from absolute terror.

Aldrin's entire face falls, and the roots of my bindings slacken around me. "You are not a slave. You never were." His voice breaks.

"Your prisoner, then. What is the difference?" I laugh bitterly.

"You are not my prisoner." He takes a few steps to close the distance between us, then falters.

"What do you mean? You had me carried away from that battle against my will. You held me in your camp with the ward and kept me up in that tower so I couldn't escape."

"No," Aldrin says, eyes wide. "We rescued you, healed your wounds, and gave you food and shelter. We allowed you to roam freely in our camp. Gods, the ward is an illusion spell to keep us hidden, not a barrier. I even offered to help rescue your sister."

"You offered me a bargain!" I yell. "I know nothing about you, Aldrin, but you hold me against my will and expect me to feed you information about my realm. Why would I trust you? Betray my people to you? For all I know, you were one of the fae lords who lived in my realm and took our lands before the portals were closed."

I am hyperventilating. My chest heaves against my loose bonds and it is all I can do to stop myself from shattering into a million pieces and crying in front of this cruel fae man.

"I wasn't even alive back then," he says slowly, deflated. "Few fae are left who lived in your lands during the Dividing War."

I blink at him. "I thought high fae were immortal."

Aldrin raises an eyebrow at me. "Do you really think it is possible for anyone to be immortal? Our time moves slower here. If a fae visited the human realm every twenty-five of our years, almost a human lifetime would have passed in your realm. That's how your myth started. True, we live a lot longer than humans, but no one is immortal. I think a lot of what you *know* about fae are myths, distortions and pure fabrications created by the humans who closed the portals and needed to justify their actions in your histories."

Confusion rolls through me, chased by bone-deep fatigue. I am so sick of his games. I can't tell the lies from the truth anymore. Maybe my assumptions and prejudice created my own prison. Maybe not. The moment I escaped, he chased me down. A cage without bars is still a cage.

"I am not your prisoner?" I waver.

"No. You never were." A deep sadness rolls over him as he looks at me.

I don't believe him. The events of the last two days rearrange themselves within my head and I see it, exactly how this man can rationalize to himself that he hasn't taken a human slave.

Maybe he believes he is better than other high fae, that he won't force his will on a human woman, but he is holding what is not his to keep.

We are dancing in the gray space between captive and companion.

# CHAPTER 14
# ALDRIN

Horror runs through me as I stare at the brave and strong woman before me. Keira fought every step of the way like a creature of the shadows, and now I know why.

This whole time, she thought she was a slave captured by an enemy force. That I was going to force her to — The thought is too confronting.

How many warriors would have been crushed under the weight of those circumstances? And here she is, still battling for her freedom. This is a woman I could respect.

A deep sadness fills me at what the humans clearly think of us. What she thought of *me*.

I am at a loss for how to gain her trust, until a terrible idea comes to me. Completely foolish, really.

"I will pledge a blood oath to you, Keira," I say with as much grandiose as I can muster. She raises mocking eyebrows at me. "I will never hold you against your will, enslave you, make you a prisoner or a forced consort. This oath will stand as long as I live."

I pull a knife from its sheath at my waist and slice it across my palm.

Glittering spheres of white lights gently float up from my

outstretched hand, hovering above our heads, then shattering into hundreds of fragments and raining down on both of us. A tinkling sound fills the air like the ringing of a hundred tiny bells.

Keira places out a hand and catches the sparkles on her palm. They absorb into her skin, lighting up the flesh for a single moment.

The roots that bind her at my command slacken completely, falling to drape across her hips and legs. I can never restrict her like this again.

Not unless she wants to be tied up beneath me.

The image flashes in my mind. Her arms tied to the posts of my bed and her stunning eyes hooded with hunger as they stare into mine. A light flush over her freckled cheeks and lips parted as rough breaths escape them, as I hover over her.

I blink hard to return to the present.

"Yet, here I am, bound up by your power for a second time. I'm starting to think you enjoy tying up vulnerable women." The smirk that forms on her lips is absolutely wicked.

I am a fool for not taking an oath to her earlier. For not proving to her that she is safe with me. If only she knew what I have endured because of my respect for humans.

I grin stupidly and lazily retract the roots.

"Wait. Let me try." Keira's brow furrows and sparks of light flow through her hair, lighting up the red, orange and gold strands. Interesting. There is a lot this little human is not telling me. The tree's roots are whole one moment and turn to dust the next, the particles holding the original shape for a heartbeat, then floating away into motes.

Keira sighs. "My magic is different here. Stronger. I've never done anything like this before."

It is autumn magic. The command over elemental wind, fire and earth magic to destroy and sow back into the ground. It is the opposite of my earth magic of spring, creation and growth.

I hold out a hand to guide her over the broken ground and she takes it.

Actually allows me to touch her this time.

The skin of her fingers is soft and pale, and her nails are well-shaped and clean. These are not the hands of a laborer. I try to ignore the weary, measured look she gives me and how she pulls away from me the moment her feet are on level ground.

I analyze her from the corner of my eye. The regal straightness of her back, the fact that she holds my eye when she argues with me, rather than showing the subservience of a peasant. She has a light scattering of freckles on her face that would intensify if she worked under the sun.

And she is incredibly articulate.

Keira is no commoner who accidentally crossed into my realm while foraging for berries.

Nor is she a druid, the only humans who seem to cross between worlds with regularity anymore. Not with her level of ignorance.

I have to find out her story, and I know I will not like it.

I lead Keira back toward the camp, Drake and Silvan following behind but giving us space. When Keira turns to me, head slightly cocked to the side, there is an analyzing look in her eyes. I become caught in them and suddenly there is nothing else in the world. The night retracts to only the two of us.

"You keep defending your ancestors." A frown deepens on her face. "Saying my history books have been corrupted, but what if your histories are wrong?"

I let out a long-suffering sigh. I had been enjoying the few minutes of peace between us. "Tell me, please, what do humans say of the fae?"

She bites on one of those perfect rosebud lips. "The lower fae are devious and wild. They are as likely to attack a human as they are to bring her to their wild parties in meadows and make her a lover."

"Is that why humans come here, to take a lover?" I feign a laugh, but it is a very real question.

Keira laughs. "No. No, of course not. The reputation of this realm has a certain appeal. Of beautiful fae with wings and colorful skin, lavishing attention on a girl and taking her to festivals where she can enjoy herself with complete abandon. Of absolute freedom. This realm is enchanted compared to ours. There is wondrous magic everywhere. Human women are expected to behave, to cover up and hide any aspect of their sexuality. To get married, have children, then die. Here, a woman could be something else, whatever she wants."

There is such longing in her voice. I wonder if she too was trapped back in her realm.

"And the high fae?" I ask as we approach a denser part of the woods, lighting more orbs to illuminate our way.

I have very, very little fire magic, left over from a distant Summer Court ancestor, but these are simple tricks.

The smile fades from her lips and the space between us suddenly widens as though she remembers I am some terrible predator. It only twists a dagger in my heart a little.

"The high fae are known for kidnapping our women. For taking them to bear their children, because fae women are near barren." She shoots a nervous, apologetic glance at me. "That a human should avoid high fae at all costs or be used and destroyed by them. That wars are fought between courts over the possession of a single human woman."

Tension coils through me at her revelations. I knew we would have to break prejudices within the human world, but I didn't think they would be this bad.

"The threat we pose to your kind is that dire, and yet still you choose to wander into my realm?" I muse.

"I didn't—" Keira turns abruptly to face me and almost walks straight into a low-hanging branch. I reach out and lift the thin limb before it can strike her, bringing our bodies close for a fraction of a moment. Keira doesn't flinch away and it makes something swell within me.

"And do we eat our own babies as well?" I ask in a perfectly innocent tone. "Or are we supposed to kidnap human children to eat? I need to know how I should behave."

Keira shoots me a dark look.

I shake my head. "Do you realize this is the most common propaganda monarchs use to turn their people against a perceived enemy? Stealing brides and babies?"

"Do you know what every single fae does in this court?" she throws at me. "Are you aware of their every action in other courts? Can you guarantee that a high fae has never hurt a human woman? Never tried to keep her against her will? Never kidnapped a plaything?"

"Well, no." I rear away from her intensity.

"These sorts of stories come from somewhere." Keira picks up her pace and stomps through the woods ahead of me.

"It is not a systemic issue," I call after her, then speed up so I am walking next to her. "It's not normal fae behavior and would not go unpunished. That is the difference. It sickens me that humans think all high fae indulge in violence and rape and slavery."

Keira stops abruptly and we glare at each other. Her lips work, but no sound comes.

There are cracks in her anger, as though the rationality of my words got through to her.

I chance taking a step closer. "Think about it, Keira. Do you not have criminals in your realm? It doesn't mean all humans are corrupt. What do the druids say to your people? Do they counter these lies?"

"The druids?" Confusion crosses her face.

I nod. "They are the only humans who cross between realms every alignment, and who truly know us fae. There are communities of them in each court. I have visited their city here in the Spring Court. They could tell you that your histories are full of lies. That their females aren't harassed."

Keira stares at me for a long moment. "Their order is incredibly secretive. The masses don't even know druids still live in this realm. I wouldn't be surprised if they don't even share information between their factions."

Disgust fills me. These people allowed hatred and fear to fester in their realm without bringing the truth to light. We walk at a slow pace, and I grind my teeth. A glower forms on my face as I stare at the darkness ahead.

"So they allowed prejudice to grow," I say finally. "And they become complicit in their silence."

145

Keira gives me a sidelong glance, delicately lifting herself up over a fallen log. "I once found a book in our library of court transcripts that were a couple hundred years old. Multiple druids were burned at the stake for contradicting the known history of the Great Fae War. For trying to disband what you claim to be lies.

"They were charged with treachery, abuse of their position of power and conspiring with the enemy. Maybe they decided their version of the truth wasn't worth their lives, especially when no one else was getting hurt."

I raise my eyebrows at her. "A peasant girl who forages for berries can read? Has access to a library and the time to go through old court documents?"

A blush blooms across her cheeks. "All people are given the opportunity to learn to read where I am from."

My smirk widens. She is becoming more and more interesting.

"Well, what do the fae think of humans?" She shoots me a hard glance. "Cyprien accused you of a crime when he thought you had opened the portal."

"It's not what we *think*, it's what we know," I venture, then realize how arrogant that must sound. "The portals between worlds were once permanently kept open so humans and fae could pass through the checkpoints at will, and people of both races lived in both realms."

"Yes, and the fae high lords stole half of our kingdom, becoming our rulers." Keira doesn't miss a beat.

"Not exactly. A fae could not own land in the human realm. But some married humans and became custodians of their land when their spouses died and their children were too young to rule over the land. Some did this for many generations of their family, stepping in whenever they were needed. I cannot imagine the trauma of outliving so many loved ones."

I shake my head, but quickly press on before she can interrupt. "A black market rose in the trade of 'magical flesh.' Vulnerable fae were hunted and slaughtered so humans with little of their own magic could consume our bodies and steal what was ours. The human kings did nothing to stop this trade; some even indulged in it. Evidence of the practice was clear when a king who had no magic suddenly showed new abilities.

"When we fae decided to protect ourselves and created a warrior band that tracked down and destroyed the human traders, war broke out between the realms. It was us who closed the gates and knocked them out of alignment, so it would be very difficult for humans to travel here."

Keira gives me a disbelieving glare.

"*We* could open the portals again if we wished, but it is a crime," I say. "You see, many of us believe humans slip into our lands to hunt our lower fae to continue the ancient black market flesh trade. That *they* steal *our* babies when they prey on our males for their seed and return home with a child in their belly."

A darkness crosses Keira's face and for a moment I think she is going to be sick. "And what do you believe?" she almost whispers.

"I believe it. The perfect society doesn't exist. A people where every single one of them is good and just. It's not possible." My boots crunch over frost dusted across the wild grasses, but I hardly feel the cold. I pull aside the broad fronds of a fern to allow Keira to pass.

"There are humans who would march an army on us to slaughter every fae, to remove the threat we pose and steal every drop of our magic," I continue. "There are fae who would occupy human lands, hoard their resources and enslave their people. I am sure there were fae lords who abused their custodianship when our realms were connected. A system of laws and consequences is needed that makes corrupt individuals accountable. To ensure no race gets away with exploiting the other. Keeping the realms apart is not the answer. We both suffer from it."

"And this is what you are fighting for?" she mutters, those huge, pretty eyes gazing up at me. Something changes in her expression. Like she finally hears me.

"One of many things, yes." I soften from looking at her.

A silence stretches out between us as she chews on my words. It is peaceful. The silvery moonlight casts the forest in soft hues and the chilled air swirls around us in a gentle breeze, carrying the scent of disturbed soil and bruised leaves. Puka skitter in the branches high above our heads, the mostly nocturnal low fae only visible as small blurs of black fur and huge ears fleeing our approach.

"Tell me," Keira says softly. "Why are you so sure that my histories are corrupted but yours are accurate?"

I scratch at the stubble on my face. "Because we don't only write our histories in books. We extract a copy of the memories from people who lived through the events, seal them with magic and preserve them in libraries. Anyone can view them."

"Memories are tainted with the bias of the people they belong to. You preserve the prejudice of those fae as well." She throws me a hard look.

"Yes, we do, but it doesn't mean their experience is any less authentic. Our Living Memory Scrolls cannot be tampered with later. They are experiences seen, heard, tasted and felt firsthand."

"A snippet can be taken out of context," she snaps. I don't understand why she is fighting me on this.

"Often, dozens of memories are preserved after a significant event," I counter, and Keira opens her mouth, but I throw my hands up in the air. "Perhaps you need to view the Living Memory Scrolls before you can judge if they are valid or not."

"Perhaps I will." She shoots off through the brush ahead of me.

"Are you normally this argumentative?" I call out.

"No. People normally find me quite agreeable." She slaps foliage out of her way with exaggerated aggression. "But people don't often villainize my entire race."

"Villainize?" My voice pitches high in my shock. "But you said — but I — you're trying to get under my skin now."

She laughs at my reaction, but then her face turns somber. "Are you going to get into trouble for fraternizing with humans?"

This woman makes my head spin. The track splits and she walks in the wrong direction. I grab her elbow and pull her toward me, onto the correct path.

"You have no idea of the grief I have suffered for being sympathetic to humans," I say. "I suspect it's why Cyprien was surveilling me, to make sure I was behaving — which I was. Your timing was very unfortunate for me."

"Are you some sort of rogue party?" Her eyebrows crease into a frown.

I exhale, long and slow. "You could say that. Exiled. To the wildlands. We cannot set foot into the capital city unless summoned."

"Is that why you were fighting Cyprien? There was so much anger between the two of you."

A flash of red-hot fury boils within me at the thought of the man. "Cyprien is a fool. A blind, rash fool." Bitter betrayal floods through me. "We are enemies because he killed my sister."

Keira stops suddenly and stares at me, stunned. I almost crash into her. The blood drains from her face and her skin turns deathly pale. "And now he has *my* sister."

Unshed tears glaze her eyes and her hands start to tremble.

"No," I say, wiping a tear that escapes her eye with my thumb. "No, it's not like that. He is not a cruel man, just stupid."

Keira angles her whole body away from me, as though she has remembered I am a monstrous high fae. It hurts more than it should.

"I will make that bargain with you, Aldrin." Her entire countenance is cold once more. "I want my sister freed from Cyprien, but I will not return to the human realm until I am ready to leave. I have hardly experienced this realm."

A distance opens up between us and all I want to do is close it back up again. I don't want her to leave, either. I have a feeling I am going to need her.

"A bargain." I hold out my arm to her. "I will help you release Caitlin from Cyprien's capture. Once your sister is free, you will tell me your story and why you traveled to this realm when I ask."

Keira takes my hand. "It is a bargain."

I slide my palm up her wrist so that we grasp arms instead, then shake it firmly twice. Thick ribbons of bright white magic wrap around our clasped arms, tying them together with multiple loops. They feel like silk brushing against my skin, warm like a ray of sunlight on a cold day. My skin tingles where it meets Keira's.

The glow of the magic dissipates, leaving silvery loops etched into the skin of our wrists in matching tattoos. Keira looks down at them, then up at me, horror growing on her face. Those pink lips part in shock as she struggles to speak.

"Don't fret." I brush away the strands of curling red hair that fall across her face. "A fae bargain isn't the horrendous thing I am sure you have been warned about. They are our most valuable currency. The only one that binds a person to their word."

I scan her face, tipped up at me, large doe eyes wide. It is an effort to keep my hands at my sides when I want to grab her chin and turn her face from side to side, so I can inspect every detail of her beauty. I want to brush those lips with my own, to see how they would taste. If they are as soft and supple as they look.

Perhaps this is why only young, beautiful women wander into this realm: because we fae find them so irresistibly beautiful. So delicate and fleeting.

Her chest heaves. My hand somehow clutches her wrist, and I lift it to examine the markings of the bargain there. Her creamy flesh is pale and iridescent compared to the tan of my own. Smooth, where mine is full of calluses from years of handling weapons.

Keira doesn't pull away from me, but I let go of her anyway. "We will leave in the morning. I expect to find Cyprien by nightfall."

I am almost certain I know where he has set up camp. The man is far too predictable.

## CHAPTER 15

# KEIRA

A large yawn cracks my jaw as I sit huddled by the fire with a mug of sweetened coffee in my hands. Morning came too quickly.

I stare at the silvery lines of the bargain that run up my hand to my lower arm, turning it around so I can view the entire faint marking in the morning light.

I have lost my mind.

There is a sincerity about Aldrin that I almost find myself trusting. We have a common enemy for the moment. To get Caitlin back, I only need to tell Aldrin my story. Then we will see if I am truly his prisoner or if he will let me go.

He never specified how much of my story was required.

I won't need to betray the priestesses or give away the purpose of our pilgrimages. I came to this realm on a journey of self-discovery. That is my story.

Not to steal relics or heart-stones or an unborn babe. The details of my secondary mission, to convince a Lake Maiden to give me a seed-stone, I mean to leave out. I will not give a fae any information on my people. Not when they could use it against us.

I am staring into the fire, utterly lost in thought, when a large figure joins me on the mossy log. His weight causes it to roll slightly and I jolt out of my daydream. I whip my head to the side to find Aldrin beside me, shoveling a spiced porridge-like breakfast into his mouth with sweet flatbread.

"Not a monster. Only me," he says as he practically inhales his food.

"Oh really? And here I was thinking you were one and the same." I can't help the smile that creeps onto my face. I get pure joy from taunting the man. It is absolutely different from flirting.

"Well, that hurts," He grunts.

"It's hard to lose the association when my first impression of you was made while you were dripping with black blood and slicing a spriggan in half."

"You can talk." He looks up at me with a growing grin. What is it about this man that thoroughly breaks down my defenses?

"What?" I snap. *"What?"*

"Really? You don't know?" His smile widens at the blank look I give him. "Do you have any idea how many spikes of those vines you pierced me with when we first met? Why do you think we sat around all day yesterday? I had to heal, too."

I frown at him. The bastard is taunting me. I hit him in the chest, but his smile widens. "You shouldn't have tied me up in the middle of a damned battlefield! And it still didn't deter you from doing it a second time! You must really like it."

"Needed to keep innocents out of the battle. I didn't know you were a seasoned fae killer." I give him a dark look, knowing he speaks of the Cú Sídhe from last night. If he had any idea of the full truth, he would hate me. Aldrin eyes my coffee. "Where did you get that?"

"Klara made it for me. She also told me I look like shit — her exact words — and asked if a bunch of puka had dragged me around the forest for half the night." I swallow.

Klara had produced a small mirror, the kind many of the men use to shave on the go, and the woman staring back at me was not one I recognized. There were leaves in my knotted hair, dark rings under my eyes and tiny scratches on my face. I looked like cats, or puka, had gotten to me.

Aldrin stands, turning to Klara halfway across the camp. "Hey, Klara! Make me a coffee?"

"Make it yourself, Your Royal Highness," she throws back. "The kettle is on the fire."

"Worth a try. I think she likes you better than me." He winks at me as he sits down.

How did I not see this side of him? It makes my chest flutter when I should be wary of this dangerous man. I will be done with him soon enough.

He searches my face as though he is trying to see into the depths of my soul. "Tell me, how does a human woman have so much magic? I thought it would be bred out of humans by now."

I choose my words so carefully. "I come from a province where the veil between our realms is thinnest. Entire rifts open up when the worlds align. Magic leaks through, enriching our soil and water. Sometimes low fae get lost and wander in. There is an underwater river beneath our orchards that flows straight from this realm." I don't mention the hunts that prey on low fae or that my grandmother became pregnant to a fae.

"Hmmm." Aldrin scratches his chin, which is now clean-shaven.

He doesn't believe me. The story sounds feeble to my own ears.

"The magic has always run deep in my family line," I venture, but it doesn't change his expression.

He considers me. "You have no idea how much magic you have. What you are capable of. I can train you, if you like?"

I give him a long look. "Why would you do that?"

"Because I am bored and curious and I hate to see talent wasted. Maybe I feel bad about the way you have been treated here. Let me make it up to you."

Aldrin wants something from me, but I don't quite know what. It makes every instinct for caution rear within me. But there is so much I can gain in this, so I nod.

"Great. But I have a price." A smug smirk grows on his face.

I roll my eyes. "Of course. Fae always have a price."

"I teach you how to better wield your magic…" He raises an eyebrow. "In exchange for a kiss."

I stand, kiss him on the side of the forehead as I would my father and start to walk away, before glancing over my shoulder. "You have your payment in advance."

The man expected me to squirm or blush like a maiden.

He grabs my wrist lightly, playfully tugging me back to him. "Not exactly what I meant."

"Well, you should have specified." I slip my arm away.

Silvan and Drake approach, unintentionally blocking my escape. Their focus is on Aldrin alone.

"We found Cyprien's camp. It's exactly where we thought it would be." Silvan frowns profusely. Despite the tight curls of reddish-blond hair that drape down to his shoulder, he looks mean, with the other half of his head shaved and his eyes permanently narrowed.

"Gods be damned," Aldrin grumbles. "It's going to be bloody difficult to root him out. We'll go for the backup plan."

I glance between all three men, utterly lost in the undercurrents. Not for the first time, I feel like a rabbit surrounded by wolves, holding my breath and hoping they don't notice me.

Aldrin stands and scales a stone table that still has food spread out on it, his boots bringing mud to the clean surface. His features pinch with anger and his eyebrows furrow in a deep scowl. Those branching horns grow at either side of his head, a crown of twigs. Beneath his tanned skin, black bands emerge, streaks that highlight the sharpness of his cheekbones, jaw and brow.

The man I had been teasing a moment ago is gone, and this fae who took his place half terrifies me all over again. I came close to forgetting what he is.

"Everybody listen here!" Aldrin's voice booms through the space, enhanced by the wind, and they all crowd around him, even the kelpies. "Cyprien and his men have set up their encampment at the Frozen River Fortress, on Winter's border. While this makes it harder to penetrate their defenses, it also has benefits. The location is an hour's hike to the Dividing Cliffs, where we *know* the evidence is laid bare to support our claims. No one can look upon those lands and still disbelieve us!"

Muttering breaks out through the amassed people. I scan them wildly for any hints as to what they are talking about.

"Will we be able to come out of exile?" Drake asks with eagerness.

"Let's not get ahead of ourselves," Aldrin says. "You know how stubborn the man is. It could be an effort in itself to get him to look at the view from the Dividing Cliffs. Not to mention we need to infiltrate his camp first. Having one ally will not get the council to believe us, but it is a start. You have all been incredibly loyal, and as always, it does not go unnoticed or unappreciated."

Aldrin claps his hands. "Pack up the camp. We leave immediately. It is a day's hike to get there and I want to strike tonight, in the early hours, when their sentries are at their weakest."

The space around me turns into a frenzied flurry of action. I am an island within a churning mass of movement. An incredibly awkward one.

People work with swift efficiency to clean away the breakfast spread and pack any belongings. I sit back down on my log, feeling useless, especially after a fae rips the unfinished coffee from my hands, throws it on the fire and rinses the mug with a splash of water magic.

My satchel is already packed and over my shoulder. It always is. I grope around for something to do, but it seems this dance is so well practiced, it is complete before I get a chance to join.

I am all but collected by the crowd as the march through the forest begins. The muscles in my legs protest after the strain of the night I just had, but I push through.

Our band stretches out in a long line for the duration of the trek, people clustering in groups of twos or threes to talk. The scouts at the front disappear from my view and the kelpies whizz up and down the line with a tremendous amount of energy. I can't help wondering how much faster we would get there if we had enough kelpies for us all to ride. Perhaps such a thing isn't commonplace here.

I find Klara at my side, crunching on a large, crispy fruit with navy-blue skin that has iridescent, milk-white flesh within. It almost looks like an apple, and I wonder if it would taste similar.

She sees my curiosity and pulls another from her pack, offering it to me wordlessly.

"Is it normal for kelpies to join a roaming band?" I ask to fill the silence. I turn the fruit over and over in my hand, considering it. "Shouldn't they be linked to a specific body of water?"

Klara tosses her core into a bush and licks the juices from her fingers. "No. Kelpies are nomads and typically travel the realm to visit different rivers and lakes and oceans. They don't normally swear allegiance to anyone, but Aldrin fights for the survival of all fae. Their pack has been greatly affected by the corruption. Kai, Iris and Freya are all that are left. That is why they have joined us."

I open my mouth to ask about the corruption — it must be whatever is creating the Twisted Ones — when a grating voice cuts through my thoughts.

"I would like to taste the water of the human realm." Kai trots beside me, half horse and half man.

My gaze reaches his navel, then his bare chest, and having to slide up all that skin to his eyes.

I hadn't noticed before that his humanoid skin has a blue sheen to it, flecked with transparent scales where a human man would have chest hair.

During the battle, Kai had a thick layer of hard, blue scales coating his shoulders like armor, but they are gone now.

His nose is wide and almost completely flat with two long slits at its base, and his hair is the color of old seaweed, a green so dark it's almost black, with streaks of navy. Kai's eyes are the most unnerving, the brown iris occupying the entire space with no white shown, the eye of a horse instead of a man.

It is unsettling how his features change so much between form and the way they blur sometimes. I have seen his face look much like that of a high fae, with regular eyes and a straight nose. Sometimes, his cheeks have scales and long fins that drift on the air like they would in water.

He can pull at will any aspect of the three shapes he can take, without having to commit to a full transformation.

"I don't think you should visit my realm." Tension ripples through me.

"And why not?" he asks.

I swallow. How do I answer such a question without admitting that we hunt fae? That we treat their bodies as trophies and delicacies?

"The fae are not permitted into the human realm," I say. "It is punishable by death in my kingdom."

"And yet here you are, walking free in our realm. Humans are hypocrites," Kai spits.

I stumble on a branch caught between my feet and quickly catch myself.

"Fearful hypocrites," Klara chimes in.

"But Aldrin says we need them," Kai adds.

It is incredibly difficult to get a read on his emotions. The expression on his face never changes from stern disapproval and that voice is always so gruff.

"The portals have been closed for a very long time." I find myself on the defensive. "My people only remember the war."

"Hmmm," is all that Kai responds with. He leaps over a fallen log and transforms into his full horse form midair before galloping away.

"He does that a lot. It makes it hard to win an argument," Klara mutters beside me.

The hours tick by and the walk through the woods is long and brutal.

Pain sings out in my thighs and my lower back aches by the time we reach a site to stop for lunch. Klara uses most of the time to draw the fatigue out of my body, but guilt radiates through me at taking away her strength.

"It is nothing," she reassures me.

"Aren't you tired? Don't you need to conserve your strength?" I ask her.

"I am fae. This walk is nothing for me. Actually, we could run and be there within an hour, but I don't think you'd like to ride a kelpie again, and we can't tire ourselves out if we want to attack Cyprien's base tonight."

The woods change as we navigate through them.

Trees with full canopies and trunks slick with moss give way to bare branches with only pale leaf buds or white flowers decorating them. Wild grasses become coated in glistening frost, which intensifies until patches of snow dot the ground, and I have to step over them in large bounds to avoid wetting my boots.

It is as though we are walking backward through time and experiencing seasons in reverse.

A realization smashes into me: we are literally marching toward the moment when winter melts into spring. It is the border between the two courts.

I shiver and rub my hands together. I didn't dress for winter.

I jog to warm my frozen body and overtake some of the fae in the loose column of our band.

I spot Aldrin at the front, talking with Drake and Silvan. The two depart the group, most likely to scout ahead, and I find myself drawn to Aldrin's side, as much as I know I should stay away from him. He stares straight ahead, eyes dark as he grinds his teeth.

"When you break into Cyprien's camp tonight, I'm coming with you." I raise my chin and my spine goes stiff and straight.

He doesn't even look at me. "No."

"No?" I repeat incredulously. The bastard speeds up his long steps and I am forced to almost run to stay at his side. He is not getting rid of me that easily. "I *will* be part of the team that rescues my sister. No man can stop me."

"No, you won't be." Aldrin turns a simmering glare upon me that would make even the bravest warrior wither, but I am far too used to being in the warpath of men. "I am the commander of this unit, and I decide who will come. I will not bring a fragile human into a battle because she misses her sister."

I raise a single eyebrow at him. "Fragile?" I snap. "Fragile! You know nothing about me." I don't back down, despite how he towers over me and how his shoulders are almost double the width of mine in his spiked armor. Despite how I shiver from the cold.

"Interesting, that." He unclasps his cloak and wraps it around my shoulders. His warmth envelops me, and his earthy, floral scent fills my nose. "It's not like I haven't tried." My head spins at the contrast between his harsh tone and his kind actions.

I glare at him. "Here are a few facts for you. I am a huntress, trained in stealth and survival. I may have no experience in fighting a battle, but sneaking into an encampment undetected, in the middle of the night? That plays into my strengths."

Aldrin's mood shifts as his eyes roam over me. "Maybe you can show me some of your moves and impress me, then?" He purrs mockingly.

I breathe in, then breathe out, forcing the rage to seep out of me. "And then you will allow me to come?"

Aldrin smiles. It is a predator's smirk. "We will spar after we make camp and wait for darkness. If you can disarm me of my favorite blade, you can come. I'll even make it easy for you and wear a blindfold."

He pulls a jeweled knife from his belt and shows it to me. There is a large, oval ruby right where the hilt and guard meet the blade, with a handful of smaller rubies scattered across it. Decorative swirls adorn the surface in silver wire.

It is absolutely stunning, but does not look like the kind of dagger that would be used in battle. It is far too ornate. Unless it is imbued with magic.

"Done," I say before he can change his mind. The man has no idea what I am capable of. He gives me a side glance with a coy smile. It sets my nerves on end and destroys my carefully cultivated calm, digging beneath my skin. How does he know exactly how to aggravate me? "Did I say something amusing?" I peer sweetly back.

"You are very confident in your abilities," he ventures.

"The hunts back home saved my sanity. Participating in them. Training for them. It enriched a mundane life of waiting." I am suddenly flooded with that feeling of loneliness. Of having no identity of my own to hold on to and putting my life on hold while I dreamed of Finan.

"Waiting for…a man?" Aldrin probes, giving me a sidelong glance.

I cringe as Finan's betrayals come crashing down into me.

"And he wasn't worth it," Aldrin murmurs.

"That remains to be seen." I keep walking, chewing over my thoughts, but Aldrin watches me.

I let out a long breath. "It is my duty to marry him. Both our families are relying on our union, but his loyalty to me came into question. I ended the commitment between us before I crossed into this realm. I told him I needed time for self-discovery and he said he would wait, but I don't know for how long."

The pain of those wounds rips open afresh. I haven't thought once about Finan or the mess of my life back home since I crossed to this realm. Hysteria begins to bubble through me.

"Well, he sounds like a bit of a prick to me." Aldrin scans the tree-line ahead.

I laugh. The sound is half choked, but damn, it feels good. "Yeah, he is a bit of a prick. Self-absorbed, too."

"Who cares about duty and marriage right now? You are a world away from your life. Gods, stay here with me and my band of merry misfits if you like." Aldrin flashes me a charming smile. It should feel like a threat, especially since I have no idea if he will let me leave, but the way he said it is so disarming, like it is my choice.

For a moment, I believe him. Right until my sanity comes flooding back.

I look over his shoulder to the grim-faced, hardened band of warriors behind him, who look anything but merry.

The forest gives way to a small clearing, encircling an impossibly immense tree, both in girth and height. My breath hitches in my throat as I crane my neck to look up and up, but the gnarled trunk reaches far above the canopy of the woods. Its own foliage is almost out of sight. It is taller than Appleshield Castle, hill and all. It could rival a small mountain.

"We will wait here for night to fall," Aldrin commands the entire band as we file out of the treeline. "Let me talk to them first."

Talk to who? I glance around, trying to spot more fae.

Everyone seems to stop in the meadow that surrounds the giant tree, and Aldrin walks ahead of the group.

There is a massive doorway set in the tree's base, between two snaking roots that run along the clearing, wide enough to fit half a dozen men shoulder to shoulder. A gate barricades it, woven of brambles, thick branches and vines, and dotted with red roses. The thorns among them are as long as my forearm.

"Coroliss. Embla. Myrthe. Saga. Tauriel," Aldrin bellows, his words echoing back to us as his voice bounces around the clearing. "I summon thee!"

His roar fades and silence stretches out. The muscles in his shoulders ripple with tension, causing the spiked shoulder guards of his bronze armor to rise. Aldrin turns and gives a worried glance to Silvan, who shrugs back.

My attention is still on the gate as I try to peer through it at this distance. The tree is completely hollow and a massive, grassy field occupies its center, dotted with patches of snow and the colorful shock of tulips breaking up the mottled green and white.

The shock of realization hits me. This is not one trunk.

It is multiple trees grown together and warped into the shape of a tower, each trunk like an arm that reaches out of the ground, and its canopy a cupped palm forming a large platform. The trunks are woven and twisted around their neighbors, but there are distinct color differences that belong to each tree. Ash, caramel, tan, pistachio and cinnamon.

I blink as branches unravel and re-twist, not believing my eyes as a humanoid shape forms from them.

Twigs wrap around each other until two perfect calves form, a blanket of fuzzy moss sprouts around full hips of vines, and a stomach of brambles curves out. Branches grow from the torso to form arms and moss to create full breasts. The branch still connected to the tree resolves into a head, the wood thinning and trailing away into twigs that fall like hair and snap away from the mother tree. Leaves immediately bloom across them.

I stare at the beautiful tree nymph with my lips parted.

Another transforms into a full humanoid figure, with blunt woody spikes jutting from his elbows, knees and spine and cascading horns of curling branches on his head. His entire body is modestly covered in spongy yellow lichen.

A female appears, a twisting trunk giving way to multiple thick roots where a human's legs would be. The last two males remain connected to the mother trees, showing only humanoid faces of wood peering out from coiling branches and leaves.

I can't drag my eyes away from these majestic creatures. Tree nymphs. And to think we humans dare to steal their heart-stones, their souls, and condemn them to death. Again I am flooded with the realization that we are as much the villains as the fae who steal brides.

"Aldrin. Aldrin. Aldrin. Aldrin." Their voices sing like the wind, rippled over the top of each other.

"The golden hope of spring. We heard you had been exiled. You are not here to plan a rebellion, are you?" one almost wails.

"And if he is?" another responds. "And if he is? We do not follow the whims of the council. We could not deny him. Would not deny him."

"The golden hope of spring. Bring us hope. Bring us salvation." That singing, over and over.

"Aldrin. The protector of all fae. High and low. High and low. Your brothers and sisters have forgotten us."

"Is this war? Rebellion? Retribution?"

Those voices overlap and repeat in my head, ringing in my ears, around and around.

Aldrin holds up his hands. "Good Fair Folk, I simply ask for shelter for one night in your watchtower. I do not come here with the intent of war. It has not come to that."

162

"Welcome."

"Welcome, golden one."

"Welcome."

I knead my temples, trying to release the pressure from those voices laden with emotion.

The branches of the gates groan as they retract back into the trees, opening a narrow portal through the gate wide enough for us to walk through in single file, with Aldrin at our head.

I try not to touch the curling and swaying tendrils of thin creepers as I pass under. The thorns of the brambles are each as long and thick as a carving knife, and I bet they would turn into weapons against an enemy trying to penetrate this gate.

The space inside the trees could easily fit a camp of a thousand men, dwarfing our tiny band of eleven high fae, three kelpies and me. I turn around in a circle, taking in the meadow within, the impenetrable wall of trunks around us, and the wooden staircases and platforms that scale the fortifications to the canopy above.

"What is this place?" I ask, half to myself.

"This is a Watchtower Tree." A tall figure stops beside me.

I turn to Silvan in shock. The man rarely speaks. I can't help feeling unnerved around him. His words are always bitten off and there is a constant whipcord tension within the muscles of his lean build, as though he is permanently ready to strike. The coldness of his narrow gaze never seems to warm, like it promises death alone.

"What does that mean?"

"They are watchtowers," Silvan offers most unhelpfully, then stalks off, bellowing orders to a group in his path setting up a tent. I stare after him.

I find myself utterly alone within a crowd of people for the second time today, idle while they busily set up the camp and rush by me. I don't know how to make myself useful and am too intimidated to approach anyone.

"Hey, Keira, if you're looking for something to do, you can help me skin and gut this."

I whip around toward Drake, who has an entire deer hoisted over his shoulder, two arrows extending from its back. Well, not quite a deer, but close enough.

He gives me a wide, mischievous grin, as though he expects me to balk at a bit of blood. His eyes dance while he waits for me to take his bait.

"Well, that is something I can do." I pull my knife from my belt as I approach him. I have skinned and butchered a beast plenty of times on a hunt.

Drake dumps the creature on the ground by a pile of large sheets of slate. "Really?" He raises his eyebrows.

"Sure," I say, squatting down. "I didn't know this realm had deer."

The creature has antlers of pure, branching crystal, so pale it is transparent, and the fawn fur has green moss growing through it, with drapes of vines hanging from its spine and in place of a tail.

"I think the moss-deer originated in your realm." Drake wipes his hands on his britches. "But traveled here through the veil and perhaps mated with our creatures." He pauses. "You don't really need to help me with…"

Drake trails off as I get to work on the kill, then falls into line beside me.

# CHAPTER 16

# KEIRA

Drake whistles as he takes thin steaks and lays them out on slabs of granite, brushing a mixture of spices onto them. Zinnia touches those rocks with the tips of her fingers, her pale flesh flaring to the brilliant orange of metal held in a fire, transferring heat from her magic. The meat immediately begins to sizzle and my mouth waters at the aroma rising from it.

"I guess tree nymphs don't appreciate a woodfire in their midst." I try to make conversation.

Despite Drake's teasing sense of humor, the broad-shouldered man still makes me nervous.

And Zinnia—she is slight but angry and deadly like a viper. There is definitely something snakelike in the hard, yellow glare she pins people beneath. Her severely angled eyebrows seem to have a permanent furrow between them. Her black hair is a shock against her fair skin, and it hangs loosely to her waist.

"Tree nymphs don't like fire." Zinnia turns her unnerving stare on me, and I can't help feeling like every layer of my being is being unraveled and assessed by them.

"I wouldn't enjoy being near a damn fire either if I were made of wood and leaves." Drake laughs, chopping a cooked slab of meat with a butcher's blade and moving it to a cooler rock, flicking a piece into his mouth.

"You're no less flammable," Zinnia snaps at him.

"Yes, but I can run from a fucking fire. I'm not rooted to the ground like a tree," Drake counters.

"What if the whole forest was burning down around you?" Zinnia leans toward him. "How fast can you run?"

"Are—are you planning my death?" Drake glances from Zinnia to me and back, his eyes widening in mock horror, then a slow smile grows on his lips.

"A woman can dream," Zinnia says in such a low, deadpan tone that my stomach tumbles.

Drake moves to pop another piece of meat in his mouth, but Zinnia reaches out with lightning-quick speed and grabs his wrist. "There won't be any food for anyone else if you keep eating it all." She slaps Drake's cheek lightly, but a smirk splits her lips. "This one is always good for a laugh," she tosses over her shoulder at me. I can't help staring after her as she gets up and leaves.

"She terrifies me a little," Drake admits, watching her walk away.

"Terrifies *you*? I was about to wet myself," I admit.

Drake laughs, busying himself cooking.

"Is she always that intense?" I venture.

"Yes. No. When you get to know her, you can see through the cracks in the mask. It becomes easier to tell when she is amused."

I swallow nervously. Somehow, I think Caitlin would love this woman.

A pang of grief twists within my chest at the thought of my sister. I am so damn afraid for her. This Cyprien seems like a monster.

Drake's movements catch my attention. He takes a thick slice of flatbread and spoons chopped meat onto it in a line. Spiced vegetables are added on top, along with a red sauce, then he passes the meal to me. I take the leaf plate in both hands and stare at the food, trying to decide how to eat it.

All the toppings are in a neat row in the middle. I nibble an edge of the flatbread, then glance at Drake, who has his lips pressed tight as though he is trying not to laugh. I take another bite, trying to get more than bread in my mouth.

This thing is impossible.

A rumbling laughter rolls behind me and I turn to Aldrin. My heart skips a beat as he walks toward me and I try to ignore the fact. His fingers brush mine as he takes the plate from me, wraps the bread into a cylinder with one side tucked in, then hands it back to me.

"I see humans have forgotten more than our history. It's your loss. Our food is bloody amazing." Aldrin's amber eyes dance as they hold mine.

I take a bite of the roll and flavor bursts within my mouth, the meaty juices popping with the tang of spices and a hint of chili.

Aldrin clicks his fingers at Drake and gestures toward the food, then a plate.

Drake spreads out his arms with feigned confusion on his face.

Aldrin grunts. "Bread and meat. Pass it. Extra sambelini."

"Manners, Aldrin, manners. You don't need to be a brute because we are in the wildlands," Drake baits him.

"Please, oh protector of the Spring Court, Commander of the Special Forces, pass me some dinner so I can get on with my pressing duties." Aldrin half bows at him.

Triumph flickers across Drake's face as he prepares another open wrap for Aldrin and hands the leaf plate over. My gaze flicks from him to Aldrin and back. Why is Drake not the leader of this band, when he has such a title? How in the darkest realm did they get exiled?

Aldrin turns to me. "Would you like to see the view from the top of watchtower?"

"That's your pressing business?" Drake asks, his voice pitched high.

"Very pressing," Aldrin says around a mouthful of food, then swallows. "Keira wants to prove that I should let her come tonight."

Drake raises his eyebrows and looks at me, as though he sees me in a different light. "Good luck." He tips his head.

There is no condescension in his tone. No comment on how unladylike it would be or how a human woman should do as she is told. I could be friends with this man.

Aldrin flicks his head in my direction and starts walking toward the staircases that run in a zigzag up the wall of the tree, broken up every so often by platforms. Something about the teasing glint in his eye as he glances at me over his shoulder forces me to follow like a puppy, even though those stairs fill me with apprehension. It could take a lifetime to climb to the top of them.

I am curious. That is all. It has nothing to do with the fact that I can't drag my eyes away from the rippling of his muscles as he moves, or the way his fitted pants hug his perfectly sculpted ass. Damn. This man is dangerous. He is going to make me lose my mind if I don't get away from him soon enough.

I have to half run to catch up to his long stride. "We aren't going to climb *that*, are we?"

Aldrin glances at the stairs. "Gods, no. There is a lift. I hope you're not afraid of heights, because it is a little...airy."

He brings me to a small platform of interwoven branches against the wall, and as we step on it, wooden limbs grow swiftly around the perimeter, forming a cage that completely closes us in. Taut vines extend up from the two far sides, reaching way above us in a loop, and they suddenly tug the entire enclosure upward.

I stagger, and grab Aldrin, the most stable thing in the lift.

That railing looks as though I could easily fall straight through it.

I ignore the low chuckle reverberating through him. My entire body is rigid as my fingers curl into the hard panels of his leather armor, and after a heartbeat, he wraps a tight arm around my shoulders.

My breaths come in hard, sharp gasps.

Our rushing ascent sets a breeze blowing my hair away from my face and my stomach does somersaults. A sense of weightlessness fills me as the ground drags away, turning everything miniature before me. I try to ignore the fact that I can see right through the many small holes in the basket.

This is exhilarating and terrifying.

My head spins as we stop at solid ground, but I find I cannot move. I struggle not to vomit. It takes a long moment for the fear to ease from my nerves.

"Are you okay?" Aldrin says gently, peering down into my face.

I am practically wrapped around him, my arms encircling his waist and my head buried against his chest. His strong arm pins me to his side. I drag in a long breath that only fills my nose with his scent and remove myself from him. I take a shaky step from the basket to the ground beyond. Aldrin doesn't let go of me, but instead guides me by the elbow.

"Sorry." He finally lets go of me. "I probably should have warned you."

I hit him in the chest, then hit him again. It is like striking a stone wall. "Yes, you should have warned me! I wasn't expecting *that*. It took only a minute for us to rise so high."

I stagger away from him while he lets out a low laugh at my back.

The sight of the canopy snags my attention. I expected nothing but branches up here, but there is a flat, woody ground that stretches out and is covered in spongy moss and wildflowers. Pools of water collect in the crags and ferns grow in soil in nooks.

The treetop appears like a sparse forest, the topmost branches reaching up from the ground in long appendages that explode with sprays of emerald leaves.

The canopy of the nymphs' trees forms a great platform in a ring, and its foliage creates a defensive barrier around the outside edge. There are slits in the woven branches of the walls for archers and viewing balconies with a hint of a vista visible beyond.

The diffraction of intense orange light from the rays of the evening sun catches my attention. I turn to find a massive plinth, then another and another. There are five evenly spaced across the platform, so similar to the jade plinths we use to open the portals.

They are double Aldrin's height and as wide as him. I walk up to the closest and run my hands across the runes carved into the orange stone veined with red and brown.

"The jasper plinths are beacons," Aldrin says beside me. "This tower is one of many that watches over our border with the Winter Court. If an invading army crosses into our lands, the nymphs light up the jasper plinths. They send out a beam of red light and magic, which sets off every other watchtower in the Spring Court. The alarm lets us know of the threat immediately, and the signature of the magic tells us where it comes from."

"That is ingenious," I murmur.

"Come." Aldrin takes my hand and pulls me toward one of the balconies. "The view is breathtaking from up here."

The vista stretches out before us, all the way to the horizon, where the forest thins, then finally gives way to a stark white plain of snow. There is very little leaf canopy on any of the trees here, but as the land inches toward winter, the skeletal branches become more prominent and the flower buds disappear.

"Is there a physical divide between courts?" I ask.

"There are magical wards," Aldrin says. "But those are more deterrents than fortified barriers, with plenty of gaps in them. It would take considerable effort to get an army through, but it won't stop an invading force. It's just another obstacle."

A silence grows as I take in every detail of the forest, noticing the outline of another distant Watchtower Tree.

Aldrin shuffles beside me. "Come. The sun will slip behind the horizon in an hour. It gets dark fast so close to winter. I brought you up here so we wouldn't have an audience when you try to steal my dagger." He taps the blade at his belt.

"I appreciate that." Nervousness rolls through me.

I must be insane. The man is a head taller than me, full of taut muscle and built broadly for strength. I've seen how lightning-fast his movements are. I am grateful that he took off his spiked armor.

He is fae and I challenged him. I am definitely losing my mind.

Aldrin leads me to a clearing of sorts that is encircled by a bit of a thicket. He stops in its middle, and a sly grin grows on his lips and fills his face.

"It's not too late to back down, Keira." He pulls a blindfold from his pocket and lets it hang in an outstretched hand.

I take the strip of fabric from him and stand on the tips of my toes to tie it around his eyes. My fingers brush the lines of his face, gliding over his freshly shaven skin and threading into his pulled-back hair as I knot the fabric. The masculine tang of sweat mixed with the floral notes of spring hits me.

A strong urge overtakes me to run my hands across his cheek and down his chest. The motion would distract him, and I should use every weapon at my disposal with this man. My stomach tumbles at the idea, but I force myself to step back.

Aldrin lifts part of the blindfold and catches my eye. "Walk back to the lift. When you get there, it will begin. I will remain in this spot, only moving to defend myself. You have until sunset to take my dagger."

"You're going to regret going easy on me." I pinch the blindfold and pull it back over his eye. He grunts in response.

I do as I am told, lingering at the lift to think. This is no deer that I hunt. His other senses will be far stronger than my own. I have spent hours thinking on how to mitigate each.

I creep through the thin brush littered with twigs, carefully picking each silent step and gently pushing between ferns so they don't make a sound.

Golden rays of sun fall upon Aldrin's tanned skin as he stands incredibly still in the clearing, his nostrils flaring as he tries to catch my scent on the gentle breeze.

I approach the edge of the trees, spans from him and pull off my shawl, tying it to a branch. The site I selected is downwind from him. I make noise, enough to be believable, and he turns straight to me with a smile on his face.

"You'll have to do better than that." His tone is so arrogant, so self-assured, I can't help smiling.

I grasp a long limb of a tree and turn a segment of the woody flesh to ash, breaking it away from the trunk. My magic whittles the limb until I have a staff the same height as myself.

I slip away on silent feet. I collect leaves and bruise them in my hand, rubbing the sharp scent of the vegetation on myself, then send a steady air wield rippling through my shawl, wafting a breeze straight at him.

He faces the wrong direction as I stalk him ever so slowly, step by step. I feel like a graceful, vicious mountain lion hunting its prey. With a gentle flick of my earth magic, I snap a twig a span away from my shawl, and hope he thinks I'm still standing in that direction and nowhere near him.

The rubies of the blade in his belt glitter in the dying sunlight.

I hardly breathe as I near, creeping until I am almost close enough to touch him. I snap a large branch from a distant tree and as the weight of it crashes down, I use the sound to cover my attack.

With a roll of my wrist, my earth magic corrodes the woody ground Aldrin stands upon, and my staff swings through the air and takes his feet out from under him. I throw a blast of air at him to knock him off balance for good measure. My body swings around him with the momentum of my attack.

He falls, grunting in surprise, and I thrust a knot of solid air at his belt to knock the knife from its scabbard. Aldrin dissipates my magic effortlessly. He rolls into his fall and uses the momentum to spring back to his feet, his hand over the prize.

I retreat, sliding back into the trees.

I need a new plan. His mastery of magic is immense, as is his skill as a fighter. There is no way I can take him on in a direct attack. I didn't even know it was possible to unweave another person's threads of magic.

Aldrin's rumbling laughter reverberates through the clearing. "Show me what else you have."

That arrogance could be a weakness.

He turns his head around, clearly trying to pick up a trace of me with his senses. I grab a pebble and flick it with wind to bounce straight off his forehead. Gods, it's satisfying.

"Ouch!" he says. "Now you're toying with me." He turns to face me and my smile slips. I just showed him my location, but it gave me an idea.

I circle around him, closer and closer, getting myself into position.

I whip up a breeze, encasing him in a gentle whirlwind, then weave another and another, until there are a dozen different flows whipping around him. Aldrin raises an eyebrow, as though he is going to allow my magic for now. I suddenly feel more like an angry kitten attempting to claw at him than a prowling mountain lion.

The currents of my whirlwinds pick up leaf litter, pebbles and twigs, and I flick them at him from every direction, like pestering flies. All that magic puts a strain on me and sweat drips down my forehead and back, but there are too many flows for him to dissipate at once.

The ground ripples and groans as I take control of it, suddenly ripping it out from beneath one of his feet. I rarely use my earth magic, normally relying on air instead, but being in this realm has uncovered a depth of power I didn't know I had.

Aldrin slips to one knee and I run at him. I direct a thrust of air to grab the dagger from his belt, but I am holding on to too many flows to have precise control. The blade rushes upward instead, flung directly above his head. I don't hesitate for a heartbeat. I leap upon his upturned knee and propel myself skyward after my prize.

My reaching fingers curl around the hilt of the blade at the same moment Aldrin's arms wrap around my waist. We must look like a pair of professional dance partners mid-performance for a heartbeat, until we crash to the ground together.

A bed of spongy moss springs up beneath us as I hit the ground and Aldrin falls on top of me. My whirlwind still pelts him with debris, but his first thought was to soften my landing. I drop my magic abruptly.

Laughter explodes from me, building and building until my chest shakes with it and tears pour down my face, and I am no longer in control. It is high-pitched and loud, a sound made with complete abandon.

The warmth of the moment spreads throughout me, taking away my worries with each breath, and I realize I haven't felt like this in a long, long time.

The thought is like a bucket of icy water over my emotions.

Aldrin is still consumed by a fit of laughter. It vibrates through me, his jolting breaths and shaking chest. He is half sprawled on top of me, half trapped under, as our bodies awkwardly intertwine. I realize he landed with his face buried in my chest, and the ridiculousness of it makes me lose myself to laughter all over again, really making the situation worse.

Aldrin pulls off the blindfold and stares down at me with awe. "What part of the underworld did you come from? Are you a member of the wild hunt I didn't recognize? I have to give you points for creativity." His head collapses on me again, this time on my stomach as he gives in to another bout of laughter. I think he is completely incapacitated.

His blade is still clutched in my outstretched hand, and I flash it before him. "I told you I'm coming tonight."

"Yes." His eyes sober. "You're coming tonight."

I can tell the moment the giggles leave him and he realizes the position we are in. Realizes that his body pins me down and I haven't tried to move him.

Aldrin's amber gaze turns liquid-hot, running up my body. It lingers on the lacing of my dress' neckline that has become dangerously loosened and shows the generous curves of my breasts beneath. How the rest of the fabric pulls taut over their heaving swells. Heat flushes through my skin under the intensity of that appraising gaze.

He is so incredibly close. The hard planes of his body are pressed against my torso, and one of his thick thighs somehow fell between my thighs. I want him to press it harder. To drag it against me and light up a fire at my core from the friction.

My gaze darts across the chiseled muscle of his arms, exposed beneath his rolled-up tunic, to where they cage me beneath him. His own neckline gapes as he hovers over me, and the most beautiful sight of tanned abdominals and pectoral muscles greets me.

I have to drag my attention away from them, to the sharp angles of his face, still hovering over my bosom.

When his gaze locks with mine, there is heat in his eyes. "You know, no one is going to miss us for at least another hour or two."

He drags a finger along my cheek, across my lips, then down my neck, my chest, going lower and lower. Aldrin stares at me, daring me to stop him, as he reaches my breasts and drags his finger between them, right down my exposed cleavage. A shuddering breath leaves me as I arch into his touch. I want him to do it again with his tongue.

"Do we care if they do?" I thread my fingers through his hair.

Those eyes rove across my body and face again, searching for something.

My heart thunders as the most beautiful man I have ever seen looks at me with such open lust.

A wild gleam enters his gaze as he crawls up my body until we are face to face. "You *are* wicked."

Heat rushes through my every extremity and my stomach tumbles with anticipation as his breath caresses my cheek. I run my hands down his chest and the hard ridges of his muscles feel exactly as I thought they would. I want him. Need consumes me, hot and fast.

I came here to embrace this pilgrimage and the experiences it throws at me. To find myself. To put my needs first, and doesn't that include my own pleasure?

His face lowers toward mine until I think he is going to kiss me, but he whispers in my ear. "Do you want a fae lover?" His breath tickles my skin.

Everything within me freezes at his boldness. While I take a fraction of a second to consider, he kisses a line down the side of my neck. It almost drives out all rational thought. I snake my arms behind his neck, savoring the feel of his lips against my skin. It makes the muscles of my core tighten.

I didn't come here for a lover. I've taken steps to make sure a magical pregnancy won't happen. All I know is that I want to experience him. That this is a man who could make me feel alive.

Aldrin pulls himself up onto one elbow as he lazily looks at me. Any hesitation I may have had disappears.

"Yes," I breathe. "I want a fae lover."

His entire body stiffens, and he pulls himself off me abruptly.

I stare at him with utter confusion at the sudden mood change while my body prickles from the cold in the absence of his embrace. He gets to his feet and glares down at me as I pull myself up.

"I should have known. You are like the rest of them," he spits at me, and tension coils in his muscled shoulders. "Here to take a lover and sneak off home with the unborn baby."

"What!" I find myself yelling as all that building passion turns to anger. "*You* tried to seduce *me*! I haven't made a pass at you."

Aldrin gives me a hard look, as though I am caught in a lie.

"Does it even matter to you humans which fae gets you pregnant?" His voice is low, stone cold, and somehow that feels worse than shouting. "Don't think you and your sister are the first women to come here. You said it yourself, human women come here for lovers."

"I said they are enticed by the freedoms here." I am angry enough to throw something at him. "We get to actually *live* when we are in this realm. But of course, any woman with a healthy sexuality must be a villain, right?"

Aldrin's features darken. "Isn't this what your family does? Sends its women to this realm looking for lover?s How else is your magic so strong? You must be half fae. Was it your mother who went to the autumn realm? Your blood is brimming with their destructive earth magic."

I hiss. "My grandmother—"

"Your grandmother. And I wonder which poor fool she seduced, then stole his baby." Venom pours out of him, so at odds with the man whispering in my ear a moment ago.

"A dead fool who tried to hurt her and keep her prisoner!" I walk right up to him and speak slowly into his face. "If you want to end the prejudice between our people, then you have to learn to trust me. Stop assuming I'm going to do to you any and every bad thing my people have been accused of. Didn't I agree to trust you?"

His grim countenance doesn't change.

I don't drop my eyes from his. "Do I need to make an oath that I won't steal any babies while I'm here? Not even a spare changeling."

He lets out a barked laugh, catching my ironic joke. For centuries, it was us humans who accused the fae of stealing our babies.

"Fine. Fine." He throws up his arms. "But I had to know. I *had to know*. And why else did you agree to…"

I raise my eyebrows at him and he swears, looking away from me for a single moment.

"I'm not a complete prude. I just like privacy," I say softly.

Tension crackles between us and he looks at me differently, analyzing and appraising. "Look, I—"

He reaches out a hand toward me and I turn my back on him, stalking toward the lift.

"How did I end up the asshole in this situation?" he mutters behind my back.

I hold his jeweled blade in the air. "I'm keeping this."

Aldrin continues to grumble as he follows me, but doesn't protest. Magic hums through the dagger. This relic would be enough if I decide to get Caitlin and go straight back home, but I won't let this stupid, beautiful man make me miss the once-in-a-lifetime opportunity of exploring this realm. Of living.

Gods, is it too much to ask to take a lover who knows what he is doing? One who would care about feminine pleasure as much as the fae are famed to? I don't want to live a life where all I know is the dissatisfaction of Finan's fumbling hands.

# CHAPTER 17

# ALDRIN

That woman will be my undoing. I cannot think straight when Keira is around. Those large eyes drink me in whenever I am near, like she can't drag them away before she has examined every inch of me. Like she is dying of thirst and only I can quench it.

When I smile at her, those red lips part and her breath turns shallow as a slight rosy glow creeps across her skin. The way she constantly looks back over her shoulder at me drives me insane, swaying those beautiful, rounded hips as she walks and flicking that long red-gold hair.

I grind my teeth in frustration as my blood runs hot.

Keira always seems to find herself somewhat exposed around me, hiding naked within the caves of the lagoon but still drawing my attention to her. Clothes torn by Cú Sídhe and showing tantalizing amounts of her flesh. The entire neckline of her dress unlaced halfway to her navel, extracting my jeweled blade while practically shoving those generous breasts into my face, then pulling me down onto her.

And I was stupid enough to think she was trying to manipulate me, rather than being as attracted to me as I am to her.

"Aldrin! Are you even listening to me?" Klara snaps.

I run a hand through my hair. "Sorry. I got distracted."

"That much of a shock to you that a human woman bested you?" she asks.

"You have no idea," I mutter. Keira bested me in more ways than one.

"I've spent the entire evening hunting out these mushrooms and painstakingly isolating their aerosol spores—at your request—and you're too distracted to listen to me?" She tosses her head with agitation, throwing violet braids.

I motion for her to go on.

"I was saying." Klara rolls her eyes to Drake and Silvan. "You can knock out Cyprien's guards with a whiff of this potion. His sentries will remain unconscious for at least an hour. Do not—I repeat—do not breathe in any yourself."

I nod. I have learned to trust her advice. There is a reason she was once the Spring Court's Minister of Specialized Battle Tactics. She gave up that title and position for me.

The night deepens as we drill the plan into each of my fighters, then we march.

We trudge up a long, winding path with minimal tree cover that follows a wide river, slabs of ice floating on its surface. A thin mist curls up from the body of water.

Blue and green lights bob above the surface and others swim in fast arcs beneath, the sprites of air and water playing with each other. Its vibrancy tells me the Lake Maiden still thrives in these parts.

I rub my hands together to chase away the chill.

My party wears thick coats of white fur taken from the watchtower's stores. They are musty, but warm, and will keep us hidden. I examine my fighters, noting the grim determination etched into each face. Even Keira wears the same expression, without a hint of fear. Brave girl.

It takes a little over an hour to reach the Frozen River Fortress. It sits at the apex of a dam, and its domed spires colonize both sides of the many-tiered waterfalls that cascade into the river. A great wall encircles both halves of the fortress, and they are connected by multiple arching bridges.

A sharply ascending path cut into jagged stone leads to the nearly impenetrable fortress. A surprise attack would be impossible if it were fully manned, but I know it is empty except for Cyprien's small force.

We split into two predetermined groups as we reach the base of the fortress. One to focus on knocking out the guards and binding them, and the other to penetrate Cyprien's chambers and secure him.

I slink through the shadows and approach the wall beneath the cover of evergreen trees that should never have been allowed to grow this close to it. Silvan, Klara, Drake and Keira follow close behind, not making a sound. A sentry passes over the wall above our heads, stopping at its midpoint to scan the field before continuing.

Klara opens a jam jar of the mushroom spores, holding it away from us and wielding careful tendrils of air to blow them up to the top of that wall. The flow diffracts the moonlight ever so slightly.

The sentry crumples and falls from the wall.

I swear softly and throw out a buffeting layer of wind to slow his descent, while ripping out of the ground a network of tree roots in a net to catch him. I lower the man to a bed of moss, binding him there in roots, then glance at Klara.

"Shit," she hisses. "I didn't expect it to be so potent."

"Haven't you made this before?" I whisper back, and she shakes her head.

We wait for someone to call an alarm, but when none comes, I create a ladder out of roots up the wall.

Silvan moves first, running across the empty space while holding a ward of invisibility around himself. The magic is difficult and imperfect, especially on a moving target.

There are hints of his silhouette still visible as a ripple of warped air shooting across the bare land, but it is damn near hard to spot by the unsuspecting eye. A guard would need to scrutinize the right spot to see him. It's a pity the talent is so rare and only two of my band have the ability.

His footprints in the sparse snow disappear immediately as he brushes air over them as he passes. My soldiers are well trained, by Cyprien himself.

Silvan's distorted body flies up the ladder, then disappears completely as he reaches the top of the wall. A minute passes. My heart crashes painfully in anticipation and every muscle in my shoulders ripples with the need for action.

A disembodied hand beckons us from the top of the wall. There are no nearby guards.

I push Drake forward at Silvan's signal. He makes the mad, vulnerable dash to the wall and up its height, completely exposed. It is difficult to watch, his whole body visible and completely defenseless while he climbs.

I breathe easier when he joins the protection of Silvan's invisibility ward and winks out of view. I clap Keira on the back to push her next. She glances over her shoulder, eyes sparkling with exhilaration and a half-smile on her face.

Keira actually smiles in the face of battle.

Nervous sweat drips down my spine as she scales the wall and joins Silvan.

I tap Klara to go next.

"No," she whispers. "You go first. I will protect your flank, sire."

I don't like it, but it makes sense.

I spring into action, my long, silent bounds chewing up the spans to the wall in seconds. The ropes of the ladder burn my hands from the friction of my ascent, then I swing over the top of the wall and search for the distortion of Silvan's ward.

A disembodied hand grabs my fur coat and pulls me a few steps into it, then I am suddenly pressed into the warm bodies of Drake, Silvan and Keira. The air is stagnant under the invisibility ward, as though we huddle under a blanket and exchange breath.

Klara joins us within a few heartbeats.

The layout of the fortress sprawls before us. A series of buildings wrap around a circular core, each level set at a sharp incline, until at its peak a single huge tower stands, with a large hall with sleeping quarters for whoever commands this military outpost on its top. This is where we will find Cyprien's head-quarters.

We march in a double-row column down the length of the wall, our movements slow and awkward. Two guards appear suddenly as we round a corner and Klara takes them out with her spores. Both crumple to the ground.

A staircase takes us down from the wall to the grounds, then we pick our way through the fortress. It is slow going. Enough to set my teeth on edge and my blood crashing in my ears.

We move in a stop-start trek through the streets, constantly scouting for enemies.

The buildings here are mostly cylindrical, painted in bright shades of red, pink, yellow and blue. The broad door frames and windows are of quartz that glows under the slivers of the twin moons. Spires of moonstone shimmer like beacons at the top of the domed, tiled roofs. The streets would be completely lit up under a full moon.

If this fortress housed a full army instead of being practically abandoned, the stone would have been powered by fae to chase away shadows an invading force could hide within. It would reveal the shimmer of Silvan's invisibility ward that we hide beneath.

We take an indirect path through the fortress, up narrow stairways and alleys hidden between buildings and avoiding direct roads that would have more eyes on them.

I memorized every inch of this place during the last war with the Winter Court.

The night is silent except for the rush of the waterfalls cascading beneath us. Not even the footsteps or chatter of guards float to my ears, though it is well past midnight.

Something sits wrong within my gut, but I cannot quite put my finger on it. We pass two more of Cyprien's people, already dispatched by my own, and I wonder why there hasn't even been a scuffle yet. Perhaps they are all sleeping, as I anticipated.

A final alley brings us to the courtyard before the grand hall. I hold up a hand and my party stops immediately. I scan the area from our hidden position for a long moment.

There should be guards on those immense double doors framed in moonstone, regardless of the time of night and the limited numbers of Cyprien's force. He is a brilliant strategist, but he has always been arrogant enough to assume he is untouchable.

Surely it can't be this easy.

We have to enter through the main doors. If we try to scale the outside of the Tower to reach the bedroom on top, we would be visible across the entire fortress. Not even Silvan could keep the invisibility ward over all of us that spread out. The slit windows are too narrow for any of us to climb through regardless.

A single fern leaf lies across the step of the main doors. A signal from the other half of my force. They are here already, waiting under the invisibility ward formed by Zinnia, the only other member of my band capable of the magic.

I take in a deep breath to steel my nerves, rolling my shoulders to ease some of the tension. The space around the main hall is completely empty of soldiers; the grounds, the walls and the shadows.

I lead my party out of hiding.

Another distortion of air follows us, crude enough that I spot it straight away. We are sitting ducks out here. My entire force, right in Cyprien's clutches. These people rely on me and their fates are tied to mine. They joined my exile willingly, and that is not a thing easily forgiven by the high chancellor.

I grasp the latch on the door and twist it. It isn't barred. It's not even locked. The bright light and warmth of roaring fireplaces leak out of the gap in the door as I slowly swing it open. The hinges don't make a sound.

I know my doom immediately.

Time slows, so each heartbeat extends a lifetime. The scent of sweat and leather floats out of the hall, too potent to be impressions lingering from the day. The slightest grinding of metal reaches my ears, armor moving upon adjusting bodies.

The door swings to reveal a room full of guards lining both sides of the hall, their bodies creating a wide tunnel to the dais.

Two thrones sit upon it. Cyprien occupies the larger one, with his back completely straight and utter stillness on his stony features. Not even a hint of surprise shows. In the other smaller throne lounges a human woman with an arm hanging over the edge, clutching a goblet of wine casually around its rim. Keira's sister. Their similarities are striking.

"It's about time you arrived, Aldrin." A wide, cocky smile fills Cyprien's face, and he spreads his arms. "We have organized a little party for you and your human friend."

My blood turns to ice as thoughts whirl in my head and I look for a way out.

A retreat.

A horn blows from outside and resounds within the room, followed by boots crashing on cobblestones behind me. I throw a glance over my shoulder to where a dozen soldiers file out of the two buildings behind us, wedging my loyal band of warriors between two forces on this doorstep.

I step out of Silvan's invisibility ward, onto the elaborate mosaic floor of the hall, exposed beneath all that bright light. I don't spare a second thought for the guards clutching spears around me.

I send a glare of pure hatred at Cyprien. "You're sitting in my fucking chair," I growl.

# CHAPTER 18

# ALDRIN

Cyprien rises and slowly claps his hands at me, stepping down from the dais. "You took your time in coming here. And no, it stopped being your chair when you were exiled. Are you going to let the rest of your people in from the cold?"

I curse under my breath, then motion for them to enter. The wards ripple then fall away, and the entire band is visible, with grim expressions and taut bodies, ready for a fight.

Except we are grossly outnumbered.

Keira stares at her sister sitting on that dais, examining every inch of her as though looking for signs of abuse. She takes a hesitant step forward, but I put a hand on her shoulder to still her. To keep her behind me. Caitlin's eyes narrow on my touch.

I focus my gaze on Cyprien. "How did you know we were coming?"

He stops his approach halfway down the hall and raises his eyebrows at the viciousness in my tone. "I would love to say I outwitted you. That I know you so well, I anticipated your every move, but that would be a lie. In fact, it was the human woman who helped me."

Cyprien glances back at her over his shoulder. "Caitlin wanted her sister back. She had the audacity to demand I muster my entire force and chase you through the woods to find her. But I wouldn't. Didn't need to, because I knew you would come for Hawthorne. That you would have to hunt me down and force me to listen to your explanations on why my hasty assumptions were wrong, and why I should be on your side."

"Get to the point, Cyprien," I growl at him.

"Did you know that these women have the most fascinating bracelets made from moonstone? Caitlin told me they were created from chips taken from the portals so they could find their way back to the human realm, but they also gravitate toward each other. So when your little party marched here and snuck in so effectively that my guards wouldn't have been able to stop you, we were sitting here tracking your progress." Cyprien laughs. "The irony, that something so small was your undoing."

I turn my simmering scowl on Keira, now hidden behind Klara, who whispers in her ear, and I beckon her forward. As she reaches my side, her sister's facade of nonchalance falls away and Caitlin suddenly perches on the edge of her seat.

I place a hand on Keira's arm. "Did you feel the bracelet?" I ask in a low tone.

"No, but I was too terrified to notice," she murmurs.

"Keira, are you okay? He promised me you wouldn't be hurt." Caitlin stalks right off the dais and tries to charge past Cyprien, but he holds out his arm like a wall. She turns on him like a hissing wildcat. "You said she would be safe. He brought her to a damned ambush!"

"I said he would treat her well. I never promised she wouldn't die from his stupidity." Cyprien doesn't lift his gaze from me. "Sit back down, Caitlin."

The woman analyzes Keira for so long I think she is going to defy him, but then she returns to her throne.

"I'm fine, Caitlin," Keira says and the coiled tension falls from Caitlin's shoulders.

I turn my hostility back to Cyprien. "Well, I'm here. What do you want from me? I assume there is a reason you traveled all the way to the borderlands from the capital."

The smugness drops from his face and his eyebrows knit. "Aldrin, I've come to realize that I was wrong. That—"

"I'm sorry. Can you say that again?" I can't help the grin that grows on my face. He has always been too easy to rile up.

Cyprien gives me a deadpan look. "I was wrong." He suddenly claps his hands. "Everyone out. We have things to discuss."

Soldiers file out of the room. They are a volley with multiple currents, and my people are an island of stillness within them. Around us, metal plate armor clanks, chain mail rattles and leather swishes.

Hawthorne resolves out of the mass of soldiers and approaches me. I look him up and down, searching for signs of assault, but the young man's skin and clothes are clean. His hair is pulled into its usual neat topknot, with the sides of his head freshly shaven. There is a scar that runs over his right eye and down his cheek, but it is old.

I slap him on the back. "Were you treated well?"

"Yeah, like the rest of them," Hawthorne says. "They shoved me in the barracks and I caught up with a few old friends. Kept an eye on me, though, so I couldn't escape or get word to you." I nod and he leaves with the rest of them.

I grab hold of Keira and motion for Silvan, Drake and Klara to remain. They slink into the shadows, watching and waiting for any threat. I walk to the dais with Keira in tow, but Cyprien makes a show of taking *my* seat again.

Lilly resolves out of the shadows and stands at Cyprien's side, behind the throne, clearly still his second in command. I didn't realize how much I missed her calm presence until her honey-gold eyes land on me, glowing with warmth.

She dips her head to me in acknowledgment, and the firelight shimmers off the tattoo of long lines and swirling runes that covers her forehead and entirely bald scalp in an intricate cap, in perfect harmony with her caramel skin. Earrings that run up her peaked ears and are connected by a chain dance with the motion.

I drag my attention back to Cyprien and stop just below the dais, though it kills me. "Tell me. Will you back me? Do you believe in the corruption now?"

Cyprien holds up a hand. "Not so fast. I was merely saying I was wrong in assuming you went so far as to let two human women into this realm. Not even you would push it so far."

Disappointment crashes through me. I may have won the first battle before I walked in the door, but the greater one still lies ahead of me.

"No. I did not," I mutter.

"We have become fast friends, Caitlin and I. She has told me a lot of interesting things about humans." Cyprien raises a hand in her direction.

"Not fast enough friends, since you still hold me as your prisoner," Caitlin snaps at him.

"You are my guest." Cyprien gives her a sidelong glance, as though they have had this conversation countless times. "Have you not made friends here?"

Her cheeks color, but she mutters under her breath, "A guest that can't leave."

Cyprien leans forward in his seat, the thick braids of his long, dark hair flicking forward over his shoulder and the gold beads threaded into them clinking. "Do you know that when we brought her back here, she knocked three of my soldiers unconscious and almost burned down an entire building in her attempt to escape and rescue her sister?"

I nudge Keira beside me. "The two of you are similar, then?"

She gives me a long, withering look. "I am still not happy with you. Do not forget our bargain."

The reproach burns.

Perhaps I was not fair in my test of her. Even the thought of it, of what she was willing to do with me, is enough to heat my blood and make my head explode. The frustration makes me mad.

I turn that energy back to Cyprien instead. "Tell me again about how you were wrong. How you made yet another fast assumption and turned your forces against me over it, without talking to me first. Without asking a single question. You should have known me better."

"I don't know you at all anymore, Aldrin!" Cyprien erupts, standing from the throne. "What were you doing at the border of Winter, killing the twisted creations that they sent into our lands? Destroying the evidence of it? Can you not see the land grab into Spring the Winter King is making? There is snow everywhere here. The Frozen River once had ice in it the size of my fist. There are platforms of ice now, the size of a barge. The dam above is almost completely crusted with ice. The Winter King is using his love of technology to force the season in our lands."

A deep fury builds within me until fire runs through my veins and I cannot contain it any longer. My every muscle is taut, twitching with pained restraint, because all I want to do is hit the man in his face.

"This is the kind of narrow-sightedness that got my sister killed," I growl at him.

"Don't you dare bring Lorrella into this! Don't. You. DARE. Do you think losing my wife and our unborn child did not kill me also? We had never heard of a woman dying in childbirth before. How was I to know? I did the best I could." Cyprien's face turns red and tears build at the corners of his eyes.

I run a hand through my hair as grief threatens to overwhelm me. It shivers through every extremity of my body, but I cannot turn into a howling, crying mess here. Not in front of this man. "You should have taken her to the druids. The humans would have known what to do. Their women sometimes die in childbirth."

"Like you said. Their women die in childbirth. They can't always prevent it." Cyprien's eyes are cold. Dead. "I lost my wife. My child. And the friend who had been my brother since before I married his sister."

A silence extends as we glare at each other, all the anger and pain at Lorrella's death thrown between us instead us unpacking the grief behind it.

"Every day I wake up and still look for her in my bed, as though my sleep-ridden brain cannot understand that she is gone. Even after all these years," Cyprien murmurs, and the gods help me, his voice cracks.

I shake my head in an attempt to violently remove the emotions I cannot handle. Otherwise, that darkness will swallow me whole.

Before I know what I am doing, my treacherous legs take me up the steps to the dais. I grab Cyprien and crush him in a bear hug and hold him there for a long time, like I can't let him go. His entire body goes completely rigid within my grasp and he holds his arms out, away from me, before awkwardly patting me on the back.

"I am sorry," I say hoarsely. "That I blamed you. That we have hardly talked since."

"As am I," he says. "I should have listened to you, then and many times over the years since."

I let him go, then pull away. "Listen to me now, Cyprien. The Winter King is *not* making a land grab, despite what the high chancellor is claiming. *She* does not even believe it. Would this fortress be empty if we were about to go to war with Winter? Claims of an old enemy at our gates and the fear-mongering that goes with it is the best way to unify a people. The best sleight of hand so they cannot see the truth."

Cyprien gives me his classic thin-lipped frown. "And what truth is that?"

I have to get through to this man. To resist the urge to shake him. "You saw the spriggan my soldiers put down. The creatures were suffering, many hardly able to function. Their bodies were rotting away and turning to ash, dissipating on the breeze while they still lived. Why would the Winter King do such a thing?"

"The official word is that he has unleashed a disease that attacks our low fae." Cyprien's voice is chipped with ice.

"The spriggan are of both Winter and Spring courts—why disease his own subjects?" I whip back.

"Maybe something went wrong. Maybe he doesn't care about his own subjects."

I raise an eyebrow at him. "You have met Erik. A man doesn't change that much, Winter King or no. He is not his father. Do not forget the war ended between our courts because he worked hard for the peace treaty."

Cyprien taps his temple with a long finger while thinking, but that frown is gone.

I pounce. "The lowest fae, those with the smallest drops of magic, they're falling apart. Fading away, because there is not enough power left in these lands to sustain them. The lands are dying where the courts border and the magic is at its thinnest.

"What you see here isn't a Winter land grab, it is a spread of the desolation at the borders. There is now an icy wasteland where our court meets Winter—not their usual snowy plains, but a place devoid of life, with immense cracks of darkness running through it. These are voids where all matter has been sucked away, as though the rifts are gates to another realm that is absolute nothingness. Like the night sky without the stars. The earth around them turns to ash drifting on the breeze, just like those spriggan. The magic is fading away from our realm and our entire world will die when it is gone."

I need Cyprien on my side. Need him to listen to me. He still has influence in this court. "Come to the Dividing Cliffs, Cyprien. See the evidence for yourself."

He shifts uncomfortably. "If there is evidence, then why do the high chancellor and the entire council believe as they do? Why is no one looking at it?" The fight has gone out of him.

"Because no one cares to see. They are too stupid or too afraid," I counter. "It is easier to deny what is right in front of our faces than to acknowledge this threat that none of us know how to deal with. To admit that this was our doing, and that we don't want to change our comfortable lifestyles to fix it. War with Winter is easy in comparison. It is our oldest dance. We all understand it."

Cyprien rolls his neck. "I will think on it." He turns to Lilly. "We have a lot to discuss."

"Yes. It seems that we do." Lilly tips her head to me ever so slightly again. "It was nice to see you again, Aldrin, and witness your unique perceptions. I hope you will stay at this fortress while we deliberate," She says without a hint of mockery, and her motherly tone makes me feel like a boy running around the palace again, when she used to give me treats.

Both turn away from me to slip out the back door beside the dais, but I block them with my body. "Why did you come here, Cyprien? Surely it wasn't to monitor me. If the high chancellor wanted to know if I were a threat, she could have sent anyone."

"I am here," Cyprien says, "because I am losing faith in the high chancellor. I have wondered for months if I was wrong in allowing her to remove my king from his seat of power and send him into exile."

Cyprien looks me straight in the eye. "Aldrin, my King of the Spring Court, please do not prove my most recent change of heart wrong. Because if you are indeed worthy, if you prove to me that everything you have said is true, I will fight to the ends of this realm and into the next to return you to your rightful place. But first…" He holds up a finger. "First, I need to be convinced."

Those words smack into me with the force of a stampede of crazed kelpies. Cyprien turns on his heel, nods to Lilly at his side, and both leave the room.

## CHAPTER 19

# KEIRA

I t feels like a cold bucket of water has been poured over my head as Cyprien disappears and the exchange is finished.

I am left gaping at Aldrin. "You're a king?"

"I was." He shrugs at me, but his attention is far away.

"You didn't negotiate for my sister to be freed from that man's clutches!" I push at his chest as hard as I can, but he doesn't move. I hold on to the anger that burns through me like hot oil, because the panic that rises alongside it is enough to undo me.

"Clearly, I am a king with no power." Aldrin tries to brush me off again, but double takes as the tips of my hair start to sizzle with the hint of flames. "One battle at a time, Keira. I will win him over, and then his prisoner will be my prisoner, and I will release her immediately." I keep glaring death at him and he sighs, holding up both hands. "Okay, okay, I will talk to him and find out why he cares to hold on to her."

Impotent frustration flows through me, but I have no choice. This high fae, this *king*, he has his own battles to face.

I suddenly feel like a fool, challenging royalty from another realm. I almost made him my *lover*.

So much for staying away from the high fae.

My head spins and I run my hands over my face. I am making every mistake my grandmother warned me against.

The streaks of war paint across Aldrin's face slowly fade back to the regular tanned tone of his skin and the thin, curling and branching antlers dissipate into shimmering motes. They seems to only come out when he fights or is angry. Just like my hair.

Caitlin approaches me gingerly where I still hide behind Aldrin, giving him a wide berth. She grabs me by the shoulders and examines me from head to toe, her face twisting with emotion at the sight of me.

"Were you hurt?" she demands.

"Only from my own magic, but they healed me. Were you hurt?" My voice breaks.

"Same." She laughs, then pulls me into a tight embrace, and her body shakes. "I was so scared for you, Keira. Terrified I'd never find you again."

I realize she is crying. The dampness of her tears is in my hair and across my cheek. "It's okay. I'm here." I pat her back and squeeze her.

Caitlin has never been good at expressing her emotions. She builds up such a strong, severe facade to prevent anything getting close enough to hurt her, but she doesn't let emotions out either. It allows her to weather a storm, to destroy anyone who would harm her people, but when she breaks, it is all at once and she utterly shatters.

It is always the people who put on the strongest fronts who are the most fragile within.

"Has Cyprien treated you well?" I whisper.

"Yeah." Caitlin gulps. "I actually like the stony bastard."

"Yeah, me too, unfortunately," Aldrin grumbles, still beside us. "But he is a terrible host. I'm not leaving this fortress until I get my answer."

Caitlin lets go of me to examine Aldrin. He gives her a formal bow. "Nice to meet you, Caitlin. It was much anticipated."

She gives him a curt nod. "Thank you for taking care of Keira while I dealt with this fool." She flicks her head in the direction Cyprien went.

I give Caitlin a wide smile. She has a sense of humor, if you know where to look for it. Then I round on Aldrin again. "You are a *king?* When were you going to tell me?"

I still can't believe I almost seduced a fae *king* for fun. It would have been insanity. I can't bind myself to another king.

"Probably whenever you told me a single detail about your life," Aldrin quips back.

I turn to Caitlin and she tips her head to the side, eyes dancing from me to Aldrin and back.

A team of servants bursts into the hall, ushering us out with promises of hot, spiced wine and rooms prepared with comforts. There is even an offer of a hot bath, but I dismiss the indulgence of the idea at this time of night, requesting one for the morning instead. Drake, Silvan and Klara materialize out of the shadows and follow us.

As we are pushed up to the domestic quarters, I raise my eyebrows at Aldrin. "Cyprien marches an army with a team of servants?"

He cracks a smile. "It is common to have smiths and cooks travel with an army. Cyprien takes it to the extreme on this small excursion."

My room is next to Caitlin's, with a bed set up with pillows and blankets that are only a little musty. There is a chest for my belongings, a small dresser with a mirror and a table with two chairs. I can sense the wards on everything to keep out the elements and decay. Every inch of the walls is painted with elaborate designs of flowers and vines.

The basic but cozy room is surprising in a fortress, but if it is meant to be constantly guarded in peacetime, the generals would need rooms for their wives or highborn guests.

I linger at the small table that has a counter of moonstone and a crystal decanter on top, with a matching goblet and a wash bowl. Fresh rose petals grace the top of the water. I dip a single finger in, wondering if I should wash, then swiftly pull it out at the shock of the icy water.

My sister knocks on the door, then enters.

"Why are we being treated with luxury?" I ask. "Why not put us in the barracks with the other men and women, or with the servants?"

Caitlin bites her lower lip. "I may have told Cyprien I am the heir to the Appleshield Protectorate."

"Caitlin!" I protest.

"He didn't know what to do with me when he dragged me back here, whether or not to lock me up in a cell. I almost escaped while he was still deciding, incapacitating the guards he had put on the door of a small, empty room. When he saw I could fight, and wield magic, he knew I wasn't some simple peasant. He has treated me as an equal since I swore an oath that it was the truth. It means I got a seat at the table when they discussed what to do about Aldrin and you."

My mouth hangs open. Caitlin found herself captured by our enemy and instead of becoming another one of their victims, she negotiated a position of power.

"I cannot leave these grounds. Cyprien has put a spell on me that makes it physically impossible unless he personally escorts me, but I can roam freely. What about you? Are you Aldrin's prisoner?"

I chew over that thought. "Honestly, I have no idea. He says I'm not, that I can go back to the portal and leave this realm any time, but also not without an escort. These fae are nothing like we were warned about. He won't have me wander these lands freely. It makes it really hard to achieve what we came here for."

Caitlin holds up a hand and whispers into my ear. "She can hear everything that is said here." She pulls away and speaks loudly again. "You came here for an adventure. We both did. Is this not an adventure?"

I nod, too tired to even ask who *she* is, but then another thought takes me. "I made a bargain with Aldrin." The color drains from Caitlin's face, but I press on. "He must set you free, and then I will tell him my story. It was the only leverage I had over him. He seems very, very interested in our realm and our people. But Aldrin never specified how much I must share, and I do not intend on betraying any secrets."

She nods. "It is a dangerous game you play."

"I know."

"Keira…there is someone I want you to meet. Cyprien introduced us, and I have spent most of my time here speaking with her," Caitlin says with such vulnerability.

I don't question her as she leads me through the winding walk-ways of the fortress, down to the lowest level that hugs the base of the wall.

The moonstone window frames are like large glowing eyes, breaking up the thickness of the shadows.

Caitlin fashions multiple orbs of fire to light up the night, hovering in the air above us and following our progress. It helps to chase away the chill of the air but does nothing for the bite of the wind. I hug the fur coat tighter around me.

She takes me to a bridge that arcs over the frozen river. It looks like spider webs of spun silver glimmering in the half-light, the railing a delicate design of arches overlapping each other and the path a thickly woven netting.

I take a step onto it, expecting the entire structure to sway, but it is completely rigid. The railing is taller than any person, a protective cage over the bridge with regular slits, so defending soldiers can fire arrows but are protected from enemy missiles.

The bridge reaches an intersection that branches in two, but at its center there is a narrow, descending spiral staircase. A column of the same silver wire encircles and protects it.

Caitlin leads me swiftly down the stairs, turning around the support pillar of the bridge. Twin waterfalls roar on either side, splashing sparse droplets onto us. We step out onto an isolated plat-form of rough stone, covered in patches of blue lichen and sprays of ferns.

There is a circle of large moss-covered stones in its center, and Caitlin takes a seat on one, indicating for me to do the same, but I stand rooted to the spot.

I burn with curiosity, trying to examine every last detail of the space.

Caitlin sings a soft, winding melody I have never heard before. It takes a few heartbeats for me to realize the words are not in our language. It is in pure, formal Fae. The language I wanted to learn. She creates multiple orbs of fire, so it feels like we sit before a roaring hearth, rather than on an exposed platform above a frozen river.

Before I can ask her where she learned such a song, the waterfall beside us stops flowing. It is the eeriest sight. All that crashing water halts and defies gravity, the loud white noise it created oddly missing. Then the waterfall parts like curtains and a figure steps through onto our platform.

The female is made of iridescent water, glowing with blue light. She assembles herself before our eyes from ribbons of water still connected to the motionless waterfall. They encircle her silhouette, thickening arms and thighs, reaching out from the top of her head, before cascading down into hair.

Within a few heartbeats, the fae is fully formed, her curvy figure shrouded in layers upon layers of light, gauzy fabric that is almost sheer. Puffs of it stand erect at her shoulders like webbed fins and ribbons trail down her back.

As she steps forward, her body completely detaches from the waterfall, which crashes down into a torrent again. Her skin turns a pale pink, not dissimilar from my own, but her hands, forearms, chest and cheeks all have a flush of blue. Small, shimmering scales are scattered across the areas where a human might have freckles.

Her long hair is white as snow, and it drapes to her waist, pulled back from her face with combs of shells from the creatures that live in her waters.

I can't stop staring at the beauty and otherworldliness of her.

"You have returned." The Lake Maiden's voice is like a song. "And you have brought a friend."

"My sister." Caitlin approaches as she would a wild animal she is afraid to frighten away. "The one I told you about."

"Yes. I can see the kindness in her eyes. The warmth in her soul. She is strong and fragile. Vulnerable but fierce. I have met many kinds who have crossed my waters over many years, but never one like you. Tell me, dear sister, of your quest. Of your desire to save your people." The Lake Maiden holds out her hand to me and I take it. Her grasp feels like ice dripping through my fingers, but she smiles kindly at me as she leads me to the seats.

I glance at Caitlin and she nods. *Tell her the truth.*

"What is your name, Lake Maiden?" I ask.

She cocks her head to one side. "Odiane."

I shuffle on the frozen rock, trying to get comfortable on the seat. "I have traveled from the human realm, Odiane, from a region that brushes up against this one. We are losing our magic, just as the fae of this realm are losing theirs. Our lands may not be dying, but our way of life is, and our world is returning to the mundane. Without magic, we will return to the dark ages from before the Tuatha Dé Danann gods visited our realm and created the fae.

"We will become vulnerable to disease and famine again. Subject to the whims of untamed weather in hovels that cannot protect us. Already we have lost the ability to reproduce the technology we rely on. Soon, we won't have the power to maintain them. It is my quest to ask for a token of magic to return to my realm, and in exchange, I will offer my service to take your seed-stones to other bodies of water in this realm, so that your children can grow there."

A jitteriness fills me. I did not expect to meet a Lake Maiden and immediately proposition her, but from one look at Caitlin, it is clear she has been forming a bond with this fae over days.

Odiane turns to my sister. "You are right—this one has a conscience and heart. Many humans have tried to slay me and steal my heart-stones. Many fae have tried to do the same for my power. To take my seeds, so they can have the privilege of a Lake Maiden guarding and nurturing the waters in their lands. But some would see my daughter as their slave, a pet to be used up by them. We could never be tamed."

Odiane's huge, strange eyes hold my gaze. They are dark pools of rapidly moving blue, like her waterfalls. "I have been a part of these waters for centuries and seen countless armies clash. Sometimes I join the fighting and sometimes I watch from the sidelines, with my own amphibious court the only one to benefit from the slaughter and the feast it provides them. Rarely have I chosen to surrender a seed-stone freely."

Her white hair ripples through air as it would below the surface of the pool, and trickles of water run down her body and away from her in small rivulets, back to the waterfall.

I wonder how long she can last on land, before her whole entity crashes down and returns to its home.

"Do you want your seed-stones to be spread to other waters? For your children to grow and reside there?" I ask her. It won't be much of a bargain if she doesn't care for children.

"Oh, yes." Euphoria crosses her face. "I desire to hear the songs of my daughters from their waters across the lands. To hear their stories of what their homes are like, of the people they meet. As I once sang with my mother and my sisters. Not many of my sisters are left, and I have so few daughters."

"That sounds very lonely," I venture. "I also know what it feels like to be surrounded by people"—I indicate the fortress around us and the fae within it—"but to feel utterly alone. Like there is no one who quite understands you or is the same. I lived a privileged life before crossing into this realm, but one devoit of meaning or purpose other than waiting on the man I would marry."

I take in a shuddered breath, but continue. "Everyone around me had their busy roles. Caitlin preparing to become the next lord protector and dealing with the political maneuvering that comes with it. Our brother training to become a druid. My younger sister has the greatest powers in our generation of our family, and she practically manages the orchards with my father.

"But I was to wait and bide my time until the prince was ready to marry me. To educate myself on history, on the customs of the other kingdoms, on finance and trade, but every time I saw him, he didn't care for my opinions. I came here to live. To forge my own path and achieve something that was mine, before I return to my duty and live for everyone else again. I can't complain. I'm not hungry or poor or oppressed, but to me, my struggle is still very real."

The Lake Maiden examines me for a long time, drinking in my emotion like a person dying of thirst.

"We can bring your seed-stones to waters of your choosing," Caitlin ventures. "Where they will be safe and valued, and you won't be so alone anymore."

Caitlin's greatest strength as a leader is finding out what a person needs at the depth of their soul, not only the shallow little things they want, then dangling it in front of them for a bargain that would benefit both parties.

Perhaps she is more fae than we realize.

"Maybe I will allow you to take my seeds to other waters. Maybe I won't," Odiane says. "Before I can trust you, I need to know you. But if you earn my trust, if you bring my daughters to other lakes and rivers and springs in this realm, I may let you bring one back to your land. Your sister tells me the magic from my realm bleeds into yours. Into the air, the water, the soil. If my seed is closest to the veil between our lands, in the waters that flow from here to there, perhaps my daughter would be born with a soul, a body and a mind. If I come to trust you both, I might give you two daughters, each in very different forms."

Odiane looks to Caitlin, whose skin is flushed as she stares at her with such open hope. She could give Caitlin the magical pregnancy she desires, without the requirement of a male fae touching her. And she could give me a seed-stone to put into a lake back home.

The Lake Maiden smiles warmly at me, her cold hand squeezing mine again. "Keira, return here every night while you stay at my frozen river and tell me of your world. Of this prince that you feel obligated to marry. Of your hunts for wild fae who cross into your lands.

"I will not balk at the stories of glory and death as my king might. He too once took pleasure in such things, before our world began to unravel. Tell me of the oppression of your women, the things so subtle that men believe them nonexistent."

And I do. I speak to the Lake Maiden as the night deepens and the clouds part to reveal an indigo sky filled with the pinprick lights of stars, the space around them bleeding vibrant purple light. Their constellations are so very different from my own.

I tell Odiane about Finan, my hopes, my desires, my disappointments, with Caitlin as my silent support. The Lake Maiden's body drips away, bit by bit, until her rounded curves are wraith-thin and her hair is almost all gone.

As the day is born and pink light glows from the horizon, chasing away the blackness of the sky, Odiane sighs, then fades into heavy droplets of mist that hit the ground. I jolt mid-sentence, and shoot a shocked look at Caitlin.

"She does that." My sister tips her head to the pool on the ground.

It is only then that I notice the channels cut into the rock, allowing the water to flow back to the river.

"I don't think it is a true form that she takes. If someone decided to capture all the water of that body and move it elsewhere, Odiane's presence would remain here, with her heart-stones. She would appear here again, in another body of water."

I nod absentmindedly.

We hardly talk as we make our way up the staircase and through the levels of the fortress to our bedrooms. Fatigue slams into me as soon as I see that inviting bed, my limbs turning leaden, and it is not only because we stayed up the entire night.

The remnants of adrenaline fade away, and the exertion of the last day finally takes its toll. From walking an entire day to this base to creeping into the fortress with fear and anxiety rolling through me like a sickness, only to fall into our enemy's trap.

I have never felt fear like when those fae soldiers closed around us. Normally, I feel nothing at all.

My eyes keep drooping shut, and it is a struggle to pull off my clothes and slip into the nightdress laid out on the bed before melting into it. I drop off into oblivion immediately.

# CHAPTER 20

# KEIRA

anging echoes throughout my room, loud enough to make the door rattle in its frame. I take in a sharp breath and sit up abruptly, the blankets falling around my waist. The crashing bounces around inside my head, pain cutting through it. Someone is banging on *my* door. I take groggy steps across the room and open it.

Aldrin stands there, folding his muscular arms across his broad chest, with bright sunlight beaming into the room behind him. I want to slam the door shut in his face, but he shoves a foot in the doorway so I cannot close it. I am too tired for his games.

"You weren't sleeping, were you?" A smile creeps onto his face. "Because it's midday."

I groan in response, not caring that my hair is a mess of curls that half hangs over my face.

"Get changed. We are going to train your magic," he says, trying so hard to keep his eyes on mine and failing as they flick to my neckline and back up.

I am wearing nothing but a thin nightdress, askew across my chest and with the sharp peaks of my nipples clear beneath the silky fabric.

*Gods damn it.*

Mortification rises within me, and he takes a step back, allowing me to slam the door in his face, throwing my back against it. His laughter from the other side reverberates through the door, only igniting my rage further.

"Be out in five minutes," Aldrin calls.

I run my hands down my face as I try to slow my heart rate. I was up half the night with the Lake Maiden. And the night before that. Every night since I met her.

The deep urge rises within me to tell Aldrin to come back later. To crawl back under those blankets, but I need training. This knowledge could empower my people.

"Give me ten minutes," I respond.

"Five," Aldrin shoots back. "I'll be waiting out here."

The infuriating man has nowhere else to be. By this time, he has probably had a yelling match with Cyprien at least once.

I pull a tunic over my head, drag on a pale blue skirt that is narrow and divided for riding, the kind that looks more like gathered, flowing pants, and then tie a cotton corset over the top.

The cool splash of water as I wash my face helps to wake me up, then I grab the pastry and cold coffee a servant left on a tray while I slept. There are still flecks of powdered sugar on my face as I open the door and I quickly brush them off.

Aldrin leans against a thick pillar, lost in brooding thought. The loose curls of his dark hair are tied back into a knot at the nape of his neck, and strands escape to frame his face. Those thick eyebrows are pinched over amber eyes lost in shadows.

Hints of the black war paint that shimmers into existence on his skin whenever anger or fight takes him are visible across his cheekbones, his forehead and neck. They accentuate the sharp planes of his face and make him look very much the high fae warlord. A king.

I swear I stop breathing at the sight. At his terrifying beauty.

Aldrin turns to me and shakes his head. "Cyprien is driving me insane."

"He seems to be good at it." I fall into step beside Aldrin as he leads me down the long portico. "What are you afraid of?"

"I'm not—" Aldrin turns to me, then exhales. "Cyprien is one of the most stubborn, by-the-book people I know. To him, hosting my party here, hearing me out, it borders on treason. Maybe he justifies it by telling himself that I am technically being held by him for questioning. But traveling with me to the border of our supposed enemy, to witness evidence that I claim will convert him to my cause, would be viewed as a betrayal by the high chancellor. I am afraid he won't take that leap of faith, despite what I have already shown him."

"What did you do that was so terrible?" I ask. "Why were you exiled?"

A bitter laugh rumbles through him. "I had an idea that made people uncomfortable. A solution to a problem they didn't want to admit existed. Change is so...inconvenient. Especially when the people in power aren't directly affected by the threat yet."

We travel across the colonnade that wraps around the upper levels of the apartments.

I frown. "It's hard to change people, especially when the issue becomes entrenched with emotion, like the mistruths your people seem to cling to. Sometimes, all you can do is chip away at the lies."

Aldrin grunts and leads me down multiple levels, through alley-ways and out to a private, walled courtyard of packed earth we have been using as a training field. A frozen breeze curls through the space, and I regret not wearing that ancient fur coat.

"What am I going to learn today?" I ask.

"I have seen you wield air magic to propel weapons, knives and arrows, but I want you to use it to hinder an opponent's moves. To create micro-shields against the impact of their blows, and to rein-force your own strikes." He removes a sword from across his back, and places it on the ground. "Tomorrow, base jumping."

"Base jumping?" My voice pitches high.

"Think of it as running across air while creating hard discs of it to step on as you go. It takes some skill and strong nerves, but I think you will manage."

"I will manage?" My eyebrows shoot up. "What if I fall?"

"Don't worry. I'll catch you." He grins at me. It is bait. I know this for a fact, as his smug smile widens.

"Oh, good, as long as there is a big, strong man here to save me." I poke him in the ribs. "Too bad every time you try to save me, you make matters worse."

"Hmmm," he replies. "Maybe I need to focus on saving fae from you." I raise my eyebrows, but he continues anyway. "Does the Lake Maiden need saving, perhaps? Don't think I haven't noticed you working your innocent little human girl charms on her. 'Odiane, I will help you and your daughters take over the realm. No, I don't want much in return.'" He imitates me in a ridiculous, high-pitched voice.

I throw a shaft of solid air straight at his stomach, hard enough to make him double over protectively and grunt, but not to inflict pain. "Maybe you should focus on protecting yourself."

He shows me no mercy after that, drilling me hard with our training.

Aldrin demonstrates the weaving of an air net that is so fine it can be thrown up and dissipated in heartbeats, but strong enough to stop a blade.

Then he tests me, striking blows with the sides of his hands that fly for my arms, my chest, my back, as I clumsily throw air between us. When they connect, they are taps that pepper my body, and when I am successful in shielding, they crack audibly on the hard air.

"You see that?" Aldrin says between huffs of breath. "That shield could break a person's hand if they came at you with full force, but—" He kicks the backs of my legs so my knees buckle forward. "It took too long to form. Occupied too much focus and energy. You couldn't shield yourself from the next attack."

We keep dancing, sweat dripping down both of our bodies as he dips in toward me, so close my head clogs with the sweet scent of him and his breath tickles my neck. His face is inches from mine, and it would be so easy to lean in and press my lips against his. I wonder what he would feel like. Taste like.

His perfect face is all I can see as his hand taps my waist, then slides away, only to hit my arms, my chest, my lower back. It feels like his hands are all over me.

I forget to shield, utterly distracted by his nearness, and he gets a few good blows in.

Aldrin laughs, taunting me. There is golden light swirling in his eyes as he circles me like a predator. I take control of the thinnest layer of air between his feet and the ground and pull it out from under him. His smile falls as he slips for a single heartbeat, then braces himself on a wall of air he throws up.

"Good," Aldrin grunts. "Use your imagination. Now let's practice hand-to-hand combat maneuvers with fortified air."

Weaves of air form around his chest, arms and thighs, colored in golden light so I can see them. It reminds me of the pads Gwyneth uses when she trains me. I lean forward and poke the one at his chest. It is soft but solid under the gentle impact.

"Start with a side kick," he demands.

I ready my stance, then kick the side of his thigh, wrapping my shin in a thin layer of soft air padding and building a hard plate of air over the top. I use the same vein of magic to increase the power of my blow.

Aldrin grunts as our bodies connect. "Again. Harder."

I kick the same spot multiple times in fast succession. The magic increases both my strength and speed.

"A foot jab to the chest now," he barks, and I oblige, moving my shielding without pausing a beat.

He holds up his hands, the air cushioning there expanding. "Strike with your fists."

I breathe as I throw myself into the motions. One, two. One, two. My muscles burn from the exertion, the pain rippling up my thighs and through my abdomen. I stop and pant, leaning forward on my knees while the blood rushes from my head. There are a few beads of sweat on Aldrin's forehead, but he looks otherwise unfazed.

"If I didn't know better..." He gives me a slow smile. "I'd say you've had professional training. Strange for a peasant girl who stumbled into this realm while foraging for berries. Tell me, Keira, daughter of the Lord Protector of Appleshield, have you ever had to forage for anything in your life?"

"I guess my end of the bargain is fulfilled, then, if you have heard my story from my sister, or Cyprien." I try to joke to lighten the mood.

He raises an eyebrow, suddenly deadly serious. "I'd rather hear it from you. Every. Last. Detail."

"Can you blame me for lying to you? I was half terrified out of my mind when I first met you." My breaths leave me in sharp puffs. "I won't give you any more until the bargain is called in. Otherwise I'll have nothing left to leverage with."

"Keira, the bargain was never necessary. I was always going to free your sister. She might die of boredom in Cyprien's clutches," Aldrin says. "But your lies, they are hurtful."

"Hold on. You withheld information from me, too!" I poke him in the chest. "You never told me you were the king of these lands!"

Aldrin looks down at me, leaning in with amusement. "What was I supposed to say? *Hey, human, you know how you are terrified of high fae and believe them to be slavers? Well I'm the worst of them, their king.* You would have been running in the opposite direction, screaming."

"Who says I won't still?" I ask, heart racing, but not from the exercise.

My hand is flat against his chest and the muscles ripple beneath it as he laughs. The warmth of his body envelops mine as I gravitate into him, now only inches away. I cannot help it, as though I am being pulled in by some invisible force.

"I don't know. You seem to enjoy getting pretty close to me." His eyes search my face, then settle on my parted lips. A single finger tips my chin up toward him.

My arms snake up his chest, gliding across the firm ridges of his pectorals to settle around his neck, fingers toying with his hair. He holds me low around my waist, pulling me tightly to him.

I want those roaming hands all over me, touching my bare flesh, teasing and pleasuring.

This is a man who understands how to utterly undo a woman. Anticipation coils deep within my stomach, then lower.

I reach upward on the tips of my toes as Aldrin bends down into me and his lips gently brush against mine in the most tantalizing way. He does it a second time, probing, teasing, testing.

Testing. Just like last time.

I pull back and slap him across the side of the head, then shove his chest hard until our bodies separate. "This better not be another one of your damned tests!" I spit at him. This man makes my head spin. "You can't keep playing games with me."

Aldrin holds a hand to the side of his head and I don't feel the least bit guilty. "Ouch. Yeah. I deserve that." He gives me a look that is both coy and appraising. It makes my legs go weak.

I glare at him. "That's not much of an apology!" I am ready to turn on my heel and stalk away, because I can't handle making myself a fool in front of this man a second time.

He grabs my wrist and pulls me a step closer to him. "I'm sorry for being an asshole. It was a cruel thing to do. You kept giving me these heated looks and found excuses to be half exposed in front of me."

"I did not!" I pound at his chest, but he doesn't let me go and I don't try to pull away.

A huge, teasing smile fills his face. "And I was afraid you were a seductress from the human realm here to take my baby."

"I am not!" Indignation roars within me.

He cocks his head to the side. "Are you sure you're not a seductress from the other realm?"

"Do I need to dangle my contraceptive tea in front of you?" I snap.

His eyebrows rise dangerously high, his charm breaking with the shock of my admission. "You're on a contraceptive?"

"That's none of your business!" Gods, I want to die.

"But you just said—" He shakes his head. "No more games, I promise. And I'm sorry."

I scowl at him, scrutinizing his expression. "Why should I trust you again?"

He raises an eyebrow at me. "Do you want me to beg? To get on my knees? I will, if you like." My stomach does somersaults at his implications. He pulls me in so close he hardly has to lean in to whisper in my ear. "Trust me, because I will make it worth your while. I already know you want me." I groan. Damn, he is good.

Shivers run down my spine and I melt in his arms.

His hands move slowly across my waist, probing and stroking in caressing motions, moving toward my hips. Then his lips work their way down the sensitive skin of my neck.

I gasp, pulling back enough to look into his hooded eyes.

I wrap my arms around his neck as we reach in toward each other, our lips colliding in a hard, brutal kiss. It is hungry, devouring, as our lips move against each other, desperate to taste and touch.

My fingers run across the sharpness of his jaw, down the ropey muscle of his neck and broad shoulders. He only wears a thin tunic, but gods, I want to slip my hands under it and touch his bare flesh. To run my fingernails across the grooves of those washboard abdominals I have glimpsed.

A deep desire fills me to peel the clothes off him, right here. For my skin to rub against his, my bare breasts to be crushed on that hard chest.

Aldrin bites my lower lip, sucking it between his, then parts them to slip his tongue inside. He is all passion and chaos, and the intensity of it makes my stomach tumble as I try to keep up.

My entire existence reduces down to the taste of him, sweet as ripe berries, as his tongue caresses mine. Those thick arms tighten around me, squeezing me to his chest, and still I want more.

I press my hips against his to feel the hard length of him against my stomach. Thrills shoot through me at the thought of his arousal. It is massive. I grind my body against it just to test his reaction.

Aldrin lets out a ragged groan, pulling his lips away from mine for a heartbeat.

I need more.

I run my hands down his chest, across his ribs and lower, to his hips, as Aldrin peppers kisses on my neck, from my ear to my collarbone. My skin tingles delightfully with each touch of his lips.

My hands reach the line of his pants, and I am met with the difficult choice of ducking them upward under his tunic and exploring all that flesh, or dipping them inside his trousers. I dare them lower, pulling open the strings of his pants and sliding my hand within.

I close my eyes and heat floods my blood as my fingers glide across the tip of that hardness. Then I follow its length down and down until my hand brushes over the entirety of it. I smirk as Aldrin shudders and hisses in a breath. It makes me feel powerful.

One of Aldrin's hands roams up my stomach to the neckline of my tunic, air tugging apart the laces so his hand seamlessly slips beneath the fabric. His fingers brush over the peaked tip of my nipple, rolling it between them and sending hot waves of pleasure shooting out from it.

I run my hand across his cock even harder, then I grasp it in my fist and pump. Again and again, enjoying the hitches in his breath and the little sounds he makes. We both breathe hard, especially as he reveals my other breast and leans down to take it in his mouth.

Then Aldrin's other hand slips down to the fabric between my legs, but there is no way in. Not with the top band of my skirt sitting around my waist and restrained under my tightly laced corset that reaches my hips. He would have to half undress me to get access.

I shudder as he rubs his fingers across the sensitive apex of my thighs through the fabric, the friction shooting bursts of pleasure through my body. I curse myself for wearing this damn dress. He can't even lift the hem because the skirts are divided.

If I had been wearing pants, his hands, *those fingers*, would be plunged deep within me right now.

Aldrin presses his mouth over mine, forcing his tongue within, as the tension builds within me. His fingers swirl over that perfect spot again and again, flooding my core with heat and intense sensual friction. Pleasure sparks through my entire body, flooding my brain until all I register are the many ways we touch each other with desperate urgency.

I could come apart with this alone, and my body shivers as I edge toward that precipice. Tension coils tighter and tighter within me and still those expert fingers don't let up.

The sound of a throat clearing rumbles behind us.

"If the two of you aren't too busy, I have decided I will inspect the Dividing Cliffs. Today. Right now." Cyprien bites off each word.

Aldrin stiffens within my embrace as my face burns with mortification, and I swiftly pull my hand out of his pants and adjust my neckline. His body begins to reverberate, and I realize it is with laughter.

"For fuck's sake, Cyprien," Aldrin says into the crook of my neck, then pulls his face away from me. "Can we go in an hour or two?"

I glance over my shoulder. Cyprien stands in the entrance to the courtyard, frowning profusely but otherwise completely unabashed by what he has walked in on.

"We go now, if you are serious about this threat. Otherwise don't waste my time. Meet me in the main hall." Cyprien turns and walks briskly away.

Aldrin gazes down into my face with such tenderness, running a finger across my lips, that I think I am going to be undone. My heart flutters wildly in my chest.

"Hold that thought for me," he murmurs, then lets me go.

Frozen air wraps around me in place of his arms, and I shiver. My body craves the hard press of his. Bitter disappointment crashes down into me as the laces at my neckline are retied by Aldrin's threads of magic.

His hair is disheveled from my touch and his hardness is still painfully visible through his leather pants. There is a light in the eyes that look me up and down with an unspoken promise, but then he sighs as he smooths his clothing.

"I'm sorry about Cyprien, but—" Aldrin shakes his head. "I need him to believe me."

There is such vulnerability on his face that I forgive him immediately. My mind does, anyway. My body still screams for his touch and my blood races at the memory of it. I nod, not ready to speak, knowing my voice will waver with unsatiated hunger.

I watch his tight, muscled ass as he walks away and regret that I didn't squeeze it when I had the chance.

I should never have touched him, but I couldn't help myself.

The last thing I need is to become entwined with another king who might think he has a claim over me. It was different when I thought he was an outlaw. One I could enjoy, then leave behind when I return home. But a king? Nothing is ever simple with a king.

The image of Finan's face the last time I saw him comes to mind, emotion brimming within those ice-blue eyes as he said goodbye to me. I try to summon a scrap of guilt, but I feel nothing.

Aldrin glances over his shoulder and winks at me. "Are you coming?"

"Not...in the way I wanted to." The words slip out of my mouth and the look he gives me is utterly devious.

# CHAPTER 21

# ALDRIN

The wind howls around us, making the magic weave of our domed air shield flicker visibly. It protects us from the harshness of these frozen barrens, somewhat. Klara and Drake focus on that weave, patching it as the torrent of air corrodes its surface.

Multiple orbs burn inside, but the fire magic of my people is slight, and the heat generated only takes the edge off the chill.

Nothing can change the fact that we climb through deep snow.

The apex of this region of the Dividing Cliffs is just ahead of us, the seam between Spring and Winter. A landscape of pure white stretches out in all directions as snow coats everything, and the sky is a gloomy mass of clouds. Falling snowflakes are tossed sideways by the wind.

We reach the edge of the cliffs that overlook Winter. I do not focus on the desolation beyond. I have seen it a hundred times before. I watch the reactions of my companions instead.

Silence has a grip on the group. They stare at the undeniable devastation laid out before us. Cyprien and Lilly stand rigid with shock, their faces slack. A deep frown forms on Cyprien's features and his lips compress to a thin line. A tear slips down Lilly's face, freezing upon her cheek.

My people have witnessed this corruption multiple times before. We have checked the entire length of the border in our exile, but the horror of it never seems to fade. The severity of the place keeps getting worse.

I look for Keira, because I desperately need her to see what I fight for, to understand.

Maybe then she will be open to helping me.

She is next to her sister, shivering uncontrollably. I don't know if it is from the cold or the realization of what threatens this world. I create another orb and place it in front of her.

Tears are frozen on her cheeks. I take her hands in mine and rub them to return the heat to her flesh. Even through her gloves, I can feel the iciness of her fingers.

"Are you okay? Can you handle this cold?" I murmur. Who knows where the limits of humans lie?

"I am so sorry, Aldrin. This is the plague on your lands?" The howling wind almost whisks her words away.

"Come. I would like you to hear what I tell Cyprien," I say, pulling her by the hand.

We trudge a handful of steps through knee-high snow to Cyprien. Despite the short distance, it is hard work. I place a hand on his shoulder. The muscles are rigid beneath my touch.

He doesn't turn to me. "These lands have never looked like this before. Winter has never been a wasteland. There has always been life."

I nod. "At a glance, a person might think Winter is attempting a takeover. The ice and snow have crept deeper into our lands and the deepness of the freeze here has intensified. But *this* before us is not winter. It is a void. A desolation. This is what happens when the magic is stripped from a place. There is no substance, because our world is made of pure magic. Remove it, allow it to fade away, and there is nothing to remain."

I look at the barrens before us.

There is a long drop from these cliffs to a field of ice and snow, which stretches as far as the eye can see. The plain is rippled, as though a god ran huge claws through the land. In each valley, there is a pit of blackness, with great flakes of ash rising from it.

These immense rifts are as wide as rivers, dividing the field. The darkness within is so complete it is utterly devoid of light or substance. There is no hole to fall into, no bottom to crash upon. Inside those rifts is nothingness. Tears in space and time. The threat that will consume this entire world until there is nothing left of it.

We are sleepwalking toward a disaster.

Cyprien's eyes are glazed. "The whole border looks like this?" he asks.

"Yes." I swallow. "And the border with Summer is exactly the same, except it is a wasteland of sand and heat and those horrible rifts."

Lilly stalks to my side. "Why has the council not acknowledged this? We should be debating solutions in the Senate." Anger pinches her features. It is so rare that any emotion ruffles her usual calm.

"Because neither the members of the council nor the high chancellor have traveled here to view the evidence before shunning the idea that this threat could be real. It is much easier to deny this truth than to accept it and fight it."

Cyprien and Lilly's faces drain of color.

They have always supported the council, and the high chancellor after she became an elected official. I was removed from my throne and exiled over this issue and my solution to it. They were drawn into the web of convenient half-truths and fabrications, like the rest of my people.

"How did this high chancellor usurp your place, Aldrin?" Horror fills Keira's face.

From the corner of my eye, I notice Cyprien look away and a red flush of shame creep up his neck. This is new.

I let out a long breath. "The high chancellor is a brilliant politician. She has an air of both authority and wisdom, and thoroughly discredits any who oppose her. I have heard of her utterly destroying the businesses of minor merchants who threatened her own trades. She knows how to make the right promises to convince unwary people of even the most ridiculous things. To tap into people's fear and greed, and she does it shamelessly. Ruthlessly."

Lilly shuffles beside me. "Her smear campaign against Aldrin was relentless."

The air is heavy between us, filled with regrets. Cyprien still won't look at me. Keira's eyes dart between us, her lips parted in shock.

I continue. "She attacked right when I needed my people to trust my judgment. When I presented my evidence and solutions, and I was most vulnerable. The high chancellor scented my weakness and took full advantage of it. By the time I limped into my exile, I had begun to thoroughly doubt myself, my abilities and my predicted disaster."

I rub my temples. There is so much more to the story than that.

Had the council shown a unified front with me, I could have convinced the people of what we need to do. Of the sacrifices we high fae must make. It astounds me that I could have called them to war, and they would have followed. But asking them to leave the comforts of the city to tend to the wilds, as is our duty, was an outrage.

"The high chancellor is a great politician, but a terrible leader." Cyprien's cold words send chills down my spine.

I hold his gaze. "You have seen spriggan turn to rot and ash as their magic dissipates. You witness the rifts across this border. As you traveled through our lands, I'm sure you noticed lakes that no longer hold a Maiden and groves of trees with no nymphs. We passed through a Watchtower Tree on our way to the Frozen River Fortress, and two of the nymphs didn't have enough magic to form a body and disconnect from their tree. Have you seen enough to believe me?"

Cyprien glances at the frozen plains for a long time without responding. When he finally speaks, it is with a hoarse voice. "I have been urging the high chancellor to send an emissary to the Winter Court for a year now. To arrange a meeting between our ruling powers to parley. To question Erik on the increasing frosts and snow and ice in our land. She immediately refused, and recalled our ambassador to the Winter Court."

He falls into silence and Lilly picks up the tale. "It's almost as though our probing made her tighten her grip on the communication between the two courts. It became a treasonable offence for people to contact *anyone* in Winter. We have communities of high fae who were originally of that court, or who belong to both, and cannot speak with their family across the border. It is wrong. She claims to protect against spies, but I wonder if she is only protecting herself."

Anger runs through my muscles, causing them to ripple and twitch with the need for action.

Cyprien looks as though he has bitten down on something bitter. "I tried to talk to our ambassador Joven as soon as he returned, to glean what he knew of the brewing war in Winter, but he only remained in the capital for a day. He was immediately reassigned to a country estate. I wanted to visit him, but he hasn't responded to my messages or anyone else's on the council.

"Aldrin, you should have seen him that one day he was in the capital. It was as if he were a man hunted by the Soul Ripper itself, looking for threats in every corner and always accompanied by guards. At first, I thought he had seen things in the Winter Court that terrified him, but I came to wonder if the real threat to his life was in our court.

"So much has changed since you left," Cyprien says. "New laws. Different members of the council. I started to truly lose my faith in the high chancellor when soldiers were pulled from the border of Winter after they started returning home from rotations speaking of things that gave substance to your claims. As you said, what kind of leader would pull soldiers from the boundary of an enemy they believed was planning an attack? One who is either vastly incompetent, or who is covering for her own lies."

He shakes his head. "I had to come to witness the truth for myself. I had to talk to you. Properly. We haven't had a conversation since—" His voice breaks.

"Since Lorrella died," I finish for him gently, that all-too-familiar throb of pain building in my chest.

"I heard your proposal to the council." Cyprien runs a hand across his face. "I listened to your arguments and your evidence, but I was still too far gone in my grief and pain and anger to truly hear you. And when everyone turned against you, one by one, I too got swept away by the current."

I touch Cyprien's shoulder and he flinches at the contact. "Listen to me now."

"This is a lot to take in." He motions with an arm to the sight before us. "Let me think first. Tonight we will talk."

I nod, fighting the wave of emotion that rolls through me. It is much more than I expected and I am afraid to dare to hope. Not when he has let me down before.

Cyprien and Lilly stalk away to another bluff to take in more of the view, creating their own air shields. My thoughts fall into a brooding cyclone that whips as harshly as the frozen wind around us. Keira takes my hand in hers. I had forgotten she was there.

"I'm sorry that happened to you, Aldrin." She peers up at me, the wild curls of her red-gold hair erupting from her fur cap. Those strands are the most vibrant thing up here. "Not only that an imposter used deception to steal your birthright and smear your name, but that your friends did not stand by you. That you *still* have to convince them."

I blink at her, surprised by her warmth. "Too many of my friends followed me into this exile. Ten was enough. More would have joined, left their positions in the Senate or the army, but the Spring Court needed them. Perhaps I will still have friends in places of influence when I return to the capital."

If I ever return to the seat of my power. That old pain radiates through my chest, seizing my heart. Longing floods me, to see my city once more. To have a chance for redemption and to save my people. It has been a distant hope for too long.

We leave the howling edge of the Dividing Cliffs in huddled groups, with shields of air tucked around the clusters of people, a fire orb in each. Warmth spreads through my body from the hike back.

Cyprien is deep in thought by my side, a severe frown pulling at his stern features as we descend the cliffs through a path cut into the stone. An outcrop scoops over our heads, shielding us from the worst of the snow and wind.

"Are you planning on taking a human consort?" Cyprien suddenly asks.

"What?" I choke on the word.

"It's why you are keeping the girl near, is it not?"

"Do not say that in front of humans." I grab him by the arm. "Our realm has been separated from theirs for hundreds of years and they do not remember us favorably."

Cyprien gives me one of his probing, questioning glances.

I pinch the bridge of my nose. This is the worst place to have this conversation, but I know Cyprien won't let it go. "In our history with humans, there have been fae who have kidnapped human consorts. A corrupt minority, but it seems this is the only part they remember of our relations. I have been told that even recently, human women have been held against their will after wandering into our realm. The humans seem to think we are all slavers and rapists wanting to take their women. It doesn't help that we have both tried to contain these two." I tip my head in Keira and Caitlin's direction.

"They'd end up dead if they wandered through the forest on their own," Cyprien snaps.

"Would they?" I raise an eyebrow at him. "You've seen them fight."

He gives me a conceding bow of the head. "You didn't answer my question."

I huff out a breath. "I'm not looking for a consort, Cyprien. She promised me information, that is all."

"You have a very interesting way of trying to get *information* from a woman's mouth." His lips actually curl up into something that resembles a smirk.

"Making jokes now, are you?" I laugh at him. "I thought you were challenging the frozen plains for iciness."

"You give a man far too much ammunition, Aldrin. You ever like to dance on a knife's edge." His eyes glitter with amusement. The irony is that I have always thought the same of him.

Cyprien shakes his head, then removes my hand from his arm. "You are far too distracting. I need to think."

I raise both my hands. "I was respecting your silence. You started the conversation with your inappropriate questions."

Cyprien pats my shoulder, then joins Lilly, immediately talking in tones that I cannot hear. I watch them for any hints as to what they will decide.

The path leads out of the stone cavity and a winter wonderland sprawls out before us. Cold dread pumps through my veins at its presence in *my* lands. Every inch of me screams that this is wrong.

A thin layer of snow completely covers the plateau, crunching beneath our boots, with only the green leaves of the odd tulip or daffodil sprout poking through. No flowers. Pine trees dot the plain, a light dusting of snow on top of their broad branches, alongside skeletal oaks.

Everything is far too monochrome for my tastes: the white of the frosty ground, the frozen lakes and overcast sky against the almost black of the trees.

As we enter a forest and the snow thins to mere patches, Keira joins me at my side.

"Would you believe that I had never seen snow before crossing to this realm? The winters of my home are mild." Her pale cheeks are flushed a pretty shade of pink.

"Is that so?" I ask. "What do you think of it?"

"Not a fan. Too cold." Her breaths come out as streams of mist. "Too wet."

I lean in towards her, close enough for her to feel my breath on her skin. "Do you want to know a secret?" She nods vigorously and I almost smile at her eagerness. "Neither am I. It's too...white. Boring. Where are the different colors and textures of the scenery? There are no leaves or flowers to give the landscape a hundred shades. I can't hear the gurgling of a stream or the buzzing of bees, smell the pollen and dirt or the sharpness of bruised herbs. It's all more of the same."

She smiles. "I agree with that, though I'm sure there are people who believe otherwise."

"Yeah," I say. "There's a whole Winter Court of them."

"Aldrin…" Keira bites her lower lip, and I remember how she did that to mine this morning.

"Yes?" I purr.

"Why are your lands dying?" Her voice is gentle, and so innocent.

I look away. "In short, because most of us have abandoned our posts in the forests for the comforts of the cities." Those doe eyes continue to stare at me, unsatisfied. I stare at the ground, watching patches of snow turn brown from the mud of my boots.

"This entire realm is made of magic, created by the powers of the Tuatha Dé Danann," I say. "Without high fae tending the lands and nurturing them with our magic, they fade. It is a cycle, where the more magic we put into a place, the more it generates in return, like a farmer tending their crop."

Light motes of snow drift down and land on my skin. They dust Keira's hair. I am entranced by the beauty of her, but I drag myself back to our conversation.

"Once, fae were spread throughout the court. The fortresses and villages of the forests, mountains and meadows were brimming with high fae and the wild parts with low fae. But then my ancestors erected a sprawling metropolis modeled on those in the human realm, and after each war, refugees fled to it. The lords amongst our people took up residence there, realizing the depth of power they could hold if they were permanently around their king, forming the council.

"The city became places of culture and comforts, where delicacies are imported from other courts. Anything a fae desires is available: bars, restaurants, venues that host parties all day and night. There is an abundance of work in the city, much of it far easier than the country life and an existence in the wildlands. The people there keep all their magic for themselves, funneling it into businesses or self-indulgences, rather than sowing it back into the earth."

Keira sucks in a breath. "I would love to visit your city. See how the people live there."

I shake my head. "The problem is, we became lazy, greedy and self-ish. We sold our souls for comfort and extravagance. When my people stopped giving part of themselves back to the land, the land stopped returning the magic. Our powers began to fade, and our very life force with them. Conceiving a child gradually became near impossible. There isn't enough magic to go around. Then..." Words escape me for a moment. "Then our women started dying in childbirth."

It takes me a long time to pick up the narrative again. "Our numbers dropped drastically, and it wasn't clear what was happening at first. When the magic dipped below a crucial threshold, our world started to fall apart. You have seen this. The lower fae whose bodies dissipate on the wind. The land falling away to nothingness in great rifts."

Keira moves a branch from her path, the staircase up the rocky incline to the Frozen River Fortress barely wide enough for us side by side. She pants at the pace I set in my frustration, but pushes to remain at my side. I slow my strides, forcing myself to not take two steps at a time.

"What is your solution?" she asks. "I know it's controversial."

I give her a sidelong glance.

My answer might terrify her, but she will find out eventually. "It's a two-pronged attack. Fae need to move back to the outposts of this court and nurture their land, rather than being concentrated in one city. There will be incentives, land given away, much smaller cities built, trade expanded so commodities are available throughout the court.

"But we also need to vastly increase our population. You must understand—low fae take their magic from nature, but we high fae generate it within ourselves. More high fae means more magic in this realm. My grand plan, the one that got me exiled, was to invite humans to migrate to these lands as full citizens, and hope they would interbreed with our kind to produce the next generation."

Keira raises her eyebrows at me.

"Don't look at me like that," I mutter.

"I didn't say anything." Her expression is unreadable.

But she hasn't run away from me screaming, and that is something.

"I know what you are thinking." Vulnerability rolls through me. "I promised you we don't steal human consorts, and here I am suggesting breeding between our races. But *this* is different. A solution that relies on choice and freedom. Our people once wanted to live in each other's lands. To intermingle. Humans have a far longer lifespan here, so close to the source of their magic. Their power is vastly increased. I hope they would make a home in these lands."

"The idea of having humans here was that repulsive to your people that they exiled you?" Her eyebrows shoot up.

"Humans have their prejudices and we have ours," I grumble. "I think the bigger outrage was suggesting they move to the forests, where they would initially lead a more primitive existence."

By the time we return to the Frozen River Fortress, the cold has thoroughly seeped into my bones and I don't know if I will ever feel warm again. We drop the air shields as the icy claws of the wind are cut off by the high walls.

I turn to Cyprien. "Are you ready to talk? I think you have had enough time to mull over what you have seen here."

"I am ready to talk."

"Lilly?" I ask. A shadow of a smile curls her lips, and she dips her head in agreement.

I lead the party to the great hall, stalking with built-up frustration.

The hearths rage with crackling fires and a wall of warmth hits me upon entering, making my frozen skin sting with a thousand prickles. A banquet table is set with hot, spiced wine and a spread of nuts and dried fruits, but I ignore them, rounding on Cyprien.

"Do you stand with me?" I demand. "Or do you stand against me?"

I have had enough of uncertainty.

Cyprien kneels. "I stand with you, my king. My loyalty is to you and my soldiers are yours. I will help you dispose of the high chancellor and gain your throne again."

There is a blaze of passion in his eyes, and he is going to need it to do half of what he pledges.

Lilly kneels beside him, an arm crossed over her chest, fist clenched. "I stand with you, my king."

"Good." I reach down an arm to each of them and pull them up. I grasp Cyprien by the shoulders, and he places his arms on mine. "I have needed you. The gods know I have I *needed* you."

He gives me a curt nod.

I hide the wave of relief that crashes through me. This man doesn't know it, but he had the power to break me. I never want to be that weak and vulnerable again.

# CHAPTER 22
# KEIRA

My heart hammers violently in my chest as Cyprien kneels before Aldrin, then is helped to his feet. A monumental shift in power has just occurred. Events have spiraled faster than I can keep up with over the last handful of days and I am in over my head.

I never anticipated talks of rebellion and of a king being reinstated on his throne during my pilgrimage.

Caitlin clutches my arm, her fingernails digging into my flesh. She feels it too. The urge that screams: run, run, RUN. Get away before we become embroiled in a civil war.

"Do you yield your prisoner to me?" Aldrin asks Cyprien, and my stomach tumbles.

The man throws a quick glance at Caitlin, then back. "Yes. I had no plans for her, besides tossing her through a portal as soon as I got the chance."

Aldrin's gaze turns to Caitlin. "You are free."

Magic brims within me, swelling in my chest until the pressure feels like I will explode. The sound of trilling bells fills my ears as the skin beneath the tattoo tingles. He has completed his side of the bargain.

Aldrin beckons me forward with a single finger, and I move as though through water. My feet take one step at a time of their own accord, my mind too dazed to be in control.

He puts an arm around my shoulders and leads me to a chair, depositing me in it. One of the thrones. He takes the other, leaning forward so his elbows are on top of his knees, gazing into my face intently. Our legs touch.

"Keira. Tell me your story." White tendrils of magic curl away from his lips with his breath.

My mind becomes groggy. It moves so slowly, like I am intoxicated and have no mastery over it. There was something I was supposed to remember.

I greedily scan Aldrin, as though the answer lies there. The sharp angles of his tanned face. The broad chest with unbound hair draping down it. Bulky, muscular thighs with large, calloused hands hanging casually between them. I should be afraid of him, but I can't pinpoint why.

My throat dries, and I swallow hard. "I didn't plan to take the pilgrimage. I didn't think I deserved it, that I had the right to an adventure for self-discovery. How could I risk myself when the entire kingdom needs me?" The information is forced right out of my mouth. I should feel horror, but I can't muster any emotion at all.

Caitlin's sharp intake of air is a distant thing sliding over my senses. Aldrin's expression as he raises his eyebrows and turns to Cyprien means nothing to me.

"I spent my life preparing for the day Prince Finan finally committed to marrying me, for when I was to become queen." A shudder ripples through me. "I studied alone with my tutor. History. Battle tactics. Foreign politics. Diplomacy. Except no one in the royal family cared to hear my ideas. I devoted my life to him, but then discovered he would toss me aside if a better bride came along. He would take my own sister if the king demanded it. My carefully planned future crashed down around me."

A tear rolls down my cheek, but I have no idea why. More words spill from my lips. "I chose the dangerous pilgrimage because meeting the fae and learning their culture was my dream as a child. I came here to experience life before becoming locked away in another castle. Before becoming bound to Prince Finan."

I fall silent, panting with exertion and staring at nothing. A great void opens within me and I tumble into it, falling deeper and deeper into that despair.

The magic tugs at me, and I hear Aldrin as though he is very far away. "More. Tell me more. What is the pilgrimage?"

I hardly register the words that fall from me. "It is the greatest honor. Women who take it and return are celebrated. We become priestesses, and are offered a comfortable life in the temple if we want it. Upon taking up the call, women are schooled in all we know about this realm, but it is precious little. We are trained to defend ourselves, and then we are guided through the portal, like lambs to a slaughter. Our mission is to bring magic back to our lands, sometimes a relic or a heart-stone. Sometimes a woman returns pregnant. Some never return at all."

Anger ripples across Aldrin's features and I can hear Caitlin telling them to stop what they are doing to me, that none of it is true.

I was supposed to hide any information that would betray my realm. How can a single woman hold back the tides of the ocean?

"Was that your intent?" Aldrin's low rumble is filled with fury. "To return pregnant?"

"No." My every muscle is limp and I wonder if I will fall out of this chair. "No. I came to look after Caitlin. To learn about the fae, not to gather information on an enemy, but to write an academic tome. To learn the magic of these lands and the language of the runes. We planned to make a bargain with a Lake Maiden and return home with the gift of her seed-stones, one in my pocket and one in Caitlin's belly."

"Not all humans are so considerate. Some would steal and lie and kill in their desperation to return magic to our realm and save our way of life. Fae slip into our world to kidnap our women and turn them into breeding slaves. They take from us what they need, and we do the same. It is not moral, but it is necessary to save thousands of human lives."

"Is this celebration of the pilgrimage, of killing fae, revered universally in your realm?" Aldrin practically growls.

"Yes," I half choke, trying to keep the word in.

"How do you feel about this cruelty and prosecution of the fae by humans?" he probes.

"It is wrong. It weighs heavily on my conscience. I am powerless to it," I say.

"How would humans react to the portals opening permanently again? To the idea of an alliance and coexistence?" Aldrin's voice is rough.

I glance around the room and find Cyprien holding Caitlin back from me while she kicks and claws at him.

"Fear. Mistrust," I mutter. "If the portals opened without prior agreement, they would be met with a human army."

I try to focus on my breathing, in and out. On tensing each individual muscle to bring myself back in control of my body, but the haze is so thick.

I want to clamp my lips down, but the words keep escaping. "The priestesses would have the power and influence to make an alliance. They reside in every province in the kingdom and are almost as powerful as the king. These women have traveled to these lands, and they are an authority on the Otherworld and magic itself. If any could convince the lords of the benefits of connecting our realms, it would be them, but it would incite a bloody civil war. Prejudice is strong."

I sway in my seat as my vision blurs in and out. "The lords could combine their forces to push the king into an alliance. But not the current king. Not King Willard. He is too old and hateful. But Prince Finan, the man I am to marry—I could convince him. The lords, the priestesses, and the druids could convince him. My grandmother is the high priestess my brother a druid and my father the lord protector of the lands that border this realm."

Aldrin leans in towards me, his face so close to mine. "If you became queen, would you push for an alliance between our lands?"

"If I am convinced your people would treat mine with respect and as equals, then yes, I would," I say.

229

There is a long pause. I can almost see the gears turning within Aldrin's mind as he looks away from me.

"Do you want to marry Prince Finan?" Aldrin speaks ever so gently.

"No. I do not." My statement hangs between us. "What I want doesn't matter. If I do not become his queen, if I do not control and guide him, his reign will be a disaster that will be felt across the kingdom."

A series of expressions pass across Aldrin's face and I can't read a single one of them. "I have one last question for you." He seems to hesitate, eyes utterly vulnerable. "Are you the second daughter of Edmund, Lord Protector of Appleshield?"

What a strange question for him to ask.

"Yes," I whisper, and he recoils as though slapped. Aldrin collapses back into his chair. I watch him, still drowning in the magic swirling in my head.

He raises an arm. "Thank you for telling me your story. You're released from the bargain."

Conscious thought crashes down on me like a physical weight. That damper on my senses lifts abruptly and I am overwhelmed by the crackling roar of the fires, the heat that threatens to suffocate me and the scent of smoke. The ragged breathing of each person around me as their stares remain fixed on me.

Confusion whirls in my head as I stare at them, then at Aldrin. My arm stings and I pull back the sleeve to watch the wisps of magic curl away from it in silvery light, the tattoo disappearing.

"What did you do?" I turn to Aldrin, but the memory slams into me of what he compelled me to say. "What did you *do*?" I leap to my feet and back away from him. The anger at the abuse roars within me, clashing with terror. "You forced me to speak against my will. To tell you things that are a betrayal of my people. How did you get inside my mind like that? It's a violation."

Aldrin stand and reaches out for me, and I take another step back, just outside of his grasp.

"A violation?" His voice is pitched high in shock. "Keira, this is what you agreed to in our bargain. To tell me your story."

"My story is about the horrible man I am promised to and my girl-hood dreams. Not tactical details about the power structure in my realm or the intricacies of the pilgrimage!" I yell, tears running freely down my face.

How stupid was I to think I knew this fae? That I could trust him at all. Trust any of them.

The fae are known for taking what they want.

I am horrified that I betrayed my people, to a fae king, no less. It is so much easier to throw that anger at Aldrin instead of myself.

"The intricacies of the pilgrimage!" He growls back. "*That* is the violation here. These practices are the reason we fae closed the portals in the first place. And you are one of them."

His hands clench into fists at his sides and he towers near me, but he doesn't yell or get in my space.

Self-righteous rage rolls through me, hot and hard and bitter, but it's tainted with deep shame. He is right. Not his methods, but his judgments of us.

"The practices of her people are not this woman's fault. She came here with no ill will," Cyprien chimes in.

I let another man near my heart, and he betrayed my trust.

"It is not my fault you don't understand the nature of a bargain." Aldrin doesn't meet my eye.

"Well, maybe you should have informed me before you trapped me in one," I snap at him.

"How could I have known it was going to compel you to speak truths you didn't plan to share?"

"But you took advantage of it anyway." Pain radiates through my chest. *He is a king of the fae. Of course he took advantage of you, you silly girl.*

"I will not use the information to harm your people. You know that," Aldrin replies. "Even if humans have been committing crimes against us for generations."

"I don't know anything about you," I spit, then turn on my heel and stalk out of the grand hall.

Caitlin follows me out into the frozen night, gripping me tightly around my arm and leading me to our rooms.

"What am I doing here, Caitlin?" I sniff as I hold my emotions in. "I cannot trust my own instincts anymore. He used me."

She quickens her pace. "Keep it together, Keira, until we have privacy."

I need to kill this softness in me, if I am to be queen. I trust too soon, too easily, and am devastated when that trust is broken. We rush through an alleyway, down winding paths and up the staircase that hugs the apartment building.

I can't get Aldrin out of my head. Those golden eyes that swirl with fire. The quick half-smile that warms me from head to toe, that penetrates to the depths of my soul. Aldrin is a man I could love. By the gods, he might drive me to insanity, but I could love him with my whole heart. The emotion he flares within me puts to shame the pitiful spark I hold for Prince Finan, and it will only grow the longer I let him in.

After witnessing the devastation of these lands, I know for certain that I have to marry Finan. The fate of two worlds depends on me. My shoulders sag from the sheer weight of it. From the heartache of having to tie myself to that man.

Caitlin rounds on me as soon as we are in my chambers. "I know you want to leave, but we need to finish what we started. We will complete our mission and have something to bring home. And you will stay with Aldrin long enough to work out what he is going to do with the information he took from you."

I lock away that pain deep within my chest. "He is high fae and outmaneuvered me. I shouldn't be shocked. There won't be a next time." I toss myself onto the bed and let out a shuddering breath. "By the darkest realm, I was enjoying his company too much. Of course it wasn't real." I laugh bitterly. The pain will come later, in the depths of the night when I am alone in my blankets.

"He has probably had hundreds of years to learn how to manipulate and get what he wants," Caitlin offers.

I sit up on the bed. "We need a plan."

Caitlin smiles wickedly. "We will learn theirs. If high fae open the portals, the Appleshield Protectorate must be prepared for them."

# CHAPTER 23

# ALDRIN

I run my hands through my hair then down my face, and collapse into my chair. I watch the doors, as though I expect Keira to return.

"I made a mistake, didn't I?" I mutter. "In the way I handled that."

"It would seem that way." Cyprien takes the smaller throne next to mine. "She is the one Lorrella prophesied about, isn't she? The second daughter of the Lord Protector of Appleshield, who will help you bring our two cultures together."

I close my eyes for a long moment. "Yes. Yes, she is. I thought at the time—that maybe—who knows what seers mean with the riddles they give?"

Cyprien's lips press into a thin line. "Are you going to tell her?"

"Yes. No. I honestly have no idea. You know what happened the last time I spoke of that prophecy."

"She has a right to know." Cyprien's tone is low.

I look at him, then look away. "I will scare her away entirely. Let me get the timing right."

A frown pinches his brow. "It appears she will help you through this Prince Finan. You can't keep seducing the future wife of a king you want as an ally."

"Can't I?" I raise an eyebrow at him. "It sounds like the man is a fool, and Keira as queen would be my ally."

"Regardless. Casual sex will complicate an alliance. This is more important than your *urges*, Aldrin."

I slump back into my chair. "Maybe you should have some *urges* of your own and lighten up," I grumble. "Maybe that's why there is a stick up your ass. You just need a good f—"

"Aldrin. Careful." Cyprien gives me a hard look, but a quirk to his lips hints at a smile. For Cyprien, he might as well be beaming.

I've been spending too much time with Drake and his horrible humor is rubbing off on me.

I cannot get the smell of Keira out of my head. The taste of her.

How her hands ran over my body like she wanted every inch of me, and the way her fingers curled around my cock. The memory of her stroking and pumping my length is enough to drive me insane. I need more of her. To try everything with her.

Something deep within my soul calls to hers, but Cyprien is right.

I have to tread carefully with my next steps. The fate of this entire realm could depend on her. For all I know, Keira has taken her sister and left.

I rub my eyes. "For years, I have been trying to work out a path to the humans. When Keira was compelled by the bargain, I couldn't stop myself from asking every question that has plagued me since I was exiled. The answers to all my problems were offered up on a silver platter, and all I had to do was reach out and take them. I didn't mean to hurt her, or abuse her trust, but I did it anyway." Shame slices through me.

"Why are you telling me?" Cyprien barks. "Take a jug of wine and a platter of food to her chambers, and tell *her* you are sorry."

Cyprien points to the banquet tables laid out with hot meats, spiced vegetables on skewers and wine. I didn't notice the servants enter. I do as he tells me, balancing a tray and jug as I leave the hall and descend through the fortress.

I try to practice what I am going to say in my head, but the words won't come.

Cold sweat trickles down my back as I reach the door to her chamber. I cannot hear sobbing through it, and a wave of relief rushes through me. Muffled voices drift through as I juggle the items in my hands and knock on the door. A silence falls in the room, then footsteps approach. I swallow nervously.

Keira opens the door, her expression masked. She doesn't frown or scold or show signs of tears. Behind her, Caitlin sits on the floor cross-legged, sharpening a blade with a whetstone.

"Very considerate of you, Aldrin." Keira takes the platter of food and the jug of wine from my hands, and uses her foot to shut the door in my face.

I stand there on the threshold for a long moment, in complete disbelief. She just dismissed me.

I knock on the door again. "I came here to talk to you."

"I'm busy, Aldrin," she calls back.

Dread fills me. She is definitely angry. "Hear me out. I want to apologize."

The door cracks open a notch, only enough to reveal half her face. "Not tonight, Aldrin," Keira says simply, as though the fatigue of a hundred years rests upon her soul. "Not tonight." She closes the door again, gently this time.

At least she hasn't disappeared into the night. I don't think I could handle never seeing her again.

I return to the feast hall, blinking as the light burns my eyes in contrast with the blackness outside.

"I'm guessing it didn't go well?" Drake laughs and chucks a strip of meat in his mouth.

Klara nudges him in the ribs and he almost falls out of his seat at one of the banquet tables. "Don't be a nosy bastard." She turns her violet gaze on me. "Are you okay?"

The question jolts me out of my reverie. How has Keira gotten so far under my skin? The armor of a king, of a leader, snaps back into place over my emotions and expression alike.

"Fine. It's bloody cold and dark out there."

"Yeah," Drake says. "I told Kai he was insane, swimming in the

Frozen River. The damn kelpies have spent this entire time fawning over the Lake Maiden. Something to do with giving her the worship that is her due."

I nod. I had wondered where they had gotten to.

There's no use trying to keep track of kelpies or relying on them to stay where you want them.

I walk away as Klara explains to Drake that the whole reason kelpies are nomads and travel the courts is to pay their respects to the different waters and their guardians, in a near religious pilgrimage. She says it as though he is stupid for not knowing. There is such a huge grin on his face, I wonder if he is baiting her again.

I return to that throne on the dais, not feeling like mingling with the dozen of soldiers who now drink and eat and talk in the hall, both mine and Cyprien's. While I was gone, long tables and benches were brought in, including a table at the throne, already laden with food. Cyprien joins me, perching on the edge of the smaller throne.

"She's definitely still angry," I admit.

"Losing your touch with women, Aldrin?" A cruel smile curls Cyprien's lips. "Maybe you should spend less time in the wildlands and return to the Senate."

I whip my head toward him. "You know I can't do that. I have been exiled. The council will refuse to hear me."

"But they will hear me," Cyprien urges, tapping his foot rapidly. "If I invite you to give evidence on what we have all seen at the border here, then they have to allow you into the city and the Senate."

I let out a bitter laugh. "We will have to be clever about it. I will struggle to set foot into the city, but the Senate house? The high chancellor would never allow it."

"Then we won't announce your presence until I raise my concerns before the council and call on you into the house to give evidence." He is deadly serious. There is that half-mad glint in his eyes, the one he gets when he forms a daring plan. The very look that has won me many battles.

I drink from a chalice of wine. "Will it be enough? If they didn't believe me all those years ago when I was their king, why would they believe us now? How can adding your testimony help so much?"

Cyprien presses his lips into a thin line. "Things have changed a lot since then. The high chancellor has shown her true colors, her ruthlessness and disregard for fact. The people are far worse off under her. Titania has fixed none of the problems you faced under your reign, and they have only grown worse. I believe our court is ready to accept the real threat that faces us, especially without a new and shiny politician making promises and discrediting you."

"Oh, she will still discredit me," I retort.

"She will," he allows. "But this time, she too has lost the confidence of the Senate and people."

I ponder that thought for a long time. Returning to my city and my home.

"Your people need you back in power, Aldrin," Cyprien says, and the gravity of it radiates through me.

I have known him for most of my life, inside and out, and he is not a man to play political games. I can trust him in this, because if he wanted to destroy me, he would have arrested me for treason by now.

"Okay," I say. "Let's do this. Let's return to the capital and take on the high chancellor." I tap the armrest of the golden throne with a finger. "We need more evidence than our words and memories. Even if we bring corrupted low fae, it won't be enough. I will collect an entire party of nymphs from the borderlands to speak of how their magic is disappearing, along with that of the land, and the great scars upon this realm. We will demand the council visit the border themselves."

"Titania will argue that you have betrayed us to the Winter Court and that it is a trap," Cyprien says.

"Then we will take them to the border of Summer," I quickly cut in. "It is just as devastating. There is no way she could spin the same lies about our oldest ally."

"It could work." A rare smile grows on his face. "It could work."

The idea grows rapidly within my mind. "I have to take the risk. I am achieving precious little out here. Killing corrupted fae helps to redistribute their magic back into the ground, but there is always more."

Cyprien takes a flatbread and tears pieces from it, placing them in his mouth. "We should structure your journey to collect low fae witnesses to coincide with the human women's mission to spread Odiane's seed-stones. It is a noble cause, and it will allow you more time to win back Keira as an ally."

"I don't even know where to start with that," I admit, halting the piece of meat I was about to bring to my lips. My appetite suddenly disappears.

Cyprien continues as though I never spoke. "Perhaps she may be a queen one day, perhaps not. She already has the connections we need, as does her sister, with easy access to these priestesses and their lord protector." He leans closer to me, an intensity in his voice as he drops it low enough for only me to hear. "You need to work out what capacity you want her to be in your life before it gets messy: friend, lover, wife."

I recoil from him. "Hold up there, Cyprien. You see a man kiss a beautiful woman once, and assume we are going to marry." I try to laugh it off.

"You forget, I know you, Aldrin." Cyprien pulls himself up and walks away without a glance back, leaving me stunned.

I am not looking for a romance. How could I when my life is in tatters? I am facing the potential death of my realm and civil war of my court.

But if Keira asked me to her bed tonight, I could not stop myself.

## CHAPTER 24

# KEIRA

Water trickles down Odiane's heart-shaped face, between her large eyes and over her small lips. Her skin is milk-white, dotted with transparent, glittering scales, her with cheeks flushed blue.

This morning gills slit the sides of her throat, and large fins fan from her ears and shoulders like ornamentations. Her white hair is as short and shaggy as a human man's, with a lock hanging between her eyebrows. She is utterly beautiful.

"You are leaving me this morning," she practically sings as she runs a hand down Caitlin's face. "But you will come back to me on swift legs. Humans always do things in such a hurry. Your lifespans are so short, but bursting with adventure."

"We will." Caitlin's shoulders are tight. There is moisture at the corners of her eyes that could not be from the waterfalls. We stand too far away.

"Oh, to walk this realm and see the many things the high fae speak of!" A look of pure longing fills the Lake Maiden's face. "You will be fortunate indeed."

"Soon you will have new daughters to sing to and they will tell you of the same sights," I offer to her.

Odiane stands tall, stretching out both her arms and reaching a hand toward each of us. The sleeves of her dress are made of thousands of tiny shells woven together, and water mists down from them to the ground, so it appears like the fabric of her sleeve is wide and gaping.

"Shall we make a bargain?" the Lake Maiden asks, and my stomach twists with nervousness.

I was told to never make a bargain with a fae, and I am about to make my second. The first didn't go so well for me. I take her hand anyway, and those long fingers are ice cold as they interlock between mine. Caitlin grips her other hand, then reaches for my grasp, so our three bodies make a circle.

"I set a task upon you, Caitlin and Keira Appleshield, to take my seed-stones and set them into bodies of water that are unoccupied by a Lake Maiden. Once each of my daughters is placed in their new home, you may return to me in your own time and I shall give you two seed-stones. One for Keira to place in your homeland of the Appleshield Protectorate, in water where the magic is strongest. One for Caitlin to place in her womb and create a half-human child with the blood and magic of the fae."

"I accept the terms of this bargain," I say as one with Caitlin.

A chill runs through my fingers, up my arm and into my center. It builds across my collarbone and chest until blue light illuminates through the fabric at my neckline.

I turn to Caitlin, lips parted.

The shining brilliance fades, and the flowing strokes of runes are visible along her skin above her neckline, like a necklace tattooed in faint blue ink. Odiane releases my hand, and I quickly unlace the neckline of my dress with shaky fingers to reveal the same mark.

"I hope you like my touch upon your skin." The Lake Maiden laughs. "Is it not beautiful, this caressing of the heart?"

The waterfall suddenly rushes out to meet Odiane, and a bundle materializes in her hands. It is a circular bubble of water, with a thick, calcified netting of segmented coral encasing it. Swishing around in the water are three seed-stones. They are the same shape and size as a chicken's egg, but that is where the similarities end. These are completely transparent, bound within a soft membrane, and have a navy center of dense matter encased in thick jelly.

"My daughters." Odiane offers the bundle to us.

I take it, the coral netting rough beneath my fingers and the magical barrier on the water slick under my touch. Caitlin holds out a leather satchel and I place it within.

"How do we take a seed-stone out?" Caitlin asks.

"Place your hand inside with intent, and the magic will part for you. Do not leave the seed-stones out of water for too long, or they may dry."

Great rivulets run from Odiane's arms, their form lost in the escaping water. Her stomach is a twisting void and her hips and legs have diminished greatly in girth to make her appear skeletal. She must have used a lot of magic in the bargain.

Despite her fading body, her eyes glow with hope. "Farewell and travel safe. Deliver my offspring and return to me, lovely ones."

I jump as the mass of her body loses its shape and the water crashes to the ground. I will never get used to it.

I turn to Caitlin. "I honestly thought getting here and holding the seed-stones of a fae would be an impossible feat."

She gives me a thin-lipped smile. "Somehow, I wonder if we are just getting started."

We pick our way across the rough surface of the rocky platform, avoiding the rockpools Odiane's body created. I stop on the bottom step, still clutching the railing, and turn back to Caitlin.

"If you don't mind me asking, how do you...when Odiane gives you the seed for your womb, how..." My words trail off. There is no easy way to ask. Maybe I shouldn't have brought it up, but curiosity burns within me.

A flush creeps across Caitlin's face. "She said her seed-stones can be created in many forms. That I will need to insert it up...the usual place for a pregnancy. She wanted to do it, to lie with me, but it would be a betrayal of Gwyneth. I don't want to be touched like that by anyone else."

I place a hand on her shoulder. "I am glad you have a chance for a pregnancy on your terms. We will do everything in our power to make sure it happens. I promise you that."

My eyes glaze with emotion.

It is the thing I have feared the most for her, as our heir: the potential of her having to take a man to conceive a baby. Or living her entire life without bearing the child she so desperately craves.

At the end of our journey in this realm, we will return to Odiane, collect our promised seed-stones, then leave through the same portal we entered from. It is only half a day's leisurely walk from here.

"Are you offering me a bargain?" Caitlin smiles.

I laugh. "Gods, no. I think I have done enough of those for a lifetime."

We climb back up the staircase in a comfortable silence, each lost in our own thoughts. I jolt to a stop when I reach the top of the bridge. My heart crashes painfully at the sight of Aldrin leaning against the far rail.

A thousand emotions collide within me. The thrill of seeing him. Fear of how this man could easily betray and break me. Hope...for something I am not quite sure of. Something foolish, no doubt.

The sun has just peeked above the horizon behind Aldrin and it illuminates him in a brilliant gold glow. His tanned skin shines with vibrancy and the flowing locks of his brown hair are gilded, as though some celestial power radiates from within him.

A slow smile creeps onto his face as his gaze meets mine, as I hungrily take in every glorious inch of his body. I find myself stunned and frozen to the spot. Caitlin almost crashes into my back.

I harden my heart, shoving down the turmoil he seems to induce in me. I will not give blind faith to another royal or be taken advantage of again. I grasp the boiling anger that began to simmer last night.

"Have you taken to spying on me, Aldrin?" My tone is short as I step out of Caitlin's path. "Was forcing every last private detail of my life out of me not enough for you?"

His smile falters and his thick eyebrows pinch. "About that. I want to—"

"I don't need to witness this." Caitlin maneuvers her way around me. "Let me get out of earshot before you start whatever this"—she waves a hand at the two of us—"is going to be."

Aldrin glances between us, clearly thrown off.

Part of me understands why he did it, the necessity of it, but by the gods, it reminded me of who I was getting close to.

A fae king.

Of course he is going to manipulate a silly human girl to save his lands. If I were clever, I would stay well away from him, but I need to know what his plans are for my people.

"You were going to say something, Aldrin?" I ask in a sickly-sweet tone. I am so sick of men and their excuses.

"Yes. About last night—I'm sorry. You were vulnerable, and I took advantage of that. There is no justification for it." Aldrin peers down into my eyes, his finger lightly tracing my jaw. "I put my own desires and realm first. I should have taken the time to earn your trust instead, and prove to you that any information about your people will always be safe with me. That it would benefit both our races."

My smile drops. I wasn't expecting a genuine apology. He makes it so damned hard to hate him. His finger brushes over my lower lip and I almost forget my anger.

"I'm going to become a queen, Aldrin. I better get used to being manipulated and used for the greater good of my people." My laugh is bitter.

Aldrin tries to grab my hand, but I rip it away from him.

"No," he says. "A queen should be respected and empowered, not used as a commodity."

He stands so close to me. Too close. Electricity seems to crackle between our bodies as the warmth and scent of him wash over me. I want to reach out and touch his broad chest, to feel the hard planes of him against me in a lover's embrace.

I shove him backward instead. "You need to focus your efforts on regaining your throne, Aldrin. Prince Finan will take my hand in marriage as soon as I return. It won't be long before he becomes king, especially in fae years. Then, we can collaborate. This will be best for both our realms."

A tightness constricts my chest. My teeth grind and I shiver with restrained passion.

I don't know what makes me angrier: the fact that Aldrin is so good at weaving a spell around me, at making me almost believe he cares, or that I have to return to Finan and put this beautiful, kind man in my past.

"I don't want you to be someone else's queen."

My body freezes. "What happened between us, the way we touched and kissed—it can't happen again, Aldrin. I can't get involved with another man."

My entire world condenses down to this moment, to this man, as his face drops and his eyebrows knit. Those haunted eyes focus on me intently. His hands reach for my face, to caress the lines of it, then fall as he realizes his mistake.

"Did you not like it?" he asks softly.

"You know I did." Passion raises the pitch of my voice.

"Then what is the problem? He will never know—"

"But *I* will know." I toss my head away from him, but his gravity drags me back. "It will be a thing I carry with me. I don't think it could ever be casual for me. I can't—I can't get attached to you like that. Not when I have to go back to *him*. Please don't make this harder than it needs to be."

Aldrin opens his mouth, to say something sultry and sexy, or maybe to tell me not to go back, but I cannot hear it. He may convince me.

"No, Aldrin. No more." I place two fingers to his lips to stop him.

We stare at each other, and his shoulders deflate as though I took the very life out of him. Pain radiates from my chest, shooting through my limbs, and I may combust from the heartache I hold in.

It is absolute insanity, the intensity of these emotions. I have known this man for little over a week, but more has blossomed between us than in the years I thought I loved Finan. I only liked the idea of my prince and what I wanted him to be, never the reality of the man.

What a foolish girl I am, to feel this way about a fae, a foreign king, our oldest enemy.

A crash echoes beneath us, and I glance to where Kai and the other kelpies are leaping from the lowest bridge into the frozen river beneath. Their bodies transform midair from pure horse to an equine form covered in blue scales glittering in the early sun, each with a long, sleek tail.

They crash into the water below, creating huge rippling waves churning from the site of impact and shattering the thin sheets of ice that float like islands. Their whining calls and loud splashes echo across the morning as they leap through the water like dolphins.

From the corner of my eye, I notice Aldrin examining me, as though he is afraid if he turns away, he might never see me again.

"Where does this leave us?" he finally asks.

I shake my head. "I don't know. That is something we need to work out. Allies? Friends? Traveling companions?"

"I would like you to join me on my journey back to the capital. We will visit much of the court to see how the lower fae are faring. There will be opportunities for you to find homes for the seed-stones." Aldrin's entire body is incredibly stiff as he awaits my answer.

"I would like that," I reply, and he lets out a breath.

He tips his head toward the kelpies. "If they find out you are carrying the seed-stones for the Lake Maiden, they will follow and guard you like you are on a divine quest. To them, Odiane is a queen and goddess. The kelpies are nomads, and when it is time for them to breed, they leave their eggs under the care of a Lake Maiden."

Silvan approaches us from the far side of the bridge, his quick steps slowing to a pause as he notices the dynamic between us. Aldrin nods and he joins us.

"We have captured two corrupted baby spriggan to bring to the court as evidence," Silvan reports.

"Good," Aldrin says, utterly deflated. "Send them ahead to be held in the stables at Cyprien's residence in the capital, so they will be ready when we arrive. Make sure you stress to the guards who transport them that utter discretion is required."

Silvan gives a curt nod in response.

Aldrin looks to me, then to his man. "We will leave for the road immediately."

Excitement curls within my stomach. It is everything I have ever wanted. Endless possibilities of discovery stretch out before me, but it is all tainted with the sick, oily feeling of the complete loss of what I could have had with Aldrin.

# CHAPTER 25
# KEIRA

Aldrin stands before the immense Watchtower Tree we visited before infiltrating Cyprien's camp, conversing with its five tree nymphs. They are dwarfed by its towering height. My eyes glide up to the canopy at its peak and a shiver runs down my spine at the memory of the first time Aldrin touched me up there on the defensive platforms.

It is getting harder to hate him. To remember that he broke my trust.

"I didn't believe you when you told me how big this tree is." Caitlin rides up next to me, her horse nudging mine with its nose. I stroke the mane of the horse I ride bareback absentmindedly, then quickly pull my hand back. Not a horse. A kelpie. Kai.

They became fervent when they realized our mission, insisting we ride them despite how uncomfortable it makes me. Aldrin gently pushed the idea, considering how slowly we walk and how quickly we tire. We agreed to ride, sometimes.

"Five trees," I explain to Caitlin. "Intertwined. That is why there are five nymphs."

Caitlin frowns. "Five..."

"Some don't have enough power to form bodies and leave their trees." A deep sadness fills me for those low fae trapped within their bodies and unable to travel.

Enough of their singsong voices and Aldrin's deep rumble travel to us that I know he is trying to convince them to join us.

I watch Klara and Drake enter the watchtower carrying the jackets we borrowed, then walk back out with the equipment and supplies we left behind. All five of the tree nymphs return to their trunks, their flesh becoming engulfed in moving vines and branches and bark, until they are no longer visible.

My heart sinks and I wonder if Aldrin has failed here, until he shoots a wide, boyish grin back at Cyprien. One that fades from his lips as his gaze shifts to mine.

Two nymphs materialize out of the watchtower, holding their heart-stones that shine with brilliant green light.

One has hair of wiry twigs coated in yellow lichen and vines with golden leaves encircling her wooden limbs. As she places her heart-stone into her chest, a great change takes over her body, bark turning into skin that is highly freckled and tattooed with the vines that had been real a moment ago. She wears a crown of twigs encircling a face akin to that of a high fae, and the lichen has turned into tightly curled blond hair.

The male nymph has blunt woody spikes jutting from his elbows, knees and spine, with cascading horns of curling branches on his head. His entire body is modestly covered in spongy yellow lichen. When his form combines with his heart-stone, golden skin covers his body, also freckled, and long white dreadlocks cascade down his back. Spines still poke out of his skin, but they are muted in size.

Somehow the nymphs are even more beautiful in this form.

Aldrin leads us with renewed purpose. We travel for days through endless woods, and when the sun sets, we camp under stars visible through the canopies. There is peace in the fresh air that rustles through my hair and the scent of bruised vegetation rising from beneath my boots. I could lose myself in this court.

A forest of ancient trees surrounds us. Staircases of red- and orange-capped mushrooms the size of dinner plates colonize the wide trunks and sprout between tall roots that snake along the ground.

Creatures leap and scurry across those platforms as we pass. The furry black forms of the puka with pointed ears scramble up the branches. Tiny goblin-like fae with long beards, pale skin and mushroom hats run to small doors in the trunk and slam them shut.

A shudder passes through me at the sight of their fingers ending in long claws. They may be shorter than my forearm, but I wouldn't want one dropping on me from the trees.

Over days, the landscape changes. The trees become tall and thin, like arrows jutting out of the ground, and a rainbow of flowers blooms in the spaces around them. Tulips in shades of purple, pink and red. Daffodils in white, yellow and orange. Irises and hyacinths. Sprites of tiny white light dart between them as bees would in my own realm. The floral scent of pollen fills my head.

When we stop for lunch, I have Caitlin weave flowers into my hair. Aldrin approaches, carrying a mug of hot herbal tea for each of us, but he freezes at the sight of me. The motion is so brief, a mere hesitation in his step, but I catch it along with the fire that flares within his eyes, then dies.

"You look beautiful," he murmurs, as though he cannot stop himself.

I hardly notice as Caitlin gets up and leaves us, muttering angrily.

Aldrin sits on a rocky outcrop beside me and passes a cup of tea. The warm, damp steam rising from it caresses my face and fills my nose with the scent of peppermint and chamomile. I watch him wearily, as I would a wolf circling its prey, but he just sits there, content with silence.

I let out a long sigh. Talk of small things cannot hurt. "Everything in this realm is so sculpted and elegant, as though a god arranged each tree, every flower and leaf, fashioning the ultimate artwork. It is like I am walking through a painting."

A slow smile forms on Aldrin's lips, his arms casually leaning on his outstretched legs. "You like my court? There is so much I want to show you."

He tells me about the different regions of the land and I become lost in the vivid descriptions. Not once does he ask about my own realm or try to pry more information out of me.

"You will love my capital, Keira. The City of Vertical Gardens rises into the sky like a mountain of both a forest and thousands of immense buildings. The palace itself sits in the clouds."

I weave flowers into his hair as he speaks. It is so hard to remember the threat he poses when his eyes are filled with passion. Half of his long brown hair is tied up into a low knot, and by the time I am done, he has a crown of white daisies and daffodils in it.

We travel to a high-altitude meadow shrouded with veils of mist. Green hills roll as far as my eye can see, and touch the clouds. A ring of jagged mountains adorns the horizon before us. At a not-too-distant rise, the waters of a lake glimmer like diamonds as they reflect the late-morning sunlight. The kelpies whicker at the sight of all that water.

"We will camp here for a few days," Aldrin announces to the group, then turns to me and Caitlin. "You will find the Sky Lake is uninhabited."

Kai prances beneath me, still in his horse form. I slip from his back and he rapidly transforms his upper body and face to his humanoid form.

"You will find, my exiled king, that we kelpies know the waters of this land better than you do." There is an extra edge to his gravelly voice.

Aldrin raises his eyebrows as Kai canters away. "He's a bit snappy." He laughs. "The kelpies have been away from deep water for too long."

"Kai has been jittery in anticipation all morning," I say, then quickly chase after him as I notice he and the other kelpies practically dragging Caitlin and her satchel of seed-stones toward that lake.

My thighs burn with exhaustion by the time I reach the top of the hill. The grassy meadow gives way to a shore of ragged boulders and polished stones. It is as though the clouds reach down to kiss the lake, shrouding it in mist. The still surface is an eerily perfect mirror of the sky. I shiver. It is much cooler up here.

Caitlin approaches me at the pool's edge, but doesn't make a move toward it. We wait as the kelpies near the waters with caution, dipping their hooves in, then taking slow steps that don't disturb the inky surface. The liquid parts, but there are no ripples expanding out from the light impact. It is the oddest sight.

Iris suddenly rears up, her two front hooves dancing in the air, before bringing them down on the water's surface, and they strike something hard. It is as though the water suddenly turned to glass. She lifts them again and slowly eases them back into the depths of the lake. I share a look with Caitlin, but we say nothing.

They submerge in the lake, transforming their lower halves into the fins, gills and scales of their aquatic form, and disappear under the surface completely.

We wait and wait. The utter silence is unnerving. Minutes pass and I bite my lip as apprehension rolls through me, but the kelpies return to the surface and exit the lake.

Their sleek bodies transform into part horse, part humanoid once more. It seems their preferred form. Beads of water shimmer as they fall from their skin. The droplets are most curious, silver in color like a liquefied mirror.

"Powerful wards protect these waters," Iris grunts. Nothing covers her bare chest but her long, pale green hair. I force myself not to give in to curiosity and keep my eyes level with hers. "Old magic lies here. This is the deathbed of a god."

I stare at her with my lips parted, wanting to ask what that means, but Kai speaks first. "It is a favorable territory for a Lake Maiden to be born, live and die. Very favorable," he states.

"She shall absorb the power here. Meld it with her own. Give it all back to the lake when she dies," Iris responds to our stunned expressions.

"Okay." Caitlin nods at me. "No point in wasting time."

We unlace our boots and I bunch up my leggings. I loop as much of the skirts of my dress over my elbow, and Caitlin rolls up her pants to reveal cream-white skin.

The pebbles of the shore are smooth and slippery beneath my feet.

We tiptoe into the water, ever so gently. It is like molasses. A thick presence within it pushes back against us. My feet and legs almost immediately feel numb and disconnected from my body.

I wonder if it's the magic of this place doing strange things to my flesh or the iciness of the water.

I hold the sack of eggs bundled against my chest as Caitlin places both hands inside and pulls out a seed-stone. She scrunches up her nose as the gelatinous mass wobbles in her cupped palms. Its bathing solution trickles between the gaps in her fingers.

"It feels so strange," Caitlin mutters as she holds her hands just above the waters and releases it into the Sky Lake. We watch in silence as it drops below the mirrored surface and disappears.

Anxiety ripples through me and I turn to Kai. "There aren't any predators here that can eat it, are there?"

The kelpie laughs. "She cannot be destroyed that easily."

I begin to relax, then realize he didn't say there were no predators. "Let's get out of here." I pull Caitlin by the arm.

We return to the meadow and find the camp is completely set up, a ring of basic canvas tents built around a fire. The scent of coffee drifts on the breeze and I follow my nose straight to it. A kettle sits on glowing embers, while Drake spreads doughy flatbread across hot rocks to bake.

"How did you get the short straw of cooking *again*?" I take one of the piled mugs and help myself to the coffee.

"Can't keep my mouth shut," Drake grumbles.

"I already knew that. How did you piss him off this time?" I flash a quick grin and sit by the fire, warming my frozen feet.

"Cyprien was being an arrogant fuck, and I pointed out how many years he spent with his head up his ass instead of supporting Aldrin."

I laugh. I can't help it.

"Consider yourself lucky." He flicks his gaze at me. "We usually rotate. The only reason you're never on cooking duty is because humans can't cook for shit."

"Harsh...but probably true. We don't have many native spices."

I am halfway through my coffee when Aldrin catches my eye and beckons me to follow him by tipping his head. My stomach dips. A hundred good reasons why I should keep away from him flood my mind, but my body makes the decision for me. I drain the rest of the hot liquid, burning my mouth, then place the mug in a pile of dirty dishes before scurrying off. I need to get close enough to him to find out what his plans are for my realm, after all.

"Hey, you can't leave that there!" Drake calls after me.

"Sorry!" I call over my shoulder. "I'll clean it when I get back."

"Do you want to meet some pixies?" Aldrin's amber eyes dance as they take me in.

I nod, hardly able to contain my excitement. "I would love to speak to them."

Aldrin frowns as he walks beside me, so close that the warmth that rolls off him sets my skin prickling. "I believe these ones only speak the old language. They are pretty isolated up here."

"The old language?" I ask. "The one written in runes across the portals?"

"Yes."

"I want to learn it," I breathe.

Aldrin glances at me with surprise. "It would take years to master."

"Surely you have a book or two in your library." I hold my breath.

"Yeah, if you want to learn from a child's education manual. But it won't be easy," he says.

He has no idea it is my dream. "I have nothing but time in my realm. Even after I marry Finan, it will be years before I become queen and take on an active role."

Aldrin visibly flinches. I open my mouth, but I don't know what to say. Instead, I glance over my shoulder at Lilly and Silvan trailing behind us to break the moment.

A sharp pain pinches the skin of my neck. A buzzing fills my ear, then another sting bites into the exposed flesh of my lower arm. "Something bit me!" I yelp, trying to swat it away.

Aldrin grabs my wrist, stilling me, and a breeze envelops us. The smoky scent of burning pine fills my nostrils and thin tendrils of it become visible.

"The pixies are a feisty bunch. Territorial. They also enjoy the taste of blood. We must be close to their nest," he says.

I raise my eyebrows at him. "And you want to talk to them?"

"More than that, I want some to join my quest. They are intelligent, and will behave...mostly."

I place my thumb into my mouth, sucking on a third bite, and the iron tang of blood hits my tongue. Aldrin's eyes linger on my mouth, his gaze flaring with heat.

I turn away from him before he notices the flush building across my cheeks, in time to see Silvan madly swatting at a small cloud of pixies darting at him. A laugh bubbles out of my lips and the tense man sends me a look that promises death.

There is a city of pixie mounds hidden in a valley. Each one looks like a bundle of long pipes connected at their base, ascending in height to form a peaked shape. They are constructed from gray granite, with shimmering speckles of white, black and pink. I cannot shake the similarities with termite hills from my mind.

The air around the city buzzes with thousands of pixies. Their moving forms are flashes of bright colors. Aldrin leads us down the slope and through the edge of the city, full of ruins of mounds that are nothing but collapsed rubble.

"I wonder if this damage is from warfare or if these pixies have lost so much magic they can no longer sustain them," Lilly ponders.

"That is what I plan to find out," Aldrin says.

We pick our way through the intact regions of the cityscape, where many mounds are as tall as Aldrin. They are beautiful in their own way, with spiraling runes carved into the stone.

Swirls of flying figures spin around us like an angry tornado and Aldrin bellows the same words in old fae again and again.

A pixie stops right before my face, inspecting me as I stare at her. The tiny female has lilac skin covered in places with the palest fur. Violet eyes with no whites linger on my rounded ears. Her heart-shaped face tips to one side, ruffling the fur that grows on her cheeks and forehead, and sticks up in a short puff on top of her head. Fuzzy antlers move around furiously.

It is not the striking dragonfly wings that catch my attention, but the long, indigo fingers that end in sharp black claws.

My heart hammers from being surrounded by thousands of those creatures. They could tear me apart with their hands. I grip Aldrin's bicep as another pixie whizzes past and fear flashes within me.

More dart in to look at me, chittering in that language I so desperately want to learn. They are a rainbow of colors. I have to resist the urge to swat them away as they lift strands of my hair and pull at my clothing. I am bitten on the side of my neck and I gasp loudly.

Aldrin frowns deeply and grits his teeth. "These low fae have forgotten their king."

He speaks an enchantment in a low voice. The words swirl around in my head, building and building, overlapping with each other like he has a dozen voices. My skin prickles and my mind feels like it is being squeezed by an iron vise.

The swarm of pixies shudders as one, as an intense ripple of power explodes out of Aldrin. It crashes through me, and I am filled with an urge to kneel before him. I turn in a circle instead, still on my feet, and witness all of those airborne pixies on the ground, prostrate toward him. Even Lilly and Silvan kneel with an arm crossed over their chests.

"Gods, I hate to do this," he mutters, urging his companions up.

"Why didn't it affect me?" I whisper to Lilly.

She gives me a warm smile. "Because you are not of his court and cannot be urged to bow before him." She pats my shoulder, then walks ahead of me.

As the pixies rouse, Aldrin barks orders at them in that old tongue.

Multiple pixies of pure gold appear, beckoning us to the center of their city, toward a mound of glittering quartz that dwarfs the rest. It is large enough for Aldrin to duck his head and enter comfortably. Their queen sits on a throne on a dais, her pure white skin sparkling like a thousand tiny diamonds. She immediately starts bowing and scraping before Aldrin.

I peer into the mounds next to me, through little windows to the cozy interiors. They have comforts inside, beds and couches made of mushrooms and flowers. Rushes of dried leaves across the floors. Tables of large nuts with tiny pastries laid out upon them. There are vines that loop across the ceilings, with cured meats or dried herbs strung from them. It looks like a dollhouse.

It is familiar and foreign at the same time.

"Hmmm," Silvan grumbles. "So the corruption affects them too."

"That explains the destroyed mounds," Lilly chimes in, tipping her head as she listens to the conversation. The golden swirls of the tattoo across her forehead and scalp shimmer in the direct sunlight like precious metal.

I glance between them. "Tell me what they are saying."

"Aldrin is listening to their complaints, as a king should." She has a motherly air to her, clearly much older than the rest with a few signs of aging around her eyes. "About their struggles with the fading magic. How the high chancellor would not hear them out. Apparently they sent emissaries to ask for help from Aldrin and were shocked to find he no longer ruled. The Senate never even met them. Their story was told to an administrator, then they were ushered out of the capital with hostility."

"Aldrin has more allies than he realizes." Silvan picks the dirt from beneath his fingernails with a small blade. "Especially if it comes to civil war."

"It won't come to war," Lilly says, sharp as steel. "Aldrin won't allow it. Why do you think he went into exile in the first place? He respected the wishes of the Senate and people alike, against my advice."

Silvan raises his eyebrows at Lilly. "I didn't know you wanted him to fight."

"I recommended an assassination, or ten."

A silent understanding passes between the two of them as they turn to Aldrin again. I desperately try to understand the undercurrents.

"Do you believe he can win back his throne with diplomacy?" Silvan asks.

"Perhaps. To a degree. But there will be bloodshed by the end. There always is," Lilly says.

A chill runs down my spine. It would be insanity for me to remain here when that happens, but it is getting harder and harder to drag myself away from him.

I watch Aldrin as the pixie queen talks rapidly for long periods of time. He doesn't rush her, and each time he speaks, more of the tension seems to fall from her small body.

Aldrin is nothing like my world's stereotypes of the high fae.

Lilly leans in toward me. "Aldrin promised we will stay here for three days, and the high fae will take turns fueling magic into these lands. The throne room is a siphon that distributes the raw power into the earth. These are the duties high fae neglect."

I stare with rapt fascination as Aldrin, Lilly and Silvan place their hands on the quartz pipes of the pixies' mound and the stone illuminates beneath their touch.

A soft, low-pitched whistle fills the air as the light of their raw power grows, engulfing the entire structure and pulsating downward. A wave of static energy washes over me, making strands of my hair float upward. By the time they are done, all three fae are panting and their faces shine with sweat.

The pixie queen beams a smile at Aldrin.

~

On our second day in the meadow, I borrow a bow and quiver of arrows from Drake and practice shooting at a target he creates for me from roots and earth. He pulls them up from the ankle-length grasses and sets the woody tentacles to sway defensively around my mark. I attempt to take control of their motion to allow my arrows in.

My earth magic was undiscovered before I came to this realm. I cannot grow roots or branches, but I can manipulate what is already there. I can destroy it.

I nock my arrow and line it up with my target, a large, ripe fruit akin to an apple. A light breeze slips through my hair and ripples my long tunic around my legs, held in place by my tightly laced cotton corset. I abandoned my dress today, opting for thick leggings instead.

I thread a weave of air upon the arrow's shaft so I can guide its trajectory with precision. Tendrils of my earth magic run toward those moving roots to lasso them in place, but my grip on the weave keeps slipping.

Closing my eyes for a long moment, I thrust my power into the ground through my feet. My awareness follows it as the magic links each bit of vegetation growing in the dirt between my feet and that target, like forging a tunnel through them. I struggle to hold on to hundreds of sprouts of grass across the distance all at once.

The whipping motions of the roots around my target slow to a snail's pace.

I shoot my arrow.

It rushes toward the target. I nudge it with air while still wrestling the roots. This is where all my weaves usually unravel, but this time the arrow flies true and the roots merely twitch. I suck in a breath with anticipation as the arrow flies toward the fruit.

It is an inch away when a root snaps out of my feeble control and snatches the arrow out of its trajectory, wrapping its feeler around the shaft and snapping it in half.

I stare with utter confusion and impotent rage, until a rumbling laugh echoes behind me.

I swing around to Aldrin. "You!" I practically roar.

"Me." He has the audacity to grin.

"I almost had it!" I slap his chest hard as he makes the mistake of walking right up to me. "You broke my arrow."

"You're doing it wrong," he says. The roots toss the apple-like fruit toward us and he catches it and takes a bite. "It took so much of your focus; you didn't even notice me approaching."

"Maybe I was ignoring you," I say.

His teeth sink into the crisp flesh of the fruit again. "You don't want to wrestle with your earth magic. Use it as a gentle caress, convincing the plants to do your will. Let me show you."

He tosses the core over his shoulder, but his focus is on me. I give him a curt nod. Aldrin turns me toward the target so his hard chest lightly presses against my back, and places his palms on either side of my face, his fingers at my temples. I become hyper-aware of his closeness and my breath hitches.

I relax into his touch, that strangest of embraces. Aldrin tethers his magical wield to my awareness and the core of my power. He tugs on it, and my senses tumble forward.

Then he leads us down and through the ground, his magic hopping between each set of roots along its path instead of trying to hold them all. His magic runs right up the roots around my target, stroking them to relax and wilt.

It feels like he caresses fingers down my own awareness and my mind melts into him, my magic a calmed beast. There is an intimacy in the way his power touches my own, like he fondles my depths.

"This is a simple trick to undo another's magic on a plant," Aldrin murmurs into my ear.

"And…how did Drake…" I try to hold on to my train of thought as his breath tickles my neck. "How did he make the roots move?"

Aldrin sends a pinch through that tether to the plant, making it writher with agitation. That same sensation grasps my power and awareness, sharp and sweet, as though he pinched my bottom. I gasp, a shiver running through me. I wonder if he knows the effect he has on me.

Likely, he is doing it on purpose.

"And this is how to move it with your direction." He pushes his will into the roots, gentle as a lover's kiss yet firm as steel, gliding across my essence as well. His hands stay at my temples; they don't physically touch my body, but it *feels* like they are all over me.

"But I cannot make them grow like you do." I turn in his embrace to look up at him, and his arms wrap around my waist. I am terrible at keeping my distance from this man.

Aldrin peers into my face. "No," he says, his eyes flicking down to my lips. "You don't have any spring magic."

My heart stammers at the heat in his hooded eyes. The bastard knew exactly the reaction his magic had over me, and I can't say I didn't enjoy it.

"Let me do one more thing." His hands cup my face and tip it upward, his fingers gliding to my temples. "I want to check something."

"Okay," I half whisper. I don't think I could deny him a thing in this moment.

Aldrin's power thrusts into me, hot and hard like a shot of whiskey burning through me, reaching depths I never knew I had.

My breath hitches as cold sweat breaks out over my skin, but he buries his power further. It strokes and caresses in the most delicious manner all the way down. A smug grin pulls on the corners of his lips, until he suddenly staggers away from me.

"What?" I manage. "What is it?"

He runs a hand through his dark hair. "You have an immense well of power, Keira, but there is a massive block on it. You hardly access a fraction of it. What are you, to have that much power?"

"Human. I'm human, Aldrin."

"Yeah. Human, with a hell of a lot of fae," he retorts.

The fact that my grandmother was impregnated by a fae spring to mind. One she claims was incredibly powerful. "It doesn't really matter, Aldrin," I throw back. "I am duty-bound to the human realm regardless of what is in my blood."

He seems to shake himself. "I need to think of a way to break that block. But I came here now because I didn't get to teach you how to base jump. We got...distracted last time."

My stomach tumbles at the idea of falling from the sky. "Gods," I mutter. "Do we have to?"

Aldrin turns deadly serious as he forms a staircase of platforms hanging above the ground. They are made of hardened air, but thick enough that their shape distorts the light and they are clearly visible.

"This is what you don't want to do." He walks up the steps. His floating body is an eerie sight.

I raise my eyebrows. "You start by showing me the wrong way to do it?"

"Yes. It takes too much time and magic reserves," Aldrin continues. "But you get the basic concept. Create a platform, step on it, then retract the one behind you." The lowest air base disappears as more form above him.

I watch Aldrin in awe, my lips parted, as he reaches the height of a house, then simply leaps to the ground, landing in a crouch. Dust and small stones plume up in a cloud around him, but he stands and strides over to me, completely unaffected.

"Let me demonstrate the correct way to base jump," he says.

Aldrin moves lightning-fast, leaping upward in staggered jolts as thin platforms of air form beneath his feet then rapidly disintegrate. It is a beautiful dance through the sky.

He reaches the same height again, before misplacing a foot and landing in a heavy crouch. Sweat glistens on the muscles of his bare arms below his rolled-up sleeves and fire burns in his amber eyes as he looks up at me. A hint of a smile plays across his lips.

"Now you try," Aldrin commands.

"I can't do *that*," I half whisper.

"You can and you will."

I weave a single platform, then step on it. Pride fills me and I turn to Aldrin, beaming, but it disintegrates beneath my feet. I stumble to the ground, lurching forward, and Aldrin hooks an arm around my waist and pulls me against his chest.

"I already know I'm going to enjoy this," he murmurs into my hair before letting me go.

I shoot him a dark look, but try again. I fall so many times, stumbling off the side of platforms, forgetting to hold my wield or simply losing sight of where I built them and leaping into thin air.

Aldrin catches me again and again, with his strong arms and tendrils of air. Each time, he places me gently back on my feet as though I am the most precious thing in the world.

My head spins after a fall from my own height and my blood rushes. I allow Aldrin to hold me close to him while I regain my bearings.

"Can we do something else? Anything," I pant out. "This is too hard."

"Anything?" He raises an eyebrow at me, but just as my blood heats, waiting for sensual promises to leave his lips that I know I'll have to deny, he gives me an intense, serious gaze. "How about we practice your destructive earth magic?" He leans right in to speak in my ear. "Just try not to pierce me with a hundred needles this time."

A slow grin forms on my lips. "I can't make any promises. Perhaps you need a few needles to burst your overinflated ego."

A laugh reverberates through his chest, still pressed to mine. "You are going to regret those threats."

Before I have a chance to loose more witty, teasing remarks, the ground rumbles beneath my feet. Thick, rough bark brushes against my back as a whole damned tree grows behind me. Its girth thickens and its canopy branches out overhead, as though it has been there for a decade. The casual use of so much magic is staggering.

"Redecorating, are you?" I say, tipping my head toward it, but Aldrin ignores me. He grabs me by the shoulders and pushes me back slowly into the trunk, pinning me there.

My lips part and my breath catches. I should be afraid of a fae restraining me, but the way he touches me is far too seductive for me to think straight.

The look in his hooded eyes has heat pooling in my stomach, and lower. Then he presses his thick, muscular thigh between my legs and his broad chest crushing mine leaves no space between us.

Aldrin's body forces me against the tree, but that isn't enough for him. He watches my face for any signs of resistance as he takes each of my hands and holds them above my head, in the foliage of hanging vines.

My stomach flips and a small whimper leaves me as tendrils curl around my wrists and tie me to the tree.

I could break them easily by ripping my hand away. I could tell him to get off me and he would, but I don't want to.

My breaths become ragged as Aldrin leans down, his lips so close to mine that I could lean forward and kiss him. He glides a hand across my cheek, then runs his thumb down my lips.

I gaze up, at him motionless. Stunned and not wanting to break this moment.

His voice is soft and hoarse. "I have been wanting to test that blood oath I made to you, Keira." His hand runs up the sensitive skin of my exposed arm, where the sleeve of my tunic has fallen away, until he touches his restraints. "You see, I cannot bind you with vines, I can't even pin you with my leg, unless you want it. Now show me your autumn magic, and destroy these bindings before I lose control of myself."

Aldrin pulls back from me, smirking, and the cool air rushes in.

"No," I say.

He freezes. "No?"

I wield air to push him between the shoulder blades and force him back towards me. "No," I repeat. "I am enjoying this." I know I have gone too far when Aldrin's gaze falls to my lips and he brings his face so tantalizingly close. Panic rears up in me and I tense. "Wait—" My chest heaves as I try to summon rational thought. I cannot trust him, cannot allow him to get too close. He is fae. Ruthless. Brutal. Manipulative. Except he has shown me he is nothing like that, time and time again.

"I—Aldrin, we can't...we shouldn't..." I pant, still arching my back and pressing into him.

"Then why is your air wield still pushing me against you?" He raises a single eyebrow at me, and the corners of his lips kick up. I can hardly hold on to my train of thought, much less answer him. "You don't want to get too attached to me when you have to leave this realm. Tell me to stop, and I'll stop." Aldrin doesn't release his grip on me.

"I don't want to, but..." I close my eyes as he trails kisses up my exposed neck.

"Just once, Keira, to level the score. To satisfy a burning need. Once can't do much harm."

"Level the score?" I ask. My chest heaves as his kisses travel down my collarbone and toward my cleavage. He slowly pulls at the laces of my tunic to get better access, searching my face once more. I let out a groan as his lips touch my skin again. If they travel any lower, he will expose my whole breast.

"The last time we touched, your hand disappeared into my trousers, but I never got to return the favor." To accentuate the point, Aldrin drags his thigh up my throbbing core and the friction shoots intense sparks of pleasure through me.

I cannot think straight when he touches me like this. "Just this once. To level the score," I murmur.

His amber eyes flash and his mouth is on mine in a heartbeat. Our lips and tongues collide with desperate need as he presses harder against me. I forget about my earlier protest and disintegrate the vines at one wrist so I can thread my fingers through his hair.

Those hands rove all over my body, slipping under the hem of my tunic to grasp at my breasts, while mine slide down to the curve of his ass.

Every inch of him is perfect.

Aldrin rubs his thigh across my core a second time and I hiss in a sharp breath of air at the explosion of sensation. He removes his leg from between mine, pushing them further apart with the motion.

He watches my face closely as his hand runs down my breast, over my sensitive stomach and to the band of my leggings. It glides beneath, slipping under my panties as well, until those calloused fingers reach the apex of my core. I shudder under that touch and arch my back. Aldrin groans as he feels just how wet and ready I am for him.

I grip his shoulder tightly as his finger rolls my clitoris again and again, my body jolting with each swirl.

An arrogant grin grows upon those sensual lips as he soaks in my every expression, especially when he slides two fingers deep within me. Then they start to curl.

I melt, right there in his arms, and moans fall from me.

"That's what I've been dying to hear from your lips," Aldrin growls in my ear.

Those punishing fingers work me hard, thrusting and curling deep inside, his thumb tracing circles on my most sensitive part. Waves of pleasure crash over me, building and tightening within me.

I need more of him, but I can't take too much. Can't pass a point of no return. I free my other hand by vaporizing the vines and undo the lacing of Aldrin's trousers, fingertips grazing over his erection in the process. He grunts in surprise, but doesn't stop his wicked fingers moving within me.

I pull him free and gaze down to catch the sight of his hardness arching out of his pants. It is almost enough to make me crash into a violent climax. I slide my fingers across its length, pausing to run circles over its head with my thumb, delighting in the feel of it.

Aldrin's breaths become harsh and throaty, and when I palm his cock and pump it rhythmically, he lets out ragged, soft growls right in my ear.

A deep tension grows within me with each volley of pleasure he rings from me. It becomes so intense my legs shake and I think my heart will give out, but those fingers continue to rub and caress my inner walls until they clamp down on him.

All the sensations clash within me until I reach a boiling point, and I tip over the edge and into a release so strong I cry out from it. Aldrin doesn't let up as he guides me through wave after wave of bliss, until I collapse in his arms.

My hand still moves across that massive cock, forward and backward, until Aldrin's bulky body tenses around me and a choked groan leaves his lips, his seed shooting over my hand in hot spurts.

He buries his head in the crook of my neck and we stay like that for a long moment, panting and reeling. I wrap my arm low around his waist and tip my head to his shoulder. It feels so right, buried within his embrace.

"I didn't think you'd actually let me touch you," he admits, voice muffled.

"Just this once, Aldrin," I say, and he nods, but I don't know if either of us believe me. I have terrible self-control, and he has none at all.

This is only going to end in heartbreak.

Regardless of what grows between us, I have to return home.

# CHAPTER 26
# KEIRA

We travel across a wide road chiseled into the rocky terrain of low mountains with a sheer vertical drop on one side. My skin prickles with fear as we cross an immense bridge that arches over a gulf, its support pillars disappearing into the swirling vapors of hot, misty air below.

Caitlin gives me a wide-eyed look and her face pales, but neither of us protests.

The altitude and humidity don't seem to affect the fae, who laugh and joke as they jog all around us. It makes it hard for me to catch my breath and forces me to ride Kai.

We pass through many villages carved into the very stone of the mountainside in sprawls of ornate domed caverns, but they are practically deserted. An inn beckons to us halfway up a mountain, and I dream of a warm bed and hot bath as we approach.

Its courtyard is utterly empty as we enter. The banquet hall and levels of apartments are silent, dashing my hopes. The only sound is the ringing footfalls on the pavers, until two elderly high fae rush out to greet us. I wait at the back of our group as they trap Aldrin in a long-winded story about their woes and the fact that they haven't had a customer in a year.

Apparently, this was once a busy pilgrimage trial for a religious ceremony to a temple at the mountain's peak.

I join Caitlin where she peers over the railing at the edge of the courtyard, inspecting a waterfall that crashes down the mountain and disappears into the steam. It must pass directly under the inn. Multiple water wheels spin within its cascade.

"There are hot springs here. Inside the mountain." Caitlin points at a sign swinging in the breeze, advertising the pools. "It might make a pleasant home for a Lake Maiden."

"Yes. That sounds lovely." I turn, examining the unbroken face of the mountain around the inn, looking for the entrance. I catch Aldrin's eye instead.

I approach, but direct my attention to the innkeeper. "Can we visit the hot springs?"

"Yes. Yes. I can take you there. It's full of fire sprites, mind you," the woman says, then rushes off, barking orders at her partner.

Aldrin raises an eyebrow. "Fancy a swim? I could escort you, especially if you are planning to take these off." He pulls at the fabric of my clothes.

I nudge him in the ribs, giving him a dark look. He plays dangerous games. "We are looking for a home for the second seed-stone."

He continues to grin at me. "Careful what you get yourself into, sweet little human. Fire sprites have a temper. You almost got eaten alive by pixies last time you were surrounded by low fae."

"Are you offering yourself as my big fae protector?" I roll my eyes at him.

He spreads his arms wide. "Well, I'm here if you need me."

"If I recall, they were biting you as well." I poke him in the chest, then freeze as a thought comes to me. "Why are there fire sprites inside the mountain?"

"Because this is an active volcano." His smirk is oily as he waits for me to react.

"We are standing on an active volcano?" I practically yell, and everyone stops and turns to me.

Caitlin stalks over with fury lining her face. "Are you bloody seri-ous?" She pokes Aldrin in the chest. "Are you insane, making us hike up a volcano for days? What if it erupts? I don't know about you, Aldrin, but I don't have a death wish." She storms off.

"I see why she and Cyprien became fast friends," Aldrin mumbles.

"She has a point." I don't let him bait me. I wait for the explanation I know he has.

"It rarely erupts and the fire sprites give us plenty of warning when it is about to." He shrugs. "This inn has survived five eruptions, because it has wards layered upon wards. We'll be fine."

"Have you forgotten I'm human?"

"How could I forget?" He murmurs so low I wonder if I was meant to hear it.

We are led through a series of tunnels filled with hot steam. Water drips from the low ceiling and runs down the walls. The way opens up to an immense cavern filled with dozens of baths.

Another tunnel takes us to a great, bubbling lake with multiple streams converging and gushing water into it.

My skin flushes from the heat and my clothes and hair are damp from sweat and vapor. I take a few steps toward the edge of the lake but it feels like walking toward a raging bonfire.

Cyprien grabs my arm and pulls me back a pace. "Do not touch the water." His gaze is hard as he holds my eye. "It will sear the flesh off your bones." A great splash drags my attention back to the lake, as all three kelpies dive in. Cyprien gives me an apologetic half-smile. "They are fae, and you are not."

Caitlin slaps him on the back as she passes. "Thanks for the tip, Cyprien, but I think we will manage."

A crackling, scraping sound echoes from a tunnel and I whip around to it. They are footsteps of a whole horde of creatures, becoming louder and louder. The rock walls illuminate with an intense red glow, only growing brighter.

My mouth goes dry and every muscle tenses in preparation to fight whatever hellish beasts are about to march out. If they are half as violent as the Cú Sídhe, I won't have a chance to run.

"Ouch, Keira. Why are you clawing into me?" Cyprien frowns at me and I realize I have a death grip on his arm, and my nails are digging in.

Drake glances at me, then at the tunnel, and laughs. "Are you afraid of a few fire sprites?"

"Aldrin said…"

"Oh, this is going to be good. What story did he tell you?" Drake beams.

Cyprien drags my hands off him. "They are bad-tempered but not dangerous. This wouldn't be a tourist spot if violent creatures lived here."

It makes sense. Drake is still staring at me, his lips clamped tight like he wants to laugh again, and I give him a hard look.

My heart freezes regardless when the fire sprites step into the cavern.

Their forms are humanoid but completely composed of flames that move and flicker and crackle. Their hair, fingers and feet are tongues of fire and their eyes are black as charcoal. It is like their entire bodies are ever-changing mosaics of red, orange and yellow. The heat that radiates from them is distinct, even in this sauna.

The innkeeper hurries over to the elemental fae, inquiring about their families. It is the strangest sight, that motherly, graying woman laughing with these demons.

"Big bastards, these ones," Aldrin muses as he passes us to greet them.

"Sometimes a fire sprite is the size of a candle flame. Sometimes they are as big as a tree," Cyprien says. "Aldrin will try to convince them to join us, so try not to be afraid."

"I think I'd prefer the sprites the size of a candle flame." Caitlin grinds her teeth as she approaches me. "Shall we get to work? The kelpies said these waters are suitable."

Our bargain with Odiane means that only Caitlin or I can take the seed-stones out of their sack and place them into the water. Kai can only help once it is done.

We squat by the rim of the pool and Kai waits with outstretched arms held below the water's surface. He holds a form that is half man, half fish, like the legends of mermaids.

Sweat drips down my face as the heat rolling off the water threatens to suffocate me. I pull a slippery seed-stone out of its protective sack and hold my cupped hands as close to the water as I can bear. Pain pricks my skin as boiling droplets splash onto my hands.

I pour the seed-stone into that shimmering cauldron and quickly rip my hands back. Kai swoops it up and dives into the depths of the water with his precious cargo.

I suck on my burns, but it doesn't help.

Caitlin helps me to my feet and together we stagger out of the caves and into the cool night air, leaving the fae behind us. It rains gently outside, and those droplets are cold kisses on my overheated skin. We lean against the rocky wall and pant, both of us flushed a deep shade of red.

It takes a long time for my head to stop spinning and my skin to return to its usual shade of creamy white.

Caitlin gives me a sidelong glance. One that is scrutinizing and disapproving.

"What?" I ask. Her frown deepens. "What?"

"Have you lain with Aldrin?"

I almost choke.

"Because if you have, if your plans have changed, I need to know." There is no hint of judgment in her. "If you get pregnant, we need to run. Already I have been watching him for the signs of becoming a crazed, possessive fae."

A cold sweat breaks across my skin. "My plans have not changed," I say in a rush. "I am still taking the contraceptive herbs." Gods, the last thing I want right now is a pregnancy.

She tips her head at me. "But have you lain with him? Do you plan to? Because he could still turn and entrap you, just like the fae did to our grandmother."

"Gods, Caitlin, I don't know." I toss my head from side to side. "He won't hold me against my will if he gets attached—"

My sister grips my shoulders tightly and stares into my eyes. "No woman thinks it will happen to her."

It sends cold chills running down my spine and my stomach twists with dread. "He made a blood oath to me; he physically cannot hold me prisoner against my will," I say. Her hands fall from me and the tension bleeds from her shoulders. "Being in this realm is the only time in my life I get to *live*," I half whisper, and a tear rolls down my cheek at the admission.

Caitlin glances away from me. "I was scared for you, Keira. He seems to be everywhere you are, getting too close and finding excuses to touch. Don't forget that we *have* to go back, no matter what. That our time here is only temporary. Live, but don't get attached."

～

When we leave the mountain range, two fire sprites join our party.

Our journey takes us toward the coastline. The taste of salt hangs in the air and the roaring of waves bounces off the scraggy, wind-blown trees of the woods. We trek through them until they thin, then disappear.

The shore meets the ocean in a series of broken cliffs. Those rock faces are beaten away by the sea, and each time the two clash, a clap of thunder echoes. Our entire band stops to admire their battle. I near the edge of a cliff and peer down the sheer height of it, mesmerized as the waves roll in.

"Careful not to fall." Aldrin loops an arm around my waist and pulls me against his chest and away from the edge. I laugh with delight and bat at his hands. "Sharp winds have been known to pick up a person and deposit them over."

We take a narrow staircase carved into the cliff face down to a beach protected by a natural alcove in the coastline. The warmth of a mid-spring sun bakes my back. It blows my mind that the seasons progress here not with time, but with location. As one travels through the Spring Court, they go from the thawing of winter to the kiss of mid-spring, and end at the beginning of summer.

A dozen seals sunbathe lazily on rocky platforms on the far side of the small beach. Aldrin calls out a greeting as he approaches, and a few roll from their backs to glance over.

My step falters as one stands fully erect on its back flippers. Its neck extends unnaturally, then its entire head flops back, and a woman's face emerges. Like a person unbuttoning a coat, she peels off that sealskin and steps out of it, completely naked.

She fastens her sealskin around her like a cloak that reaches to the middle of her thighs. More of their number transform as our party approaches.

I can't help staring in wonder at those selkies, but I fall behind as Aldrin starts to address them.

I rush across the sand, my boots digging in deep, to hear their exchange as they bow before their king. I join the rag-tag band behind Aldrin, of high fae, low fae and humans.

Drake raises his eyebrows at me. "You're a nosy one, aren't you?"

"You have no idea," I murmur back.

Drake opens his mouth again, probably to say something *he* thinks is witty, but I shush him instead, straining to hear the selkies.

"Did you just shush me?" He somehow makes a whisper sound indignant, but the hints of a smile are on his lips.

"Someone should do it more often," Klara cuts in. "You talk too much."

I turn my attention back to the selkies while Klara and Drake speak in hushed voices.

"My king, we did not expect you in these parts," the female selkie leader says. "We heard you were exiled for trying to fix these lands."

"It is true, but it will not stop me from fighting the plague of corruption that has fallen on us." Aldrin spreads his arms wide.

The woman falls to her knees before Aldrin, tears running down her face as she hugs his legs. His entire body turns rigid and he casts a glance back at Cyprien, who merely shrugs.

"Oh, my liege, we have suffered. Only you understand. The fae at Fort Saltcrest turned us out!"

Many of the selkies wail. It is a horrible chorus behind her words that breaks my heart.

Aldrin grabs her hand and lifts her to her feet. "What is your name?" he probes gently.

"Wren, my king." She stares and stares into his eyes.

"Tell me of this plague on your tribe."

She wipes away a tear. "It is our children. They are born...they cannot remove their skin and take their second form. There is no indication that they have the higher intelligence of a selkie. In all ways, they are born just *seals*! Animals. We don't understand why." A loud sob escapes her.

"And your magic?" Aldrin holds both her hands.

"It dwindles with each generation. We have only a drop left," she says.

Aldrin nods. "You are losing your magic and that is why your children are not born selkie. Those high fae in their fortress above the coast should have set that right." Anger rises in his tone and the selkie leader begins to sob again.

"What of my pregnancy?" another woman calls out from among the rocks.

"And mine?" says a second.

Aldrin's eyes run over the amassed selkies. "Those I can save. My followers here can give each of you a top-up of power, but the same problem will occur again if we do not return the magic to these lands. The children that have already been born..." Aldrin shakes his head. "We cannot give magic to creatures that don't have any to begin with."

The selkie's features crumble as she glances over to a seal pup. Her child, trapped in seal form.

Tears burn at the corners of my eyes, and I force myself to look away and stop listening.

I turn back to Klara and Drake instead. "How do you give a selkie your magic?"

"It is much like healing." Klara's violet gaze focuses on me. "We do not give them our specific powers, but top up their own reservoirs. I have done the same to you. The low fae take their magic from the lands, whereas we high fae generate it within ourselves."

"It is exhausting, physically and mentally, and takes time for a high fae to recover." Drake runs a hand over his shaved head. "That's why some fae don't like doing it. The process is very inefficient when it is done from fae to fae."

"People are inherently selfish," Klara states. "And prefer to hoard their resources to advance themselves. Most people need to be forced to do the right thing."

Caitlin is silent, a severe frown occupying her pale face as we place the last of Odiane's seed-stones within a cavern with multiple deep pools of water that connect with the bay at high tide. The significance of the deed hardly registers within me on the back of the selkies' pain. Silent tears roll down Caitlin's face as our side of the bargain is completed and wisps of blue light evaporate from the runes on our skin.

We have almost completed the mission of our pilgrimage. There is nothing holding us back from returning to Odiane, collecting our prizes and leaving this realm forever, except there is so much I still want to see and do.

The fact that I only have a finite time here comes crashing down on me.

The look Caitlin gives me is one of pure understanding, because she knows what I have to go back to. I finger my moonstone bracelet. It still glows brightly enough. I have at least another month before the portals close.

We set up camp on the cliffs that overlook the ocean, within a natural depression that shields us from the unforgiving wind but doesn't steal the view.

A small cooking fire crackles in the center of our ring of tents, and we sit around it, eating shellfish and drinking.

Silvan pulls out a set of panpipes and plays a fast-paced tune. Drake adds to the music by clapping his hands against his thighs and beating his feet on the ground, while Lilly sings a high-pitched, word-less song that weaves in and out of the music.

Fae pair up and dance, swapping partners every few heartbeats. It is raw and chaotic compared to the stiff, structured waltzes of my home.

My eyes are only for the lone man who walks upon the beach, the moonlight shining off his naked body. Aldrin's muscles ripple with each step he takes into the waves. My attention is attuned to the flex of each tight butt cheek and the specks of water that glitter on his huge biceps and across his broad back.

When the waves reach his waist, Aldrin dives into the water and disappears.

The people revel around me, but all I can think of is my growing dread for the day I must return home.

Aldrin returns as most of his band retire for the night, talking to a few of them in hushed whispers outside of the firelight. When they leave, he sits alone in the grassy field dotted with closed blooms and stares out to the ocean, far away enough that I can hardly make out his profile in the shadows.

Something pulls me toward him. I'm unable to leave him alone in his struggles.

I grab a canteen of wine and make my way over. There is a deep scowl on his face and every chiseled muscle of his neck and shoulders is taut, slightly exposed through the half-unbuttoned neckline of his tunic.

I sit in the soft grass beside him, but I don't say a thing. I just stare out at that same view. I hand him the canteen of wine. Aldrin looks at me for a long moment, then relaxes marginally and takes a swig of the wine.

"It is easy to lose hope. Seeing the gravity of the situation," he says softly, letting out a long breath. "I have been so blind. For years of my exile, I believed the high chancellor would do a better job at ruling these lands than I did. That because the people voted her in, I must respect their choice.

"I thought I could still achieve my aims in the background, convincing the lords to invest in their lands, but very few would even grant me an audience. When I realized my error, most of my influence had been whittled away, and now I am far too powerless to stop what is happening."

He falls into silence.

I take his hand in mine and squeeze it. "You are not powerless, Aldrin. Far from it. You will open the people's eyes; I am sure of it."

"I don't have a choice. My people need me," he murmurs. "But regaining my throne will be the first challenge of many."

"I will help you negotiate with my people," I say. "My family will have the connections you need to open the portals between our realms. We could have trade and migration flowing freely again. It could save both our realms."

A cool breeze whips off the ocean, ruffling my hair and making a shiver run down my spine. Aldrin frowns as he notices, then puts his arm around my shoulders, pulling me in until my head rests on his chest. His warmth and scent immediately envelop me.

"No mention of your prince this time," Aldrin murmurs. "Or of you becoming his queen."

I shudder and Aldrin's grip tightens. "I don't want to be his queen. I know we should use every resource at our fingertips, but I don't want to spend my life in an unhappy marriage. Is that selfish of me?"

Aldrin stares into my face, his expression searching. "I don't want you to marry him either." I swear there is hope within his amber eyes. I pull away from him.

The heavy guilt of my duty threatens to suffocate me. In the end, I will do what is required of me.

I force a smile onto my face. "I would love to import your spices into my realm. I don't think I can go back to human food."

"Hmmm. Humans are known for having terrible food," Aldrin rumbles.

I elbow him in the ribs playfully.

"What?" He grins at me. "You pretty much said the same thing."

"You have never tried our food," I protest. "There is so much to gain from combining our cultures, for both sides. Maybe my people will become as liberal and progressive as yours. Our women will be free to choose their own destinies." I glance over my shoulder to where Klara, Lilly and Caitlin share battle stories.

Aldrin lies back in the grass, gazing at the stars. "Those are a lot of pretty thoughts, but there will be great upheaval and battles between here and there. We may not get to live in those golden times. Great social change can take generations."

I lie beside him while those words hang in the air.

A peaceful silence stretches out between us. I examine the sky, a broad expanse of indigo and purple, streaked with a thick slash of bright stars.

"Your constellations are wrong," I tease.

"Excuse me?" Aldrin actually sounds indignant.

"Every time I get comfortable here and almost forget I am in another realm, something incredibly off reminds me I am on another world. Your constellations are completely different to those in my night sky."

"Do you want me to tell you the stories behind them?" he asks, turning his face to mine. There is less than a handspan between us.

"I would love that."

At some point in the night, I fall asleep right there beside him in the long grass. I wake up when the sky is still dark, with my head nuzzled into the center of his chest and my leg bent across his hip. My hand somehow found its way under his tunic in my sleep and rests on the hard planes of his bare abdomen.

Worse is the placement of his hands, one wrapped around my back and cupping my rump and the other with the tips of his fingers plunged below my neckline and resting on the top of my breast.

I remain like that, enjoying the weight of his hands on me and listening to his breaths as his chest rises and falls beneath me. He murmurs something in his sleep and his head thrashes slightly from side to side. I crawl up his body to peer into his face and check if he is having a nightmare.

With the motion, Aldrin's hand dips deeper beneath my neckline, and his calloused fingers graze my nipple. I take in a shuddering breath at the sensation, and heat suddenly pools between my thighs.

His eyes move rapidly under his lids and his fingers twitch slightly on me as he murmurs some more. I bite my lip, wondering if I should wake him in case some trauma plagues his dreams. Worry fills me as I move to place my hands on either side of his shoulders and stare closer at his face, but then I feel it pressing into my stomach.

Aldrin is completely erect.

And then he whispers my name.

Sensual shivers ripple across my flesh as that single word does wicked things to me. Is he having a sex dream about me? My breath hitches. I want to know every last detail of what he does to my body in it.

Arousal runs hot through me in waves, making my skin burn as I watch the perfect lines of his face. His dark hair curls freely in the blades of grass and I just want to run my hands through it. I want to kiss those lips.

I teeter on the edge of indecision. My entire body tingles with desire and need, screaming at me to wake him up and make his dream a reality. My brain is still in control enough to tell me it is a terrible idea.

Aldrin's eyes flick open, then darken with something primal. They glance from my face hovering over his to my body pressed against his chest, then to his hand still tucked deep beneath my neckline that gapes open and reveals my breasts.

In a heartbeat, he flips us so my back is pressed into the grass and he lies on the top of me. His face is just inches from mine, his legs pressed between mine, and that erection pushes hard right over my core. My eyes roll back in my head.

"Aldrin." It is meant to come out as a warning, but it sounds like a moan.

"Is there something you want from me, Keira?" He takes my lips with his before I have a chance to respond. My back arches, as his tongue slips into my mouth, caressing my own with wild passion. He bites my lower lip and all rational thought floods my mind.

My hands grip his back, pulling him impossibly closer, and my legs wrap around his hips, reveling in the feel of him right there.

"I will stop if you ask it of me. But you have to ask it," Aldrin growls in my ear, palming my hip and holding it in place as he grinds the length of his hard cock along my core.

White-hot sparks of pleasure shoot out through my body at the friction and a choked sound leaves my throat. I jolt from the intensity of the sensation.

I don't want him to ever stop.

A smugness curls his lips as he peers into my face, then drags his hardness against my most sensitive parts again and again. My fingernails dig into his back as shudders run through me and I am lost in the utter bliss of the moment.

That chest pressing me into the grass, that cock lighting up every one of my nerve endings as it rubs into me with each delicious rock of his hips. I roll mine, drawing out every last bit of friction.

I let out a low moan and Aldrin cups a hand over my lips. "Scream if you want to, but you'll need to be quiet if you don't want to wake up the camp."

I whimper in response as the pleasure builds within me, coiling tighter and tighter until my breaths are ragged.

Aldrin fists the hem of my skirts in his hand and bunches them until they rise high enough that he can glide his hand across the bare skin of my thigh. He raises his body from mine to give himself access and drags his clutch on my skirts ever so slowly up and up until the fabric pools above my hips.

Aldrin's gaze flicks up to mine to read my face for a mere moment, then he loops his fingers into my panties and drags them down my legs.

I help him by lifting my hips.

By the time he tosses them aside, my hands are at the waistband of his pants, fumbling with the laces. My whole body shivers with need for him. I so desperately want to join our bodies. There is awe on his face as he looks down at my legs parted around him and my core bared and ready to take him.

I don't get the first loop undone on his trousers before the voices reach us. They are so damned close. Panic flares within me. It is then that I notice the sky has turned a silvery blue with dawn and the sounds of the camp waking nearby register. And there are muffled footfalls approaching our direction.

Aldrin groans, then rolls off me. I quickly thrust down my skirts over my bare body.

A handful of moments later, Drake and Hawthorne pass by in the long grass, swinging pots to fill with water from the river to boil for breakfast. They almost pass us completely, but Drake happens to glance over the distance and notices us lying in the long grass. A slow smile fills his face, but he says nothing.

I turn onto my side and face Aldrin, my lips parted as I pant. He presses his forehead to mine.

"Fuuuck, Keira." His voice is low and hoarse, his breaths as ragged as mine. There is so much emotion threaded into those two words. "The next time I get you like this, I'm not letting you go."

Shivers run across my flesh with anticipation.

When his eyes open, they are filled with such raw need and tenderness, as though I am the most precious thing in his world. That look sends liquid fire through me, warming my very soul. It is so much more than desire for my body. His gentle fingers brush away the hair from my face and trace my cheek.

In this moment, I know I am in trouble. If I give this man up, it will not only destroy me. It will kill him too.

# CHAPTER 27

# KEIRA

The most magnificent city I have ever seen sprawls across the horizon. At first glance it appears to be built into a small mountain, but then I realize the city *is* the mountain, with structures reaching higher than I thought possible.

Each cluster of buildings has spires and domes and towers at every level, with arching bridges reaching between them, and immense, external flights of stairs scaling the structures. Multiple streams run through the layers of buildings, ending in dainty waterfalls, and great trees rise alongside the structures.

It puts to shame the boxy, lifeless structure of Appleshield Castle.

There are many roads leading to the City of Vertical Gardens, and they are all brimming with people. All except for the one that takes a traveler through the wilds of the forest. The path we have been using.

We watch that far-off city from the height of its closest Watchtower Tree, our party of high and low fae hidden within its gates.

It is far smaller than the one we stayed in near the border, not designed to hold an army but to receive messages from across the court. The only place to camp is on the platform of the canopy.

Aldrin stands stiff-backed on the balcony facing the view of his home, the one that betrayed him. I sit with Drake, Klara and Silvan, but they are in a somber mood, sharpening their weapons and saying very little.

This isn't the homecoming they wanted.

Caitlin brings me a cup of tea, infusing her minor fire magic straight into the water to boil it, and sits down beside me on the carpet of moss. She picks up a weapon from the sharpened pile and silently oils the blade with expert hands.

Cyprien joins Aldrin's side on the balcony, and I strain my ears to hear their conversation.

"Are you sure you are ready to do this?" Cyprien asks.

"What choice do I have?" Aldrin practically growls. "My eyes have been opened since you came to me. I will not turn my back on my people."

"There will be significant risks," Cyprien states softly.

"The risks are greater if I don't return to the Senate." Aldrin runs a hand through his hair and looks over his people. "It is my head the high chancellor wants, and I don't think she would be ruthless enough to take it when the Senate and the entire city are aware I am in the capital to petition them."

The starkness of the threat to him, and his acceptance of it, makes my blood freeze. Caitlin shoots me a startled look as she too realizes the gravity of Aldrin's situation. The risk we put ourselves in by staying with him.

But I can't walk away.

Not yet. Maybe I could help him before we leave.

"Let me go into the city first, and pave the way for you," Cyprien urges, placing a hand on Aldrin's shoulder. "I will ensure the corrupted spriggan have arrived at my estate and that our evidence is still intact. Give me time to call on allies in the Senate and begin to plant the seeds of your revelation. The day you enter the city, I can have sympathetic guards on the gate. I will take our low fae witnesses with me, have them in position when you need them."

Aldrin nods, but it is clear from his sagging shoulders that the necessity of those actions pains him. That he will not be welcomed home.

"How long do you need?" He murmurs.

"Give me a week, then I will send for you." Cyprien slaps him on the shoulder, then walks away, calling his soldiers to him.

The vulnerability in every taut line of Aldrin's body as he watches Cyprien leave makes something tighten and twist within my chest.

"That settles it, then. We will be returning in a week," Silvan grunts. He puts so much force into the whetstone running across his blade that it slips and he cuts his finger.

Drake grabs his hand and runs his thumb over the small gash, a dim white light glowing between them, then the cut is gone. "Does it terrify anyone else? What will we find there? How the people we left behind have fared?" Drake chokes on those last words.

Klara immediately rises to her knees beside him, wraps her arms around his neck and pulls his head to her chest. Drake closes his eyes for a long moment as she kisses his forehead. "Rainier will be fine. He was always a tough boy."

I stare at the unexpected intimacy between them.

Drake's gaze falls on me and a hint of a smirk plays on his lips as he catches me gawking at them. "Keira, why do you look so surprised that a woman loves me? Am I that much of a fae beast to you?" He hides his emotions in humor.

"No. No. It's just that the two of you always seem to be fighting." I can't hide my fluster.

"Fighting like an old married couple?" he quips. Suddenly their every interaction reframes itself in my mind. The arguments without heat, instead met with smiles. The fact that they are always together. Not every couple shows their affections in public.

"Someone needs to put him in his place." Klara smiles.

"Come on, wife, you just love to flirt with me." Drake stares up at her.

Klara disengages herself from him and sits down again. "When Aldrin lost his throne, a huge rift formed in the ruling class. Families were dragged apart as some supported their king and others Titania. Any who strongly opposed the high chancellor were placed under house arrest indefinitely on their own estates. To even visit them is to risk your neck. We chose exile with Aldrin, but our son, Rainier—he was fresh in his political career and was ensnarled in Titania's lies, becoming a devoted supporter…" She trails off.

Drake runs the back of his hand across his eyes. "The last time we saw him, it ended in a heated argument. I don't know how he will receive us on our return."

"I'm so sorry," I say, and it feels inadequate.

Silvan stands up abruptly, tosses his whetstone to the ground and stalks away with anger rippling through his tense body.

"When Silvan followed Aldrin, his partner remained behind in the palace." Drake watches him go. "I have never met two men more dedicated to each other, but Silvan saw this as a personal betrayal, and it almost broke him."

My heart squeezes with the amount of pain they have all endured. Beside me, Caitlin scrubs a tear from her eyes.

"At least being in exile hasn't been all bad." Klara lets out a laugh that is riddled with sadness. "It has done wondrous things for our relationship. Drake was away far too often on his missions for Aldrin."

"What were your roles in his court?" Caitlin asks, using the tip of the blade to indicate the fae around us.

"Most of them worked for Silvan," Klara states. "He was the captain of Aldrin's personal guard. Still is, I guess. I was his Minister of Specialized Battle Tactics, and Drake—"

"Spy Master." He gives us a massive grin.

Klara nudges him in the ribs. "Commander of the Special Forces. Scouting a target, taking a specialized team into the field and handling it. Mostly collecting information."

I smile at Drake. "So, master of assassins and spies?"

"See, she gets it." Drake glances at his wife, who rolls her eyes.

Caitlin leans forward over her knees. "And Cyprien is the commander of the army, if I'm correct. I want to know why Titania kept Aldrin's brother-in-law in that position."

Drake scratches the side of his face. "Because their falling out over Lorrella's death was well known and fresh at the time. She had only just passed."

I glance over to Aldrin as a deep sadness for him rolls through me. He lost everything all at once. As he catches my eye, his frown softens and the tightness of his jaw releases.

My blood races at the look in his eyes as he approaches, then stands over me. "Can we talk for a few moments?"

I take the hand he holds out for me and stand. "Can we go for a walk?" The Watchtower Tree and the emotion clogging it suddenly feel suffocating.

Aldrin runs his thumb over the top of my hand as he stares into my eyes. "I know a trek near here that you might like." Shivers run down my spine as I hope for undercurrents in his words.

Drake glances from me to Aldrin and back, a huge smile growing on his face, but I ignore him, along with the scowl deepening on Caitlin's features.

We are only a few steps out of the Watchtower Tree when Aldrin rounds on me, his expression guarded and unreadable. "You are free to leave this realm whenever you want to," he says, so gently.

"S-sorry?" I stumble on the word.

"Your obligation to the Lake Maiden was completed two days ago. You can collect your seeds and leave this realm. That was your mission, wasn't it?" His voice is emotionless. Dead.

"Would you stop me?" It feels like a wild animal is clawing its way out of me.

"If Odiane is okay with it, who am I to stop you?"

"That's not what I meant, Aldrin." I toss my head. "Do you want me to go?"

"Gods, Keira, it's not about what I want." He closes the space between us and grips my arms. "Things may get incredibly dangerous once we enter the city. Neither you nor Caitlin need to risk that. So if you plan to leave in the next few days anyway—"

I suddenly understand the fear flashing in his eyes. I cut him off. "I *want* to stay longer with you, Aldrin. I can testify before your Senate and tell them who I am and what I can do with my family connections."

"They are treacherous and may try to harm you." That simmering gaze bores into my soul. "And you will leave eventually."

"The wild hunt themselves couldn't prevent me from seeing your city. A *fae city*. It would be a dream come true for me. And my offer to speak with the Senate isn't completely selfless. Your people are not the only ones who need this alliance," I say.

Aldrin lets out a ragged breath. He looks away from me, but his eyes are dragged back like he can't help himself. "Keira, there is something I haven't told you. Please, by the darkest realm, please try to understand why and forgive me." He takes a step back from me.

Fear shudders through my entire body, because I have no idea what to expect. "Tell me, Aldrin."

"My sister was a seer, and she prophesied a fate for me. Lorrella said a woman would come from the human realm with hair of fire." Aldrin takes a lock of mine and lets it slowly drop through his fingers, spreading out the red and gold strands glittering in the sun. "This woman is to stand by my side to return the magic to this realm. At first I thought she meant—well, that doesn't matter. She spoke of you, Keira. How you will help me. Whether you will do it in your realm or mine, I'm not sure yet."

I step away from him as icy claws grip my chest.

"Why didn't you tell me, Aldrin? How long have you thought it was me?" I am almost yelling as hot tears form at the corners of my eyes and he gives me a pained look. Then the true reason for my explosive reaction slips from my lips. "This means I *must* go home and marry Finan."

"Not necessarily," Aldrin cuts in. "Seers speak in riddles. Who knows what they truly mean?"

A tear slips down my cheek and a tortured frown pinches Aldrin's brow as he watches me with caution.

I pound his chest with my hand. "Why didn't you tell me earlier?" I growl, all that fear, all the bitter disappointment in my fate being forced, bubbling out of me.

Aldrin runs a hand through his hair. "I didn't know how to tell you, Keira. I didn't realize it was you until you told me your story, and

I had lost your trust by that point. I've tried a dozen times since then, but I was scared it would push you away."

The self-righteous anger fizzles out of me at the vulnerability in his expression. "I don't want to think of my duty right now. There is a month before the portals close and I have to return home. I want to enjoy my time here."

He gives me a curt nod. "Shall we go for that walk?"

I follow Aldrin down a narrow path that cuts through the rainforest, alive with the sounds of chittering puka and dripping water. Ferns colonize the ground and grow within the nooks of trees. Huge butterflies with colorful wings the size of my hands flutter around us.

Massive purple blooms hang from vines and red mushrooms poke through the grass. It is beautiful, but I don't care for any of it.

Nothing exists except for the man before me.

We pass a narrow creek gurgling over rocks and Aldrin wraps his hands around my waist and lifts me over the water with an excuse about not getting my boots wet. He does it with such ease, as though I weigh nothing at all.

Aldrin stops at a fork in the path and examines it for a long moment, then glances over his shoulder at me.

"Keira," he says, stalking toward me until he grips one arm and tilts my chin up to peer into his face with a single finger. "I am going to ask you a question, and I want you to answer me *very* honestly. Can you do that?"

My mouth turns dry and I manage a nod.

"That morning in the grass, when I had your skirts hitched up around your waist, would you have had regrets if we weren't interrupted?" he rumbles.

My stomach dips and my breath hitches. "No," I whisper. "My regret was that we didn't get to..." I let my words trail off.

Aldrin nuzzles his head into my neck, kissing the sensitive flesh until he reaches my ear. "Do you have any idea how much the image of you spread wide and bare beneath me has plagued me for the last two days?" he growls.

"Yes," I pant. "Yes. I think I do." He pulls away eyes hooded. "Aldrin?"

"Hmmmm?"

"Before I woke you...were you having a dirty dream about me?" Heat flushes through me at the idea, pooling low in my body.

"Probably," he says, as though it happens all the time.

Aldrin grabs my hand and tugs me down one of those paths. The sudden change in pace has my head spinning. The heated look he gives me over his shoulder tells me he is taking me somewhere to utterly devour me.

I bite my lower lip as the last of my reservations flee me.

Why should I spare a thought for Finan, for my kingdom or even tomorrow, when I have this beautiful man here, right now?

The path opens to a pool of water enclosed by thick tree cover. The surface shimmers like thousands of jewels, and its cyan depths are completely transparent.

Aldrin gives me a wolfish grin as he pulls me to him and kisses me so tenderly, a soft brush of our lips and a slow caress of our tongues. I step out of his grasp before he can pin me to his chest. The hint of a frown pinches his eyebrows as he reaches for me and I take another step back.

I give him a sly smile. "Don't touch me until I say you can. I want you to watch."

Heat simmers within his eyes, but his lips quirk up in a cocky half-smile as he raises his hands, then takes a seat on a low boulder.

I hold Aldrin's gaze as I unlace my cotton corset, my breasts spilling out of the restraining garment, covered only by a thin tunic beneath. I unthread each loop with a painstaking slowness, revealing more and more of my breasts until he looks like he is going to combust.

Tendrils of air pull at those strings, making them fall apart faster, and I give him a sharp look. He smiles at me wickedly as I toss my corset to the ground.

The shape of my breasts and peaked nipples is abundantly clear through the gathered fabric of the tunic. I undo my belt and chuck it to the side, then I loosen the fastening on my pale blue riding skirt and slowly shimmy it down my hips until it falls to the ground.

Aldrin sucks in a sharp breath as my legs are almost completely exposed, the loose tunic the only thing that covers my hips.

Light dances in his eyes as he reaches out a hand for me, but I take another step back. A light breeze curls around my hips, flicking up the hem of the soft fabric covering them.

I bite down a smile at Aldrin's impatience.

I pull free the laces of my tunic until generous amounts of my breasts are visible through the gap down to my waist.

Aldrin's gaze follows my fingers eagerly as I teasingly drag out every motion.

He swallows when I pull at one sleeve, revealing a shoulder, my entire arm, and then a single breast. I repeat on the other side until there is nothing holding up my tunic and the thin fabric floats to the ground and pools around my legs.

I am completely naked except for a lacy undergarment that covers very little.

A heated flush creeps across my skin at the look Aldrin gives me, roaming up and down my body, lingering at my breasts, down my stomach to the mound between my legs, to the curve of my hips and thighs, and back up.

He is like a man dying of thirst but too afraid to take a drink. It has anticipation rolling through my stomach.

I step out of my clothes, toward him, and slowly remove the pins from my hair. The crimson and gold strands fall across my chest as I toss my head. I take another slow step to close the space between us, and he leans forward eagerly in his seat.

"Gods, Keira. You are going to be the end of me." His every muscle is taut, as though he struggles to restrain himself from pouncing on me.

A self-satisfied smile grows on my face as I stamp my boot in the space between his thighs on the boulder. His hands immediately wrap around my bare calf, unable to help himself.

"Unlace these for me," I command.

His eyebrows shoot up and the quirk of his lips promises a hundred wicked things to me, but he does as he is told and pulls the boots off, running his fingers across my freshly washed foot, then repeating with the other.

Aldrin's eyes flick up the length of my bare leg at his eye level and across my body, then he stands suddenly. "I am done waiting. Tell me I can touch you," he growls, his face inches from mine.

Shivers run down my spine. "Touch me."

Those large hands wrap around me, sliding across my waist and hooking me in toward him. They run across my flesh, one sliding upward to squeeze my breast and roll my nipple with his thumb, the other gliding over my hip and across my ass, tugging at the undergarment. Fire radiates out from wherever his fingers glide over my skin and my breaths come fast as desire coils deep within me.

Then he loops his fingers in the waistband of my undergarment and drops it to my feet.

I kick the scrap of lace away.

I undo the buckles of his boiled leather armor and toss it to the ground. My fingers shake slightly as I unbutton his dark tunic, revealing bit by bit those perfectly sculpted pectorals and two rows of washboard abdominals.

Heat pools between my legs at the sight of him, and I run my fingers down all that golden skin that gleams with sweat. I want to lick the grooves of that chest, but my hand meets the belt of his pants and I become distracted.

Aldrin looks down at me with simmering heat as I fiddle with his buckle. He leans down and takes one of my nipples in his mouth, flicking his tongue over it again and again. I shudder with pleasure. My fingers keep sliding off the buckle. I can't function when he touches me like this. He laughs and removes his belt for me.

I pull his pants down and the glorious length of his cock springs out. He kicks his trousers away. I stroke the bare length of him. It is so big that the thought of it inside me makes delicious shivers run down my spine. I run my finger over the tip and watch his face as his head tips back and his breath turns rough. I pump it ever so slowly, wanting to soak up all the lust rippling through him.

Aldrin focuses on my face with determination as he slips a finger between my thighs, gliding it across the dampness there.

His thumb rubs circular motions across my clitoris with expert skill. He slips two fingers inside me, curling deep within. Pleasure explodes through me in ripples, building as my breaths come short and fast. Aldrin watches the ecstasy across my face with intensity. With an arrogant smirk.

"I am only getting started with you." His voice is hoarse and threatening. It makes my heart skip a beat. He takes me by the shoulders and pushes me to the water's edge.

The pool is warm, with waves of colors rippling across it as we disturb its surface and wade in deep enough to reach my shoulders. Most of Aldrin's chiseled chest is exposed above the waterline.

He grabs my waist and lifts me up onto his hips in a tight embrace. I wrap my legs around him and thread my hands through his dark hair. The hardness of his cock is pressed against my core and reaches up to my belly.

Aldrin moves my body through the water, lifting me up and down as though I don't weigh a thing, gliding his hardness against the outside of my most intimate parts, making every nerve ending light up with each grind of our bare flesh. His face raises, tipped back and eyes shut, as he savors me.

Then our lips crash together with the desperate need that has been building over two months. He bites my lower lip, then parts my mouth to slide his tongue against mine. Shivers run through me as I rake my nails down his back.

"What happened to that prince of yours?" he growls into my ear, right before nipping the lobe.

"Fuck him," I groan as he kisses my neck. "It's not my problem that he is a complete idiot."

"Good," Aldrin rasps. "I want to hear you moan."

He lifts me out of the water and deposits me onto a smooth ledge, so my back lies flat across it with my breasts pointing to the sky. I am lost for a moment in the sight of all that glittering water falling from his dark hair, running in rivulets between the grooves of his muscles. Until he takes my thighs in his hands and separates my legs.

I almost protest when he leans forward and kisses me right at their apex.

The shock of intense pleasure ripples through me, stealing my breath. I let out a whimper, followed by a long groan as I forget who and where and what I am, until there is nothing but me and him, and what he is doing to my body.

It is like nothing I have ever felt before. His tongue rasps over my clitoris, making tight little circles as his fingers dig into my thighs. I shiver and shudder as jolts of pleasure run through me, overlapping each other, coursing through the very foundations of my existence. Then he enters two fingers inside me, thrusting and curling in perfect synchrony with his teasing mouth.

He knows exactly how to touch me, making my back arch and my body jolt under the pressure of his swirling tongue. The friction almost becomes too much and I try to shimmy back from him, but he grips my hip with his free hand and holds me in place. I cry out as the tension reaches an explosive point and still keeps mounting.

"Come for me, Keira," he demands, his breath brushing my core, then his punishing tongue sets to work on me again.

I crash straight over the precipice of pleasure and my body contorts as my mind bursts into shattered starlight and ecstasy. My release courses like fire through my veins, and Aldrin's mouth is still on me, licking and flicking, guiding me through each crashing wave of it.

My body turns completely limp and I lie there, panting. A cocky laugh rumbles through him, then he plants kisses up my belly, between my breasts and along my collarbone. When I open my eyes, he is hovering over me, his hooded gaze drinking in the sight of me. I glance down the expanse of all that tanned skin of his chest, to his hardness that hangs between us.

I need it pounding inside of me.

"Fuck me, Aldrin," I moan.

"Say it again."

"Fuck me, Aldrin."

"Beg." His body shivers.

"Pleeease." I throw my head back. "I need you."

He climbs higher up me, his legs separating mine further until his hard cock rubs up my clitoris in a swift motion that makes me gasp. Thick, muscular arms cage me on either side and his chest hovers over me.

"How could I deny you?" He looks at me with a predatory expression that is savagery and beauty, all wrapped into one.

Aldrin guides himself to my entrance, pausing with just the head inside me, then plunges the entire length of his hardness in to the hilt, stretching and filling me up. I let out a whimper, digging my nails into his powerful shoulder blades that ripple under my touch.

Then he rocks his hips against mine.

My whole body lights up with pleasure as he drives his cock in and out, in and out. Each thrust is harder than the last, hitting that spot deep within me that forces out all rational thought. Tension builds and builds until it is almost unbearable.

I need more.

I wrap my legs around his hips and grip his ass as I move against him, pushing him deeper and chasing that friction that sends me wild. Making each plunge hit harder. His breath comes hard and fast right in my ear and he grunts with primal need.

Aldrin lifts one of my legs, angling me so his pounding movements hit new depths, each stroke more powerful, faster, until my whole body jolts with each delicious impact.

I revel in the way his body wraps around mine. How his bare skin glides against my bare skin. I never want to be separated from him.

My chest swells until I think I will combust, and the pleasure builds to an almost unbearable intensity, and still his hips rock and roll into mine. The utter bliss notches up and up and up until my inner walls clamp down around him, then convulse as a violent climax rips through me.

I cry out and arch into him. My entire essence is torn away by those currents of utter euphoria, until I know nothing at all but the man pressed on top of me.

My release sends Aldrin over the edge, his movements becoming wild until his entire body tenses as he grunts out a choked sound and spills his seed into me.

We lie there for a long time, still joined and breathing heavily, as his hot seed slips down my leg. I wrap my arms around his back and lazily stroke each toned muscle as he buries his head in my neck. His grip tightens on me, as though he never wants to let me go.

There is something so sweet in the gesture.

I could live an eternity here, in this moment.

Aldrin pulls himself onto his elbows, our entire bodies still touching, and studies my face with tenderness. His finger draws the line of my lips, runs across my cheek and my jaw.

"Did you enjoy yourself?" There is a smug grin on his lips. He already knows the answer. His hand brushes small circles along the skin of my thigh that still brackets his hips.

"No one has ever made me feel like that," I murmur, and my eyes roll back into my head just at the thought.

Aldrin freezes and his body tenses around me. "Not even your prince?"

I'm still too far away and riding that wave to think clearly. "He has never made me climax."

"You were going to marry a man who has never made you climax?"

I blink at him. "A woman's pleasure is considered unimportant where I come from. Taboo, even."

"Unimportant? It's a basic right." Horror fills his face.

I kiss his lips with a brush of mine. "Good thing you know exactly how to give me that basic right."

He searches my face for so long that I wonder what he sees. If he pities me. I could become lost in those amber eyes, so vulnerable and open in this moment.

I can't help tracing a hand down his face, the light stubble catching against my skin. His huge biceps bulge as he wraps his arms tightly around me and rolls us so he is suddenly on his back and I am sprawled across him. He pulls me into his chest and I bury my cheek into those perfect pectorals.

Aldrin kisses the top of my head.

"You have awoken something within me I thought died a long time ago," he murmurs. His pulse accelerates beneath my ear as he clearly searches for words and is lost. I don't care as long as his arms remain around me.

"I care for you, Keira," he finally manages, his fingers tangled in my hair. "And it terrifies me because I don't know where this is going, but I will take whatever you are willing to give."

Both joy and pain twist in my chest. I want to give him everything. I could love this man, if I allowed myself to fall. It would be as easy as breathing.

But I have my duties to my realm and he has his.

"I care for you, too," I say, knowing I can never take it back. It could change everything, and nothing at all.

## CHAPTER 28

# ALDRIN

There was a time when I thought I would never set foot into my city again. When I dreamed of this moment. We walk the wide promenade of the capital's main entrance, a long bridge that spans the granite roots of the city. Streams run through the channels on either side of the road, cascading in thin waterfalls over the edge into the deep valley below.

Overhead, a series of immense golden gates arch over the road, dwarfing us with pillars as wide as an ancient tree, covered in blooming vines. Between each gate stand larger-than-life statues of every king and queen who has ruled this court, facing their consorts on the opposite side. My ancestors.

Keira sucks in a sharp breath as she passes my likeliness in the last colossus, then turns wide eyes to me, as though she didn't quite believe I am a king. The space for my queen remains empty.

All I can do is shrug.

It takes all my willpower not to pull her in by the waist and sink my lips into her neck. To whisk her away to the nearest place of privacy and have all of her.

The city opens up before us as we pass under the last golden gate, and my companions audibly sigh. Silvan wipes a tear from his eye.

Drake laughs, a huge smile on his face. Klara looks up to the sky, ignoring the layers upon layers of buildings, to the golden palace at the apex of the city that we grew up in.

Only my original band travels with me, as well as Keira and Caitlin. Cyprien has already smuggled in my lower fae followers.

As I breathe in the amalgamation of scents of my city, spice, pollen and coffee, a weight lifts from my shoulders.

Many of the streets of the City of Vertical Gardens are flanked by lazy streams, dotted with lily pads. Dozens of bridges arch away from each main road, crossing over each other and chaotically leading to clusters of shops, restaurants, bars or apartments.

There must be a hundred pools of water that break up the city blocks, and as many waterfalls trickling down the buildings, hydrating the thick canopies of blooms that occupy any available space on roofs and walls.

Clusters of buildings rise as tall as mountains, always with a base of shops and a patchwork of apartments above, in different shapes and sizes. Walkways with arched railings hug every level and bridges or great staircases span the air between the megastructures, giving the illusion of webs between mountains.

A person can travel from one side of the city to the other without ever having to descend to the lower platforms.

All manner of domes, spires and towers grace the capital, jutting out of the sides and hanging in the air in many places. Every inch of the golden stone is adorned with engravings of flowers, leaves or runes.

An intense wave of pride rolls through me at not only the beauty of my city, but the pure ingenuity of it. The feat of magic and engineering to create such a wonder. My ancestors, along with the Tuatha Dé Danann gods, pulled the bedrock up from the ground to form its base.

Keira gravitates toward me, her rosebud lips parted as her doe eyes drink in the sight. Immediately, another image of her face flashes in my mind, flushed prettily and moaning as I pound into her.

"Aldrin, I had no idea a city could be so enchanting," she gasps.

I give her a sidelong glance. "Would you like a quick tour?"

I need to be seen by enough people that they whisper about my return. It is my assurance that will keep the high chancellor's hand in check. Word will spread while the Senate enters its session, still allowing me my element of surprise.

I want Keira to fall in love with my home. I want to bask in her wonderment as she takes in all its glory.

Her entire face lights up at my suggestion. "Oh, Aldrin, I would love that!"

I place a hand on the small of her back and lead our party down an offshoot from the main boulevard.

Klara raises an eyebrow at me. "Is this wise? Should we not head straight to the palace?"

I pull my pocket watch out of my travel pack and inspect the time. "Let's live a little. Twenty minutes to enjoy the city."

I lead us through an open-air bazaar. It is on the ground level of an immense building on stilts, with only wide arches walling it in. Those regularly positioned columns are engraved with images of nymphs and vines.

Keira gawks and turns in full circles as she takes in the many stores.

We pass a shop that has spices arranged in pyramids of red, yellow, brown and green, with dried herbs hanging from its ceiling. We practically have to pull Caitlin away, with promises to return.

Another stall has displays of flowers in every color imaginable, some larger than my hand. Some sell chocolates, perfumes, twenty types of olives, or fresh fruits. The entire space smells of the tang and richness of spices, vinegar and pollen.

Caitlin stops dead at a store that sells artisan-painted glass lamps. There are fire orbs within them, illuminating the leadlights and casting their colors across the floor. Klara pulls her along by the elbow, and I am surprised for a moment, because I never took her for one to care for pretty things.

"All those fire orbs would be worth enough to buy a small estate back home," Caitlin mutters.

"They are cheap and common here," Klara informs her. "Most high fae have enough fire magic to create their own. It is mainly low fae and elementals who buy them."

Keira's eyes dart around, as though she is trying to commit every detail to memory. A huge smile graces her lips. It fills me with pure happiness. I wrap an arm around her waist and lead her out of the bazaar.

We take a winding avenue up the vertical city. The platforms and staircases here are constructed from the roots and branches of a series of wisteria trees, their huge trunks melding with the buildings.

The way is surrounded on both sides by cafes, restaurants and bars, framed by the curtains of purple wisteria flowers, their fallen petals creating a carpet beneath our feet.

Tables and chairs and patrons spill out of each restaurant. The area buzzes with activity. There are musicians and street performers everywhere, lone artists playing instruments for diners or bands taking up one of the many daises built for them.

A lute player serenades us for a handful of steps, staring into Keira's eyes while singing, until I toss him a coin. Keira comes to a full stop before a fae who creates flowing, colorful images in the air with light, her art a story of dragons battling each other, their long bodies fluttering and thrashing above our heads.

"It is beautiful," Keira says.

While she is transfixed by the show, I am mesmerized by her breathtaking loveliness. The colored lights reflect upon her skin, accentuating the soft curve of her generous lips, the vibrancy of her tightly curling hair and that line of cleavage I can see from my vantage point down the neckline of her dress.

Keira turns to say something to me, then notices the subject of my attention, and that open mouth turns into a smile so wicked it doesn't seem to belong to the same woman.

Gods, I could take her right now.

I feel like the king of the world when she gives herself to me. It is an utter privilege.

"We can't linger here." Klara breaks the tension.

I hate that she is right. I want the people to glimpse me, to question whether I am their king returned, but I must be gone before any form the conviction to approach me.

We continue upward, across golden bridges that span glittering waterfalls and past gardens of miniature rainforests nestled between buildings. Puka run rampant in some of the wilder parts, swiping food from the carts of unwary street vendors and scurrying up the sides of buildings in a flurry of black fur, long pointed ears and claws.

Of course, I have to stop to buy street food from those same vendors to see the look on Keira's face as she eats it. They have some of the best food in the realm. I settle on skewers of spiced, charcoal-roasted meats and flaky pastries with berries and nuts.

"Damn, I have missed this!" Drake takes another bite of meat, then sighs and throws back his head.

Keira licks the juices from her fingers. "And I thought the camp food was good!"

"Oh, my cooking is good." Drake gives her a slow smile. "But I haven't had the right resources in the wilds."

"Are there no bounds to your ego, Drake?" Klara asks in a flat voice, but her lips quirk.

"Why should it have bounds?" Drake raises his eyebrows. "Especially if it's true." Klara gives him a deadpan look. "Come on, admit that you love my food." He pokes her in the ribs.

Caitlin stares at a skewer, turning the stick around in her hand as though she is trying to unpack every flavor on it. Her eyes flick up to her sister. "I want to buy spices to bring home. As much as we can carry." Keira gives her a wide smile.

I glance at my pocket watch again. "On another day." I hurry them along.

We take one of the many bridges that lead to the mouth of the palace. My heart fills with equal parts nostalgia and dread upon returning to my home.

The golden palace is perched at the highest reach of the city. It consists of immense, circular buildings adorned with arches, columns and staircases that lead to levels of gardens and open platforms.

Waterfalls run down the curved faces of the palace that are otherwise occupied by massive leadlight windows.

The highest garden has a circle of arched gateways at its top, with a diamond plinth in its center, once a portal to the world of the gods. At its apex is an open-air temple to the Tuatha Dé Danann. Once, we worshiped and summoned our patrons from that site, until they stopped coming.

I would have loved to witness our creators stepping out of those portals, to bask in their glory, but it has been hundreds of years since they have visited us. Some believe our gods are dead. Maybe that is another reason our lands are dying.

Both Cyprien and Lilly wait for us in the courtyard that leads to the servant's entrance of the palace, casually leaning against a railing. They straighten as they spy us. Lilly collects my band and leads them away to their position for our move.

Cyprien is at my side, leading me through the garden. "Did you make sure you were seen in the city?"

"Yes. Rumor of my return will travel fast."

"Good." He nods curtly, setting the gold beads of his black hair clinking, despite how the braids are pulled back by a leather thong.

We exit the garden and take a staircase down to the Senate house, a small, cylindrical building with all the same golden features of the palace.

Cyprien holds open the back door for me and we make our way through narrow corridors of marble floors and walls, and into a waiting room. It is here that witnesses are called to give accounts during the Senate.

All my low fae companions wait here: the pixies, nymphs, fire sprites, selkies and kelpies. I greet each of them by name.

I stand behind the door, the sound of muttering and footsteps on the other side as the senators fill the room beyond.

"Don't wait for an official summoning, because you won't get it," Cyprien whispers in my ear. "You'll know your cue."

He disappears the same way we came in, and within moments, his voice travels from the other side of that door, greeting his fellow senators. The buzz within the room increases, becoming so loud it is difficult to pull one conversation from another.

What I would give to have an eyehole into the room.

The sound cuts off all at once as the clicking of heels on marble rings out.

"I declare the Senate is now in session," a musical, feminine voice rings out. It sets my blood to ice and has my mind recoiling with rage. Titania. The woman who calls herself the high chancellor. "We have many, many issues to discuss. First on the agenda are the food shortages and low fae riots—"

Titania stops speaking abruptly as more footsteps echo off the stone floors, accompanied by gasps and murmurs.

"Cyprien? What are you doing?" There is a feral note to her outrage.

"I invoke the right to speak first! On the gravest of matters!" His statement cuts over the top of increasing murmurs.

"No. No, you cannot speak first!" she snaps at him.

"It is his right!" a man calls out.

"It has always been the way of the Senate," another supporter chimes in.

"Let him speak!"

Cyprien roars, "I have discovered a betrayal of this Senate, of our people and the entire Spring Court." The room falls silent. Not even the high chancellor speaks.

Anticipation has a cold sweat prickling my skin and sliding down my back. It would be so easy for Cyprien to betray me at this point. To hand me over to Titania for treason. I have considered it a thousand times, and dismissed it as many. But you never truly know a man.

"We have been lied to." Cyprien pauses to let it sink in. "By this woman here! The high chancellor who calls herself the representative of the people and Senate."

"You *dare* lay such charges at my feet!" Titania roars.

"I do," Cyprien replies.

"What evidence do you have?" that same supporter calls out. I recognize the voice as Bryce's, and know they have struck an alliance before the session. Cyprien would be insane to make these accusations without lining up his supporters.

"I traveled to our border with the Winter Court—" Cyprien starts.

"Who gave you leave to go to the border?" Titania cuts in.

"Do I need permission to travel the territory? Should I have applied to leave the city?" Cyprien yells back, and the murmurs of agreement around him tell me how bad things have become, that this is almost a reality.

"As general of the armed forces, it is my job to inspect the border, the watchtowers and fortresses, and check on the soldiers there. For years, I have been barred from doing this for one reason or another. My position is slowly becoming a title only, as my powers and authority are siphoned away by her secretaries. So I went on a covert mission, and do you know what I found on our border with an enemy that Titania claims is readying to go to war with us? Our fortresses and watchtowers were empty. Utterly empty! All of our soldiers have been moved away from the border with Winter."

Sharp gasps precede the eruption of yells and cries.

I tap my foot with agitation. It is killing me that I cannot see what is happening, the expression on each person's face. There is much that can be told about a person's true stance by watching their initial reaction to news like that.

"That is enough!" The high chancellor shuts the room down. "You will take his word over mine? The threat from Winter is not coming from the borders, it's coming from their technology! From plagues!" She is making it up as she goes, I can tell.

Some people fall so deep into the web of their own lies that they convince themselves too.

The truth of the corruption is an inconvenience to her family's business. If the people were to leave the capital in large numbers and return to their posts in the wilds, her personal costs of selling them all the delicacies and commodities she trades in would skyrocket. Her family's wealth would collapse and her base of power with it.

Titania has no noble blood and no ancestral right to the ruling class. In my reign, I made it so anyone could rise up the ranks. Titania bought her way in.

"The threat is very much evident at the borders," Cyprien replies, venom for venom. "But not from Winter. The high chancellor won't let anyone near there because she doesn't want you to see the true nature of it. Our magic is fading, we all know that, but at the border there are huge rips through the land, and within those rips are voids of complete nothingness. This realm is falling apart!

"The low fae are being born without half their limbs, and their flesh is rotting and turning to ash while they still live. I have proof and witnesses! Any person who travels there will see the truth of it first-hand. And you know what else I found at the border? Our rightful king, the only one with the nerve to address the problem, returning the corrupted low fae back to the earth so their magic could be redistributed. So I invited him here."

A raging passion runs through my blood. This is *my* kingdom she is destroying. *My* people she is bringing to their knees. All because she cannot face the truth.

"Follow me," I growl to my low fae supporters.

I slam open the door. The room turns dead silent as I stride across the mosaic floor and stand before the concentric rings of senators.

Titania sits in *my* throne facing the Senate, with a diadem on her forehead as though she were royalty. I send a single scathing glance over my shoulder at her.

Those eyes of pure, swirling firelight narrow on me, lined thickly in black to match the tattooed midnight of her lips and her long hair. Runes glitter and move in swirls on the pale skin of her forehead, her hairline shaved back to give more space to the parlor tricks of the tattoos.

All of it is someone else's magic imbued into her skin and eyes, because I know she has very little magic of her own. Those ears hidden beneath peaked caps of silver jewelry are almost rounded like a human's.

Titania is irrelevant here.

As I turn away, I glimpse the ripple of fear that crosses her face before she schools it into a haughty mask. She had power here, because I allowed it. The vote, the election and her reign all happened because I respected the will of the Senate and people. But I was wrong.

I scrutinize the reactions of the thirty senators before me. How light grows in some eyes and resentment and distrust in others. There are so many new faces. Titania removes any senators who are an inconvenience to her, until only those who are too afraid to challenge are left.

A ruler is not meant to have that kind of power.

It could work in my favor. All these alienated lords and ladies.

My low fae witnesses line up behind me. The flames of the fire sprites suddenly rush upward, their presence becoming larger than life. The kelpies rear back onto their hind legs and kick the air.

Pixies dart rapidly around the room, examining many of the senators by suddenly appearing in front of their faces before dashing away. Only the selkies remain calm, completely in their land form with their sealskins draped around them like cloaks.

"This is the gravest threat we have ever faced," I boom with passion. "Our world is unraveling, fae are suffering, and this woman would have you pretend it is not happening. If we do nothing, our way of life will collapse. Everything we know will die."

Unhappy murmuring builds around me. Fear coils in my stomach that my pleas will fall on deaf ears again.

"Is this a military coup, Cyprien?" Titania's smile is cruel, taking advantage of the hesitation of the Senate. Her tongue is ever golden. "Is that why you are spinning these lies, to get your brother-in-law back in power?"

"How can it be a military coup when I have no idea where you have stationed the soldiers I lead?" Cyprien snaps back.

"Aldrin should be arrested on sight. He has been exiled by the Senate and people," Titania states in a bored voice, clicking her fingers at two guards, who do not move.

"Not when he has been invited here by me, as a witness against your crimes," Cyprien jumps in.

I glance sidelong at Cyprien, then at the powerhouse before me. "What do you say? Do you want to believe Titania's lies again at face value, or do you want concrete evidence?" I raise my eyebrows at them, holding the eyes of key players. "How has her rule been going for you? I hear the food shortages have gone from a prediction in my reign to a reality under hers. And riots?" I turn to Titania and tisk.

She launches out of my throne and for a moment I wonder if she will try to claw my face with the stupidly long, red-lacquered claws of her fingernails.

Her facade of fake charm has vanished now that she rules by fear and bullying tactics. She stands there, seething at me, jaw clenched with black lips pulled back to reveal her teeth. Tendons stick out on her all-too-skinny neck.

Titania's mouth works and her arm thrashes out, a single finger pointed to the door, but no words come out. I cock an eyebrow at her. I hold a sound barrier of air around her vocal cords, because I am done with hearing the poison she spews.

Only a king or queen of this court can use magic in this room, and it is incredibly satisfying to remind her of who I am. Her eyes narrow on me, literal fire swirling in them, as she mouths: *I will destroy you.* The problem is, she already did, and I survived.

Cyprien leans toward me. "Is it a good idea to antagonize her?"

The senators argue, yelling over the top of each other like school-children.

"I needed to know her hand," I murmur, noting the fact that not a single person notices her silence. "She has gutted the Senate of power, hasn't she?"

Cyprien nods. "Mostly. For now. She forgets the lords speak directly to the people, and can revolutionize them to invoke the power of the mob."

"Too messy." I shudder at the thought of the bloodshed that would entail.

Bryce slams a fist on the table before him, his huge form standing over it. "I want to hear from the low fae witnesses. Then, I want to go to the border myself to see what the flaming fuck is happening there."

A clash of voices greet him, some for his idea and others against.

"What are you so afraid of?" Bryce yells to the clustered groups that argue with him. "If our king is wrong, then we will go there and see nothing. There will be no harm in it!"

I hold up both my hands and send out a commanding wave of magic, the kind that could force every person here to bow before me for a few heartbeats, but I dilute it enough that it shuts them up and forces their attention on me.

"I have companions here who traveled a long way to tell you their stories." I spread out my arms toward the low fae. "Each of their tribes has sent representatives to petition the Senate, and *all* were blocked by Titania's secretaries. Since when do we send away fae in need before even hearing them?" My tirade ends in a furious roar.

Everyone turns to Titania, where she has returned to lounge on the throne, legs crossed so that a heeled shoe hangs in the air. She flicks a clawed hand in the air a few times, rolling her eyes as though she is allowing me to speak, to damn myself.

As I turn away, one of her secretaries rushes over to her.

Damn. I'm running out of time.

"Get to the point, Aldrin. Her personal guards will swarm this room in minutes," Cyprien whispers.

"I suggest a full tribunal and trial," I say. "An investigation into the evidence I have brought you today. Send people to the borders. Do not dismiss these low fae in their time of need. It is our duty to help them. *That* is why we are the ruling class."

Both sides latch on to the idea of a tribunal, and senators stand and clap.

I hold up a hand. "I stepped down from my rule of my own accord when the Senate and people voted me out. When I believed a competent ruler was going to take my place. But Titania has brought nothing but lies, corruption and gross negligence. I will not allow her to destroy us."

The room explodes into chaos, and falls silent again as soon as I speak. "I will remain in the capital and the royal quarters for the entire duration of the inquiry. My doors and receiving room will be open to any who want to speak to me, or my witnesses."

The crashing footsteps of guards rushing down the back corridors of the Senate house reach my ears. Cyprien shoots me a panicked glance.

I have no idea how far Titania will take things in the heat of the moment.

I half turn and smirk at her. "Titania, I assume you were not arrogant enough to move into the royal quarters?" I laugh as I step toward the front doors of the Senate house, knowing full well that she did. A calculated slap to her authority. A ridicule of it.

I step out the main doors as Titania's private guards burst into the room. My loyal band surrounds me immediately, hands on the hilts of their swords, as well as Cyprien's loyalists. They were my original King's Guard, dedicated to *me*.

Silvan grasps my arm and leads me away from the Senate house. "I do not like you being put at risk without me there," he growls as he slips straight back into the role of Captain of the King's Guard.

I shoot a single glance back through the open doors of the Senate. At the mess I left in my wake. Every member is on their feet and yelling. Papers scatter everywhere as tempers fly. My smile falters as my eyes fall upon the armed guard in their midst. I do not recognize their faces, or the foreign uniform.

The high chancellor has taken far too many liberties.

# CHAPTER 29

# KEIRA

Aldrin paces across the royal bedroom in nothing but a white bathrobe, the hem swishing against his powerful thighs. It is tied loosely across his waist, exposing the tanned skin of his chiseled chest. I bite my lip as I hungrily take in the sight of him, my stomach tightening with need.

I sit on the edge of his four-poster bed, the pale curtains pulled back. Behind him, immense arched windows give a floor-to-ceiling view of a blue sky and fluffy clouds. Thick rays of sunlight pierce through, making the gold veins of the marble floor glitter.

This single room is massive, with a roaring fireplace, sitting couches and a writing desk, large amounts of empty space around them. Potted trees fill the corners, giving the space an almost wild feel.

"They are utterly spineless!" Aldrin runs a hand through his loose, damp hair. "I have given the Senate everything they need to start an inquiry. The evidence is laid out for them, but still some refuse to see what is right before their eyes. Some are terrified of the truth and make themselves willfully blind. Others don't want the inconvenience of correcting the issue. There are those who believe me, but are too incompetent and afraid of Titania to do anything about it."

I get up and take Aldrin's hands, then lead him to the bed, pushing his chest to force him to sit down and stop pacing. He grunts in response. That bathrobe rides further up his thighs, almost, *almost*, giving me a glimpse of that manhood beneath.

I blink and force myself to focus. "It has been three weeks, Aldrin, and the Senate are nowhere near setting up an inquiry."

Three glorious weeks of exploring every inch of each other's bodies and joining them in every way imaginable.

He turns those amber eyes on me, a flash of panic within them.

I squeeze his hand. "You said it yourself. Titania has hamstrung the council with cowards. All they know how to do is spiral into useless debate. Look for other allies in the people, the soldiers, and the lords that have been ostracized."

"I will not start a civil war," he grumbles. "I will not do that to these people."

"No," I say gently. "But this palace seems like a great place to lay a siege. Sometimes we can't achieve what we need to with diplomacy alone. If a battle were fought in this palace, and the blood of Titania's guards was spilled, but the citizens of the city spared, would that be such a bad thing?"

"I had hoped to regain my power in the same way I lost it." Aldrin's eyebrows furrow and shadows dance in his eyes.

"You're an idealist. I respect that." I straighten the sides of his bathrobe, then gaze up at him. "You once said history is written by the victors of war. Inciting the lords and mob to your cause is still winning the popular vote. The high chancellor will not walk away peacefully like you did."

Many fae have visited Aldrin over the weeks, meeting him in the sitting rooms or study of this apartment. Lords, senators, heads of merchant guilds and chiefs of low fae tribes, all to determine his ambitions and to hear from his own mouth the disaster that will befall this realm.

Sometimes, they come just to speak to Caitlin and myself. To hear our claims of what we can do to open the portals between realms again. We make no promises, only speak the truth. There are high fae who are prejudiced against humans. Who fear that we will flood their realm in droves and dilute their bloodlines until there are no fae left.

It is a stretch of the imagination, and they are few.

Of all these purists, Titania is the worst. Strange, considering there is so much human blood in her lineage that her family has only a drop of magic and many are born with rounded ears. Or maybe it is because of this fact. Her own inadequacies and frustrations fuel her hatred for us.

"I like it when you speak politics with me, Keira. You are better schooled than the fools in the Senate." Heat burns in Aldrin's eyes.

I lean in toward him. "I'm not sure if that is a compliment."

"You're smarter than me, though I'm not sure if that is a compliment either." Aldrin grabs me by the waist and swings me into his lap as though I weigh nothing.

I immediately straddle him, the silk of my skirts shifting up my thighs. "Don't depreciate yourself," I laugh, slapping his hard chest lightly.

He buries his head between my breasts and grumbles an incoherent reply. I draw in a ragged breath as his fingers brush strokes across the bare skin of my legs, bunching the fabric of my skirts and dragging it up my thighs.

A thought occurs to me, and I pull back from him. "If you leave the city to pursue other avenues for supporters, your push for an inquiry by the Senate will die, am I right?"

"Yes. And Titania will do everything she can to make sure I can never enter the city again," he replies.

"Then summon your supporters here." I place my hands on either side of his face as I stare into his eyes. "Call back the ex-senators and lords and ladies and anyone else who supported you the first time. We need them."

"It would be seen as a threat. A gathering of my forces," Aldrin counters. "I'm not prepared for that yet."

"Your armed forces, they won't march on the capital at her command, will they? Who is their loyalty to?"

"I don't believe so," he says. "Cyprien says they believe they are under the direction of the Senate, but it is Titania's secretaries who have hidden and spread them wide. She is a fool to treat this court's armed forces as a personal threat to her rule and attempt to disperse them."

"Does Cyprien truly not know where they are?" I ask.

A smug grin grows on Aldrin's face. "What do you think? Does the man come across as incompetent to you, or sneaky and crafty?" My lips part with surprise, but Aldrin continues. "Let Titania believe she is more powerful than she actually is. She will overplay her hand."

"Could you muster them for—" My words are cut off when Aldrin places a finger to my lips.

"No talk of civil war," he says, his grip tightening around my waist. "That army could easily split in half and fight each other, if she whispers poison in their ears. They are better off far from here for now."

I cock my head to the side. "You have an army in this city that could be at your disposal. Every lord and lady who supports you has their body of guards to defend their estates. Even just the threat of using the people as a mob can go a long way in getting your throne back."

I play idly with his hair as I think back on every book I read about politics and battle tactics as I prepared to become a queen. "You need to discover the loyalties of the palace guards and the serving staff. They can move without being seen. You will quickly be able to overwhelm her personal guard in numbers," I say.

Aldrin crushes me into him and kisses me deeply. Passionately. It is a rough bruising of lips and a colliding of tongues. By the time he releases me, I am thoroughly breathless.

"You have a fucking brilliant mind. Do you know that?" His calloused fingers brush hair from my face.

I think back to the numerous family dinners where we discussed news of wars and politics outside of our kingdom, and my father drilled each of his children on what we thought the nations might do, how a battle may play out, what techniques each side should take. He treated his son and daughters the same.

"Does it threaten you? My brilliance?" I brush my lips against his and feel them curve into a smile.

"Only if you were on the opposite side of a battle to me," he says.

"Never," I whisper back.

I push him until he lies flat on his back on the bed. I tug that damned bathrobe open and my stomach tightens all the way down to my core. Aldrin lies bare beneath me, every muscle of his chest and abdomen sculpted, with a scattering of dark hair beneath his navel that drags my gaze down to his fully erect cock.

I take it in my hand and stroke it teasingly, savoring the way his body shudders. Enjoying the feel of every pass my hand makes up and down.

He throws his head back and groans, his hands digging into the flesh of my thighs.

I lean down over him, bracing my hands on either side of his shoulders, and kiss his lips hungrily. His fingers slide lazily up my legs to the center of my thighs, passing over their apex in a rolling motion once, then twice. I let out a small whimper as my body jolts. I am already saturated for him.

He inserts two fingers inside me, curling them deep and thrusting them in and out, all while rubbing my clitoris in those delicious circles again and again.

Fire builds within me as I gasp in air, burning through my core and driving that insatiable pressure. I move my hips against his fingers, increasing the friction in all the right places, and shudder at that ecstasy that runs through me in sharp shocks.

I let go of Aldrin's hardness to pull the beautiful silk dress clean over my head and toss it across the room.

The sight of my pale thighs straddling his tanned hips, his fingers busy thrusting within me, is enough to undo me. I arch my back and let out a throaty groan as the pressure within me explodes and I cascade into an oblivion that is so sweet.

I crawl down his body, placing kisses on the grooves of his muscles. First between the corded tendons of his neck, then the ridge between his pectorals. I slide my tongue around the sculpted bulk of his abdomen, and lay kisses from his navel down and down that rock-solid stomach to his hardness.

I take it in my mouth, as much as I can fit. A thrill runs through me at the gasps that erupt from him as I set to work, running my tongue over its tip, sucking hard and deep, and pumping with my hand what doesn't fit into my throat.

Aldrin's body is coiled tight, and his beautiful face is twisted with euphoria. It is empowering to make this man, this *king*, become so utterly undone.

"Fuck me, Keira." Aldrin's breaths come hard and fast. "Literally. Fuck me."

I obey his command.

I straddle him and savor each tantalizing inch as I slowly slip onto his hardness. It fills me up in gradual increments to an almost impossible depth. I thrust my hips in hard, jolting motions as the friction within me radiates pleasure that shoots throughout my body.

Aldrin's hips move to meet mine at a brutal pace. His hands grip them and push me down harder against him with each thrust. Our bodies collide with a force that sends violent waves of pleasure bursting through me. The friction, the tension, it makes me feel like I am on fire.

His eyes are like molten gold as they watch me, darting between my lust-filled expression and breasts that bounce with each collision of our bodies. I lean forward over him, caging him with my arms on the bed, until my nipples rub against his chest as I ride him. It brings our faces inches apart.

The tension builds within me, and I am going to combust, right here, gazing into his eyes.

Aldrin wraps an arm around my waist and flips us in a fluid motion, his body rolling with mine so we never come apart. I am suddenly on my back, with the weight of his bulky frame driving me into the mattress.

His head nuzzles my neck as he pounds into me. I wrap my legs around his waist, clinging on for dear life. He drives that massive cock into me, harder and faster, until I am crying out and my inner muscles are clenching around him, because it is so deep and perfect.

I am engulfed in his scent, the earthy, almost floral aroma of his hair and the sweat that slicks his body. His low, panted growls fill my ears.

Pleasure builds to an almost unbearable point, tightening within me until I am so coiled up with tension that I explode into a cascade of blissful release. It is so intense, my vision blurs with stars and shadows, and I slip away to another plane where coherent thought is no longer possible.

Aldrin's entire body clenches tight and freezes moments later, and he lets out an incoherent grunt.

I wrap my arms and my legs tightly around him to cling on to each shudder of the climax that surges through him. He collapses onto me, body limp. I idly stroke his golden skin that shines under the rays of late-afternoon sun entering through the window.

"Sire?" A knock comes at Aldrin's bedroom door. "Your afternoon appointment will be here shortly," his royal butler, Basil, says from just outside.

"Damn. I completely forgot," Aldrin mutters against my neck, not making an effort to move.

"I have taken the liberty of running another bath for you." Basil's tone is full of deference, without a hint to what he clearly overheard through these walls.

Aldrin pulls himself up onto his forearms, peering into my face with a look of pure admiration. He brushes his fingers through my hair. Under that gaze I feel more valued than I ever have in my life.

He kisses me with a soft brush of the lips. "Care to have a bath with me?"

I respond with a smile.

His bath is more like a small pool recessed into the tiled floor, and it has an entire room of its own. The rose-scented water reaches my shoulders, and I tie up my already clean hair so it doesn't get wet.

I should have known better.

Aldrin steps into the pool and splashes a wave of water at me. I retaliate by sending my air magic into the pool and dousing as much of it as I can on top of his head. I find myself laughing, straddling his hips as I try to wrestle him, but he dumps me back into the body of water.

We don't get nearly enough time in there before Basil reminds Aldrin of his appointment, and he gets out and dries himself with a volley of air. I watch as Basil dresses him in his court finery.

He looks absolutely breathtaking in a doublet of black and gold embroidered silk, cut closely enough to accentuate his broad shoulders and thin waist, with matching slim-cut pants.

I find my own silk dress and pull it back on, smoothing out the rumples.

Aldrin kisses me before he leaves the bedroom.

Basil turns in the doorway and gives me a long, searching look. I wonder if he is analyzing me as a potential threat. There is a fierceness beneath that calm mask of subservience that makes me wonder if he is more than a butler. He has waited on Aldrin since he was a child, and seems to have a fierce, paternal love for him.

I pin up my hair slowly, completely lost in thought when another knock comes at the door.

"May I enter, my lady?" Basil's voice is soft on the other side.

"Yes," I say.

He steps through the doorway with a tray in his arms. It has a china pot of steaming tea, a matching cup and a bowl of honey.

"Forgive my assumptions, but I believe this is in order again today." Basil places the tray on the small table beside my armchair, then bows and walks out backward.

I lift the lid of the teapot and stare at the bloated herbs and flowers within, my stomach churning at the smell of it. Within is the same contraceptive tea my mother would bring me whenever Finan stayed with us, and I did my duty to attempt to bind him to our family.

Basil is definitely trying to protect Aldrin's interests.

I choke down the disgusting liquid and don't bother telling him I was already taking the herbs daily so I wouldn't get my cycle on the road.

I make my way through the opulence of the royal apartments, toward the main doors to leave. Aldrin can send someone to find me if I'm needed. I am done waiting around for men.

My steps take me through rooms with intricate marble mosaics across the floors and broad pillars of agate. The ivory walls are embossed in a multitude of metallic colors, forming intricate designs of swirls, flowers and leaves.

I pause in the entrance hall as Basil opens the door to the sitting room, balancing a tray of refreshments.

He leaves the door ajar and I catch a glimpse of low couches that face each other, and the lord sitting opposite Aldrin, still stained with dust from his travels. Their voices travel to me and I can't help pausing to listen.

"News of your arrival in the capital traveled quickly. Especially after your speech to the Senate. I still have my connections here." Every muscle in the lord's shoulders is taut as Aldrin scrutinizes him with narrowed eyes and a predatory gleam.

"You must understand, my estates are closely watched and I am practically under house arrest," the lord urges. "But when I heard word of your return, I feigned a sickness that kept me in my bed and took a covert mission to the border with my guard. My coming here was near impossible."

He leans forward in his seat. "I need you to know that I made a mistake when I voted you out. After what I saw…I believe you, Aldrin. I want to give you my oath and backing, if you will take it."

I suck in a breath. I probably shouldn't be listening in, but I can't help myself. This is exactly what we need, but Aldrin hardly reacts. He crosses an ankle over his knee and glowers at the man until he dabs sweat from his forehead with a handkerchief.

"And what does your oath and backing give me, Lord Cedar?" Aldrin's tone is as hard as steel. "I need more than pretty words."

"You know my influence in the capital has diminished since I fell out of the high chancellor's favor, but I have other resources. There are far too many like me. We still have dominion over our own provinces and together, we can be a formidable force. I can help you gain the support of others, my old allies from the Senate. I will convince them to see the border and the corruption of the low fae."

Aldrin motions to Basil, who picks up a crystal decanter and pours wine into two crystal chalices. Aldrin takes a long drink from one, and doesn't say a single thing to the lord opposite him, who loses his nerve and keeps talking.

"You have more support outside of the city than you realize. Things have been difficult in your absence. Mismanaged. Food shortages. Raised taxes on the lowest classes. The low fae are quickly becoming sub-citizens. Titania has not held up on her election promises. The time is right for you to take back your throne and for the people to hear your…unconventional ideas for saving this realm."

Aldrin scoffs. "I need to get them to believe there is a threat to our magic and realm first."

"And they will!" Lord Cedar's face lights up.

I wonder if he is actually enthusiastic about his king's return, or if he is a drowning man threatened with irrelevance and Aldrin is a rope tossed to him in a turbulent sea.

Basil leaves the sitting room, closing the door behind him and blocking out their conversation. The butler gives me a hard look, as though wondering if I am Aldrin's lover or a spy in his inner circle. I turn and leave the apartments, somehow feeling chastened.

Aldrin is a king who would value the options of his queen.

The thought is so alluring, it stops me dead in my tracks.

I am filled with heady longing to be Aldrin's partner in this. To stay here and see it to the end. To be at his side for all the good and bad moments, and pick him up each time this world grinds him down. My chest aches with how badly I want it, how badly I need him in my life, not just temporarily.

I have been considering myself as Aldrin's partner. Acting as though I will become *his* queen, not Finan's. I have forgotten myself. I have my duty to return to. *My* realm and *my* people.

My fingers fly to the moonstone bracelet at my wrist, passing over the beads and their greatly weakened pull. They are milky and dull, where they once shone bright like small beacons.

Ice forms in my stomach.

We have just over a week until the portals close, maybe two, and we still need to travel back to Odiane to collect our seed-stones. I cannot breathe at the thought of leaving Aldrin. Of having to marry Finan. My throat tightens painfully as panic engulfs me.

I was taken away by Aldrin's dreams, and thought they could be mine.

The world spins around me as I pace briskly toward my own apartments. I enter, then push my back against the closed door, running my hands across my face while my chest heaves.

I am falling for Aldrin.

If I stay here much longer, I *will* become desperately in love with him. I don't give my heart away in portions, but thrust the whole damned thing at a person. Much longer, and I will turn my back on my realm to spend my life with this man who has stolen my heart.

It is like a cold bucket of water is tipped over my head. The sacrifice required for such a choice hits home. If I remain after the portals close, I will never see my parents or siblings again. None except Caitlin would know what had happened to me.

It would destroy my father if I never returned from the pilgrimage, since he fought so hard for my right to cross. My mother would think I was ravished and harmed by high fae. The anchor to my home is so incredibly strong.

That bright light of a future with Aldrin filled with love winks out.

He may want my body and my friendship, but there is no guarantee he will make me his queen.

Bleakness hits me hard and fast.

I walk through the lavish apartment and find Caitlin waiting for me on a recliner in the sitting room. She is sprawled out, flicking through an introductory book on fae runes.

"You're a difficult person to find," she snaps, but when she glances up at me, the scowl falls from her face. Caitlin drops the book, stands and wraps me in a rigid embrace. "What happened? Who do I have to murder?"

I shiver. "I promise I haven't meant to avoid you."

"I know," she says into my hair, then pulls me back at arm's length to examine my face. "I have given you space to enjoy your time with Aldrin, but I worry about you, Keira. I'm so afraid of your heart being broken again, and I think it will be infinitely worse this time."

I almost break down and sob in her arms. "I think it is inevitable."

"Don't say that." She stares into my eyes intensely. "Tell me what you need, and I will fight to the end for you to have it. I don't know what is in your head right now."

I shake my head to clear the demons clouding it. "I don't know."

"Yes, you do. You're afraid to say it, Keira. It's just you and me here. This is a safe place."

I suck in a sharp breath. "I think I have fallen for Aldrin." Something splinters deep inside me at the admission. "But I can never have him. My duty is back home."

"Fuck your duty!" she snaps. "You know what you will return home to! I will bring enough magic back for the both of us to satisfy your *duty*. The way he looks at you and listens to your advice…gods, Keira, it's everything you have ever wanted!"

"It's not just that. If I stay here, I will never see our family again—"

Caitlin huffs a breath. "Aldrin can open the portals at will. Any fae can."

"Not without severe repercussions. Aldrin and Cyprien fought a battle over it when we first met. It's not like I would be able to come home for dinner every Sunday. I am too afraid to make myself that dependent on a man. I can't be at the mercy of anyone, even Aldrin. Not again. Not after dedicating my life to Finan and finding out it was a lie."

"Don't make Aldrin pay for Finan's mistakes," Caitlin says softly.

"Twenty-one years is a long time to wait in this realm for the portals to open if I make a mistake," I whisper.

"So is seven years in our realm, if you come home when you truly want to stay here." She pauses a moment. "Is this why you think you need to return home? Because you don't trust Aldrin?"

Gods, that cuts to the very core of my turmoil, and tears spill down my cheeks. "I trust Aldrin more than I have trusted anyone in my life, but I don't know if he loves me. If he would even want me here long term or as anything more than a lover."

Caitlin tips her head to the side and gives me a hard look. "Lie to yourself, but don't lie to me."

My throat feels like it is closing up, but I force myself to continue. "It is Finan that I don't trust. If I don't marry him and steer his reign, he will destroy our kingdom with his whims, and Aldrin will never get the human alliance he needs to save his lands.

"I am leaving Aldrin because I love him. Because my staying with him would be his ruination. I can't sit around here and watch his realm turn to ash and die."

I burst into tears, and Caitlin pulls me into her chest and cradles me while I cry and cry, my whole body shaking. She gently strokes my hair.

"Everything we have experienced of the fae is at complete odds with what we were taught," Caitlin says after a long time, when my sobs have turned silent. "I think the priestesses pushed old prejudices onto us. What if we are the first ones who actually lived among the high fae, and visited their city? What if no one else knows any better?"

"That's another reason why I need to return home, Caitlin." My throat hurts as I speak.

Caitlin's whole body tenses up. "Talk to Aldrin before you make up your mind, Keira. Hear him out. He deserves that. You should know what is on the table before you decide what to do. I will support you completely either way, but you need to choose soon. I hate to say it, but the portals are little over a week away from closing, and then the decision will be taken from you completely."

Shivers run through my entire body.

I wish I could speak to Aldrin.

He would court me with promises, but then I would never be able to leave when I know exactly how much he would offer me. I suspect he would give me the entire world on a silver platter if I asked for it.

Instead, I will give him everything he needs, by sacrificing my own happiness.

# CHAPTER 30
# KEIRA

T he sheer size and opulence of Aldrin's library takes my breath away. Two servants pull the grand doors open at my approach and the scent of musty pages rolls over me like a caress to my soul.

There are academics everywhere, poring over parchments or hidden behind towers of books, speaking in hushed whispers.

I stroll through the immense space, my footfalls echoing off the white marble floors veined with gold, and resounding off the many matching pillars. The domed ceiling reaches so high, it is difficult for me to make out the details of the elaborate scenes of fae history painted across it from the ground.

There are three levels above the main atrium that have many balconies peering down into it. Bookshelves of white lacquered wood adorned with gold take up every available surface in a sea of endless opportunities.

The entire library seems to stretch on forever.

I was paralyzed by the size and beauty of it the first time I stepped in here.

I take my usual path through the library until I reach a small room labeled *Human Histories*. I walk past the books to the cabinet taking up the entire far wall.

Within are hundreds of quartz tubes, the stone so flawless it is completely transparent, capped in moonstone. The cylinders are entwined with gold wire shaped into blooming vines. Inside each is a browned scroll of parchment, with different rough handwriting on every one.

They pulse with dim light.

Aldrin showed me these scrolls the first time he took me to the library, and imbued his magic with mine into the cabinet, so my hand can pass through the protective wards.

These are living memories, preserved from fae and humans long gone. All in this cabinet are of the Great War, or pivotal moments leading up to it, but there are others. Some from the time before, when our two realms existed as allies and trade partners.

I allow my hand to gravitate to any scroll that piques my attention. A flash of a moment plays within my mind as I hover over each, illustrating what the memory is about.

I pull on special gloves and take as many as I can safely handle, then set myself up in one of the tiny private rooms allocated for their viewing. The space has mahogany-paneled walls, low lighting from a single orb, and a table for four.

As I shut the door behind me, it blocks out the low voices and soft footsteps of the librarians. I wonder if the sound barrier is as much for my own peace as to block out my reactions to the memories from the rest of the library.

Some have left me weeping and others have made me scream.

I remove the gloves and place my bare hands upon a tube that has apples and leaves wrought in gold around it. I have watched this memory at least ten times, but I cannot get enough. The magic within grabs me with a sharp tug.

My existence winks away in a flash.

I stand within the body of a much taller fae man, inspecting the orchards at Appleshield Castle. Our consciousness melds into one, until I cannot tell myself from him.

*We fae were commissioned here to construct the greenhouses that now occupy much of the land within the keep, and I as their overseer, but I only have eyes for the lord protector's daughter and heir.*

*She is the most beautiful woman I have ever seen.*

*Black hair ripples down to her waist, and she flicks it over her shoulder as she speaks with her father. When those startling blue eyes glance over her shoulder, they catch mine, pinning me in place as my heart stumbles. Her name is Fionola. It is like a song on my lips.*

*"Elrond? Did you hear me?"*

*I have to drag myself away from the enchantment she has wielded over me and focus instead on Frode, my business partner.*

*"Are you happy for the foundation of the final greenhouse to be laid at this site?" he continues, a slight grin on his lips as he notices where my attention lies.*

*I skim over the broad parchment of the blueprints sprawled out in his hands, then give a quick nod. "Yes. Of course."*

*My eyes claw their way back to Fionola of their own accord. I hardly register the hammering of metal on metal and the whoosh created by the use of large amounts of magic. The final greenhouse. Gods. I'm not ready to leave this site.*

*The moment flashes to the next in a jarring flicker.*

*Fionola is in my arms, gazing at me with an expression that is both softness and simmering heat. One slender hand is held within mine, and my other arm is wrapped around her waist as I swish her around the ballroom in time with the music.*

*No one else matters. Nothing else matters.*

*My chest swells and my heart feels like it will explode with what her face reveals to me. Women flutter past in gowns of brightly colored silk, trying to catch my eye. Fae men are the latest novelty for a lady's lover, but I hardly see them.*

*I only register her.*

*The scent of lavender rising from her glossy hair. The feel of her small breasts pressed up against my chest and the softness of her hip as my hand drifts down her curves ever so slightly.*

*The next instant flickers, and I am surrounded by my two closest friends. Worry creases their faces.*

*"You can't get attached to a human woman, Elrond!" Frode's voice pitches high. "Take a lover, take ten for all I care, but do not fall in love with one of them. Do you know what kind of life you will have?"*

*"I am well aware of the sacrifices I will make for Fionola," I half growl.*

*"At least bring her back to our realm. You will live out your full life and hers will have an extension," Fenix practically begs me.*

*I glance between the two men, their eyes glassy. We have been inseparable since we were children, surviving the orphanage together as boys and traveling to the ends of both realms as men, going where our business led us.*

*"There is nothing left for me in our realm. You know that." My words have both of them flinching as though I lashed out with a physical blow. "Don't look at me like that. You won't be wherever I choose to settle down either."*

*We stare at each other, knowing this is the end of the road, and it is a damned shame.*

*Flicker.*

*I hold the precious weight of my infant son in my arms, rocking him in soothing motions as his eyes roll back into his head and he surrenders to sleep. I savor the peaceful expression on his tiny face, then smile in wonderment at my wife, who created this perfect bundle. She sits at her desk, glancing over the estate's accounts, but her eyes flick over to us every so often and soften.*

*I teach both my adolescent sons to fight with a sword, and we move across the paved courtyard as they attack and I defend, taking on both at once. The clacking of our wooden swords echoes within the enclosed space, along with our grunts.*

*My oldest drops his sword and I tackle him, taking Everett to the floor in a way that ensures he doesn't bang his elbows or his head as I gently deposit him. Colman seizes the opportunity to leap onto my back, his bony arms and legs wrapping around me as I mock-roar. The three of us end up in a laughing, tangled mess on the ground.*

*On the far side, hovering under the portico, my boys' trainer crosses his arms and shakes his head at us without comment. There is a reason we hire a professional to teach them to fight.*

*My wife glances up from her position on the balcony, where she is deep in conversation with an ambassador from the royal court. For a fleeting moment her frown fades and a smile replaces it. Despite the scattering of white hair among the glossy black strands, she still looks exactly like that girl I married.*

*Flicker.*

*I spin Fionola around that same ballroom we fell in love in, and hold her just as closely. Her brilliant smile increases the lines around her eyes and her hair is completely white, but she is still the most beautiful woman I have ever met, right down to her soul.*

*How could anyone ever compare to the mother of my sons? The woman who gave me love and this enriched life I never expected? When the song ends, I take her hand in mine and kiss it. I hardly notice the difference between them. The fact that mine is still smooth and youthful.*

*Flicker.*

*Tears run down my face without end as grief rolls through me. I place my hand on the cold surface of the gravestone set within my favorite garden, brushing away any dirt that has collected. I buried her here, in my favorite garden, beneath a fire-red willow tree from my homeland. Months have passed, but it feels like I lost her yesterday.*

*We had fifty years together. It wasn't enough. Nothing would ever be enough.*

*Everett finds me, places an arm around my shoulders and leads me away. When I look at him, I see the thinning of his hair and the crow's feet at his eyes, and I feel like I will break all over again.*

*Flicker.*

*My boyhood friends arrive on one of their regular visits and I laugh and hug both of them. Frode and Fenix appear as young and beautiful as the day I left their side, but I have white streaked through the braids that hang over my shoulder. Still neither has taken a wife and had children, and I think they never will. They look happy and their business has reached heights of success we never anticipated.*

*"It is never too late to rejoin us, Elrond. To become a business partner again." There is such hope on Fenix's face.*

*I smile. How could I leave my sons? My grandchildren? Our estate is my home, my life's work and my legacy.*

*After my friends leave and I am filled with the simple joy of bouncing my eighth grandchild on my knee, I know I could never regret this path. The happiness it has brought me greatly outweighs the sorrow. My adult sons still need me, and constantly seek out my advice on how to navigate this life.*

*Flicker.*

*Everett and Colman look as old and frail as I do. My greatest fear is that I won't go into the dark before my sons. All I can count on is the fact that I was no young man when I married Fionola, and that their strong fae blood has greatly extended their lives.*

*My great-granddaughter breaks my reverie as she slips into my room with a bowl of steaming hot soup. Shea feeds me as she talks about balls and suitors and the latest fashions. She looks so much like my late wife. The words slip over me and away, but I nod anyway, basking in the warmth of her presence and joy.*

*My friends visit one last time, now in their middle years, and I know they look upon me with pity. My life may have been cut short, being spent almost entirely disconnected from the raw power of my realm, but it was rich with love and experience.*

*Fionola gave me everything I ever needed.*

The power of the Living Memory Scroll ends abruptly. I jolt back into my body with tears running down my face, and grief for that beautiful life that came to its completion so long ago. I take steadying breaths and firmly remind myself that I am Keira, not Elrond.

He was my ancestor, and he left his personal journal for those who came after him. A wave of sickening disgust rolls through me that his story was not only forgotten by my family line, but utterly twisted.

I was raised to believe a cruel fae overlord once ruled my territory and stole human lands for himself. The truth couldn't have been further from that. The crimes we believed of the fae were not systemic, and that makes a difference.

I collect another Living Memory Scroll and place my hands over it. I slide straight into another person's consciousness.

*This body is smaller than mine, a human woman, but within it I brim with earthly power. The brown robes of my druid's coat swish around me as I stand on a hilltop, viewing the market sprawled out below. It is in the sand-*

hills to the north of the kingdom; a three-day walk from even the closest village. Despite its remoteness at the edge of the barrens, there are half a dozen buyers lined up.

This meat market is enough to churn my stomach and raise bile within my throat.

Both high and low fae are held in cages of iron that are exposed to the harsh sun and the sand devils that kick up and pelt their near-naked forms. Most are huddled up, their bony limbs wrapped around their middles, dirty and sunburnt.

Right before the prisoners' eyes, fae are plucked out of cages and butchered for meat, their screams and whimpers turning my blood cold. The buyers walk straight up to those live prisoners and select which piece of fresh meat they want, sometimes only purchasing a limb and leaving the maimed fae to live.

There are market stalls all around them, selling cured meat strips, bones, viscera and pelts. The fear and agony of the fae here is palpable, with wails and moans ringing out alongside the rough voice running an auction at the far side.

My stomach rolls at what I witness, and I vomit straight into the sand.

I spent months searching for this information and weeks traveling here. This realm may be the one I descend from, but it is not my home. I am ashamed of these people. My King of the Summer Court sent me on this mission to get proof of the humans' black market trade and bring it straight to the human king to help with the petition to stop these crimes against fae. And so I left my druid city of the fae realm.

Below, a caravan of multiple wagons arrives. A dozen knights spew from them and form two rows. They all wear the royal colors and crest. My heart seizes as the king himself and one of his princes step out of a carriage and walk along the aisles of the market. They are offered sizzling fae meat on skewers and eat it as they browse.

It is commonly believed here that magic-imbued meat is at its strongest when eaten fresh, and the king is clearly taking no chances. He has no magic of his own, but I suspect that is about to change. I watch from my perch with disgust as his retainers purchase large quantities of fae meat and load it into the wagons.

*There will be no help from the humans against trafficking of their fae citizens.*

*Horror at the realization washes over me. It is time that I get down there and see what I was sent here to report on.*

*I take wobbly steps down from the sand dune, slipping and sliding until I pull myself together and steel my nerves. I walk down the packed sand streets of the market, the blood pumping so loudly within my ears I can hardly hear the vendors calling out to me. Not one of them suspects I am anything other than a customer, because it is almost impossible to find this place without the right contacts.*

*The tang of blood is so strong it fills my nose. I can taste the bitter, metallic residue of it.*

*I pass cages of weeping fae broken down to little more than animals. It shatters my heart as they scurry away from me as I pass, as though I am yet another abuser. I want to yell out to them that I am trying to save them, their kind. I want to wrap my arms around them until they feel safe again. To clean the blood and grime from their skin and feed them, but my hands are tied.*

*All I can do is witness and witness and witness, so I can document these memories as evidence. It doesn't matter that my passive actions cleave my soul in two. That I have lost all faith in my own race.*

*When I reach the pavilion at the end of the market and duck my head between the folds of silk, I am greeted with the image of the king and prince seated before a banquet of various kinds of grilled meats. There is more food before them than either can eat and so much of it will go to waste.*

*The monstrosity of it all is too much. The sheer cruelty. My head spins with revulsion and it takes all of my willpower not to vomit again. A dagger twists and twists in my chest.*

*I turn, rush down the aisles and leave.*

The memory ends and I drag a long, ragged breath into my tightening throat. I heave again and again, my entire chest shuddering, but I can't get enough air. My awareness is back in the wood-paneled study, but all I can see is that market and those caged, suffering fae.

A sob escapes my lips, then my cries come hard and fast until I hold my head in my hands.

Suddenly Aldrin is right before me, prying my arms down, his eyes level with mine and swirling with concern. He is all I see, and he kisses me hard on the lips, pulling my shocked body to his and lifting me from my seat in the embrace.

That warmth. His distinctive earthy scent. Those lips. It all brings me back to the moment. Aldrin gently deposits me back into my seat and drags over another chair, sitting right next to me. He stares into my face for a long moment, wiping away my tears with his thumb, then hovers his hand over the scroll to glimpse it.

He recoils as though it struck him.

"There should be a content warning on that one," he mutters.

"It was very emotional," I murmur. "I have seen others on the black market trade, but they were more distant, analytical."

Aldrin nods. "It depends on how affected the person who created the memory was."

"Have you thought of making a Living Memory Scroll on the evidence you have witnessed of the corruption and the rifts?" I ask.

"Yes, but it won't help my cause." Aldrin sighs. "The magic is complex and takes time. Remember, these scrolls are laden with the person's thoughts and opinions. Right now, my biases will probably be called into question. I have already been exiled once for broaching this issue and failing to make the people believe me. These scrolls are best for recording history from multiple perspectives."

I sit back in my chair, mind still reeling from the scrolls.

Aldrin's hand draws small circles on my thigh, winding higher and higher. "Care to have a private dinner with me?"

"Shouldn't you be dining with your courtiers?" I ask absent-mindedly.

He waves a hand. "I've been meeting with potential supporters all day. I *want* to have dinner with you. To spend every moment I can with you, because I don't know how long this will last." There is such vulnerability in his eyes, and it pains me to see it. "I want you to stay, Keira. Not just for another week or month. I want you to *stay.*"

A tear rolls down my face and he wipes it away. A pendulum swings in my mind, and I am flying between two potential futures.

"Is the idea that horrible?" The side of his mouth quirks up and I laugh, despite the second tear that leaves my eye.

"I have no place here, Aldrin. And I can't abandon my family, never see them again or tell them what became of me." The very idea tightens my throat, suffocating me.

Aldrin quickly straightens in his chair. "You'd be able to see your family as much as you want."

"What?" I gasp. The entire world seems to tip sideways.

"I can teach you to open the portals at will. You'll have enough power if you can break through your block. Most high fae can do it. We have a gate to the Appleshield Protectorate just outside this city." He runs a hand through his hair. "I'm sorry. I never realized this was a conflict for you."

"I thought it was a crime to open a portal?"

He raises his eyebrows. "It's a crime for a *fae* to open a portal. No one stops humans from returning to their realm. The druids do it whenever the worlds align, but with your power, you won't have to wait."

My stomach launches at the idea, and hope flares then dies within me. "But you don't know how to break my block yet?"

"We can work it out. But these things take time and practice." A slow smile fills Aldrin's face as he leans in toward me. "You'll have to tell your family a story other than that you are having a love affair with a fae."

"Love affair?" My voice rises high with indignation.

"Do you want it to be more than that, Keira?" He leans so close, peering into my eyes, then brushes a kiss to my lips. "Because you already clutch my heart in your fist."

A ripple of pure joy runs through my body. It is paired with terror. I want to tell him I am falling for him. That a life without him would be like losing part of my soul. The moment he walks out of a room, he takes a part of me with him, and all the warmth and light and joy leaves.

But something holds me back.

I am a woman who usually lets every single person into her heart, and to hell with the consequences or the vulnerability to hurt it gives me, but this man—if I open myself to him, he will take everything that I am and give his everything in return. If we cross that bridge between us, there will be no going back, because our two consciousnesses will collide and fuse and there will be no me or him anymore, only us.

"But what place could I possibly have here?" I whisper.

"Oh, I don't know." He gives me a sly smile. "What place do you want here? I don't know if you've heard, but there's going to be a great social change in this court. Why not start it in my palace? Why not start with us?"

I am completely speechless.

"I brought a Living Memory Scroll for you to consider. Food for thought." He points to it on the table, then gets up and moves to the door before turning back to me. "I'll see you at dinner." An incredibly smug expression fills his face as he strides from the room.

My stomach tumbles as I touch the scroll with trepidation. Immediately, I merge with the memory.

*I run through a meadow of swishing grass that is soft beneath my bare feet. Spring blooms throw the scent of pollen into the air. I am in the body of a young human woman. Iona. Her name is Iona. Tree nymphs run alongside me, laughing. My friends.*

*A scream pierces the air, then another, turning my blood to ice. I creep back through the woods, toward that woman's wail. My friends try to tug me back to safety, but I push forward.*

*An old moonstone portal glows vibrantly. I crouch behind a bush and watch two high fae men drag a woman each from the swirling mists, snatched from the human realm. The women kick and fight to no avail. They plead to go back. To be set free. One man tosses a girl over his shoulder and the other carries his prize around the waist.*

*The opening of portals is strictly forbidden, but there have been rumors of fae traveling through them to kidnap a human consort.*

*"What do we do?" Saga whispers to me, tears running down the bark of her face.*

*I shake my head. "We follow them. Find out which village those high fae are from, then tell the druid elders."*

*Something fractures deep in my soul as we watch the abuse of those women from a distance: being pulled by their hair, tossed to the ground and finally tugged into a cellar beneath a great tree, where they will be broken into good little wives.*

*Scenes flicker by so quickly my head spins.*

*The mad dash through the trees back to the druid city. Standing before the Council of the Elders as they argue back and forth about how something must be done, but theirs is the power of healing and nurturing the earth, not of battle. A decision is made to petition the king, and my father volunteers to travel to the City of Vertical Gardens with me.*

*Flicker.*

*My breath catches as we walk down the center of the great hall of the palace. I have never seen such opulence. The floor is an elaborate mosaic of marble, depicting flowers and the low fae of the Spring Court. The walls are gilded and great velvet curtains hang over immense, arching leadlight windows.*

*But it is the sight of the king that sets my stomach tumbling. He is seated upon his throne on a dais, his bright emerald eyes glittering against the tan of his skin. I have never seen such a beautiful man.*

*His petition hall is almost empty, except for a few guards and the king's adviser. We had expected him to make us wait for the formal session in a few days' time, but as soon as we told our story to one of his stewards, he saw us immediately.*

*"King Jarrah of the Spring Court, I present to you the druid Belemor and the acolyte Iona." We are announced and we bow deeply before him.*

*King Jarrah steps down from the dais and stands before us. "No need for formalities. Speak to me. Has there been a violation of the portal treaty with the humans?" His gaze dashes between mine and my father's.*

*I tell him my story. Every last painful detail of what I witnessed. He doesn't interrupt me or turn to my father for confirmation. When I am done, he simply nods and beckons the captain of his guard over.*

*"Take a task force and investigate these allegations immediately," King Jarrah commands.*

*The soldier turns on his heel and leaves.*

*"I would like to thank you for informing me about this nasty affair. Such*

violent practices cannot go unpunished." The king's eyes dance as they hold mine. "I would like to invite you to stay at the palace for a while." He spares a glance at my father. "I get so very few chances to meet my citizens from the druid city and I would like to get to know you a little better."

My head spins as he holds my hand in his. "I would like that," I say a little breathlessly. My father speaks, but I cannot hear him over the rush of my blood.

Flicker.

The mild breeze flicks up the curls of my hair as we walk through rose gardens under the light of the moon, my arm tucked into the crook of Jarrah's. It has become a ritual of ours over the recent weeks. He smiles as he gazes down into my face and it feels like we are the only people in the world, despite the guards who trail behind us.

Music flows out of the ballroom of the palace, along with voices laughing and talking. My king throws these balls because I like to dance. Because I cannot get enough of the feel of his arms around my waist and his body pressed so close to mine. It feels like home.

We find the center of the gardens, where a grand fountain gurgles, and Jarrah seats me on a bench before it, then kneels in front of me. He takes both my hands in his, kissing each one lightly, and my head spins.

He looks up at me, burning with passion. "Iona, will you do me the honor of becoming my wife? My queen?"

I stare at him in shock. "Why me?" I whisper, but my heart swells with love for him.

He takes my chin in his hand gently. "Nobody makes me feel alive like you do. None have your sheer capacity for empathy. You put your life on hold to find justice for two women you do not know. And quite frankly, I am in love with you."

"But I am human," I say. "Will the fae accept me as their queen?"

"They will," Jarrah says with certainty. "I will make sure of it and will tolerate no less. When the portals were open and the human and fae realms coexisted as one, it was not a rarity for kings and nobility to have a human spouse."

I throw myself into his arms, and he grunts with surprise at the suddenness of my movement, then wraps his embrace around me.

"You haven't answered my question, Iona."

"Of course I will marry you," I murmur into his ear, and his grip tightens on me as his lips find mine. I taste salt on my tongue, and I don't know if it's from his tears or mine, or both.

Flicker.

I stand beside my husband and king on the palace balcony overlooking the parade of our people, chanting both our names. The crown no longer sits heavily on my head, and the rigid straightness of my back, shoulders and raised chin is now natural to me. Jarrah sends me a look of absolute adoration, then squeezes my hand.

It took us years to get here, and many political battles for me to be accepted completely, but this court isn't composed of only high fae. These lands are for low fae and humans as well, and I have become their champion.

I grip the shoulder of our young daughter, just tall enough to look over the railing. There will be no barriers left for her to fight against, because Jarrah and I will have conquered them all by the time she is grown.

I blink rapidly as the memories slide away from me.

My hand shakes violently as I remove them from the scroll.

What is Aldrin trying to tell me by showing me this Living Memory Scroll? Surely it cannot be...

For the first time in my life, I have no idea which path to take. Remaining here would be a huge leap of faith. That old fear curls within at the thought of my kingdom burning to the ground without me.

# CHAPTER 31

# KEIRA

Aldrin's breaths are long and even, deep in sleep beside me. His entire golden chest is exposed to the waist, with a light sheet draped over his hips. I examine the way the moonlight plays across the sharp angles of his face and trace the peaked tips of his ears with a finger.

He looks so peaceful in sleep.

So incredibly vulnerable.

Gone are the quick flash of expressions and the brooding frowns that often pinch his brow.

I finger the beads of my moonstone bracelet. They hardly glow, even in this dim light.

Aldrin tried so hard during our dinner to tell me how he feels, but I couldn't hear it and he is still so guarded. We were destined to fail from the start. I feel like the last grains of sand are slipping through my fingers and I have run out of time.

I made love to him tonight like it would be the last time I touched him, and it probably will be. A blade twists and twists again in my chest as I grieve him while he is right here, in my arms. As Aldrin drifted off to sleep, my mind stayed completely alert to savor every last moment.

It all comes down to a choice between the fae realm or my realm. Between what is best for me and what is best for my people, and I have never, ever put myself first. I attribute no value to my own happiness when being selfish could result in the ruination of my kingdom. It is as simple as that.

Half the night disappears as my mind runs around in circles, looking for some loophole or way out.

I finally get up and make my way to the bathroom. I splash cold water onto my face and stare at myself in the mirror for a long time. Until I decide to make the most of right now. That is all we have.

I want to wake Aldrin and feel his powerful arms wrap around me and pull me into his chest. Kiss and touch and lick his body to see how quickly he hardens for me.

I open the bathroom door and freeze in shock.

A man in a deep indigo robe stands over Aldrin's sleeping form, grasping the hilt of a longsword in two hands, preparing to drive it through Aldrin's chest. The blade shimmers and glitters with dim white light, imbued with magic. Shadows curl out from the tall figure, moving as though they are a part of his robe.

Time slows down a crawl and every second lasts an hour.

Fear roars to life within me, squeezing my heart in an iron grip. It is swiftly followed by rage, detonating all magic I hold. It feels like my chest will explode. I scream Aldrin's name and the sound echoes off the walls like the call of a banshee.

The trunks of all the potted trees in the room shatter, and those shards elongate into a hundred crude arrows, flying as one at the assassin. I wield air to drive the projectiles to my target and give them deadly force to bury into the body of that robed figure.

An air shield immediately snaps in place around the assassin, but it is not enough. The assassin's blade whips away from Aldrin in a movement so fast and fluid it registers as a blur to my eyes, and cuts down the missiles that penetrated his defenses. Then he turns his gaze toward me, barely visible beneath his hood.

My blood freezes.

His face is hidden behind a black mask, but those slitted, ice-blue eyes glow with radiance. They are lined with thick bands of charcoal and his lips are jet-black.

The assassin immediately leaps into the air, base jumping in the way Aldrin tried to teach me. He moves at dizzying speed, dragging his sword upward in a long arc to bring it down on my head in a mighty swipe. I only have a heartbeat to react. I run and slide across the stone floor, gliding under the assassin.

His blade slices clean through the doorway where I had been standing. I take control of all that wooden framing, realizing it is somehow alive, and rupture a volley of sharp missiles right in his face. A shaft pierces his thigh and cuts pepper his face, but it is nowhere near enough to stop a fae.

He turns, his hood thrown back, scowling when he realizes I am not some helpless human. Then he flicks his wrist and I am lifted off the ground and smashed into the wall, like a rag doll caught in a gust of wind.

My head cracks. Jarring pain flashes through me. I try to scramble up, but I cannot control my limbs. Air wheezes in and out of me, and I just can't get enough. I get tangled in the curtains, but finally turn back to the assassin.

Aldrin's incoherent roar fills my ears.

My heart leaps as he rises from the bed, looking like a god of death. Thick horns erupt in a crown on top of his head. Black stripes of war paint decorate his face. His biceps ripple as he throws out his arms, then curls his hands and forearms back in.

The plaster walls explode around the assassin. The trees that are clearly the living bones of the palace erupt out of them and reach for the man. He leaps out of their whipping grasp and flies across the room. His two-handed sword slices clean through wood.

It is a game of cat and mouse.

I scramble out of the curtains, but there is nowhere to go. I would only be in Aldrin's way. Branches explode out of the roof, following the trajectory of the assassin as he charges Aldrin. They stab and miss him by an inch.

The assassin leaps over Aldrin and smashes a downward blow of that white, shimmering blade toward him. Aldrin catches it on an air shield held before his upraised arm. Sparks of starlight fly from the sword, illuminating the curve of Aldrin's shield. The assassin's entire body is poised in midair above him as he uses his weight behind the blow.

The move is a mistake. Remaining still for even a moment seals the assassin's fate.

Aldrin grins in the man's face with a flash of teeth, an expression that is both terrifying and feral.

A dozen waiting branches whip out from the walls and ceiling, tearing into the assassin and coiling around him. The man wields his sword to slice away at the branches, and I shatter one into splinters and send them right through that wrist.

With a sharp blast of air, I thrust the blade from his hand.

It clatters to the floor.

Aldrin wraps the assassin up in a coiled, woody cocoon, looping again and again until he has no hope of breaking free. He hangs in the center of the room, blood dripping onto the ground in a rhythmic splatter from his wounds.

I stare with horror at what we have done.

Aldrin rushes for me, his hands gripping my shoulders as his eyes skate over me. "Are you hurt?"

"I'm okay," I chew out. I don't tell him how my head spins and my legs are unsteady.

Aldrin turns to the assassin, keeping his distance. Fury ripples through every line of his tall, broad form. "Who hired you to kill me in my home? In my sleep?"

The assassin's face contorts into a sneer, his hands and feet twitching where they are free from the woody bindings. I take a step closer to Aldrin as fear flashes within me that he is readying for an attack with magic. Tendrils of shadow seem to whip and thrash around him, but they have no physical form.

It isn't until the skin on his face mottles with blue and froth escapes from his lips that I realize the assassin is dying. A few more moments, and he hangs limp in his bindings.

"Fuck," Aldrin spits, backing away from the body. "A suicide curse."

My whole body shakes uncontrollably and I let out a whimper. It is all I can do to stop myself from vomiting. I double over and grab hold of the side of the bed. I am not used to witnessing such violence, engaging in it, let alone watching a horrible, agonizing death. I have hunted animals, but I have never seen a person die before.

Aldrin is on me in a heartbeat, his arms wrapping around me and pulling me into his lap on the bed.

He looks over me frantically. "Are you hurt? Poisoned? Did the blade touch you?" His hands tremble as they hold me.

"No," I say, unable to look away from that dead body. "I thought he was going to kill you, Aldrin. I walked into the room and he had a sword held just above your heart." Hot tears run down my face.

Aldrin shakes his head. Those curling horns are still out and black marks slash across his cheekbones and forehead. Rage is in full force within his burning eyes and his lips are pressed into a thin line. This is how he looked when I first met him, more feral animal than fae man. It absolutely terrified me before.

Now, I find safety in the monster within him.

This man would rip apart the world to protect me.

"He would have killed you for being a mere inconvenience, like swatting a fly. For getting in his way and trying to stop him. I would have ripped him to pieces if he drew even a drop of your blood. I would have found who hired him and—"

"But he didn't," I say. "And I was more than an inconvenience. I held my own until you woke up."

My fingers stroke the war pattern across his face, and they disappear beneath my touch, as though I wiped them away. I caress those horns, tracing their path, like small, thin antlers. They feel so real, so solid, until they dissipate to ash and blow away. His fingers are completely black, ending in long claws.

Only the strongest of fae reveal their roots to their gods in a physical form.

Aldrin looks away from me. "I was foolish in thinking Titania would not stoop this low. She is insane to hire an Assassin of

Belladonna to kill me." Aldrin scoops me up into his arms and places me on the bed.

"An Assassin of Belladonna?" I ask as he pulls our prepacked bags out of a trunk.

"There are places in this world that don't belong to any of the courts. They live by their own laws. The Temple of Belladonna is said to be on a mountaintop between courts, but no one knows where. They breed and train the realm's most deadly assassins."

I glance at the dead, twisted body hanging from the ceiling and an icy shiver runs down my spine.

He was someone's son. Maybe a brother or a friend, too.

What makes someone give all that up, lose everything they once were, to become an assassin? To die for such a cause, instead of risking being made to talk?

A deep sadness fills me at the loss of such a soul, not in their death, but in a life lived like that.

"Do they work for commissions only?" I ask. "Or do they have their own political motivations?"

"It's not really known," Aldrin replies over his shoulder, tossing travel clothes at me. "Get ready to flee. We can't remain in the city. There will be more coming."

"But you defeated him easily." My hands tremble, but I do exactly as he says.

Aldrin pauses and turns to me, spreading out his arms. "Very few could take down a Belladonna Assassin, but I am the King of Spring, standing within the seat of my power. That is why he came in here on silent feet and tried to kill me in my sleep." He takes my hands and looks into my eyes, pure worship shining within them. "It would have worked, if you hadn't saved my life. Thank you."

I swallow. "You saved mine too."

Aldrin shakes his head. "You wouldn't have been at risk if it hadn't been for me."

This is what I will abandon him to. Plots and assassins in the night.

Aldrin shoulders his pack and tosses mine at me, then leads me out of the room.

I try and fail to ignore that dead assassin still hanging by branches within his rooms. "Are we going to leave the body there?"

"Yes. It's evidence of an assassination attempt and I am going to make sure the entire court hears about it," Aldrin grunts. "We have to gather the rest of our band. They could have set assassins on them too, but it's unlikely that—"

"Caitlin!" I yelp, spinning to him. "Would they have gone after Caitlin?"

Aldrin pushes me gently through the entrance hall. "No. She would not be on their list, but she is coming with us just in case."

A banging resounds loudly at the main entrance of Aldrin's apartment. It starts as a frantic knocking and rattling of the handles, then the entire door frame shakes as someone throws their shoulder against it. Aldrin pulls me behind him in a swift moment and a gust of wind rapidly whips around us as he readies his magic.

"Aldrin!" Silvan cries out. "By the gods, open the door!"

My chest is pressed against Aldrin's back, and I feel the tension release from him. The breeze around us drops, and the air before the doors shimmers as Aldrin removes his ward. Silvan barrels in with Drake at his side. Both men stare at us, then their gaze passes over our shoulders to the bedroom and the dead assassin within.

"Fuuuuck," Silvan breathes, stress tightening his shoulders.

The color drains from Drake's face. "I've never heard of someone fighting a Belladonna Assassin and living."

"Well, I've never taken one on before," Aldrin snaps.

"Why did you come racing here, Silvan? What news did you hear?" I ask gently.

Silvan jolts. "There are Belladonna Assassins in the city, though I guess you already know that. We were playing cards with the palace guards in the barracks and the call came in that Cyprien's estate has been set on fire.

"One of his own guards brought us the news. He pulled me aside to tell you to get out of the city. That they slaughtered your corrupted spriggan and would have killed Cyprien if he were home. They maimed a few of his guards to find out where he was." His gaze passes to the corpse again. "They will come for you again when they find out this one failed."

Drake practically bounces on his toes with the need to get moving. "Cyprien left a message for us to meet him outside of the God's Gate."

"We leave now," Aldrin barks, leading me by the elbow. "Wake up our people and grab the emergency bags you already have packed. Leave everything else so it takes them time to realize we are gone. We knew this was a possibility."

I stare at him. *I didn't know this was a possibility.*

It takes time to gather our people. Caitlin pulls a knife to my throat as I shake her awake. Her movements are fast and sharp with years of training, and the anger that pinches her features turns to wide-eyed horror as she realizes it is me hovering over her. She dresses quickly as I grab her bag. The rest of Aldrin's guard meet us in the corridor.

The city is a different place in the early hours of the morning.

The shadows are long and nothing lights our path except the twin moons and the lady-of-the-night blooms, which have their white petals fully open and spheres of light at their core. In the darkness, it appears they colonize every surface of the buildings, breaking some of the inky darkness.

I see phantoms in every corner. Assassins that don't exist base jumping across the blackness in the corner of my eye. It doesn't help when Aldrin tells me they specialize in magics of shadows and light.

Fear rolls hard through me, making my whole body shiver. I clutch Caitlin's fingers like it would stop me from losing her and Aldrin pushes my lower back from behind.

Our party of twelve makes our slow descent through the streets from the palace at the city's apex. Both Silvan and Zinnia sprint to corners under the cover of their invisibility wards, then signal us to follow when it safe.

Acrid smoke curls into my nostrils. Up here the view is clear over the roofs of shops and between apartments, to Cyprien's walled estate on a not-too-distant rise of clustered buildings.

We pause within the shadows and gape at the travesty.

Plumes of dark ash are almost hidden against the indigo of the night sky, but the heavens around the inferno glow with yellow light. Within it, tongues of orange flames still flicker and dance and rage. They are subdued, but the intensity of blaze hints that the fire spread before it could be extinguished. The buildings themselves are black silhouettes on that backdrop.

I hold out a hand and tiny flecks of white ash land upon it like a dusting of snow. The bitter taste of it sits on my tongue.

The calls of those fighting the fire ring out, carried this far in the otherwise still night. Their intensity is suddenly amplified and descends into shouts and screams as a small building collapses in on itself, followed by a loud clap and rumble.

"I cannot believe even Titania would be this ruthless." Aldrin's voice trembles with rage. "That she would risk this whole city burning to the ground to silence Cyprien and myself. I greatly underestimated her."

"Desperate people can do unimaginable horrors, especially a tyrant who has their power threatened," Caitlin says from my side. "We cannot stay here."

"She knows you care about all your people and she sees it as a weakness to exploit," Silvan half growls.

We throw ourselves into our mad flight through the city, dashing down staircases, cutting across platforms and over bridges that take us from one tall cluster of skyscraping buildings to the next. We traverse the city both horizontally and vertically, until we reach a region of low-lying superstructures that appear to be a series of temples.

The stacked triangular roofs are constructed purely from polished moonstone, gleaming under the light of the moon and illuminating the streets. The stone walls are almost completely covered in thick brambles.

The pathway downward passes under great arches of white marble, with vines and closed blooms entwined around them. Large bells hang from each arch, their chains hanging so low I could easily reach up and grab them.

Soft chanting drifts across the air, rising in volume and fever, then dropping to almost a whisper, but never ceasing.

A chill runs down my spine. "What is this place?" I ask Aldrin.

"The Temple Sanctum. Anyone may come here looking for peace and will receive protection. Hopefully, we can pass through to the God's Gate unmolested."

My heart hammers painfully. Apprehension builds to an almost unbearable point as we creep down the staircases that circle around and around the main temple, and into thick shadows below.

The inky blackness of the few recesses seems to have a life of its own. Moving tendrils expand and sway until they engulf entire regions of the platforms between buildings and beneath overhanging roofs. My eyes dart between them. It doesn't make sense.

I suck in a sharp breath as a figure leaps through the void between buildings. Their feet bounce off hardened pockets of air and their dark robes fly out behind them. They are almost impossible to see.

"Assassin!" My hoarse voice is just above a whisper, but a ripple of alertness runs through the soldiers around me.

A silver line flashes through the air, moving so fast I can hardly track it. The blade lodges within the air right before my eyes, making a thwacking sound as though it hit wood. An air shield, thrown up by Aldrin. The throwing knife glitters as brightly as the sword that was held over Aldrin's chest.

"Shields up and run for the temple's entrance!" Aldrin roars as the knife falls to the ground. He grabs me around the waist and forces me to move. "I want you as far away from me as possible. You are not their target," he growls into my ear, and tosses me toward Drake's open arms.

Throwing blades fly toward us, peppering our shields. Each impact sends a violent jarring through my body. Even the fae grunt as their defenses are struck. Some knives shimmer like starlight and others crackle in bursts like lightning. It looks so much like my grandmother's magic that I share a panicked look with Caitlin. We could never guess which fae court her powers came from.

My head spins as we flee down spiraling staircases. Each time we run under one of those arches, Silvan leaps up at the front of our pack and rings the massive bell at its center. My head feels like it will shatter from the vibrations of their tolling.

By the time we arrive at the mouth of the temple, multiple bells sing out of sequence. The chanting voices cut off abruptly. Aldrin calls a halt on the huge balcony that wraps around the temple. Thousands of interwoven branches create the platform that could hold a hundred people and the surrounding railing. There must be a dozen ancient trees feeding branches into the structure.

The great doors of the temple slowly open, light spilling out from them.

Every fiber of my being screams at me to run. We are too exposed here, but I trust Aldrin's instincts.

I turn toward the temple's entrance, huddled by Caitlin's side. She grips my arm so tightly it hurts, like she is afraid that if she lets go, she will lose me again. Surely Aldrin intends for us to seek refuge within the temple. My legs almost give out when near fifty robed figures glide out of those doors and surround us completely.

# CHAPTER 32

# ALDRIN

I sigh a breath of relief as we are enveloped by the Worshipers of Peace. The assassins' blades of light still slam into our shields, and they must be mad, present in large numbers or truly desperate, if they are willing to awaken the temple precinct.

"We make our stand here," I growl.

The air hums and the hair on my arms prickles as the Worshipers of Peace thread their magic in layers upon our shields. We form a single dome that arches over all of us.

They don't ask a single question.

They don't care who we are or who our enemy is.

All the Worshipers of Peace see is that we are being attacked, and they will fight for our right to peace. Their temple gives refuge to any who ask for it, criminal or not.

The enemy's onslaught keeps cracking our shields, trying to find a way in, and it takes focus to keep building up this defense.

"We don't know how many of them there are," Silvan barks. "They could overwhelm even the worshipers."

"Can't exactly turn our backs and run," Klara says. "Not when their blades can weaken and penetrate our shields, and we cannot heal the poisons on their tips."

A chant rises from the Worshipers of Peace, now arranged in a full circle around us. The balcony beneath our feet groans and shudders as thick branches rise out of the railing encircling it, from the very platform itself, and a cage grows over us.

A strangled cry leaves Keira. I glance over my shoulder to make sure she is okay, then turn to the onslaught above us.

An assassin leaps through the air, base jumping toward a closing gap in the branches above me. His inky robes fly out behind him in tendrils, and shadows twist and twirl around him. He moves so fast, cloaked in darkness itself, it becomes incredibly difficult to track his movements.

I grab hold of brambles and pump my magic into them, whipping out the huge, woody arms toward the assassin. Trying to snare him in my trap. The assassin darts around and through it easily.

This is their strength, flying about in open spaces with such speed they are difficult to catch.

I throw those spiky branches at him again and again, recruiting more foliage until there are a dozen whipping cords for him to weave through. He lands on the canopy directly above me and slices the ward between us with his longsword, shattering it instantly. The assassin moves too fast for the Worshipers of Peace to close the gap in our wooden cage. For me to drop one thread of earth magic and create another.

The assassin throws a knife at my chest, readying another.

I pluck the first out of the air with a swiftly growing vine, which shrivels to dust immediately as its flesh is pierced. I don't have the space to wield my sword.

I throw a dagger at him, but the assassin is gone and back again, dodging the knife easily, getting ready to toss another of his own. I try to grab him with the dozens of brambles around him, but they shatter with a roaring intensity, and a sharp gust of air sends hundreds of spikes into his body.

Keira and Caitlin each hold an arm stretched out toward him, the echo of the weave still connecting a line of magic from them to the brambles. They pooled their power.

The assassin's body slides off the side of the cage and freefalls into the bowels of the city.

I take in a jagged breath. It all happened within a few heartbeats.

Keira's legs give out beneath her, and I catch her with an arm around the waist and lower her to the ground. Her eyes are glazed and distant, and her magic is completely spent.

Caitlin still sways on her feet and Klara helps to lower her.

My every instinct roars at me to keep Keira safe. To protect her behind my body, but I alone am the assassin's target and that would put her in the line of fire. Drake and Klara drag the sisters into the protective center of the circle and work on replenishing some of their reserves.

I face the battle once more. The woody cage around us is still intact, now a fine mesh with holes the size of my thumb. The air shield upon it is even finer, dotted with daggers.

A rain of white needles falls upon us, so thick I cannot see anything beyond it. The wards shatter the barbs of light at first, but then they begin to pierce the shield, their length sticking deeper and deeper into our defense. The walls become a pincushion.

"We cannot wait here." I pace.

"It is near impossible to fight hand-to-hand with an assassin and survive," Silvan growls back. "We cannot leave."

"Our forces are at a disadvantage here. I will rip apart the city if I move the bedrock or disturb the trees too much," I admit.

The robed Worshipers of Peace take up their chanting again, and as it reaches a crescendo, the wards shatter completely. A great whoosh of air propels the needle-embedded pieces away from us, impaling an assassin who had been lunging toward us. His body contorts as he is thrown backward into a building, then falls from these heights.

The rain momentarily pauses.

Twenty Worshipers of Peace step out of our fortifications, then fresh wards snap into place. They are near suicidal in their protection of peace. They draw long swords from their backs in unison, then leap into the air, riding growing branches under their control, toward three assassins.

Worshipers of Peace and assassins fly through the air around us, fighting and leaping off hardened air or vegetation. Sparks fly off swords as they clash. The screeching of metal on metal is almost deafening.

I bark orders at my people, some to focus on strengthening that shield, others to thrust away any blades of light and poison that arc toward us, and the rest to stay with me, trying to catch those agents of death in a grip of thorny brambles.

It is difficult to see the battle raging beyond that intermittent rain of deadly projectiles, but each time the assassins are completely engaged in combat with the Worshipers of Peace, the onslaught stops.

It tells me that there isn't another assassin lurking elsewhere, controlling those needles.

My attention zones in on three worshipers fighting a single assassin. I weave a spider web thin network of branches all around them. One worshiper swings their sword in a low, disemboweling swipe, sending the assassin staggering backward on steps of air to avoid it. Another takes a lunge at his hamstrings, but the assassin leaps upward, somersaulting in the air, right into my near-invisible network.

My power rushes into those brambles.

In seconds, they thicken tenfold, and razor-sharp thorns blast out in rapid growth along them. The assassin is torn apart in their tangle.

The rain of poisoned projectiles falling upon us lessens.

The blood rushes in my ears as I search for the other two assassins. A Worshiper for Peace falls from the air before my scanning gaze, their golden robe streaked with red, followed by another. The assassin who took them out only has two more warriors pairing with him.

I set up the same trap as before, and use a few thicker tendrils to block the assassin's attacks. To snag an ankle or wrist and pull open his defenses. I tug the assassin off balance for a single moment, and a worshiper cleaves him in half with a swing of her huge battle axe.

More Worshipers of Peace fall through the air, their limp bodies arching in their descent into the darkness and their robes fluttering around them. A constant stream of worshipers runs out of the temple to join our original protectors, and more slip out of our protections to join the battle.

The final assassin runs along the roof of our fortification, dropping bombs of light and raw energy in his wake. The entire balcony shakes with each blinding blast, and I am forced to half crouch to keep my footing. My ears ring with a high-pitched whine and a crack resounds around us.

The wards have been breached. I can feel the fissure in them, but I cannot see a damned thing. My entire vision is saturated with pure light. I blink and blink again.

Sight returns and that assassin is running straight for me. I take hold of the cage of branches around us and slam all those woody limbs straight into him, like a hammer striking an anvil. At the same moment, I wield hands of air to pluck my people right out of my way, placing them roughly back onto their feet. In a fraction of a second before the assassin's body crushes, he throws a thick blade of poisoned light.

Its fast trajectory flies straight for my chest.

Time slows to an impossible speed, each breath lasting a lifetime. I raise an arm, but I know the blade will pierce the plates in my armor and any shield I can throw up.

The assassin didn't try to save himself. Instead he poured all of his power into that final blow. A drop of that poison in my blood could slowly kill me.

I try to turn my chest away from the path of that blade rippling with lightning, but I am too slow.

The bulk of Drake's body flies in front of me, and the dagger pierces his right shoulder, tossing his weight straight into me. Drake crumples into my arms, his eyes rolling back into his head.

"No, no, no!" My heart squeezes so painfully I think it might burst. I fall to the ground and cradle him in my lap.

The scream that leaves Klara is blood-curdling. She is immediately upon us, her hands shaking as she touches Drake's face. "No! Gods, Drake, no!"

That shaft of light that was so solid and deadly a moment ago completely disintegrates, and thick blood gurgles out of the wound. I rip away the fabric to reveal flesh already turning black around the wound.

"Someone grab me the assassin's pouch!" Klara screams over her shoulder. "Grab me the damned pouch!" Droplets of water fall on Drake's face. Klara's tears. I run my hands through my hair. I have never felt more useless.

Caitlin rushes over with the pouch clutched in her hand and Klara rifles through it immediately. The rest of my people encircle us in a protective ring, weapons at the ready and scanning the air for more attacks. I frantically look for Keira, but she is safe. Standing among my warriors without a spot of blood on her.

"Does anyone see any more assassins?" I bark out.

The predawn seeps a silver glow across the sky and melts away the thick shadows.

"It is all clear," Silvan says.

Drake moans, and it ends in a gurgled sound. I whip my head back down to him, head and shoulders still cradled in my hands. There is so much blood coating his clothes, and his usually bronze skin has become pale. Klara pulls items out of the pouch, cursing as she goes and tossing things over her shoulder.

"There has to be an antidote in here," she mutters. "Surely they have one for themselves."

I feel utterly helpless, watching his life drain away from him as the poison inhibits his ability to heal.

Klara pulls out a vial and tears the stopper from it with her teeth. She pours the liquid of pure darkness into that deep wound, and Drake instantly bucks. His back arches, chest rising from the ground and legs kicking as though they are trying to find purchase.

"Hold him still!" Klara yells and I press him down by the waist and good shoulder.

She uses up all of that antidote on the wound. The blackness of the flesh recedes, but doesn't completely disappear. She crudely stitches the wound back together, pulling a needle and thread from her own belongings.

We each hold our hands over Drake in turns, feeding our healing powers and raw magic into him until we have almost nothing left, but it is like tossing water down a drain. The poison in the wound burns it up.

It is Caitlin who forces us to stop, placing a hand on Klara's shoulder. "There is no point burning through all your reserves now, when we still need to get him out of here."

Keira brings us bandages and tightly binds the wound. Drake's eyes are wide open, and he hisses through all of it, while I pour a concoction of alcohol spirits and a drug for the pain between his lips when he can take it.

The shakes in Klara's hands steady as he becomes more alert. "The assassin's antidote isn't designed for fae outside of their order," she says. "They ingest small amounts of their poisons every day to build their tolerance. This dose will only buy Drake time. We need to get him to the healing waters of the Living Waters Lagoon."

I nod, still on my knees, holding the man who saved my life.

Silvan and Hawthorne fashion a stretcher of wood from branches to carry him in. I rise to my feet and go straight to Keira, pulling her into a tight embrace and kissing the top of her head. Her frozen hands brush the back of my neck and her entire body shivers. She is in shock.

"Are you okay?" I murmur into her ear. "Were you hurt? Depleted?"

"I'm okay," she says, but looks like a slight breeze could knock her over.

My entire being screams to make her feel safe again, but the dangers of this night aren't over yet.

I whisper to her, "I promise I will make this up to you." Keira nods, then pulls away.

"We need to keep moving," I say to my people. "More assassins could arrive at any moment." I glance up at the sky and hope to whichever gods are listening that the Assassins of Belladonna stay true to their reputation and do not attack in the light of day.

I turn toward a leader among the Worshipers of Peace. "Can I request your protection to the God's Gate?"

The woman nods. "All who pass through the Temple Sanctum will have their peace protected." The others of her order murmur the exact same words, in many voices, male and female.

We jump at shadows, at any movement in the early morning, as we descend the many staircases and traverse platforms. There are few signs of life around us, except the odd scuttling of puka scaling the faces of buildings and the gurgling of streams ending in waterfalls. The sound of dozens of boots crashing upon wood and stone announces our position for blocks, but there is no helping it.

The God's Gate stands at the base of the temple precinct, a huge yawning mouth of ribbed gold, with dainty gates adorned with swirling patterns. Beyond is the view of an open plain reaching from the foot of the city to the wilds of the forest. The plain holds the tombstones of the dead, and many portals that once connected to the realms of the gods and the humans.

Dozens of figures erupt out of the nearest temple, blocking our path to the gate. I almost unleash the might of my wrath upon them, until Cyprien's grim form steps in front of us. The black braids of his hair shimmer in the early-morning sun, the golden beads within them flashing light.

I let out a long breath, then close the distance between us. I take the hand he extends toward me, but pull him into a hug instead. Cyprien stiffens, then pats me on the back.

"Are you okay?" I ask, holding him at arm's length by the shoulders.

"I have survived worse," he says in a dry tone. "You?"

"Likewise." I shake my head. "I was attacked in the palace, and then again while fleeing through the city. We fought them off, but I don't know how many more will come. And Drake has been poisoned."

Cyprien's eyes slide over to Drake, taking in his condition. His lips compress into a thin line. "The Assassins of Belladonna will not stop hunting you until you kill the person that hired them or you convince her to cancel the order. It will be incredibly difficult for you to do either in exile."

"I know." Every muscle in my body is taut with that knowledge. Cyprien opens his mouth to say more, but I cut him off. "I will not start a military coup or civil war within the city. Especially with little preparation. I will not kill Titania, not before I convince the people of her guilt."

Cyprien scratches his jaw. "I thought you would say as much. It means you cannot remain here. What is your next move?"

I raise an eyebrow at him. "The exact thing you were thinking when you suggested we meet at this gate." I turn from Cyprien and address our combined people. "We will go back to the Frozen River Fortress. It is defensible against the assassins. Titania will call off her order when it becomes widely known, or at least rumored, that she tried to kill me. I will hold court from there and make the people who come to me witness the rifts."

They stare at me for a long moment, then nod. They would follow me to the ends of this realm and into the voids themselves.

"It is going to be a hard journey, because we are going to run there the entire way." I search Cyprien's guards until I find the kelpies. "Kai, Freya and Iris, if you could take Keira, Caitlin and Drake." Kai gives me a curt nod. "When we reach the fortress, you continue on with Drake and Klara, and take him to the healing waters of the Living Waters Lagoon."

I help pull Drake onto Freya's back and tie him in place with ropes of vines. He groans in pain with each movement, and his breaths are shallow, but they are also regular. The wound has stopped bleeding, but it is still puckered and black tendrils slowly grow out from it.

I spend a stolen moment checking on Keira. Her sister has both arms wrapped around her shoulders and speaks to her in urgent whispers as she shakes uncontrollably. Her eyes have trouble focusing on me. I want to kiss away the fear in them.

"We'll get through this, I promise you. I will keep you safe," I say.

Caitlin steps back to give us space. Keira's hands roam all over my chest, as though she is still trying to convince herself that I am alive. "So much death, and for what, Aldrin? Why did those worshipers have to die? This wasn't their fight. And those assassins? Was it for money?" She pulls away from me. "They could have killed you, Aldrin, so easily while you slept. They could have killed us both. And I—" She throws a hand to her mouth. "Oh, gods, I killed two men tonight."

"You did what you needed to, Keira. Gods, you saved my life twice tonight. If you are keeping numbers, hold on to that one." I peer down into her eyes and run a finger over her lips. "I need you to be strong for me, Keira, can you do that? Kai will carry you, and we will be in the safety of the fortress before you know it."

She nods, still dazed. It kills me to lift her up onto the kelpie's back and watch her wrap her arms around his torso instead of mine.

With a swift thanks to the Worshipers of Peace, we leave the capital through the God's Gate. Jittery tremors run through my muscles, screaming to fight, to swing my sword, as cruel anticipation pounds through me. We race through the open field of portals beyond, half expecting an attack at any time. But it doesn't come.

I set a brutal pace through the forest, only taking short breaks for food, drink and rest. I use them to sit with Keira and hold her against my chest, her legs tangled with mine. She has never seen the brutality of a true battle, and all the fear and gore that comes with it. I pull back her hair while she vomits.

I hate that her innocence was broken on my account. That I couldn't protect her from witnessing such violent death. A battle is so very different from a hunt.

When night falls, we make camp within a Watchtower Tree and the nymphs stand as our guards while we try to catch some sleep. It is no use. We all jolt at shadows and more than one of us has night terrors, waking the rest.

To my surprise, Keira sleeps solidly, held tightly in my arms while I keep an unintentional vigil over her. When she wakes, she appears as tired and ragged as I feel, with deep grooves under her eyes.

She looks at me with such sadness, it breaks my heart and sets my blood to ice. I have lost her. I know it in the depths of my soul. Maybe I never had her, and I was a fool for trying to keep her.

I have nothing to offer Keira. No home. No safety. Definitely not a crown. I am a man on the run. What right do I have to love?

We reach the Frozen River Fortress the next day, right as the sun hovers over the horizon and dusk threatens.

I bark orders, and my people scramble to see my will done. This fort can be defended against the worst of odds. There are magic plinths installed throughout the site that need powering up. Their wards cast an immense, domed shield across the entire fortress, defending against aerial attack. The act will almost completely drain each of us, but Odiane will aid us.

People rush around me in a mad flurry, every one of them with their orders, but I only have eyes for Keira. Both sisters slide from the kelpies' backs so the low fae can continue on to the healing water with Drake.

I want to scoop Keira up into my arms, to hold her close and never let her go, but she turns and embraces the man half of Kai. An expression of shock passes over his features. His eyebrows shoot up and his arms hang limply for a few heartbeats before awkwardly wrapping around her, as though he isn't quite sure where to put them.

"Oh, Kai, thank you." Keira's voice is muffled. "Thank you for everything."

"Don't get emotional on me, human." He pats her hair.

Keira embraces Klara. "I am glad you were able to speak to your son again," she murmurs, then places a light kiss on Drake's forehead, receiving an unintelligible mumbled response from him. She looks at them all with such sorrow as they leave for the healing waters, like she will never see them again.

My entire chest tightens with pain as foreboding fills me. I have to force myself to be still when I only want to bundle her up in my arms, because I get the feeling she doesn't want my touch right now.

Keira finally turns to me. We are the only two left in the courtyard. She wraps her arms around her middle, as though she is trying to hold in the pieces of herself. Her eyes are hooded with shadows and a sad frown pinches her brow.

The sight of her pain cuts through me. "Come here, Keira." I reach for her. She steps back. "Speak to me. How can I fix this?"

She shakes her head.

"I'm sorry I put you in so much danger. That you are terrified. I will do better, I promise. I won't be blindsided again." My fingers brush strands of hair like spun gold and liquid rubies from her face.

Keira shudders in a breath. "I'm so sorry, Aldrin."

"Sorry?" I ask in confusion, taking a step closer. "You have nothing to be sorry about."

She pulls away from me. Tears form at the corners of her eyes. "I want you to take me back to the portal. I am going home, Aldrin. Back to my realm. It is where I belong."

The world spins around me as reality itself seems to shudder. I knew this was coming, but I never believed it. My blood turns to ice. I cannot imagine a life without her in it. I don't want that life.

Cold sweat breaks all over my skin and a deep chill runs down my spine at the look of sheer determination in her eyes. That dagger in my heart twists and I could fall to my knees with the pain of it. My throat seems to close up, and the simple task of breathing is much too hard.

She was always going to leave me, but somewhere down the line I had hoped I was enough to make her stay.

I search her face, trying to spot the lie, needing to know that she doesn't really want to return. That she needs me as much as I need her. Tears run freely from her eyes, making tracks down her face and pooling into her hair, but she doesn't become the sobbing mess I fear I am seconds away from descending into.

Maybe she already cried all her tears.

"Take me back to the portal, Aldrin," she half whispers, and my heart absolutely shatters. "I am going home."

In my lifetime, I have been stabbed, burned, turned into a pincushion with arrows, but no physical wound has ever hurt this much.

# CHAPTER 33
# KEIRA

Aldrin stares at me, hurt rippling across his face and his body completely frozen. For the first time since I met him, he has no words. The light dies within his amber eyes and they turn stone cold as the blood drains from his face.

Bitter pressure builds and builds in my chest until I fear it will explode from raw grief. I cannot breathe around it. The sheer pain turns my limbs numb and makes my head spin. I am drowning in it.

I want to run to Aldrin; to kiss his lips and tell him I don't mean it. That I want to stay here with him, but I can't. If I give in even the slightest bit, I will collapse into his strong arms, and I won't have the strength to walk away.

"Surely you don't mean it." Aldrin's gaze tears away from me as though the sight burns him, but it is dragged straight back. "I want you to stay, Keira. I want you at my side. I—" His voice breaks. "I *need* you."

"We both knew this was coming, Aldrin," I whisper.

"Tell me what you need," he urges, "and I will give it to you. Just stay. Another week. Another month. Whatever you can give me. Don't leave now, not for fear that I can't protect you."

"Aldrin, it is ludicrous for me to become embroiled in your

civil war when my people need me. Can't you see that?" A sob escapes my lips. "I cannot help you get your throne back if I stay here. I won't be able to help restore magic to either realm. You said it yourself with that prophecy." I take in a deep breath, readying myself for the final blow. "I must become a queen in my realm and prepare the humans to make an alliance with the fae."

His beautiful features crumple at my brutality. I don't want to hurt him, but I need him to understand. "I don't care for your usefulness, Keira. You are more than your connections to me. Please tell me you are not going back for *him*."

My stomach drops and my veins turn to ice. "If it were a choice between men, I would always choose you, Aldrin, a million times over, but it is so much more than that." I shake my head. "I can't turn my back on my duty, my people and my family."

"I can't bear the thought of you with *him*. Of you being another man's queen. It would drive me to insanity." Aldrin runs a hand through his hair. "He doesn't treat you right. He doesn't worship you like I do."

I soak in every inch of his perfect face, committing it to memory. The lines of his razor-sharp cheekbones and squared jaw, his amber eyes beneath prominent, arching eyebrows. His perfectly straight nose and thin lips. I will never know a man this beautiful again.

Something within me breaks beyond repair.

It feels like it is another woman entirely who steps away from him. "I am leaving, Aldrin. You once told me you would never hold me against my will."

It is the final nail in the coffin, and Aldrin recoils as though he has been slapped.

A series of emotions rolls across his features, but they settle on utter defeat as the shadows within his eyes deepen. "If it is what you truly want, I will take you to the portal tomorrow morning. Finish up your business with Odiane tonight."

Aldrin turns and walks away from me. I watch until he disappears into the grand hall.

A numbness spreads from my chest, engulfing my every extremity, and I shiver uncontrollably.

"Are you okay?" That voice is gentle, and so familiar I almost crumble at the warmth and support in it.

I whip around to Caitlin. "How much of that did you hear?"

"All of it, to be honest," she says, unabashed. "I am your sister. If you need to fall apart, I have to be here to put you back together." A sob rolls out of me and Caitlin wraps an arm around my shoulders. "Are you sure this is what you want?"

I shrug her off me and stalk away angrily. "Don't ask me that! It's never been about what I want. Never."

She chases after me and grabs my arm, pulling me around to face her. "I'm not trying to upset you. I need to know if you are sure. There's no going back."

I run my hands across my face. "I don't want to talk about it right now. I want a distraction. Can we visit Odiane? Can we talk later?" Such desperation rolls through me that Caitlin nods.

None of this feels real. Not yet. Not while I can still reach out and touch him.

Caitlin leads me to the bridge arching over the frozen river, and down the steps to Odiane. The strangest calm falls over me in the presence of my overprotective older sister. It is as though she helps shoulder my burdens when she is near.

"Is it dangerous for us to be out here?" I suddenly feel selfish for not even thinking of her safety.

"I spoke with Cyprien," Caitlin says as she deposits me on the bench surrounded by waterfalls, then sits beside me. "This spot is protected by the wards and the assassins only fight at night."

I nod, lost in my own turmoil of thoughts. Caitlin puts an arm around my shoulder and pulls me into her side, leaning her head against the top of mine.

The surface of the river below is stained pink and orange as it reflects the sunset, white slabs of ice drifting lazily across it. Odiane steps out of the nearby waterfall, parting the gushing curtains. Her body is water made into flesh.

Many rivulets reach away from the cascading water to form her silhouette. Her hair ripples down her back in shards of ice and her gown is woven of thousands of snowflakes.

A radiant smile fills Odiane's face and her cheeks flush a deep shade of indigo. "My lovelies, you have returned to me. Already I hear my infant daughters sing of the most beautiful places."

I should be brimming with pride that we achieved such an impossible feat, but it all seems so unimportant.

Caitlin stands and approaches Odiane. "It was an honor to bring your daughters to their waters."

They speak for a while, and Caitlin retells the details of our journey to place the seed-stones in new waters. They smile as they talk. It all seems so foreign to me, so very far away. I linger a few steps behind them.

Odiane holds out the familiar shape of a seed sack, a circular bubble of water with a segmented coral net encasing it. Inside is a single seed-stone, oval in shape with a deep navy core and a transparent outer. I double take, moving closer to examine it. The center has three dense, circular masses within it, instead of the usual one.

Caitlin collects the seed sack from her. "Are these—"

"Triplets," the Lake Maiden chimes, her face brightening. "I thought long and hard on how I could gift you a seed-stone for your world without my daughters suffering from the lack of magic. Three Lake Maidens, sharing the same blood and waters, will bring magic to each other, and will starve off the loneliness until the portals open and we can hear their song."

I cannot speak for the lump that forms in my throat, and tears stream down my face. "Thank you," I finally manage.

Odiane looks at me for a long moment, not blinking once. "Young heart, it will not always hurt so. Time takes the edge off all pain, and the youth feel all their emotions tenfold."

I startle. Of course she heard my conversation with Aldrin.

Odiane turns back to Caitlin, holding out another seed sack. "And my gift of a pregnancy to you, fierce one. Our daughter will have the body of a human, but the soul of a Lake Maiden. Make sure she visits her sisters often. Both she and the triplets will find grounding by the bonds they share. Ensure her line takes care of the maidens that I have gifted upon your realm. If she is as brave as you, encourage her to take the pilgrimage to visit me."

"Thank you." Tears form at the corners of Caitlin's eyes. "A daughter is everything I have wanted, and I promise I will be the best mother I can be."

"I know. I have looked inside your heart." Odiane runs a hand down Caitlin's face, leaving a shimmering, wet trail. "Place the seed inside your womb before you leave this realm."

They exchange more words, but I struggle to focus on them, zoning in and out of reality. My mind all but shuts down to avoid the intensity of grief and heartbreak rolling through me.

I sway on my feet and struggle to pry my eyes open after every blink, and Caitlin turns to me with worry. Odiane is gone. I didn't even notice her burst into streams of water and return to the river.

My sister half carries me with her arm wrapped around my waist, leading me back up that winding staircase and through the streets of the fortress.

I don't look at her satchel that has both seed sacks in it. Every time my mind dares to acknowledge them, it skitters away from the thought.

There is a finality in this. Nothing holds me to this realm anymore. Not even Aldrin.

The fact utterly ruins me.

Caitlin should be ecstatic with the seed-stone in her possession, but instead, there is a deep frown of concern on her face. Every time she glances at me, her lips become downturned. I know Caitlin. Right now, her mind is whirling, trying to work out ways to fix this for me. To find the right thing to say that could give me a single moment of reprieve from this grief, but there isn't anything she can do.

Guilt flushes through me, so strong my knees almost buckle. I should be happy for her, but I am so sad for myself.

I return to my previous chambers and sleep fitfully. Caitlin offers to sleep next to me, but I want to be by myself.

I jolt awake with the coverings a tangled mess around me and sweat soaking my body. The twin moons are still prominent in the dark sky, but I cannot get back to sleep. A silvery glow filters in through the leadlight windows, casting a faint image of spring blooms across the floor in muted colors of green, yellow and red.

A deep, restless urge sends me out of my bed and I walk through the fortress. The assassins haven't found us yet, but there are guards on the lookout for them everywhere.

My feet take me along balconies and through streets. A protective ward domes over the entire site, leaping from plinth to plinth at the apex of the tallest buildings. The barrier shimmers and ripples in the dim light, clear to the naked eye.

I don't know how long I wander around in large circles, but as I make my way back to my room, the sun peeks over the horizon. I freeze within the shadow of a pillar across the courtyard from my chambers.

Aldrin is outside my door.

He knocks on it, then speaks my name. The sight of him waiting for me to open the door is like a dagger twisting in my heart. He knocks again, and stands in that doorway for a long time, his shoulders slowly dropping as hope fades from him. Aldrin walks a few paces away, stops and stares at the door again, shakes his head, then leaves.

A silent sob shudders through my chest. I hold a hand over my mouth and slide down the pillar to the ground.

What would I have done, if I were in my room when he knocked? Would I have lost all my resolve and let him in? I know the answer in the depths of my soul, and part of me wishes he had lured me back to him.

I get dressed, pack my few belongings and find Caitlin.

We enter the great hall together. The room is loud with voices crashing over each other as people sit and eat and talk. It turns completely silent as we step in. The heat hits me like a wall, from the roaring fireplaces and the dozens of bodies, but a chill runs down my spine.

Aldrin stands from the table he occupies with Cyprien and approaches me. "Do you want something to eat?" He is cold and brittle as he motions to the table with food set out.

I shake my head.

"Sit and talk with us a while," he almost pleads. "There is no rush."

"I would like to go to the portal now, Aldrin." I don't show the turmoil crashing through me.

He closes his eyes for a long moment, running his hands across them. "If that is what you wish."

"It is," I say.

Even Caitlin looks me with surprise at my coldness.

"Let me gather a band of guards." Aldrin turns from me, but I reach out and grab his arm, pulling him back. He looks down at my hand, then up at me.

"It is too dangerous for you to come," I say.

"I will have my last goodbye with you. The Assassins of Belladonna be damned." Anger flashes across his face, twisting his lips, but it cools rapidly. "Talk to me, Keira, tell me what you are thinking. Why is there this sudden urge for you to leave? If we can have one last private meal—"

"No, Aldrin." My voice breaks. "You promised me this. That you wouldn't hold me."

I don't tell him that if I don't leave right now, I will never be able to. If I let him in, I will lose myself.

Aldrin drags his eyes away from me and starts barking orders.

The small band amasses rapidly, and we leave the fortress in heavy silence. We make our way through the forest, the fresh chill of the morning seeping into my skin despite my cloak. Snow disappears; frost crunches under my boots, then thaws completely, the only sign of the miles we put between us and the border with Winter.

My fingers move across the beads of my moonstone bracelet in a nervous tic, and I glance at it multiple times to see its glow, ever so faint.

Aldrin walks beside me, a brooding presence of gloom. His fingers brush against my hand, but he doesn't take it in his. The man thinks I don't want to be touched by him. He has no idea how wrong he is.

"Was it me?" he asks in a low rumble. "Did I do or say something? Am I not enough?"

I turn to him, my lips parted in surprise. "You are perfect, Aldrin. You are everything."

"Then it is because you believe I cannot protect you." He searches my face. Deep shadows line beneath his eyes, evidence he didn't sleep last night.

"My time here was always only temporary. We both knew this." It is the bitterest truth.

The forest opens to the small clearing where I first saw Aldrin and the lone portal stands in its midst, seeping thin tendrils of mist. My hands shake at the sight and my throat closes up until I can hardly breathe.

Caitlin grabs me by the shoulders. "Are you sure? Are you ready?"

How could I ever be ready? But what I want doesn't really matter. I nod, because I can't speak.

My sister takes my hand as we near the portal. Its power pulls on me like a strong riptide. Light radiates through the milky depths of the moonstone, but they no longer rival the sparkle of diamonds. Their power flickers in bursts and I know it is seeping away.

The sweetest song beckons me from the depths of the portal, calling me home. Those mists swirl and tendrils of them reach out in response to our bracelets.

Aldrin's hand grasps my arm, fingers digging in ever so slightly. I whirl around to him. There is a softness on his face as he peers down at me, lifting my chin up to him with a finger. He stands so close that our bodies almost touch.

"I would have made you my queen, Keira. I would have loved you until my dying breath," he says, just above a whisper. Then he places both his hands on my face and kisses me, his lips soft and caressing. Warmth radiates through my chest at the touch, as my heart absolutely shatters. A saltiness tinges the kiss. My slow, silent tears.

I place my hands on Aldrin's chest, feeling the hard planes of it, then slowly pull away from him. I take a step backward, then another.

Caitlin's hand finds mine, but she doesn't hurry me.

I hold Aldrin's gaze as I back into the portal, his form becoming more and more shrouded by mist. He holds out an arm, reaching for me across worlds, but I am too far gone to take it. I focus every bit of my awareness on him, drinking in and committing to memory every line of his face.

Aldrin is the last thing I see as I leave his realm, just as he was the first when I entered it.

I stumble almost blindly through the thick, damp mists, allowing Caitlin to guide me. Physical pain rips through my chest. It sits within my stomach like a block of ice. I come to understand that there is a large part of me that will always regret this decision. A piece of me that will live with Aldrin. The best of my life is now behind me.

We step out into a cool, grassy meadow, with a ring of crude granite arches before us. At their center stands the tall tower in all its menacing glory, levels of arches reaching up to the jade plinth at its apex, which glows green with magic and powers the portals.

We stop at the mouth of the portal, both of us dazed.

I blink, then blink again.

It doesn't feel real, to be back here.

Everything is muted. The colors are less vibrant, the scattering of flowers and the earthy vegetation hold little fragrance, and that beam of magic, with threads woven into it from so many people, is pitiful compared to what I experienced. The power within my own veins is diminished, sluggish, weighed down like a limb suddenly turned to lead.

Calls ring out around us and the scurrying of boots follow them, but it all seems so distant.

"Hold back," a strong, familiar voice snaps. "Let me see them first."

Hands grip my shoulders painfully from behind. Caitlin is practically holding me up. Skirts swish and a lone figure dressed all in white, with hair to match, approaches us. I look into her wizened face and that frown, so similar to Caitlin's, dissolves into one of warmth.

I throw myself into my grandmother's arms. The high priestess' arms. She wraps them around me in a tight embrace, kissing my brow as though I am a small child again.

"Grandma, I did everything you told me not to do." I sob into her chest.

"Are you hurt, my child?" she asks gently. "Did a high fae harm you?"

"He—he was perfect, and returning here broke my heart," I choke out. "I—I—"

"Only time will heal that, I am afraid." My grandmother strokes my hair. "You are strong and brave for returning to us, *priestess* of the Mothers of Magic. You have made us all proud."

Those words should arouse something within me. It was once everything I wanted, but the agony within has scoured me and I can no longer feel anything else.

# CHAPTER 34

# KEIRA

I don't know how long I stay in my grandmother's arms, but she doesn't hurry me. If anyone understands, it is her. She fell in love with a fae as well.

My father materializes and practically pulls me from her, crushing me against his chest. Those thick arms wrapped around me make me feel so incredibly safe. "Do I need to fight my way through a portal and slice the flesh off whichever fae hurt you?" my father growls, his body practically shaking with rage.

"No, Father. There is no fae for you to hunt," I say.

He leans his cheek on the top of my head, and I take comfort from it.

When I finally pull myself together and scrub my tears away, I realize we have an audience.

There are pavilions set up in the meadow. Living quarters for the team who powered the portals so we could return, and any loved ones waiting for us.

Gwyneth runs to Caitlin and wraps her in an embrace, kissing her passionately. There is such bliss on her face, her eyes squeezed tight, that it is painful to look at.

Prince Finan strides across the grassy field toward me, the crowd parting around him.

My grandmother leans in to whisper in my ear. "Now is not the time for drastic decisions." Both she and my father pull away to give us a little privacy.

My blood turns to ice and I have to resist the urge to back away when Finan stops before me. A huge, cocky smile dimples his face and his ice-blue eyes light up as they roam over me, appraising my body. How have I never understood the way he looks at me, like a predator sizing up its prey?

I stand there, utterly shocked at facing him again, as unsteady as a leaf in the wind with my support drawn away.

Perfectly manicured ringlets of blue-black hair fall across his forehead, and I realize how pretty he is, in a young, girlish manner. He is at complete odds with the raw sexuality of Aldrin's masculinity. A boy compared to a man.

I wonder if I was ever truly attracted to Finan, or just the idea of him.

He sweeps me into a hug, pressing his narrow, bony body into me like he has every right, and peppers kisses across my face. My skin crawls like I am covered in insects, and the deepest need builds within me to thrust him away. He pecks my lips in that onslaught, but I don't give him anything more.

I stand there, limp.

"Keira. I am so happy you are back." Finan pulls away, his eyes level with mine. I forgot how short he is. "I waited for you, like I promised. You see, I have camped here for weeks, so I would be here when you returned. Can you imagine it? Me, camping?" His obnoxious laugh is like claws running down my spine.

Behind him, there is a massive royal pavilion in deep shades of purple, with servants teeming busily around it.

Finan folds my arm into his and leads me away. "Was it horrible?" he asks, without stopping to hear my answer. "I bet it was horrible."

My spirits sink to an even further low. This is what I came back for.

I am in a daze as I take the trek up to Lake Mistwater with the other priestesses. Nothing feels real, even as I place the Lake Maiden's seed-stone into the pool that is fed by springs that run from the Otherworld.

I should be immensely proud of this feat. Instead, my hands shake and a vise clenches my heart, winding tighter and tighter with utter agony.

Too many of the priestesses send sympathetic, understanding glances my way, and it makes me wonder how many beloved fae we have left behind collectively.

This final act means my pilgrimage is truly over.

There is nothing left holding me to Aldrin and his world.

~

I ride a white dappled mare on the journey to Appleshield Castle, and actually miss Kai's insane prancing and spurts of galloping. The pace is incredibly slow as we meander behind Finan's royal carriage.

Every time I look at the gilded thing of unnecessary opulence, my chest constricts and I fear I will suffocate.

He almost forced me to ride in it with him, but I insisted that I desperately wanted to experience the sights, sounds and scents of my home. That I longed for them. I didn't even feel guilty telling the lie.

The lands have changed with the passing of time. The spring blooming is well under way and transitioning into the summer. I have to remind myself that only a single month has passed here. It feels like a lifetime. Trees now boast a full canopy of leaves, with small, hard knots of fruit beginning to redden. Bulbs flourish across the fields, dotting them with color.

I once would have found beauty in this sight, but it is a mockery compared to the Spring Court of the fae.

We reach Appleshield Castle, my home, but the sight doesn't fill me with the relief and warmth I would have expected.

I stare at it, trying desperately to elicit an emotional response. It is like the blocky, golden towers and turrets that jut high above the immense wall suddenly mean nothing to me. Neither do the many watchtowers or the slanted roofs of red tiles that shimmer under the sunlight.

None of it screams home anymore.

Masses of the common people flank the road that winds up toward the castle, cheering our arrival and tossing petals onto our path. They must see two newly appointed priestesses, dressed in white gowns with crowns of jasmine and ivy, but I do not see them at all. My mind is completely blank, refusing the world around me.

I blink and find myself in the courtyard entrance of the castle, and an intimate group of my family and friends fills it. I am helped down from my mare and engulfed in my mother's embrace, then my father wraps his long arms around the both of us as they laugh.

In a heartbeat Diarmuid lifts me off the ground and squeezes me so tight I feel it in my ribs. My brother only lets me go so our baby sister Brianna can hug me.

I am like a limp rag doll, tossed from person to person, but it helps to melt the ice in my chest. Caitlin keeps shooting me worried glances as she talks intently with our father.

My focus drifts to my grandmother. She whispers with urgency in the ear of my mother, whose expression changes as she turns sharply to me, seeing what is before her. The grief on my face and the fact that I am struggling. My mother charges through the crowd, wraps her arm around my waist and pulls me away from all those bodies.

My bedroom is exactly as I left it. The chamber is too small and simple for the woman I have grown into.

I sleep for an entire day and night, and each time I open my eyes, either my mother or Caitlin is right there in the room with me. My father and grandmother visit multiple times, and they speak in hushed voices in the corner. Finan arrives at the door and demands to see me, and he is sent away with explanations of me needing time for recovery.

I know I can't melt down like this every time life throws me hardships. That I need to grow up and toughen up, but it is so hard to function when my brain shuts down. When my ears roar and my legs turn dangerously weak.

I have always been more prone to bouts of depression than other people. Maybe it's okay to be weak and soft and vulnerable. To feel my emotions so vividly, because it lends me great empathy.

This kingdom would be a better place if there were more people with compassion in it.

I wake to my grandmother sitting on the corner of my bed. "Sometimes, when pilgrims return to this world, they struggle to find grounding here. A piece of them still lingers in the Otherworld. I believe your heart stayed behind."

I swallow hard and nod.

"I say this from a place of love. You need to harden your heart, lock away your grief for later, and get back onto your feet. What you do next will set the course for the rest of your life. Do you understand me?" Her body is whipcord tight.

"Yes."

"Do you agree with me?"

I nod.

"Good. Because you need to decide if you are going to marry Finan, or if you are going to take on the full duties of a working priestess. You have options now, but the royal family won't wait for much longer." She places a hand on my knee through the blankets. "But first, child, tell me everything that happened. Do not leave out a single detail."

We talk for long, bitter hours, and it feels cathartic. For the first time, I hear more details of my grandmother's pilgrimage all those years ago.

Our stories are so similar, and so very different.

Aldrin never turned into the wrathful, possessive fae who tried to lock my grandmother away and stop her from returning home. Not even at the end, when I told him I was leaving. The thought starts my sobs anew.

When the shadows lengthen across my bedroom floor and bright beams of the afternoon sun burst through my window, I pull together my resolve, and find Finan.

He is in the drawing room, holding a chalice of wine lazily in one hand and reclining on a low couch, staring intently at the chess game before him. My brother sits opposite, moving a piece across the board. Finan lets out a laugh, dimples forming at his cheeks, as he grabs his queen and places it before Diarmuid's king.

"Checkmate!" Finan exclaims. "Again! I must be a natural at this game."

I carefully school my features as both men turn to me, Diarmuid raising an eyebrow and suppressing a smile. I know what he is doing. My brother is the strongest chess player in my family. Not even our father can beat him.

He is playing politics already, likely using the time spent at these games to worm his way into Finan's good graces. That will be his job when we marry.

The world spins around me and I feel like another woman moves my body. As though I am watching from the sidelines. Surely this can't be my reality.

Finan's face lights up as his gaze falls on me, and he leaps up from his seat and takes my hands. "Keira, you look stunning. They told me you were sick and I started to worry."

Behind Finan, Diarmuid catches my attention, pointing to himself, then the door, in a silent question. I nod and he makes his retreat.

"It took time to adjust. I got whiplash to my magic on the journey back, but I am far better now." The lies come easily to me.

Finan sits on the couch and pulls me into his lap, his hands wrapping around my hips. It takes all my willpower not to pry them away.

"I want you to marry me, Keira," he urges. "Be my queen. Let's go to the capital and have the ceremony immediately. I'm done waiting."

*Be my queen.* How those words make my chest ache and stomach turn. How they remind me of the man who has my heart. I push those feelings down until there is nothing but numbness to replace them.

"Yes, Finan, let's leave for the capital as soon as we can. We will marry when my family can join us there."

His lips pout. "I suppose you are right. There will be mutiny if we do not allow time for the lords to assemble for the royal wedding."

Finan's fingers start tracing circles on my hip, weaving their way through the layers of fabric to find my bare flesh. I shudder with revulsion, but he thinks it is for a very different reason, and leans in to kiss me. I place a finger on his lips, gently pushing his face away.

"We cannot do any of that. Not until we know if I am pregnant to the magic," I say.

His mouth hangs open. "Could it be possible?"

I give an alluring half-smile. "Anything could be possible, and I have been told that it is very fragile at the beginning. Any sort of excitement could make it miscarry. Besides, we won't know if I am pregnant to the magic or to you if we get too carried away."

It is a convenient lie my grandmother gave me to tell him, so I could have time to adjust to my duty. There is no chance I am pregnant.

His hand runs up my thigh and I cringe. "Does it matter how a baby is created? It will be mine either way."

"It matters to the baby," I say, taking his paws off me. "Imagine, a future monarch *and* a magical conception. The child would be celebrated across kingdoms."

A wide, satisfied smile fills Finan's face and he makes a show of lifting his hands from me and holding them up in the air. I almost feel guilty at the joy on his face. He pulls a ring from his pocket and slips it onto my finger. I don't even bother to look at it.

We are not alone for long before we are summoned to dinner.

It is a private affair, only my immediate family and Finan. I find it hard to eat, moving my food around my plate. Everything is bland compared to fae food. Boring without Drake's spices. Deep sadness rolls through me at the thought of him. I don't even know if he will live.

My parents entertain Finan with conversation, making him laugh with their stories, pretending that everything is okay. I am grateful for the fact, as I am utterly washed away by the tide of conversation, unable to follow it. Fatigue settles over me and dampens my mind.

When Finan announces our informal betrothal and fast plans for a wedding, the room turns deadly silent for a heartbeat, as all eyes fly to me.

I cannot bear the searching looks they give me. The pinch between my mother's eyebrows, or my father's flared nostrils. I give a curt nod and hold up the hand with the ring on it. That is all I can manage.

Finan has a huge grin on his face, glancing from person to person, awaiting his congratulations and not seeing what is right there before him. Immediately the room erupts in well wishes and celebration, and my father calls on a servant to bring his oldest bottle of wine.

I make my excuses to leave early, feigning that sickness again. Finan pats me on the shoulder, hardly breaking from conversation, and allows a servant to take me to my rooms. Aldrin would have dropped everything to make sure I made it to bed safely.

I don't sleep. I pace the room instead.

The hours tick by with my thoughts screaming and circling around inside my head. My chambers feel like a coffin, so I walk through the keep instead. I aim for the library, but somehow find myself at my father's study. Voices drift out from it and I stop to hear them.

"She is not in the right frame of mind to make this sort of decision. Keira all but broke it off with Finan before her pilgrimage," my mother hisses.

"Maybe she saw something on the other side that gave her clarity," my father replies.

"You need to do something, Edmund! To stop this. He should have asked you before putting a ring on her finger." Her voice has a shrill note.

"Asked me?" Fire builds in my father's tone. "I have been encouraging him for years to propose to Keira. And there is nothing I can do to stop this without causing royal offence. It needs to come from her."

The silence between them drags out for so long, I almost leave, until my father speaks again. "We set her up on this path when she was a child, Maeve. She has only ever wanted to marry the prince, except for when she heard King Willard's cruel words. We have to trust her now, and let her go on her chosen path."

"I know," Mother half sobs. "It is so hard to let go. She is still a child in my eyes. And for her to move so far away and be so vulnerable, it is terrifying."

"Diarmuid will be with her. They will take care of each other."

"I don't think she is marrying him for a great romance, but to be queen and make a difference to this kingdom. The fact that she will miss out on the kind of love we have breaks my heart," my mother chokes out.

I walk away, unable to handle their torment over my bleak future. A chill runs down my spine. I rarely witness any emotion in my mother.

The next morning, I am parceled up into the royal carriage, dressed in a puffy gown of silk and entwined in enough gems to befit a princess. It is a ludicrous way to dress for the road, but Finan expects nothing less.

The inside of the carriage is spacious, with two benches of cushioned seats facing each other and heavy drapes of purple velvet hanging open across the windows. A small table is built into the center.

Finan, Diarmuid and a lordling named Cormac play Lord's Cards. According to Finan, the game is more dignified than those played by commoners and guards, but the only difference I can see is the gold leaf lacquered onto each elaborately painted card.

I stare out the window, bored out of my mind and watching the scenery change, because card games are not becoming of a lady. Diarmuid keeps shooting me glances while he and Cormac entertain Finan. I know I am not doing my part. I should be fawning over Finan, trying to steal kisses at each stop and making sure he doesn't forget about how badly he wants me as his wife, even for a second.

I don't care.

I shouldn't have to play games and dance around in exhausting circles just to keep the interest of the man who will be my husband.

It takes almost a week of traveling to get to the capital, because the carriage can only travel at a snail's pace and must take the main highways.

A personal pavilion tent is set up for me each time we camp for the night, with its own antechamber, where I have Diarmuid sleep to protect me from nighttime visits. It's what would be expected of a lady's brother and chaperone.

The temperature increases the closer we get to Sunbright City, and I sweat in my heavy skirts in the confined space of the carriage. The deep humidity is foreign to me. Hard and heavy to breathe.

As Sunbright City comes into view, sprawling out across the horizon and ending at the mouth of a glittering bay, I prop both my hands on the window frame and stare out of it. A tall wall encircles the old parts of the city, interspersed with towers that have conical roofs of terracotta tiles.

Before it a shanty town spirals out, many of the haphazard buildings leaning against the wall and each other. The ground is of baked, cracked mud, scattered with rubbish. Dirty children run around in rags. The smell of sweat and sewage is incredibly strong.

Finan keeps talking, as though he notices none of this.

A crowd forms around our procession, watching with curiosity, but no one cheers or throws petals. Where would they even get flowers from here? There is no greenery.

We approach massive gates, and soldiers run out of the guardhouse as soon as they see us. They part the crowd waiting to enter the city with their clubs, so we can glide straight through.

I crane my neck to see a woman fall to the ground under their attack, instantly swallowed by the churning crowd. A man who tries to go to her defense is hauled away by guards. There are more blows made to those peasants even after we pass.

Horror fills me at the blatant cruelty. At the needlessness of that pain inflicted.

The carriage passes under another gate and horns blast above us to mark our presence. I jump at the sudden sound.

Finan laughs at me, placing a hand on my thigh. "Get used to it, sweetheart. They are going to trumpet our arrival at every checkpoint."

I place my hand on top of his and force a smile.

We enter the city proper, and the first thing I notice is that there is so much stone. Every inch of the ground is paved. The buildings are of tan-colored brick and the roofs fashioned in terracotta tiles. They are all of the same blocky shape and size, three stories high.

Pale travertine fountains gurgle at every corner, with water pouring from sculptures of people or animals, but these are the only artworks adorning this city.

The castle in the distance is sprawled out on a rise. I would have thought it grand, with its spires and turrets capped in terracotta, before I visited the fae realm.

It is in the same bland monochrome as the city, the high wall and a dozen guard towers setting it apart. Rather than reaching to heights like most castles, it spreads out across the hilltop like there is no shortage of land in Sunbright City.

It is merely an ugly mark on the earth compared to Aldrin's golden palace in the sky.

This entire city is dead and monotonous.

I didn't only fall in love with the King of the Spring Court; my heart was captured by his home as well.

This place, and its prince, could never compare.

# CHAPTER 35
# KEIRA

I suck in a sharp breath as I prick my finger on my sewing needle and a drop of crimson blood immediately wells up. I stick it in my mouth and ignore the snickers from two of the ladies-in-waiting, Fiona and Eliora.

The queen turns to me, looks at the messy embroidery in my hands and lets out an irritated huff of breath. Hers depicts a scenery of wildflowers, and mine—I don't even know what I was aiming for.

There are half a dozen of us in this suffocating room. The walls are painted white and decorated with purple borders and prints. Everything else matches: the couches we sit on, the tiny table loaded with pastries and tea, even the abundance of cushions scattered everywhere. I am so sick of seeing royal purple.

A knock sounds at the door, and a servant hurries to open it. The voice that drifts in releases the frustrated tension that has built within my shoulders all morning.

"I am here to escort my sister to her lessons." Diarmuid's words trail into the room.

The queen places down her embroidery, gets up from the couch with a graceful sweep of her skirts and walks to the door. "Which lesson is it today, Diarmuid?" Her tone is cold, as though her patience is stretched thin.

My brother constantly plans lessons for me, from anyone who will take me. Always to help me adjust to the royal court or to be closer to Finan. They are my escape and sanity.

"Harp lesson," Diarmuid says with a straight face. "His Highness Prince Finan has expressed an interest in having Keira play music for him."

Both Fiona and Eliora bristle, their spines snapping straight. The other two ladies-in-waiting become very interested in their needlework.

"Do you think you are the only one that Finan has taken to his bed?" Fiona hisses at me, low enough that the queen cannot hear. This is not first time she has thrown it in my face. "That he promised would be his queen?"

"Ever wondered what he was doing here in the capital, while you were in your backwater hovel? Or *who* he was doing?" Eliora cackles a most undignified laugh.

It should needle me. It should rip my heart in two. Not so long ago, the betrayal would have destroyed me.

But I don't care.

My only reaction is the sheer fatigue that rolls through me, because I have to put these women in their place. They cannot talk to me like this when I am their princess, or their queen.

I raise an eyebrow at them. "That's funny. I don't see a ring on either of your fingers. Just mine, then? Perhaps the promises he told you were lies to naive, overeager little girls, while he waited for his true bride to arrive."

They both recoil as though slapped.

"Maybe he'll keep his lovers after he is married," Fiona mutters, trying to claw any victory over me.

I exhale, glance at the queen to make sure she still cannot hear the exchange, then turn back to both women. "Envisioning yourself having his royal bastards, are you? I wonder what would happen to them upon the next ascension?"

I hate the woman I have to be to survive here.

Both Fiona and Eliora become absorbed in their embroidery again, but there is a faint smile on Nadia's face at their put-down.

The queen returns, laying out her skirts perfectly as she takes a seat on the couch, then combing her fingers through her blond hair. Her cool blue eyes capture mine. "Everyone out. I would have a private word with Keira." She doesn't even look at the other ladies as they scurry out.

I glance over at Diarmuid, still standing just inside the door, but he only raises his eyebrows and shrugs.

"I know what you are doing, Keira," Queen Andrea says. "You do not like to sit with the ladies and baronesses, to talk about silly little things while sewing cushions that do not matter, but this is how *we* hold court. A lord can be gently swayed by his wife, or have his temper calmed by her. It is important that we know them well and make sure their petty grievances are heard. That we have them in our pocket for when they are needed."

I shift uncomfortably in my seat. This is not why I agreed to marry Finan.

Queen Andrea pins me with her stare. "We may be grossly over-shadowed by the men in this family, true power may be out of our grasp, but it is our job to make sure all the little things run smoothly. You were over-indulged by Lord Appleshield. Led to believe your opinion matters as much as a man's. To think that he passed over a son, and made his daughter his heir purely because she was his oldest!" The queen laughs.

"This is your life now. You might think things are different between you and Finan. You might think that this won't happen to you when you become queen, but it will. I was once as strong-willed as you are. Finan is exactly like his father, and neither would tolerate it. I say this from a place of kindness: learn your place and learn it fast."

I gawk at the queen, absolutely dumbfounded. The blood drains from my face.

"You are dismissed for your harp lessons." She flicks her head toward the door.

I get up on unsteady feet and leave.

"Are you okay?" Diarmuid asks from behind me, as we move along a columned walkway that is open to a courtyard garden on one side.

"She voiced my worst fear," I say.

"Don't worry about the queen. She is old and bitter and gave up decades ago," he mutters back, but a frown creases his brow.

I give him a sidelong glance. Diarmuid's mousy brown hair is oiled and reaches his shoulders in the latest court fashion, and it is incredibly strange to see it in a semblance of neatness. To see any druid well put together. I guess he is trying to find his feet here.

There is a sheen of sweat on his face alongside the scattering of freckles. I wonder how he can handle wearing the brown druid's robe in this heat.

It is the attire of a court druid, tailored to fit like a long surcoat that wraps around his waist, but surely he could wear silk. Some druids, those of the wilds, wear little more than rough cotton rags for their robes and walk barefoot, even on the coldest of days.

We pass through bands of brilliant sunlight and shadow created by the columns, and each time the sunrays hit my skin, beads of sweat prickle across it. There is too much stone baking and no breeze at all in this city.

"I may have lied about the timing of your lesson." A sly smirk forms on Diarmuid's lips. "You have at least half an hour to get there. Where would you like to go? The library or the gardens?"

The thought of greenery runs a shiver down my spine. "Definitely the gardens. Take me down the route past Finan's sitting rooms, so maybe I will cross paths with him."

We get lost in talk of home as we travel through the portico passageways of the sprawling palace, until we hear someone yelling. I shoot a look at Diarmuid. I quickly realize that we are almost outside Finan's rooms, and the curses coming from within are shouted by the king.

Diarmuid pulls me into a shadowy alcove that leads to a disused servant's staircase, and we wait and listen.

"You stupid fool, Finan!" the king roars. "You brought home the wrong sister in your haste!"

"I will not be spoken to like that, Father." Finan's voice is hard.

"Do you know what this missive says? What my contact there has reported? Appleshield's oldest daughter is pregnant to the magic. Do you have any understanding of the benefit that would have had for our lineage? But instead you brought back the pretty one that sucks your cock."

I recoil sharply, but Diarmuid puts a reassuring hand on my shoulder. "It's no surprise to us that the king is an asshole. Don't let his words affect you."

"I don't care that Caitlin is pregnant to the magic," Finan growls back. "I love Keira, and she is the woman I will marry."

"We should get out of here," I whisper to Diarmuid, my heart sinking despite how Finan defends me. "I don't need to hear this."

"Agreed." Diarmuid pulls me away by the elbow.

My mind wanders as much as my feet as we stroll through the garden. I struggle to focus on the harp lesson afterward. It keeps whirling into the next day, when the king holds court to hear the petitions of the people.

The great hall is filled with royal subjects of all classes, waiting for King Willard to hear their grievances.

His throne of wrought gold and purple velvet is at the center of a white marble dais, raised multiple steps above the rest of the hall. To the king's right side, the queen sits in a smaller chair, their younger son Niall beside her. On the king's left sits Finan in a throne that almost matches the his father's. As Finan's betrothed, I sit on a stool at his side.

It is surreal to be on the dais with the royal family. To hold court with them, even though I cannot speak. My job is to be Finan's pretty accessory.

Restless people pack into the hall, commoners, merchants and lords alike. Each group is sorted depending on their station, with the poorest at the back.

A row of guards separates the people from the royal family and escorts each petitioner before the king when it is their time to speak. The king's many advisers are seated in neat rows just below the dais, with Diarmuid among them.

The white noise of hundreds of voices in constant chatter bounces off the stone walls. The only windows are high slits, so the temperature rises from all the body heat as the morning progresses. Despite the high ceilings, the space is suffocating.

I try not to cringe at the white banners draping from the ceiling and the arrangements of white flowers in great vases, a continued announcement of the coming royal wedding. It is strange that I think of it at a remove Not as *my* wedding.

Finan taps his fingers on the arm of his chair to the beat of a common tune, reclined to one side and eyes glazed, as a lord speaks of a land dispute. I try not to send him an incredulous look, but keeping such a tight rein on my features for so long is exhausting.

"I think I would like a walk through the gardens after this," Finan murmurs to me. "We could have a picnic and get the royal bard to play tunes for us." A smile passes across his face.

Even though no one else can hear us, the idea of talking about the mundane throughout these proceedings churns my stomach.

It is not only the disrespect to the people amassed.

It is the complete indifference Finan shows to running the kingdom.

A ruler must know the political currents of his land inside out, even if news of failed crops or hungry peasants bores him.

"I would love that." I force a lightness into my voice. "Is there always trouble at the border of Ethos and the Rice Plains?"

Finan actually waves a hand to dismiss the topic. "There is always something, somewhere. If you fancy, we could sneak out of the castle tonight and swim in the ocean...naked."

My skin crawls. I need to stop that visceral reaction to him. "You know I would love to, my prince, but your mother keeps such a close eye on me."

Finan grunts and returns to his tapping.

The procession of people continues, their stories and needs so vastly different. I am startled when the petitioning lords and wealthy merchants are replaced by commoners, and a woman dressed in rags with three children and a baby hanging off her kneels before the king.

She wears a scarf that hides her knotted hair, and her skin is streaked with grime. I have never seen anyone so low in the depths of poverty.

"I petition my queen, mother to mother. Our babes are dying. There is a fever in the city, but it only affects us poor, because we don't have enough food to feed the babes, or clean water to wash them. No coin for healers. As a mother, help us. Save our children," the woman sobs.

The blood drains from the queen's face. Her hands shake ever so slightly where they are placed on the armrests of her throne. It takes a long time for her to drag her gaze away from the peasant. The muscles of my shoulders are taut and my blood races as I stare at Queen Andrea with horror.

The queen goes to speak, once, twice, then stops herself and turns to the king. He has a withering gaze focused on her and raises his eyebrows.

"I will defer to the wisdom of my king on this and all matters," the queen finally says, then closes her eyes.

Something dies within me. The queen is utterly, utterly powerless, even on a matter the king would consider a small trifle.

"Do you not have access to fountains for clean water like the rest of the city?" the king immediately snaps.

The peasant woman bobs her head. "Not in the poor quarters. We must travel inside the wall for water, and it is a long trip with multiple children hugging my legs."

"But you *do* have access," the king points out.

One of the king's advisers stands from his bench. "If I might add, Your Grace, the crown distributes grain among the poor, but in times of sickness it would be prudent to give them vegetables too. An infant can die from poor nutrition alone. There is much our kitchens and the markets reject as inferior quality."

The queen gives the man the slightest nod of thanks, and the color returns to her features. I wonder if she sees this as one of her discreet wins, having a man speak for her on a whim, when she has probably put years of effort into nurturing a very unreliable alliance.

"We should send healers to investigate the situation and help where they can," Prince Niall says and his father turns a predator's glare on him. "A sickness like that can quickly spread through the city and affect all of us," Niall adjusts.

"Everyone seems to have something to say on this case. Very well." The king flicks his fingers at his guards, and the petitioner and her four children are led away. He sends a dark look to his wife, as though she could have somehow orchestrated the whole thing.

Queen Andrea's gaze follows the woman as she retreats through the parted crowd, an intensity within it. A queen should have the power to enact social change in her own city. Arrange regular food and healers for the poor. Have fountains built in their shanty town outside the city wall.

That desire burns in her, but the nervous tic of her hands shows she is a caged bird

That is what I will become.

Panic rears up within me like a beast clawing its way out, and I push it all the way down with my grief and heartache, to be pulled out and felt later.

I glance at Finan. He isn't even watching the proceedings. His mother could have used his support, and he was completely unaware. By the end of the long court session, I am absolutely fuming with him. A headache grows from grinding my teeth.

When the hall clears of petitioners and the king swaggers down the steps to speak with his advisers, I capture Diarmuid's eye and indicate for him to come to me with a flick of my head.

"You need to school your face," he murmurs. "You look like you are about to skewer a trespassing Cú Sídhe. Breathe."

"Ask Prince Niall to meet us in the library again tonight," I whisper back.

Diarmuid nods. "Don't forget to charm the prince. He looks thoroughly bored." I give him a dark look and he leans in to whisper in my ear. "Make sure I am the first person to know if you change your mind about him and we have to get the hell out of here." He squeezes my arm, then returns to the crowd of advisers.

The palace gardens calm me. We walk along paved tracks that are bordered with evergreen hedges, styled into swirling patterns and low mazes. Finan tucks my arm into the crook of his elbow and holds a frilly umbrella over us to protect our pale skin from darkening in the sun.

We cross a low bridge that spans over a man-made pond, walking until Finan finds a grassy spot that is suitable for our picnic. The servants quickly erect a small canvas pavilion over a blanket spread with delicacies.

I watch Finan as he talks, his enthusiasm lighting up his entire face. I laugh when I am expected to laugh and only speak flattery. He weaves stories of the self he wants to be, rather than exposing his truths. I try so hard to stop the bile from rising in my throat.

I miss Aldrin so damn much. Everything was real with him. He dares to care about the people of the Spring Court, not because it is his duty, but because he is full of compassion.

Those thoughts open up a well of pain so deep and intense within me, I fear I will fall in and never be able to climb my way out.

I push it all away. The memory of Aldrin's beautiful face. The amused smile that lights up his eyes and his touch that I am desperate to feel again.

I don't deserve a man like Aldrin, not when I left him at his most vulnerable point. I will not if he frees himself from the assassins, if he wins back his throne, unless he decides to open the portals. A shudder runs through me and I force myself back to the here and now.

"Are you concerned about the famine at Rockpoint Bay? That their waters no longer hold fish. It must be terribly frightening for the poor people," I say in an all-too-frivolous tone.

Finan gives me a long look. "Why do you care to talk about politics, Keira? It is unseemly for a lady, and quite frankly a bore. Leave all the petty decisions up to the advisers. It is their job, after all."

"I worry for those poor people—" I try again.

"Don't worry your pretty head about it. Here, have a sweet cake."

I try my hardest not to grit my teeth at the condescending dismissal and take the damn cake.

I left Aldrin for *this?* A wave of dread crashes over me, threatening to drown me in its intensity. My throat closes up, and it is a struggle to breathe.

I can't hear Finan talk. A loud ringing fills my ears.

Somehow, I make it through the picnic and back to my rooms, dismissing my maids immediately and stepping into the warm bath they prepared for me.

I hold my head in my hands and cry with abandon. My whole body shakes and my chest heaves with each sob that tears out of me in choked screams. I struggle to draw breath in anything other than a pant. Tears run down my face in torrents until the salt burns my skin.

All the grief I keep so tightly coiled within me comes spiraling out and I am drowning in the darkness of it. I feel like I am lost in a maze and I don't know my way out.

I am flooded by the image of Aldrin's face as I told him I was leaving. It haunts me, what I did to him. The way his features crumpled at my brutal words, and the utter defeat that crept over them. The mischievous smile disappeared from his face and the light in his eyes died. He deserved so much better.

My chest hurts from the heartache, like there is a blade inside it that keeps twisting and twisting.

I want to go back to Aldrin. To find that earlier version of myself and shake her for leaving. For putting everyone else first.

The water cools around me until I shiver, but I can't find the willpower to get out of the bath. I touch the beads of my moonstone bracelet, wishing I could still feel their pull. That the portals were not closed.

I find the single bead that bellows to the portal that led me to

Aldrin. Each bead in the bracelet is different, all milky white with flecks and swirls of green, blue and yellow, but this one has a chunk of purple right in its middle. I hold it while longing for Aldrin crashes over me like a tidal wave that rushes in and out. I picture his beautiful face when it lights up just from looking at me.

*Oh, Aldrin. I am so stupid. Aldrin, find your way back to me. I need you, more than I need to breathe. Find me. Find me. Aldrin, save me.*

It is pointless. All of this is pointless.

He is in another realm, on another world, so incredibly far away from my little kingdom of Strathia.

The bath is ice cold by the time I pull myself out of it. When I look in the mirror, my eyes are bloodshot, red-rimmed and puffy. It will not do. The future bride of the heir to the kingdom cannot be seen looking depressed.

I gaze at myself in the mirror and will my need into being. I focus on those puffy eyes. Bore into them while visualizing smooth, creamy skin, and the swelling slowly fades as the color adjusts. I shift my attention to the whites of my eyes, and now deeply veined and red, and focus my glamour magic until they too are fixed.

I had not known I was capable of glamour until I had a need for it.

For reasons I cannot explain, I strap the dagger I won from Aldrin to my upper thigh. Shivers run through my body at the memory of his being blindfolded as I attacked him, and how we landed in the grass with his face buried in my chest.

I glance down at the knife. The large ruby in the hilt glitters in the orb light and a scattering of others decorate the blade, alongside ornamental silver wire.

It is an utterly impractical design and I wonder why he kept it on him. Whether it had some sentimental value. It is the most precious thing I own. I get to keep a small part of him with me.

Diarmuid knocks on my door and escorts me to the library. I am emotionally exhausted and completely numb inside, and I think he notices despite my glamour. He gives me a long look, but doesn't say anything.

We walk through the grand doors of the library and weave

through the aisles, the familiar smell of old paper and fresh ink a salve to my mind.

My attention wanders lazily across tall bookcases that reach to the ceiling and the ladders that run across them, all the deepest mahogany. Arching pillars break up the massive hall of the library and many golden orbs illuminate the space with a warm glow. We pass busts of ancient scholars that head each aisle like guardians.

I absentmindedly read the descriptive tags that hang over each region of books. One section is set in darkness, like it is purposely trying to draw people away, but curiosity draws me in.

I grab my brother's arm. "What do you think is in there?" I effortlessly light an orb within my hand, guiding it over.

A mischievous smile forms on his lips as he glances over his shoulder. "Only one way to find out."

It is unlabeled, but crammed with books on the fae and the Otherworld. I skim my free hand over the texts, all new in their binding.

There is a doorway at the end of the aisle, guarded with an iron gate and magical wards. With a flick of my wrist, I solidify and push the air within the lock to open the mechanism, and pry open a passageway in the weak magic of the ward. It is like pulling open curtains at their seam.

We both creep in. The smile on my brother's face grows wider. He is always so easy to corrupt.

The tiny space holds a spiraling iron staircase that leads down to a room hidden below. My eyes widen at the texts within. They are so old, from the time of the Great War or earlier. History texts written about the fae at the time they lived among us.

As I run my hands over the spines, I can sense the magical oaths bound into many, the author swearing the truth of what they write, accompanied by the magic of witnesses.

There is even a cabinet of Living Memory Scrolls at the back corner, exactly as I witnessed in Aldrin's library. I take a step toward them.

"My father would not take kindly to you being down here." A voice stops me in my tracks, making cold sweat break out across my skin. I turn to Niall. "But I understand the curiosity. They put the wards on the door in the first place because I kept breaking in here as a child."

This is a treasure trove for Aldrin's cause.

The people of Strathia would trust these texts, since humans wrote them. And the fact that the king kept them means they have value. I am sure they are key to proving that despite the war, the fae weren't always an enemy. That we lived in harmony with them.

"I thought all the original texts from the Great War with the fae were destroyed," I say.

"There are too many inconvenient truths in here. Better that they remain hidden where the truth won't change anything." Niall looks at my brother. "Surely you don't have a problem with secrets, druid?"

Diarmuid coughs. There is no order more secretive than his.

Niall leads us back to the main hall of the library, past its centerpiece, multiple portals arranged in a circle. The great arches are of smooth, continuous pieces of moonstone that twist upon themselves, taller than any man and twice as wide.

They emit their own soft glow, blues and greens and yellows shimmering within the milky-white stone.

I stare longingly at them as we pass, resisting the urge to reach out and touch the stone.

When I first saw the portals here, I inspected every inch of them and felt their call. My heart leapt, because magic still brims within them and maybe, just maybe, there is still a way for me to get back to Aldrin.

It was a foolish thought.

These portals were once a gateway to the cities, castles or keeps in Strathia, and connected the royal court to the entire kingdom. Their destinations are engraved into each arch. My eyes fall on the portal that leads to Appleshield Castle and the image of its partner in the unkempt region of our gardens, covered in vegetation.

Niall catches my line of sight and gives a soft laugh. "I know you have an extraordinary amount of magic, Keira." He gives a pointed look at the simple orb that still rests in my hand. "But it would take a team of priestesses to open one of those portals now. Maybe it's not even possible anymore."

The prince leads us into a room with a small meeting table and immediately sits at it, gesturing for us to do the same. It must be his personal space. There are books and scrolls strewn everywhere.

"Did you have any success with him today?" Niall asks eagerly.

I shake my head. "Apparently, my pretty little head shouldn't worry about politics."

"Shame," Niall says, tension coiling in his shoulders. "I thought you might have more influence on Finan to get him to pay more attention. Maybe try to be more subtle. Diarmuid, how are the card games going? We need you to be one of his favorites."

"Wait, there was one thing he said." I hold a hand to my temple as I think. "He said it's the job of advisers to make the petty decisions. He means running the kingdom."

Niall writes notes and I watch him with pity. Here is a man who loves his people, who would be a good and just ruler, but is passed over because of his birth order.

He fears his brother will burn the kingdom to the ground with his apathy, and is desperately trying to take preventative measures.

Except, he has no power at all.

"Okay. Okay." Niall rubs his eyes. "That's good to know. We can expand our little group of Finan's guardians. Influence who ends up as his advisers when he ascends. I don't fully trust half the men in that role at the moment. Neither does Father, but he believes it is good to have our enemies close and hear their thoughts."

"Does he not listen to you, Niall? Would you not be the best adviser for your brother?" Diarmuid asks.

"Gods, no. Half the time he brushes me off as the little brother who knows nothing, and the other half, there is a vicious gleam in his eye, like he sees me as a threat to his ascension." A muscle ticks in Niall's jaw.

The blood turns to ice in my veins. If Finan could harm his brother from jealousy or a threatened ego, then I do not know my betrothed at all.

All of this is pointless. We will never have sway here. I cannot save this realm from Finan, and neither can Niall. I am enduring this man I somehow agreed to marry for no good reason.

I cannot help Aldrin from this position.

I cannot unite our people.

I don't even have mastery over myself.

The position of influence I thought I could work my way into will never come, that much is clear. I give Diarmuid a long look. Bitter disappointment turns my lips down and he sees exactly what I am thinking.

The pinch of his brow tells me Diarmuid has come to the same conclusion. Becoming Finan's queen is not worth the great sacrifice to myself.

Anxiety ripples through Niall as his gaze darts between us. "What I am about to tell you is not to leave this room. I fear my father's health is on the decline and we may not have much time to rein in Finan. To either make him a capable king or have competent, ethical advisers around him who will rule in his stead."

That statement is the last piece of the puzzle that makes it all so starkly clear.

Finan's queen doesn't really fit into that equation, in the same way that King Willard's doesn't. Niall sees me as a pleasant accessory to Finan, as someone who might soften him or have a small effect from whispering in his ear.

It is Diarmuid he wants.

# CHAPTER 36

# ALDRIN

I run my hand through my hair, but my fingers snag on the knots. When was the last time I even brushed it? Cyprien is talking and talking, agitation showing in the taut lines of his shoulders and his jarring hand motions, but I can't focus on a single thing he is saying.

I am so fucking tired. I wear a soul-deep, weary fatigue like a cloak.

I am an utter mess—physically, with crumpled clothes that smell of sweat and stubble across my cheeks, and emotionally.

Half the time I cannot even think straight.

The oak desk before me is covered in wrinkled parchment. Letters that have found their way to me at the Frozen River Fortress, some with their seal still unbroken. Others are in my own hand, that I started drafting before being interrupted. I am constantly being interrupted these days.

Cyprien pulls a chair from the opposite side of my desk and deposits himself in it. There are deep, black rings under his eyes. Even his usually bronzed skin looks pale.

"You'll have to repeat that." I massage my temples.

He passes me a neatly folded parchment with a gold seal. "This arrived in the mail portal. Transported straight from the palace."

I take it and inspect the seal. It is an imprint of Titania's profile. Only she would be arrogant enough to use her own face as her sigil. I tap it against the surface of the desk. "No spells or traps on the letter?"

Cyprien huffs an agitated breath. "None that I could detect."

I examine the letter for a long moment, staring at it like I have a viper ready to strike in my palms. It will be filled with just as much poison. Apprehension coils within my stomach.

"The letter will not disappear from you avoiding it," Cyprien points out.

I break the seal and open the folds. The letter doesn't shatter into a thousand needles and plunge at me. It doesn't release a choking gas or a flash of light bright enough to blind me for days. None of those kinds of spells could kill me, but I wouldn't put the pettiness past her.

I scan the lazy scrawl, anger building in my blood with each sentence.


*My dearest Aldrin,*

*Do not believe I have forgotten about you. That I will ever stop coming for you. I will strip you bare, and not in a way you will like. I have taken your crown, your title and your power. Now, your life, your dignity, your good reputation will all be mine.*

*Fear not, I am at no risk of running out of money to pay for your night-time visitors. Trade has been very good since I relieved you of your incompetent rule. The Assassins of Belladonna will keep coming to play every single night until you surrender to them. No one, and I mean absolutely no one, is coming to your defense in the Senate.*

*You see, the official word is that you were in collaboration with our oldest enemy, the Winter King. That you had sold your soul to him, shared his bed, and then attempted to sell your very people to him. That is why you tried to make them believe he is no risk to the Spring Court, all while he readies his forces for an invasion.*

*I also had them swallow—dear Aldrin, you will hate the irony of this one*

*—that the Winter King commissioned the Assassins of Belladonna to kill you. I made up some utter nonsense that you failed him and revealed your hand to me, enabling me to thwart two enemies at once. How clever your old subjects thought I was.*

*I would wish you a pleasant night, but I'd much prefer you choke in shadows and burn in molten light.*

*High Chancellor Titania*

I toss the parchment to my desk. "She is playing games," I spit.

Cyprien reaches for the letter, his eyes quickly skimming from left to right. His teeth grind so hard I can hear them. "This letter was pointless."

"Not if her aim is to taunt us," I mutter.

A high-pitched whoosh sounds as air rushes toward the letter, and the parchment still clutched in Cyprien's fingers catches fire abruptly. He drops it to the ground, cursing, and I lean over the desk to watch flames quickly lick across the page and consume it until not even ash remains.

"The only damn time she speaks the truth is when there is no evidence left of it." He shakes his head.

I don't want to think of Titania today. Not when there is nothing that can be done about her right now. It will have me stewing in impotent rage and frustration.

"What other correspondence came today?" I point to the stacks of letters beside Cyprien.

He silently hands me another one, the seal already broken, and I swiftly read over it. "Lord Cedar will not bring any potential allies to the border to witness the rifts while assassins have a commission against me. They won't risk it, not even during the day."

I rub my hands over my face and across my temples. The pain there builds and builds, raking claws across my skull. "I knew his support would disappear at the first hint of hardship."

Cyprien nods, the beads in his dark braids clinking. "Many fear they will earn their own commission with the assassins. Titania has the funds and is spiteful enough."

I read three more letters in the same vein. There is a sinking feeling in my chest, as though I am being dragged down into inky darkness and despite how I fight and claw, there is no stopping this descent. Sometimes, I feel like giving up. Handing myself over to despair.

It is so much effort to keep fighting every single day, no matter the backlash or consequences, no matter the rejection from the people I am trying to save.

It is draining me.

"This isn't going away on its own, Aldrin." Cyprien leans over the desk. "The assassins will keep coming, no matter how many we kill. Titania made that clear enough. Any support you have gathered will disappear if we let this drag on. There are only two ways to end the nightly assaults. Kill the high chancellor yourself, or put your own commission against her and have the assassins do it. I will fund it. Their order does not balk at having contradictory commissions. Both contracts will be complete when one of the clashing targets is dead."

"I will not kill Titania." My chair clatters to the ground as I rise from my seat suddenly, slamming my palms on the desk. "I will not stoop to her level. When I return to power, it will be because I have outmaneuvered her and the people have willed it. What power would I have as an unwanted dictator?"

"Your stubbornness will get us all killed, Adrin!" Cyprien gets up and stalks across the room. "It will destroy this entire realm. These are your only options." He grabs the decanter of brandy and pours himself a long drink, then drains it. He holds the decanter up as a silent offering to me, but I shake my head.

"There is another way."

"What other way?" Cyprien turns back toward me, scowling. "No. Whatever you are thinking, it's a bad idea."

"It is a terrible idea," I concede. "But it is another way. If I can make it work, then we will have a sharply honed weapon at our disposal."

Cyprien stalks right up to me and points a finger into my chest. "You have gone insane. Do not even consider it."

I push his hand off me. "Everyone has a right to take the Trials of Belladonna, to be initiated into their order. Their assassins cannot interfere with one taking the trials, and are forbidden from killing one of their members. Not only would I train with them and learn their ways, I could challenge their leader for the rule over the order. Imagine having that might at our disposal."

Cyprien stares at me with his nostrils flared wide. "Where would you even find them? The Order of Belladonna?"

"I have heard they dwell on a mountain peak shrouded in mist, in the land between the Shadow Court and the Sun Court. But all I have to do is make a formal appeal to one of their assassins, and they would be obligated to take me to their order."

"What happens to any who do not pass the trial or the training?" A deep frown occupies Cyprien's face.

I let out a long breath. "They are killed, of course, in a thousand creative ways."

"I will take this trial with you, to make sure your back is protected—"

"You can't," I cut him off. "I need you as my contingency. If anything happens to me, *you* need to become the next king."

Cyprien nods. He already knows of the plans I have for him.

I right my chair, then collapse into it.

The gold-and-oak grandfather clock in the corner of the study chimes five times and my stomach hollows out.

"Go, Cyprien, and get the soldiers ready for tonight. I need time alone with my thoughts." I rifle through the loose pages on my desk, and only notice he is gone when the door clicks shut.

I brace myself, waiting for the waves of utter devastation to drown me.

There is a pit of writhing pain within my chest, poisoning every single moment. It taints my blood, twists my innards and puts a dampening blanket across my thoughts.

The beast was born the moment Keira said she was leaving. It burst free from its bindings when she disappeared within the swirling mists of the portal, and I knew I would never touch her again. Never feel her bare body pressed against mine. Never coax a smile from her or hear her brilliant thoughts.

Those feelings are my own, and despite how they tear at me and threaten to break me, I can function while I carry them. Only just. Even as they follow my every waking moment and bleed into my nightmares.

In the hour when day turns to night, it changes. It is like the gates to my heart are ripped open and that grief and loss doubles. Triples. I swear that in these moments, the pain is not only my own, but I feel hers as well. I can *hear* her wail my name.

I turn toward the slits of windows high in the room, and examine the pink and orange stains across the late afternoon sky. It will be soon now.

The pendant of my necklace begins to burn against my skin, like a fire that runs as cold as ice. I pull on the leather thong and the chip of moonstone falls out of the neckline of my shirt.

It glows faintly.

I run a finger down its dulled edge and receive a shock of energy.

After Keira left through that portal, I took my sword and hacked at it until a shard of moonstone the length and thickness of my thumb broke free. I keep it on me at all times, so if she returns, I will know. If the portal is activated again, I will feel it.

The first time I felt the pendant brim with static charge and freeze my skin, I thought she found a way back to me. I raced through the forest as though the wild hunt themselves were after me, despite the oncoming sunset, only to find the portal utterly dormant.

The stone was dull and milky white, with none of the shimmering radiance and flashing colors present when the gateway is open.

I broke down and cried then, falling to my knees and pulling at my own hair.

My screams echoed off the trees.

If it hadn't been for Cyprien, Silvan and Klara dragging me back, I would have given up right then and there. The assassins would have found me on my knees, a broken man, and finished the job of my utter destruction.

I run my hands across my face, then place them on the desk. I riffle through the papers and find a letter to finish writing while I wait, but my hands shake too violently. A tightness forms within my chest that squeezes and squeezes until it is unbearable and I cannot breathe.

The moonstone pendant zaps charges through me again, sparking and freezing the skin of my chest, as the emotions escalate.

Keira's face appears in my mind. Those doe eyes are huge as she stares at me with awe, as she did when I taught her new magic. They glitter with green swirls among hazel.

The image changes to parted rosebud lips with ragged breaths and moans escaping them as I take her again and again.

Then to those curls of her long hair fluttering in the wind as she gazes out from a balcony in a Watchtower Tree, the sunlight causing the red, orange and gold to shimmer vibrantly.

The gods know I miss her more than I have missed anything or anyone in my life. I would give everything to touch her one more time. To the hells with regaining my crown, if I could have her.

The moonstone pendant hums with increasing power. The connection between our souls broadens, and the link of my pendant to her bracelet snaps into place again. In her world, Keira cries for me.

A sudden wave of agonizing torment and hopelessness crashes over my entire existence, the ripples of it so intense that nothing else exists. They mirror my own feelings, amplifying them tenfold.

I am dragged down and down until my thoughts are filled with nothing but churning darkness. Sobs burn up my throat and fight to break free, and I fear I will choke from the potency of them. I grip the edge of my desk and try to slow my breathing, but I have no control over the turmoil crashing within me.

*Aldrin. Oh, Aldrin.*

My heart stops dead as the words flow through my mind in Keira's voice. It feels so real, like she is wailing right next to me. But I can't put my arms around her and wipe away her tears.

*Aldrin, find your way back to me. I need you, more than I have needed to breathe.*

There is such desperation in her siren's call, but I cannot get to her. I take the moonstone pendant in my fist and grip it tightly, despite how it burns my flesh.

This is real.

It has to be.

I am not going insane or imagining this. I know because if I let go of the piece of moonstone, her calls and her emotions will disappear. They connect us somehow, my pendant and the bead on her bracelet. It allows me this tiny piece of her, and I will greedily take whatever I can.

I grit my teeth through wave after wave of pain, riding it in solidarity with her, letting my own emotions run free alongside it, until the connection ebbs and wanes and winks out.

Part of me wants to tug Keira back, pain and all, just to feel something from her. I collapse backward in my seat, utterly wrung out but still craving the sound of her voice.

I glance down at the pages beneath my hands. The ink is smudged and the parchment wrinkled from water. It takes a long moment for me to realize that the moisture is from my own tears.

Precious minutes I don't have are spent on pulling myself together, then I rise and dress myself in my battle armor. I pull on the brown leathers first, with disks of metal plate sewn into them. Next, I strap on the segmented bronze shoulder and arm guards, spikes jutting from my shoulders. I fit my chest plate last, not stopping to inspect the swirls of runes engraved into it.

I am finishing up as Cyprien ducks his head into the study. "They have arrived, but are holding back. I expect they will attack when full dark falls."

I don't need to ask who. The Assassins of Belladonna have fought us every single night we have been at this fortress, except for that first one.

Cyprien looks me up and down, his eyes lingering on my face. "Did it happen again?"

I stare at him for a long moment, contemplating how much to reveal. "It happened again. She *speaks* to me, Cyprien."

He frowns deeply as he takes a step closer to me. "None of us have slept much in days. Weeks. You have had blow after blow in that time. Countless attempts on your life. Betrayal and abandonment by your people yet again. Keira leaving. The emotional toil is expected. It would bring a lesser man to breaking point. Your strength is still needed, Aldrin, and not only for your survival. Let's not jump to rash conclusions."

"I am not imagining this," I snap at him.

He takes in a long breath, as though he is mustering his patience. "Let me inspect the moonstone shard."

I pull the thong over my head and pass it to him, the pendant still sending shocks of static into my fingers, its surface utterly frozen.

Cyprien inspects it as though it were any other inanimate object, and not one that sparks and freezes. "I don't feel anything. Are you sure—"

"Then how do you explain this?" I hold up my palm, where there is a purple-and-blue imprint of the jagged moonstone burned into it, slowly healing.

His lips compress into a thin line. "I cannot, but we have more immediate matters to deal with right now."

Cyprien turns to walk back out the door, but I grab him by the shoulders. "She is calling to me, Cyprien. Pleading for me to come find her. Keira is in trouble. I need to go to her."

He throws my arms off in disgust. "Keira made her choice, Aldrin! She chose to return to the human realm, where you *cannot* follow her. Not only will you lose all credibility with our people if you cross over, hers will kill you on sight. Have you forgotten what happened the last time you stepped into their realm? You have to respect her parting wishes, as much as you want her to call you from the Otherworld."

He stalks out the door with rage billowing off him.

"What about Lorrella's prophecy?" I toss at him, and he pauses. "Keira is meant to return the magic to both realms at my side."

Cyprien turns around very slowly. "The exact wording could mean many things. Did you tell her about the prophecy?" I nod and try to speak, but he cuts me off. "The full truth of the prophecy? About what happened when it was told to the humans?"

My entire face falls. "How could I tell her that? There never seemed a right time or way. It was so hard to gain her trust, I was terrified of losing it in a blink. Then she was leaving, and it didn't seem to matter anymore."

Cyprien gives me a withering stare for a long moment. "Come, Aldrin. We have matters of life and death to see to right now."

I glance down to my palm and see the mark has vanished from my skin. Maybe I have lost my mind.

Surely I didn't imagine it.

I march into the main hall of the fortress with Cyprien at my side. The room teems with my followers and they turn deadly silent, waiting for my command.

I skim my gaze across each of my people, falling on Drake first. He has dark stubble across his usually clean-shaven cheeks, obscuring much of the silvery tattoo of the tree of life. There is deep bruising under his eyes from lack of sleep, contrasting against the red tones of his skin. We are lucky to have him still with us and that the Living Waters saved his life.

Beside him, Klara blinks heavily as she struggles to stay awake. My gaze roves to Lilly, the oldest among us, but the only hint of her fatigue is her bloodshot eyes. Silvan has black rings beneath his slitted gaze, and I know pain from a lost lover also haunts him.

We are becoming more worn down by the day and cannot go on like this for much longer. Fighting the entire night and using much of the day to repair damage done to the fortress and replenish the magic of the ward stones.

There has been precious little time for sleep.

We are barely surviving.

I clap my hands. "Everyone to your stations. You all know your places by now."

"What exactly are we doing here, Aldrin?" Drake steps forward.

"Buying time," I grunt.

"Time for what?" He spreads his arms out. "Help isn't coming, that much is clear."

"Time for me to godsdamn think!" I growl at him.

Drake doesn't even flinch. He turns and walks out the door, grumbling under his breath, and the rest of the soldiers follow close behind him. I wonder how much longer they will continue to follow me. When they will finally have enough of being loyal to a dead man walking.

Cyprien grits his teeth but says nothing as he brushes past me.

A storm breaks overhead as I step outside. The twin moons are blotted out by thick, black clouds and thunder echoes across the sky as they collide with one another. Streams of water run in rivulets down the wards above my head.

It gives the illusion of standing inside a bubble within a crashing waterfall. A heavy mist settles upon us, penetrating the pores of the wards.

The leathers of my armor are soaked through and trickles of frozen water run down my back by the time I climb the external stairs of the highest watchtower, to the stone plinth of pure aquamarine gracing the platform at its apex.

Cyprien and Lilly already brace their hands against it. The static energy in the air raises the hairs along my skin as they funnel their raw magic into the plinth. The wards ripple with each pulse, bands of light running from the stone into them as they strengthen.

There are four other towers with plinths along the fortress, where my people are stationed in the same manner. The protective wards are at their weakest at the seams between plinths, where water trickles through the barrier and reveals our vulnerabilities.

We don't have nearly enough warriors to keep them powered.

I place my hands against the warmth of the aquamarine plinth and Cyprien grunts as he makes space for me. His drenched hair is heavy against his face and steam rises from his hands.

I can feel the wards through the plinth like an extra limb. Boots run across them, the vibration of their impact an echo jolting through my hands. I push my consciousness down the trail of magic and follow its path across the wards, counting the number of assailants. Ten upon the wards, examining our positions and weaknesses.

Thunder rumbles high above us, and a second later the sky is lit up by a great flash of forked lightning. I count another five figures clad in billowing robes of inky shadows, base jumping in the open air above the wards.

It astounds me how long the Assassins of Belladonna can maintain that kind of magic, but no fae can do it forever. Just as we won't be able to sustain the wards against their attack indefinitely.

The night sky becomes brightly illuminated, then a different kind of rain falls upon us. One of silver needles of pure light, as sharp as any knife. I am blinded by that wall of radiance cascading down and shattering upon our barrier, creating spots of weakened magic.

I focus on the area of the ward serviced by the plinth beneath my hands and channel in raw power to patch those holes before they grow.

Last night, a single assassin made it through a small breach and wreaked absolute mayhem on us before we killed him. It was almost enough to force us to drop the ward. If we had, we would have surely fallen. I feel the floods of Cyprien and Lilly's power patching other growing holes.

This is an exercise in blind trust. Each team at the separate plinths works in ignorance of each other, assuming the others aren't over-whelmed. We don't have the numbers to come to each other's aid or probe the wards beyond our designated sections.

All we can do is defend. Pour all of ourselves into the wards, because we don't have the forces to spare any on attacking the assassins.

Except for Odiane.

She materializes as a pure white silhouette from the water sluicing down the domes of the wards, like a thing of nightmares. Her fingers are long claws, her mouth filled with rows of sharp teeth an inch long and her eyes pure black with no whites. Jagged ridges climb up her bare back and spikes jut out of her shoulders, elbows and knees.

I wonder what Keira and Caitlin would think of her, if they saw her like this.

The Lake Maiden screams and the pools of water around her violently undulate. Pain slices through my ears, but the sound is diminished by the wards. The two closest assassins grab their ears and fall to their knees on the barrier, the water dripping from them tinged with their blood.

An assassin leaps toward her and slices a sword of pure, rippling starlight straight through her figure. Odiane cascades into a puddle, but a moment later two of her forms materialize out of the water. She is a queen, and we are merely squatting in her palace.

Her arms whip up from her sides, and a column of ice spikes cuts out of the water, each three feet high. The assassins dart out of that brutal path, the jagged points of the icicles narrowly missing them.

Odiane dances with the assassins the entire night, throwing her spears of ice at them and laughing with exhilaration. They dodge her attacks and dissipate her form, only to give themselves a few minutes of respite.

My high fae warriors are merely fleas on the back of a dragon, gripping on for dear life. My people channel all that is left of themselves into those wards while the assassins break their blows of light and shadow against it, trying to shatter our last defense.

With great pain, I split my channels of magic in two, sending half into the plinth and the other into attacks. I gather a tidal wave from all the water falling from the sky and running down our defenses, building it and building it, until its huge form curls over three assassins and crashes down on them, washing their bodies from the ward like ticks from my back.

I tighten my fist and force a crushing blow into the mass of water, slamming them into the frozen river below. One cracks upon a thick sheet of ice, and the other two are plunged into the water's icy depths, where I hope to the gods that Odiane's court will dispatch them.

Agony splits through my temples, but I cannot stop.

I grasp all of those trees that should never have been allowed to grow around the fortress, thrusting my power into them until they become colossuses that strike at the assassins who dart around impossibly fast. It is a crude technique, clapping immense branches together while they narrowly dart out of the way. Whipping at them with thick tendrils of roots.

It is like trying to catch a fly in my hand, but I manage to crush a few.

My head spins, my hands shake, and I don't know if my legs will hold me for much longer. I focus my efforts into the plinth, pouring all my essence into it, while Odiane continues to fight above us. I will join her with my magic again, as soon as I catch my breath.

Beside me, Cyprien has his eyes squeezed shut and his teeth gritted, as though in pain. He is on his knees, elongated fangs and tusks peeking out through his lips, his fingers the same blackened claws as my own. When his eyes open, they are completely black, with no whites.

It is rare that Cyprien reveals his more primal form. Unlike how I lose my grip on it with the first flicker of rage. Only the strongest of us still connect with the original forms of the Tuatha Dé Danann.

Lilly mutters urgently below her breath, her forehead pressed against the hot stone. Thick, curled horns erupt from her bald scalp. Her usual cap of golden runes is now black and covers the entirety of her caramel skin.

They are both stretched thin and fading.

A sudden clarity hits me. I know this is how it will end for us if I remain here. We will collapse at these plinths, and the assassins will kill not only me, but my loyal followers who will throw themselves in front of me.

Our energy and magic have been greatly taxed by weeks of these nightly battles, but the assassins keep coming, fresh and powerful, no matter how many we kill.

As dim light bleeds across the sky, Odiane's much-depleted form collapses into a pool of water and does not rise again. The assassins' assault intensifies for another hour without her harrying them, then their silver rain ends abruptly and their forms skitter away cloaked in shadows.

I let go of the plinth, lean forward over my knees and heave.

"Have you lost your mind, Aldrin?" Cyprien snaps. "We still need to power the plinths for tonight."

I examine each of them. "We don't need to charge them. I am leaving here today."

Cyprien collapses back against the plinth as relief ripples across his face. Lilly sits heavily on the soaked ground, but rolls her eyes over to me. "You have made a decision, then?"

"I am not going to bloody like it, am I?" Cyprien dries the sweat from his hands on his leathers, then grimaces at the dirt deposited on them.

"Oh no, you are going to hate it." I grin at him despite myself. A heavy weight lifts from my shoulders. "In fact, you'll think it's my worst idea yet. I will not ask anyone to come with me."

"You're not going to hand yourself over to the Assassins of Belladonna to challenge them, are you?" he asks.

"No. Not, yet anyway." I pull myself upright and stumble down those waterlogged steps encircling the outside of the Tower.

"Aren't you at least going to tell us?" Cyprien calls over the edge of the rampart.

"You can find out when everyone else does," I toss over my shoulder.

For the first time in weeks, there is a spring in my step.

# CHAPTER 37

# KEIRA

I pace the lavish sitting room of my apartments while my brother sits on the edge of a dark violet couch. Agitation makes my muscles taut, ready to flee. "I have made a horrible mistake, Diarmuid. I cannot marry him." My stomach churns at the idea.

"That error of judgment belongs to our entire family." Diarmuid tips his head back and gulps down his entire glass of sherry. "It is not right, how they treat their women here. You were not born to be silent and powerless."

I pause in front of him, frowning while the cogs of my mind whirl.

"Oh, no. I know that look." Diarmuid straightens. "You're about to do something wildly reckless and drag me into it."

"I'm going to tell Finan I will not marry him. That I will become a priestess instead."

Diarmuid leans forward in his seat, excitement rippling over his face. "Finally! I've already told you I don't want you to marry him. We have to plan carefully and do this the smart way. We will go straight to the Sanctuary of Magic in the city first thing in the morning and have them mediate on your behalf, while you are in a position of strength and safety. The Mothers of Magic will not be intimidated. We have no idea how he will react, but it won't be pleasant."

A sense of relief washes through me so hard and fast that my legs feel weak. I collapse onto a couch.

Diarmuid rises and stalks toward the bar, pouring long drinks for each of us. "We will work out the details tonight, then pack our bags. We leave at first light, before the palace wakes up, but when it is safe to walk the city streets."

My brother approaches me, arm stretched out to offer me the crystal glass, when a pounding shakes the door to my apartment in its frame. He shoots me a startled look. "Who would be visiting you at this hour of the night?"

"I have no idea." Shivers run down my spine, because I have an inkling.

"Stay here," Diarmuid orders, a rare seriousness falling over him as he curls my fingers around the glass.

My heart races and I can't sit still as I listen to the bolts being removed from my door. I take a sip of the sweet sherry to quell my nerves, but the alcohol does little for me.

"My sister has retired for the night. She doesn't take visitors at this hour." Diarmuid's anger travels to me.

"Prince Finan has requested her company," a gruff voice replies. My stomach tumbles with dread.

"Like I said, she has retired for the night. Tell him she will keep him company tomorrow. In the afternoon, perhaps. She does like to sleep in." Those words are followed by the sound of the door hitting something and reverberating, as though Diarmuid tried to slam it in the guard's face and it hit a foot obstructing it instead.

"The prince was very adamant that he would not be refused. It is not *that* late. He said he will come here if he has to," the guard grumbles. Others snicker, telling me Finan sent multiple guards. "I would hate to drag her there by force."

"It is not proper," Diarmuid grinds out.

"Look, boy, if I have to beat and restrain you just to do my job, I will. The royals don't take no for an answer. The prince said he wants to talk to her. That he has questions to be answered. That is all. Come with us and escort her, or we leave you here and take her alone."

"He. Can. Wait."

My hands shake, threatening to spill my drink as I place it on the table. There is no universe where I will allow Diarmuid to take a beating for me. I walk as though through water, finding him in the entrance, glaring almost nose to nose with the guard, lips peeled back from his teeth.

"I will talk to him," I say quickly, and Diarmuid gives me a murderous look. "But I need a few moments of privacy to fix my hair."

The guard nods and allows Diarmuid to close the door. My brother immediately turns on me. "Are you insane? Finan is a loose cannon. He clearly only wants one thing from you at this time of the night and we have no idea how he will react if you say no."

"I am aware, Diarmuid. Do not forget that I am far from helpless. My entire adult life, I have come running like an overeager puppy whenever he has called for me. If I refuse now, he will be suspicious. I cannot have him post guards on my door tonight or attempt to lock me in my chambers if we want to escape unnoticed tomorrow morning.

"I will talk to him, and I won't allow him to do anything else. If he is insistent, I will tell him we will get the priestesses' approval that it won't hurt an unborn babe on the morrow, that he only has to wait one more day. Finan is many things, but he is not a rapist, nor would he be able to physically overpower my magic."

"Fuck, Keira." Diarmuid drags his eyes away from me. "It's bloody dire when you have to reassure me about rape. I'm coming into that room with you."

We stare at each other for a long moment. "Our hands are tied. You have to trust that I can take care of myself," I say.

The doors crash open and multiple guards funnel in. One flicks his head at me. "Time to go, my lady."

It feels like I am walking to an execution, flanked by three guards, as we make our way to Finan's chambers.

There are more royal guards at Finan's door, and I wonder why I don't get the same protection. They announce our presence and Finan arrives in the doorway with a slow, self-satisfied smile growing on his face as he sees me.

Something about it is so off.

I become frozen in place.

"Ah, Keira, I have a question for you." Finan leans forward and grabs my arm, pulling me between the guards, through the doorway and behind him. Diarmuid tries to follow, but Finan puts a hand on his chest and pushes him backward. "I'll take good care of her. Your presence isn't needed here, druid."

My brother bristles at the dismissal. "I am Keira's custodian and escort. My presence is required until you are married."

"Is that so?" Finan cocks an eyebrow. "I'm sure there are some things a brother doesn't want to witness."

"Finan, don't bait him. You said you want to talk. Diarmuid can join us for that," I snap, my patience with this man wearing thin.

"Yes. We *need* to talk." Finan turns on me, anger flashing across his face then gone a moment later. With a flick of his wrist, he motions for the guards to restrain Diarmuid. I get a glimpse of my brother's red-faced fury as he tries to push through the five guards that hold him back, striking one in the face with an elbow. The prince watches them with fascination, like it is the most entertainment he has had in days.

"Diarmuid, it's okay," I say.

The two guards have him in a chokehold. "I clearly don't have a choice," he spits. "I will be right out here. Call out if you need me and I will tie these oafs up in chains of air and barge in for you."

A chill runs down my spine. If we use our superior magic on any of these people, it will be a royal offense. Gods, even Diarmuid barging into Finan's chambers without invitation is borderline treason.

A guard slams the door and all sight and sound from the corridor is shut out.

"Would you like a drink?" Finan asks in a chirpy tone, walking away without waiting for my answer. His steps are uneven as he staggers slightly. When he glances back over his shoulder and tips his head for me to follow, I notice his eyes are glazed and veined with red. Gods. He is drunk.

I follow him with my heart in my throat to a large sitting room with multiple velvet couches and a full bar. Finan moves for the crystal decanter on the low table in the center of the room, pouring red wine into two glasses but not bothering to hand mine to me.

I hover nervously beside a couch, every alarm bell going off in my head.

"Sit, Keira. I only have one question for you." Finan motions to the armchair beside the one he has taken and I crumble into it. He leans forward, so our knees are touching and his face is inches from mine. The predatory look within his eyes sends my stomach tumbling. "Are you or are you not pregnant to the magic?"

"I–I don't know yet. It is too early to—"

"LIES!" He throws his crystal glass and it smashes across the opposite wall. Crimson wine runs down it in rivulets like blood. Finan rears over me, his hands on each of my armrests so he can snarl down into my face. "I just had the most interesting dinner with my cousin. She is also a Mother of Magic. Do you know what she said to me, Keira?" I stare at him, unmoving and wide-eyed, but it only antagonizes him. "DO YOU KNOW what she said?"

I shake my head at him, too afraid to speak.

Finan takes a lock of my hair and tenderly tucks it behind my ear. "She said a Mother of Magic with even a scrap of healing ability can tell if a pilgrim returns pregnant to the magic almost immediately. That they can feel the magic growing in the womb. It doesn't take a month, and a man's touch won't hurt the unborn babe. Not even fucking. That this is the typical excuse given by a returned pilgrim who doesn't *want* to be touched."

I draw in a sharp breath and recoil from him.

"My true question, Keira, is why my future bride suddenly doesn't want to fuck me. Why she has been lying to stay out of my bed."

I forget to breathe. My brain comes to a jarring halt as rational thought seems to wither up and die. "I don't want to marry you, Finan. I want to dedicate myself to the temple instead."

Finan throws back his head and roars with laughter. In a heartbeat, he rears back from the couch, grabbing my arm and pulling me to my feet.

"What are you doing?" I trip as he drags me through the sitting room, toward the corridor beyond.

"Clearly, you need a good fuck to remember why you want me." A smile still splits his lips. "I think you spent too much time around those fae monsters in the Otherworld to remember what it's like to be with a real man."

His audacity flares up my temper, especially when *he* has never shown me true pleasure. I rip my hand out of his grasp and almost send him flying into one of the long recliners. "I am serious, Finan! I am NOT going to sleep with you. I'm NOT going to marry you."

He rights himself, then stalks to me. The hard glint in his eye and thin twist to his lips have me backing away from him, but I'm too slow. He grabs me and crushes me against his chest. I can hardly breathe from the tight vise of his arms around me.

"You *will* marry me," he growls in my ear.

"No," I sob. "It is not your choice."

His fingers dig painfully into my flesh. "You don't get to leave *me*. You are *mine*. My property. My woman. You always have been. The entire kingdom knows it." His nostrils flare and his eyes are wild with rage. "We *will* marry in two weeks."

"It is my right to dedicate myself to the temple." I struggle against him.

"You don't understand, Keira." Finan's face is inches from mine, his lips pulled into a snarl. "You. Are. Mine." He shakes me hard, my head whipping back and forth. "Your place is at my side, whether you want it or not. You will learn to accept this life. It is the only one you will get."

He finally lets go of his hold on me to jab a finger painfully into my chest, and I stumble back a step.

An ugly fear unfurls within me at the threat of violence rippling through him. I scurry back from him, around the low central table between the couches, as he stalks me.

I have never seen this side of him, and it terrifies me. It is so much like King Willard.

"Say it," Finan barks at me. "SAY IT! Say you love me. Say you will marry me."

I flinch at the aggression rolling off him and begin to cower before him. He has always held dominion over me.

Then I remember the woman I have grown into is so vastly different from that soft, naive girl who thought she loved him. I dared to cross into the fae realm. I fought against high fae and killed an Assassin of Belladonna. I outsmarted and outmaneuvered the King of the Spring Court and gained his respect. His affection.

*Oh gods, Aldrin.* The very thought of his name gives me courage. If I can find the strength to leave Finan, then maybe I could find a way back to Aldrin.

Fire courses through my veins. How dare Finan demand all of me, my life, my body and my heart, when he has never deserved any of it?

I straighten my spine. "You cannot hold me against my will, Finan. You are not my husband and you have no claim over me. I *will* become a priestess, and no one will stop me. Your guards, your armies and your father will not dare to challenge the Mothers of Magic!"

"I have no claim to you? NO CLAIM?" Finan sweeps his arm across the low table beside us, throwing the decanter and glasses to the ground. I jump at the crashing of the breaking crystal. "You will act like my wife and you will do as I say."

"No. I deserve more than to be a pretty little accessory on your arm." I lean toward him and spit, "And you are going to have to learn to accept that."

Finan moves so fast I don't stand a chance at blocking him, wrapping his hand around my throat and pushing me backward until my back crashes into the wall.

Pain radiates up my spine from the impact and explodes across my shoulders, but it is nothing compared to the vise around my windpipe. My breath wheezes as I drag it in, and those biting fingers bruise the delicate flesh around my neck.

A deep pain slices through me at the betrayal. At my own stupidity for expecting anything else from him.

"Do you see what you have made me do? I will never let you go." Finan's hand loosens only slightly. "I will never stop fighting for you. If I have to lock you up in this palace until you cooperate, then I will. If I need to beat you into submission, into a proper wife, then I will. You. Are. Mine."

For a moment, I am a startled rabbit, caught within the jaws of a wolf.

"Take your hands off me, Finan," I choke out, but he pushes his shoulder hard against my chest, slamming me against the wall a second time. My head cracks against the plaster. In a small mercy, his fingers leave my throat.

"Not until you take back what you said." His breath is hot against my ear.

"You have one last chance to take your hands off me, or I will do it for you." I don't move, push or claw at him. I don't need to.

Finan's shoulder and hips press tighter into me, making the air whoosh out of my lungs.

I am not helpless to this man. I will not be his victim anymore.

The strands of my hair rise in a phantom breeze as I gather air around me, looping thick tendrils of it between us. I wrap them around Finan like a rope, then with a quick tug he is pulled backward, away from me.

His eyes flare as he stumbles, then the color drains from his face as I bind his arms to his sides. With a thrust of air aimed at his chest, I knock him backward into an armchair, tying him to it.

"Keira—wait!" Finan yelps, fear flashing across his face. That stupid ringlet of blue-black hair I used to love so much falls over his face.

I place a gag of air in his mouth so I don't have to hear him speak again.

It is too far—by the gods, I know it—but I cannot stop myself when my temper flares.

Pushing off the wall, I approach Finan slowly and lean over him.

He wiggles desperately in his bindings, as though he thinks I'm going to slit his throat while he is vulnerable.

"No one owns me," I snarl at him. "No one has mastery over my body or my future, least of all you."

I turn on my heel and walk toward the door. Shards of crystal crunch under my feet. I give him one last glance over my shoulder. "Goodbye, Finan."

As I exit his apartment, both guards raise their eyebrows at me.

"Done already?" one asks me, while the other laughs.

"The prince doesn't need very much time," I say, winking at them. "He has gone to bed with a headache after his…exertion. He doesn't want to be disturbed."

Diarmuid pushes off the wall from his leaning position, brow furrowed and gaze roaming over me. I grab his elbow and set a fast pace.

"We need to get out of here. Immediately. Things didn't go well," I mutter under my breath.

"Did he hurt you? Touch you?" Panic flashes on Diarmuid's features.

We pass around a corner and it is all I can do to stop myself from breaking into a run. My brother grabs my shoulders, forcing me to stop, and searches my face. "Talk to me, Keira. What happened?"

I let out a long breath. "He wouldn't take no for an answer, and tried to intimidate me with aggression."

Diarmuid's eyes harden as rage flashes within them. He turns and stalks back in the direction of Finan's rooms. "I will kill him myself." Embers spark across his hair. Raw power crackles across his skin and jolts me as I touch his arm.

I pull him back. "What about your druid's oath against violence?"

"To the Soul Ripper with my oath," he snaps.

"It's dealt with, Diarmuid. I stopped him before it escalated." My stomach rolls at what I have done, but I don't regret it. "I lost my temper and tied him up in ropes of air. I left him like that. We have to get out of here before—"

"By the fucking gods, Keira!" Diarmuid exhales.

"What? You were just going to kill him!"

"I don't think I have ever been more proud of you." Diarmuid takes my arm and leads me down the corridor. "I don't know what our parents were thinking, sending the two of us to the royal court together. Between us we would have committed treason and murder."

My legs turn shaky. "I did commit treason, didn't I?"

"We can't let you fall into shock yet. We need to leave the palace now. Get out of the city before your magic wears off and Finan calls his guards," Diarmuid says.

The corridor forks and I drag him down a passageway abruptly.

"Where are you taking us? This leads away from the stables," he protests.

"To the library. Ever since I returned from the fae world, my power has grown immensely. I spent months eating their food, drinking their water and breathing their air. Everything in their lands is imbued with magic. I think I can open the Appleshield portal to take us home. There is already some charge in it."

"I should have known you would get us into huge fucking trouble within the first month of us arriving here." Diarmuid shakes his head. "Though this is on Finan."

I smile wickedly at my brother.

Freedom is so close I can taste it.

We travel through the library at a brisk place, the aisles flying past us. My heart drops as we pass that set of bookshelves leading to the fae texts, deliberately hidden in darkness. The vault beyond could have been invaluable for Aldrin's aims, full of forbidden texts with the truth of the fae and the Great War. It is a lost opportunity that could change the world.

There isn't even a single scholar down here.

The ring of portals glows faintly in the library's dimness. I pull Diarmuid by the arm to the gate that leads to Appleshield Castle. Its surface isn't smooth like I thought, but has thousands of tiny, subtle facets like the face of a gemstone. The colors embedded in the milky moonstone glitter under the minimal light.

"Do you know how to open a portal, by any chance?" I ask sheepishly.

His jaw drops. "Hold on, didn't you say you could do it? You led me here instead of the stables because you said you could open it."

"I believe I have enough power to do it…"

Diarmuid shakes his head. "I've read about it in my studies. We need to channel our raw, unformed power into the moonstone. That is all."

We place our hands on the cold stone, and a shiver runs down my spine. I close my eyes and focus on its textured surface as I pull at the power coiling within my center, feeding it into the portal.

It flows in a trickle at first, unaccustomed as I am to wielding my magic unshaped. I open myself up gradually with great effort, and streams of liquid fire and the coldest of ice course out of me. It feels like water being forced through a crack in a dam, until the wall containing it is shattered and a roaring onslaught pours in freefall from me into the moonstone.

I am being burned from the inside, scoured clean, but it doesn't hurt. A tugging sensation pulls at my essence through my hands, dragging out more of my power. It lasts for an eternity, this striving for my salvation, then ceases all at once.

Intense relief almost knocks me from my feet as I am greeted by the radiant glow of the activated portal. Swirling mists escape from within its arch, coiling around our feet as though it is eager to lead us back home.

I want to laugh and cry at the same time. It feels like I have run for hours.

"We did it?" Diarmuid pants. "We actually did it! Two people to open a portal."

I grab him by the hand and pull him toward the open gate. "You can gloat about it when we are safely home."

Diarmuid hesitates at the white nothingness within and shoots me a frantic glance.

"It doesn't hurt." I squeeze his hand and tug him through.

I expect a blank landscape of stark white that extend as far as the eye can see, like when I traveled to the Otherworld, but I am wrong. The other portal is only a dozen steps away, and the gardens of Appleshield are visible through it. A tunnel of blindingly bright mist forms walls between the two portal openings.

The contrast is a stark testament to how far away the fae world is to my own. To why we have to rely on the alignments of planets and tears in the fabric of space to reach it. A deep loneliness fills me at the distance between Aldrin and me. At the thought that I won't be able to see his planet among the stars in my night sky.

We step out into the crisp night air of a mild summer night and I want to collapse into a heap. My whole body starts to shake now that I am in the safety of my own home. Emotions roll wildly through me and my nerves are completely frayed.

The full gravity of what I have done tonight hasn't hit me yet. The consequences of it. Not only the political fallout from calling off the wedding, but the fact that I physically bound a prince and heir to the throne.

There is nothing I can do about it now.

I turn around, taking in the neglected garden. Tall weeds sprout on the gravel path and wild, overgrown rose bushes spill out of the garden beds. Behind us is the tall willow tree with fire-red blooms draping down its branches. This is the garden where I used to take Finan whenever I put his needs and his pleasure above mine. How ironic that it is my saviour when I needed to escape him.

A manic, uncontrolled laugh boils out of me.

"Don't lose it yet." Diarmuid shoots a glance at me while he crouches at the portal. "We need to shut this thing down so they cannot follow us."

I place my hands on the portal. Instinct has me drawing all that magic back into myself. The glow of the moonstone slowly fades until there is no more power humming within it.

"I didn't know we could take the power back," I murmur.

Diarmuid shrugs.

My legs are unsteady as we walk from the neglected Old Fae Garden between the greenhouses of the orchards and toward the keep. Diarmuid steers me with a hand clutching my elbow while my whole body still shakes from adrenaline.

The bridge spanning the deep valley before our fortress is an ominous sight, seeming to lead nowhere through the darkness and hovering over inky shadows. It takes all of my willpower to put one foot in front of the other and cross. My mind conjures up Assassins of Belladonna moving through the night, but that is pure fantasy. They wouldn't venture into this realm.

We approach the blocky form of the guardhouse illuminated by multiple braziers. The sentries call out an order and guards snap into a defensive formation, pointing their spears at us and blocking the passageway.

"Who approaches?" a female sentry's voice calls from the top of the wall. "Step into the light!"

Diarmuid gives me a half-smile, then leads us into the glow of multiple fire orbs hovering around the gate. Guards almost have a heart attack at the sight of us, two noble figures adorned in rich silks. Their panic rises as they recognize us. Immediately, one is sent running to the keep, probably to alert our father and a whole team of servants of our arrival.

"My lady Keira? Lord Druid Diarmuid?" a guard asks, rushing to us.

Diarmuid smirks at the title they give him. They can never quite bring themselves to address him as a druid alone.

"Are you hurt?" The guard's eyes dart across us. "Did you travel here on horseback through the night? Where are your mounts?"

"We are not hurt, Liam." I place a hand on his shoulder. He doesn't balk at the familiarity; we have joined the hunt together too many times for that. "We traveled through the portal."

The guards don't look relieved.

"I will escort you both to the castle myself." Liam turns around and barks a few orders at the soldiers left in the guardhouse. Diarmuid goes to protest, but I give him a slight shake of the head. The guards would be mortified if we took this responsibility away from them, especially Liam.

"There have been all manner of fae trespassing in the woods while the portals were held open." Liam wrings his hands as he speaks. "Somehow, some got through the priestess's wards around the portal interchange." Strange. I have never known him to fear low fae before. Surely hunts continued while I was gone.

"Have you forgotten my sister is one of our greatest fae hunters?" Diarmuid raises an eyebrow.

"No, my lady, no, my Lord Druid." Visible beads of sweat form on Liam's brow. "It is just that you don't look armed, and there have been reports of high fae lurking in the fields around the castle of late."

My heart stutters to a stop. Surely not.

"There are no high fae here, Liam," the sentry on the wall calls down to us. "The lord protector himself would know of it and hunt them down personally. What you have heard are stories that have been twisted in too many tellings."

Liam glances up to that woman, now crouching on the ramparts of the wall above us. "There *have* been strange men lurking here, armed for war."

The sentry laughs. "A few fruit thieves are not the same as high fae."

Liam scowls. He continues to mutter about high fae as he leads us through the castle grounds. A hope is born within me. One I do not dare acknowledge.

# CHAPTER 38

# KEIRA

My father stands with both hands firmly on his desk, leaning over a map of the kingdom. His eyes flare wide as they fall on me and his lips narrow to a thin line.

"What did he do to you?" he growls, and the roaring fireplaces flare up throughout the study. Murderous intent flashes within his gaze.

My mother walks into the room behind us, and she stops dead upon seeing me, her hand flying to her mouth. "Did Prince Finan do this to you?" she chokes.

I turn to Diarmuid, but he stares at me with his mouth hanging open. "Your throat. It's badly bruised, like he wrapped his hands around it. I didn't see it in the darkness."

My father breaks from his trance and rushes over, collecting me in a massive bear hug and lifting my feet from the ground as though I am still a little child.

He holds me tight against his chest, the side of his head pressed against mine. The tension I have been carrying all night melts from my body and I want to sob.

"You are safe now, Keira. I will kill the princeling. I don't care if I have to march my army to his doorstep." My father places me back on my feet and peers into my face. "How badly has Finan hurt you?"

My breath catches. "I did worse to him, Father. I made quite a mess of things."

Warm hands wrap around my shoulders and lead me to an armchair before the desk. My mother kneels in front of me, holding my hands. "Tell us what happened, Keira."

I take in both of their worried glances, and then I tell them everything.

The scowl on my father's face deepens with every word and my mother stares at me, nodding every so often.

"I told Finan I would not marry him. That I will devote my life to being a priestess. It is not the life I envisioned, but it is better than being his wife." I fall into silence.

I don't tell them about my secret hope, that by giving my life to the temple, I might be able to cross again at the next alignment event in seven years.

Where will Aldrin be in twenty-one of his years? Will he have a fae queen at his side?

I deserve as much. I need to at least try to find my way back to him. He holds half of my soul and I cannot function without him.

My father grips the edge of his desk so hard it is a wonder it doesn't splinter beneath his fingers. "That stupid bastard. That soft weakling should have known he couldn't take on one of *my* daughters."

"How did you get home, Keira?" My mother leans forward, placing her hands on my knees. There is fierceness in her delicate features. "Neither of you are dressed for travel and the guard said you didn't have horses with you."

Diarmuid takes a long swig from a cup of wine. "Oh, it was no great feat. We simply used the portal in the palace's library to travel here, to the portal in the Old Fae Garden."

"You did what?" My father's eyes dart between us, pride flickering within them.

"I did not think it was still possible," my mother murmurs.

My father motions toward the guard hovering by the door. "Get my personal guard ready to leave in the morning. I will travel to Sunbright City to clear this up."

"Is that wise, Edmund?" My mother rises, blocking his path to the door. "Think of the political ramifications."

"It's too dangerous, Father," I insist. "There is another side to Finan that we never saw. Even his brother Niall fears violence from him. King Willard might order you to send me back to Finan or face war. Appleshield cannot claim responsibility for me or harbor me."

"Keira must move to the Sanctuary of Magic," Diarmuid chimes in. "The crown cannot wage war on the Mothers of Magic. The people would not tolerate it."

My mother takes another step closer to my father. "Naomi must negotiate for Keira, as her high priestess. You know your mother will fight to the darkest realm and back for her."

My father's gaze slides over to me. "Are you sure this is what you want?"

I let out a long breath.

Is this what I want?

No. I want Aldrin. I need him. Every fiber of my being screams at me to find a way back to him. This is my only chance.

"Yes." Fatigue crashes down on me.

"Send a messenger to the Sanctuary of Magic immediately. Prepare the priestesses, especially my mother," my father says over my head to the waiting guard.

"It can wait for the morning, Edmund. Nothing is going to happen before sunrise," my mother chimes in.

I am led to my chambers, but sleep eludes me, no matter how hard I try. Thoughts whirl through my head like a swarm of angry bees. Hot tears run down my face at my sheer stupidity, because I thought I could make a difference. That I would be a queen with power and influence, achieved merely by the gravity of my personality and willpower.

Not even my grandmother, high priestess and the strongest woman I know, could have had a scrap of authority in that court.

I am so sick of being vulnerable and powerless. In the fae world, I was the master of my own fate. A force to be reckoned with. I was treated with the same respect as the men.

Opening that portal tonight was hard, but I did it without straining my power. Maybe I can open another, and find my way back to Aldrin.

Leaving him was the biggest mistake I have ever made.

I must fall asleep at some point, because I wake suddenly, my chambers still doused in darkness except for a few fire orbs hovering in the corners of the ceiling.

Caitlin is asleep on a recliner, a thin blanket tossed over her, my silent sentinel. She must have found out about my return after I fell asleep and decided she would be right here for me if I woke up crying in the middle of the night.

Guilt ripples through me as I get out of bed and tiptoe around her, throwing on a woolen riding dress and cloak. I don't wake her, not even as I soundlessly close my bedroom door.

My blood races as I tiptoe through empty corridors and out into the cool night air.

I slip into the shadows of an alcove as a patrol of two guards passes by on the wall above me, then I make my way through the maze of alleys and narrow passageways that connect the main courtyards, dipping in and out of the servants' quarters.

I reach the narrow servants' gate at the back of the wall that leads to a herb garden and unlock it easily by shifting the air within the mechanism.

When the guards pass their rotation on the wall, I dart out across the exposed space and into the tree cover beyond.

Thoughts crash through my head as I run between the orchards. Blood pumps so loudly in my ears it is deafening. I cannot think straight. Pure panic floods me. Raw need.

I claw my fingers down my face and across my temples as my feet take me to the Old Fae Garden. Mud flicks up from my boots, across the hem of my dress, leaving cold splatters on my shins.

I need to open the portal to Aldrin before the congregation of priestesses arrives at my home and I am locked within their clutches forever. I have to at least try, no matter how terrible the idea is. How unlikely.

Thorns tear at my skin and snag my clothes as I force a way through the ancient garden. It is almost pitch black, the moon already beneath the horizon.

I stumble over thick roots snaking across the gravel path and glance up to the cascading branches of the weeping willow right before my face. They are a dark outline against the night, but a breeze kicks up and the dull gleam of moonstone is visible through the parting branches.

The feel of the hanging leaves against my outstretched arm guides me around the tree, to the portal.

To both portals.

I skid to a stop before them. One has the words "Royal Palace" engraved in the stone. The other, "Fae Interchange."

My heart leaps.

It leads to the hundreds of portals where I made my crossing into the Spring Court. It was an interchange for trade and migration between the realms when we were at peace with the fae.

I grip the moonstone portal, but it takes time to focus enough to summon my magic. The stone pulls the fire of my power from me, and this time I don't hold back, flooding it quickly.

Blinding light erupts from the portal, painful in its intensity. Mists swirl within, and I don't hesitate a moment. I run beneath that arch and through the landscape of clouds, until I am staggering on uneven ground on the other side.

I am at the site of the pilgrims' crossing. The portal behind me is a beacon illuminating the ground of moss and slate near the stone circle of towering rough-hewn arches.

That foreboding tower slices through the dimness at their center, the jade plinth dull and powerless. I draw in the magic reserve from the portal at my back, closing it.

My eyes fly to the rows upon rows of portals leading to the fae world, cut into the steep hillside. I walk toward them as though each step is propelled forward by a sharp current.

A shiver runs down my spine as I stand before the moonstone gateway that took me straight to Aldrin so many months ago. It is as though fate itself brought us together. The very depths of my soul pull me toward it. Aldrin might still be at the Frozen River Fortress.

I would wander his realm for years in the hope of finding him.

I fall to my knees, not caring that the dampness of the moss seeps into my dress or that sharp edges of stone dig into my legs. My breaths are short and labored as anxiety ripples through me like fire. I reach out and put my hands on the portal.

I open all of me to the portal, pushing out huge jets of magic until my hands, then arms, are illuminated by the flow of it. I pour my very essence into it.

My legs go numb beneath me.

My fingers tingle, then burn.

The sensation travels up my arms, becoming painful, but I don't stop. By the time that scouring pain reaches my shoulders, my chest, my spine, I think I can't bear any more of it. Thousands of red-hot needles poke into my body, biting and stinging and aching. I cry out, but I don't stop.

More. I need more power.

Aldrin said I could do this if I removed the block on my magic.

My heart bleeds with the desire to open this passageway. It twists painfully. I don't care if I die trying to do it. I *need* to get back to him.

The pain hits a crescendo, and the world spins around me. That numbness creeps through me until I can't feel my entire body, but at least the pain is gone.

"Aldrin!" I scream. "Take me *home*, Aldrin!"

My pleading does nothing. The portal drags at my soul, pulling out everything I have to give, yet its milky arches only glow faintly. The vibrating hum of the moonstone resonates in my ears, engulfing me until I can't hear anything else, but it no longer grows in volume.

Blackness creeps in from the corners of my vision. My grasp on all that power slips, and it ricochets violently back into me. My essence feels like it has been tossed across a room and slammed into a wall. Thrown off a cliff and dashed upon sharp rocks.

My body crumples into the moss, limp.

Heaving sobs rip through me, constricting my chest and making it near impossible to breathe. I scream and scream incoherently, while my mind flounders.

His realm is too far away. I cannot find my way back to him.

I have defied so many odds, and it still wasn't enough.

"Please. Please. Please," I moan. "Aldrin, pleeease."

I slap at the moonstone until my palms burn, hating it so much for keeping us apart. Hating myself even more for being stupid enough to leave him.

The flash of energy leaves me and I crumple against the dormant portal. My eyes burn from the salt of my tears and are so swollen I can hardly see.

"Aldrin, how do I find my way back to you?"

The night is mild enough that I am at no risk of suffering from exposure. Perhaps I could sleep here and try again in the morning. Fatigue is like a heavy blanket, smothering my senses and dragging me down and down.

Bony hands wrap around my shoulders and fingers clutch my chin, tilting my face up. For a single crazy moment I think it must be Aldrin, here to save me, but the silhouette is far too small to be him.

"Come, child. It cannot be done," a familiar voice rings out, filled with warmth and understanding. "So many have tried before you."

"High priestess, would you like me to move her?" another asks.

All I can think is that I'm not ready to leave the portal. My mind scrambles, but my limbs are too tired to follow the command to grip the stone arch.

"Yes. Bring her down to the pass…and thank our sentries for

alerting me straight away. There is always at least one who tries to go back."

Weaves of air wrap around me and ever so gently lift me from the ground. My hair and arms fall limply out of that magical embrace. The soft swaying as I am carried away lulls me in and out of unconsciousness.

I thought I had cried out all of my tears, that nothing could hurt me this badly again, but I found a new rock bottom to my grief. I live in a world of turmoil and agony in the half-dreams that consume me.

# CHAPTER 39

# KEIRA

I blink up at a silvery sky, pierced with the light of dawn. Hopelessness floods me as I lie limp on a bed of moss beneath the stone circle.

Warmth spreads throughout my body, burning within my chest and leaking to the tips of my extremities. I am being healed. A priestess with large eyes and black hair hovers over me, pulling back as I sit up.

"You were almost completely depleted," she says softly. "Using too much magic is an immense strain on the body. It can cause your heart to give out."

She doesn't know that my heart has already been shattered to pieces.

I pull myself to my feet and my grandmother stalks over to me, her old body still moving with all the grace of a cat. Her bony fingers clutch my chin and twist my face both ways, as though inspecting cattle.

"You look far better than the sorry state we found you in. I take it you did not enjoy your time in the palace? That you have not been adjusting to life back in this realm?" she asks.

"It didn't go well. Finan doesn't like that I have a brain and a spine." I clench my fists until my fingernails bite into the soft flesh.

"Foolish man. I never liked that spoiled brat. He did this to you?" My grandmother brushes her fingers across my throat and I nod. Her lips twist in a flash of rage. "I will make him pay, don't you worry about that, and I will enjoy every moment of it. Do you feel up to walking to the temple?"

"Yes, thanks to…" I turn to the priestess with dark hair.

"Clivia," my grandmother says, and the woman nods an acknowledgment to me.

"While we walk, tell me about this fae man you were trying to get back to." Her tone is carefully neutral. That alone, in this woman who has strong opinions about everything, is enough to make me weary. Along with the fact that her first question wasn't about how I got here.

My stomach rolls in nervous anticipation.

Shame should flood me at being caught trying to abandon my realm for the fae world, but my need for him is too strong to feel anything else.

I think for a long while as we take a paved path that cuts through the slate hills and leads away from the portal interchange, deeper into the forest.

"Aldrin wasn't anything like you warned me, Grandmother," I say. "I tried to be so careful, to anticipate his betrayal at every turn, but it never came. He treated me with respect, like an equal. When I told him I was leaving his realm, he personally escorted me to the portal. He let me go, even though it broke him. Never once did he try to hold me against my will, or manipulate or control me."

My grandmother's fingers dig deeper and deeper into the flesh of my elbow as she guides me along the path, her features twisting downward in a snarl.

I bite my lower lip. "He has the kindest heart of anyone I have met. I fell for him, and in the end, it was I who betrayed him when he was at his most vulnerable." A sickness fills me at the admission. One born of bitterness and self-loathing.

"You came to love him. To trust him and his intentions," she states. The tendons in her neck stand out and a muscle feathers in her jaw.

"Yes," I say simply.

A flash of violence ripples through her. I *need* her to believe me. To *help* me.

I turn wide eyes on her. "He seeks to bring peace and open trade between our people, and I believe he can achieve it."

My grandmother is silent for a long time, her teeth audibly grinding. "I am sorry, Keira, I truly am. Please understand that everything I do is in your best interests. That I have to make hard decisions that will protect our family and our kingdom."

"What do you mean?" A chill runs down my spine.

"No high fae is kind or acts selflessly, only for their own interests. They are ruthless, brutal and manipulative. The needs or desires of a human are nothing to them. We are objects to be used. It pains me that yet another man has taken advantage of your gentle heart."

"No." I freeze in the middle of the path, right where it opens up to the Sanctuary of Magic. "No. The old prejudices were wrong. I met so many high fae and they were not like that."

"Not like that?" My grandmother grips my arm tightly. "Don't forget that I made a pilgrimage too, Keira. I hoped you would be spared the rude awakening I had on mine, but it cannot be helped." I shake my head, but she cuts me off. "And don't tell me that Aldrin is different, because he is not."

My voice rises. "Aldrin would never—"

"He *did*, child!" She grits her teeth. "He became a crazed, possessive high fae and traveled to this realm to hunt you down. To claim what he believes is his and drag you back to the Otherworld, no matter what you want. He would force you to be his consort."

The whole world seems to stop as the blood drains from my head. "I don't believe it."

"Well, you better believe it, because he is here, as our prisoner," she barks, anger rippling through her taut muscles as she points a finger at the temple before us.

The pounding of blood in my ears is all I can hear.

Aldrin came for me. He heard me. Every night I cried for him while gripping my moonstone bracelet, and called for him to find his way to me. He heard me.

I don't believe he has transformed into a monster since I last saw him. That he would do anything against my will, even less that he would drag me away if I didn't want it.

He physically can't, not with the blood oath he made to me.

My grandmother watches me closely, examining my reaction. I hold her gaze. "Take me to him. I want to speak to Aldrin."

She lets out a long breath and her shoulders sag. "I will, child. I wish you didn't have to endure what I did and see the truth of him, but a bargain is a bargain."

My grandmother leads me into the priestesses' sanctuary before I can question her.

It is a natural green bowl carved between tall hills and encircled by dense forest. Dozens of small cottages dot the perimeter of the space, trails of smoke billowing from their chimneys and flower gardens clinging to the granite masonry. The edges of vegetable patches and orchards are just visible from behind the housing.

The temple stands tall in the heart of the Sanctuary of Magic, dwarfing all other buildings. It is a hybrid structure, grown from multiple trees with immensely thick trunks and branches that interweave to form walls, with stone blocks filling in the gaps.

Leadlight windows decorate the high reaches of the temple, depicting images of summer, autumn, winter and spring, night and day. Great stone arches and doorways peek out from between barky trunks. A circle of moonstone portals wraps around the temple, connecting priestesses' sanctuaries from across the kingdom.

It is so similar to a Watchtower Tree in design that pure longing for the Otherworld crashes through me.

There is a crowd around the temple. A ring of priestesses and druids, singing and chanting and funneling their magic into the small aquamarine plinths set into the building at regular intervals. A ward ripples around the temple and I realize this is how they are holding Aldrin.

My stomach turns sick at the thought. Panic grips me at the potential of him being harmed or mistreated. Could he be badly injured? How else could they contain him?

As we near the temple, my grandmother's grip around my arm tightens. "Keira, don't allow him to manipulate you with pretty little lies. Open your eyes and see him for what he truly is, just like you did with Prince Finan. Make your peace with it."

I nod, far too exhausted to argue with her. "I want to speak with him alone."

My grandmother releases my arm. "I know. He cannot physically harm you."

I whip my head toward her. "Why? What have you done to him?"

"Oh, nothing yet, but I have my plans. Go inside and see for yourself." She turns on her heel and stalks off.

Two priestesses guard the double doors of the temple, opening them as I approach.

The large space within the temple is illuminated with bright slices of color as rays of sunlight enter through the leadlight windows high above. They cast colorful patterns across the floors, the rows of long benches and the walls. There are sleeping figures laid out across those pews, hidden under their cloaks.

I freeze just inside the doorway.

At the opposite end of the aisle, Aldrin sits on the steps of the dais leading to the altar. He is hunched forward with his elbows braced on his knees, scowling at the ground. His dark hair is pulled up in a knot, and loose strands hang across his beautiful face.

Deep shadows play beneath his eyes, throwing the angles of his high cheekbones and his razor-sharp jaw into focus.

Those pointed ears I became so accustomed to almost seem foreign to me after being in my realm for weeks. I swallow the lump in my throat. No part of Aldrin should be foreign to me.

The doors boom shut behind me, and Aldrin finally glances up. When he sees me, his entire body turns rigid.

"Keira." He stands, reaching out an arm but not daring to move. "Is it really you?"

It is as though a spell is broken, and I race toward him, barreling into his arms. Aldrin wraps them around me and holds me hard against his chest, kissing my hair and touching my face.

Silent tears run down my cheeks, and I am laughing and sobbing at the same time. I cannot help it. He only crushes me harder to him, and I finally feel safe wrapped in his strong arms.

"I'm so sorry. Aldrin, I am so sorry I got you into this mess," I choke out. "I should never have left you. You came for me."

"Yes. I came." He brushes my hair from my face. "I heard you calling for me."

I pull away from him just enough to gaze into his eyes, which soften as they hungrily take in every detail of my face like a man dying of starvation. "How? How did you hear me?"

He pulls a leather thong from beneath his tunic, and its moonstone pendant glows in the morning light. "I took this from the portal. It is somehow connected to your bracelet. I think."

I don't know how that could possibly work, but right now, I don't care how Aldrin found his way to me, only that he did.

## CHAPTER 40

# ALDRIN

Relief crashes through my body so hard I think it will knock my feet out from under me. Keira is here, in my arms, gripping my waist tightly, as though neither of us can stand without the other.

Still, I cannot believe it.

Her body is so soft against mine, and I want to lose myself in every luscious curve of it. An earthy scent rises from her hair, like crushed leaves, and I pick some of the offending vegetation from it, smoothing those golden-red curls.

I have dreamed about this reunion for a long time. Almost three months, though it has only been a few weeks in her world.

Keira is everything.

I cannot exist without her.

I don't want to.

Those calls she made, filled with raw emotion and pain that poisoned my very soul—I could not ignore them. But if she asks me to leave, I will.

I am not the wild, possessed fae they believe me to be.

Insane?

Probably.

Lovesick and foolish? Most definitely.

But not toxic. Her needs will always be put before mine.

I finally loosen my hold on her. There is so much we need to talk about and we have very little time to do it. Those stunning hazel eyes look up at me with awe, and my heart lurches, because I have missed them so damn much.

I begin to say something, but all thought flies from my mind.

A ring of purple-black bruises wraps around her throat, the size and placement of a man's fingers attempting to choke her. It drives maddening fury to rear up within me like some ugly, feral beast.

I was not there to protect her.

"Who did this to you?" I growl as I trace my fingers along her throat. "I will kill that princeling with my bare hands. If he hurt you, I will hunt him across this realm." I shake with the effort of keeping all that anger inside.

Keira's hand flies up to the cursed marks. "Yes. Finan did this. You will be proud of me, Aldrin. I tossed him across the room and left him gagged and tied up in ropes of air." A slow smile fills her face.

"He deserves to be cut into tiny pieces." I have to force my gaze away from those marks, otherwise I will tear my way out of this temple and find him, but a sense of pride at her strength fills me.

It is not an easy thing, standing up to someone who has power over you.

"I created a mess, Aldrin. I'm in a lot of trouble with the crown."

"Self-defense should never create trouble for a woman." I tenderly run a hand across her cheek. My blood runs hot as a fire of rage flares bright within. "I'm going to kill him. I'll rip him from limb from limb, nice and slow, so he can't ever hurt you again."

Keira reaches up on the tips of her toes and kisses me. Her lips are warm and soft as they press against mine. I lose myself in the sweetness of them, forcing them open and sliding my tongue between her teeth. I run my hands through her hair as her lips caress mine.

Gods, I have wanted only this for so long.

She pulls her body closer to mine and I lift her off her feet, her legs immediately wrapping around my waist. Our kiss deepens with urgency as my hands run over every curve.

My heart feels like it will explode from tasting her again.

All I know is that I need more and more. It will never be enough. I could have a lifetime of this, and I will always want more.

I pull away from her lips and place kisses down her neck. "Fuck, I have missed you," I rumble into her soft, delicate skin.

"While this is a nice reunion and all, some of us in the room don't care for a show," Silvan snaps.

"Speak for yourself. I'm bored senseless," Drake laughs.

I could kill both of them in this moment.

Keira unravels herself from me and turns to them. "Drake! You're healed!"

"Yeah." He sits up from his makeshift bed on a long pew and his cloak falls to his waist. "Apparently it takes more than a Belladonna Assassin and their poisons to kill me."

"Hmmm. We couldn't get rid of you that easily," Silvan grumbles from the other side of the temple.

My people rise from their beds, and Drake, Klara, Silvan, Hawthorne, Zinnia and the rest crowd around, though they keep their distance from Keira.

It is fair. They do not know if she will support us, or be brainwashed by the other humans.

"You're all here," Keira says in shock. "Except Cyprien and Lilly."

"I couldn't risk Cyprien getting caught up here," I admit.

Those doe eyes turn on me. "And how did you get caught, Aldrin? Surely this temple and its wards can't truly contain you."

"Hah!" Drake laughs. "Well, *that's* a story."

I shoot him a dark look, then lead Keira away by the elbow to a private room behind the altar. The last thing I need is an audience.

I look at her nervously and run a hand through my hair. "Are you pleased to see me?"

Her eyebrows raise. "Am I pleased to see you? Can you not tell?" Her hands find their way to my chest. "I am here because I tried to open the portal *on my own* to get back to you, and utterly drained myself. Because I was crazy to leave you. I cannot live without you, Aldrin. I can't deny that any longer."

Tears prick my eyes at the surge of emotions, but I hold them back.

The gods know it felt like half my soul winked out of existence the moment she left. All I want is to take her in my arms, to taste her again and strip the clothes from her, but we don't have time.

I take Keira's hands in mine. "Do you still trust me?" When she nods, I quickly continue. "We have little time and there is a lot I have to tell you. You're right, this temple and their flimsy wards would not hold us, except I made a bargain with the high priestess."

Her mouth falls open. "My grandmother made a bargain with a high fae?"

"When we arrived here, we were spotted by their scouts." The words flow out of me in a rush. "Our options were to kill the priestess, kidnap her or attempt to evade the forces she would muster. You know my feelings on the former two methods, especially when I want an alliance with the humans, so we remained on the move, setting up camp in a different site each night. There were multiple skirmishes when they caught up with us, but we got away clean without hurting anyone."

I run a hand across my face. "We made it to Appleshield Castle, infiltrated the outer wall using Silvan and Zinnia's invisibility wards, but there was no sign of you there. You had already gone to the palace and we overheard guards speaking of your wedding to that princeling in two weeks. It killed me, Keira."

My throat tightens as that pain wells up within me. I have to swallow down the lump that forms. "You were in this kingdom's capital. I considered traveling to Sunbright City and infiltrating the palace itself just to speak to you, but the risk was too great. I had to bring you to me. So I came here to the Sanctuary of Magic and offered a bargain to the high priestess. She thought I had gone mad. A fae turned possessive and feral for a human woman. I hope you believe me; it is not true."

I can no longer look Keira in the eye.

I tricked and manipulated her grandmother, and maybe she won't be able to forgive me. Perhaps I am as bad as our reputation.

Keira takes my face in her hands and forces me to look at her. "What was the bargain you made, Aldrin?" Her voice is so tender, I want to crumple into her lap and tell her everything. How I grieved for her and thought I would never see her again.

"My bargain is that we cannot harm any human until the lord protector himself arrives to give us our sentence for trespassing, on the condition that I would speak to you in private first. Each of my people made the same oath. We cannot fight to defend ourselves. It was the only way I could see you."

Keira's rosebud mouth hangs open. "Do they know that you're powerful enough to walk out of here anyway?" She laughs. "You could simply tie them up. A favorite pastime of yours." She raises an eyebrow at me. Gods, I just want to kiss her again.

"My grandmother must think she can overpower you with Appleshield's forces when they arrive." She pauses for a long moment. "Does she know you are the King of the Spring Court?"

My heart stutters.

The high priestess knows exactly who I am, but I am not quite ready to broach that with Keira. I need a few more moments of her looking at me like I am her whole world before those revelations change it forever.

I lead her to a throne-like chair and sit her down in it, then kneel before her, so our eyes are level. "Don't marry that prince, I beg of you. He doesn't deserve you. Your husband should worship you every day. You should be cherished above all else, including a crown."

I grab both her small hands in mine. "I want you at my side, Keira. You would be a true partner, my equal. I will value your thoughts, needs and independence. Be *my* queen, not his. I have little to offer other than exile, but I will cherish you above all else. We can carve out a life in this realm in some remote corner, if that will make you happy. Or we can live out the dream we spoke of, uniting the humans and fae together. I will lead whatever life you want, so long as you are at my side."

Tears run freely down Keira's face and I reach up to brush them away. "Is the idea so terrible? I can leave now and cross back to my realm if you prefer?"

"No. Gods, no. I don't want you to leave." Keira laughs, tightening her grip on the hand she still holds. "But what of your dreams, Aldrin? Your court and your realm? You can't turn your back on your people."

"Ah, Keira, they don't want me. That much is clear. I spent enough time in exile that it doesn't matter anymore. Cyprien can be the steward to sit on my throne. I will only have to return to my realm for brief intervals from time to time, to help muster the lords to him and our cause. None of that is more important to me than you."

Her eyes sparkle as she takes me in, her fingers tracing the lines of my face. A rosy glow colors her cheeks and her lips part to say something, but the yelling of men's voices draws our attention to the main body of the temple.

"Are the Assassins of Belladonna still hunting you, Aldrin?" Keira stands and spins toward the door. "Could they have followed us here?"

"No," I say, standing and pulling her nearer. "I can guarantee the assassins will not cross into this realm." Nervous anticipation rolls through me. "Your father has arrived."

The color drains from her face. "My father."

"To give my death sentence, I expect." I can't help the bitterness that rises in my throat.

"I will not allow it." The tips of her hair flicker with embers.

She tries to march straight through that door to confront the lord protector herself, but I grab her arm and pull her back. "Keira. The prophecy. There is more I haven't told you."

She shoots me an incredulous look. "We don't have time to talk about prophecies right now, Aldrin. I need to de-escalate this before an outright battle breaks out. You don't understand my father's temper when he thinks one of his own is under attack."

She is right. I have run out of time.

By their laws, they should execute us right where we stand. I will not allow it.

Cold dread washes through me, and not for the army outside. She needs to understand. Hear it from me. Or I will lose her.

"Keira, please. Let me explain. Just a few more moments. This is not the first time—"

A resounding crash echoes through the temple and we race into its main body to find the great doors flung open. Rows of human archers with iron arrows nocked and pointed at us are visible beyond the wide doorway.

I pull Keira behind my body as I approach, taking cover from that threat of fire beyond the walls of the temple. My warriors stand ready among the pews, air shields rippling before them.

"High fae of the Otherworld. I summon you out of our sacred temple to hear your judgment and sentence for trespassing into this realm," a deep, masculine voice booms, brought to us upon an amplifying air wield. It bounces off the walls of the temple.

Keira steps out from behind me, straight into the aisle and line of fire. I try to grab her and pull her back to safety, but she simply smiles at me.

"They won't harm me, Aldrin. I know every one of them." She points at the dozens of archers. "That's my father out there. Let me talk to him."

I hate it.

I absolutely hate the idea of hiding behind her. Of putting her before me, into the line of fire, but she makes sense.

I want to give her everything, to make her happy, and that includes a life with her family in it, so we need to win them over. But I will not allow her to go alone.

"Stay close to me, Keira. I could not bear it if they snatched you away and took you somewhere that I couldn't reach you."

I follow her to the doors, building an air shield before us, layer after layer until it is an inch thick. My people add their magic to my own, fortifying it until neither arrow nor sword could penetrate my defense.

I don't trust those archers. A single one of them could get spooked, and loose an arrow that finds its way to Keira instead.

An entire army amasses within the natural bowl of the sanctuary, with hundreds of soldiers behind the archers, all in a uniform of emerald surcoats and brown leather pants. I am sure there are just as many hidden within the trees and I do not discount the power of the priestesses and druids.

It could be a bloody fight to retreat from this, especially when I cannot harm a single one of them. But I never promised I wouldn't tie them up.

A man mounted on a black stallion sits at their head, and he is a truly imposing figure. The lord protector has Keira's fiery red hair that blows in the wind, with a short beard to match and a deep green gaze.

Those eyes narrow with deadly intent as they fall on me.

Recognition glows within them.

Keira tries to step over the threshold of the temple, and I grab her around the waist and hold her back.

"I can't follow you beyond here," I whisper in her ear. The building still offers us some cover. It means I don't have to hold this draining shield to my back or sides.

"Take your damn hands off my daughter!" the lord protector roars, and my hands slip away, as though they follow his command instead of my own. "Keira! Come to me, sweetheart. Stand behind our soldiers where you will be safe from him. You do not understand who he is."

"Father, he will not harm me," Keira calls out. "Aldrin has not come to kidnap me, but to make me an offer I can accept or decline of my own free will. The high fae are not what you think they are."

"Sweetheart, come here and we can talk about it." There is an edge of true fear in the man's voice. He must think I am a monster here to devour his daughter.

Keira does not move. Instead, her back becomes ramrod straight. "On my pilgrimage, Aldrin was a true friend. He helped me and protected me. He even saved my life a couple of times." I cringe, because I only saved her from the danger I put her in.

"You don't know this man." There is a hint of hysteria on the lord protector's face. "Not like you think you do."

The blood drains from me. Every single muscle in my body ripples with tension, and I think I am going to be sick.

This is the moment of truth.

Edmund is going to reveal the one damned thing I never got the chance to tell her. Because I ran out of time. Because I am a coward. This is the worst possible way for Keira to find out what I have kept secret.

"Nor do you!" Keira bellows back, finally losing her patience.

"Has Aldrin told you we have met before, he and I? That this isn't his first venture into Appleshield lands?" her father spits.

Keira whirls on the spot, staring at me with huge, vulnerable eyes and an unspoken question on her lips.

"Aldrin. King of the Spring Court." The lord protector barks my title as though it is a curse. "I told you I would kill you if you ever returned to my lands. If you tried to take my second daughter again."

"What is he saying?" Keira's face is incredibly pale.

Words escape me.

"This high fae visited our realm decades ago." Edmund moves his stallion closer to us, as though he intends to grab his daughter and pull her away from me. "To negotiate a peace treaty between our lands. He wanted open trade and migration. I was fool enough to entertain those notions, despite the treason to our crown, until he suggested a marriage to solidify the alliance. This fae wanted my second daughter to take as his consort back to the Otherworld. He wanted you, Keira. He has clearly been hunting you ever since."

Dread pumps through me.

Nothing matters but the woman before me.

Keira stares at me as though I am a stranger, or the demon the rest of the humans believe me to be.

She takes a step away from me. "Is this true, Aldrin?" she half whispers.

It shatters my very soul to see her recoil from me.

My breath catches in my throat. "It wasn't like that. I didn't come here looking for a consort, just the negotiations, but the prophecy came to my sister in a vision while we were in these lands, and I thought she saw my future wife in them. I thought she saw my m—"

"Why didn't you tell me you had been here? That you had tried to *take* me before?" Keira screams at me, taking another step backward. There is such fear in her eyes as those prejudices I worked so hard to break lock back into place. It is like a knife twists in my chest. "How can I trust you, Aldrin?"

My chest tightens to the point of pain. "I didn't know you were the same person when we first met. And then, I never found the right time to tell you. Gods, I tried so many times."

"He would have dragged you away as a child!" Edmund roars, adding fuel to the fire burning between us.

"No!" I take a step toward Keira. "Never!"

How do I tell her that when Lorrella saw the beautiful woman that would fight at my side, curvaceous and with fire-red hair, we all believed she had found my mate? That her visions were tricky, sometimes set in the past or distant future, but often they told tales only weeks or months before they transpired?

We thought the lord protector's daughter was a woman grown when I enquired about her, not a fragment of the future that hadn't been conceived yet. Edmund had been childless at the time.

It is not uncommon in my realm to seal a diplomatic agreement by suggesting a marriage. The choice always would have been hers to make in the end.

When I found her in my realm, stepping out of the portal into that battle with the spriggan and Cyprien, I didn't know she was the same person. The one whose world was fated to collide with mine. I have no doubt her pull on me is the reason I unwittingly made my way to the portal that day.

I am not a crazed fae.

I didn't enter this realm to kidnap or harm her, but from the look she gives me, she isn't so sure anymore.

"This fae has marked you as his, Keira, and he will not stop hunting you. It is what his kind does," her father bellows.

The high priestess fights her way out of the line of soldiers and faces Keira from across the field. "I once loved a high fae as well, child. Do not forget what he did to me."

It is like a spell is broken. Tears run freely down Keira's face, twisted with utter betrayal.

I reach out an arm to her. "You *know* me, Keira. You know the oath I made to you. Let me explain."

She takes another step backward, away from me, and it breaks my fucking heart. It shatters the entirety of my soul to pieces.

My hands shake, because I cannot lose her. Not again. Not over this. There is an entire army threatening me, but all I can focus on is her.

"I would never have—" Something hits me hard in the chest, making me stagger backward a step.

My eyes dart to my air shield. It shatters before me like a pane of glass, the shards falling and dissipating.

I dropped the threads of magic for a heartbeat when Keira looked at me like I was her enemy. The powerful blow of magic that destroyed it links all the way back to the lord protector himself.

He is more fae than he realizes.

In the same instant, two closely following impacts slam into my chest. Time slows. Each second drags out for a lifetime. My body is thrown backward and my legs collapse beneath me. Searing pain explodes within my chest right before my shoulders hit the ground.

Keira screams my name, but I can't see her. Her hysteria turns incoherent, becoming muffled and quieter, as though someone is dragging her away.

My hand flies to the two arrow shafts protruding from my chest and comes away sticky with hot blood. I cough and it drizzles out of my mouth. Agony ripples through me with each shallow breath, threatening to plunge me into unconsciousness, but I have to stay awake and make sure Keira is safe. For a moment, I forget why she is wailing.

The arrows. There are two of them, laced with poison.

I can feel the toxin's bite, burning at the wound where it enters my blood, slowing my heart rate and muddling my thoughts until they move so sluggishly I am hardly aware of what is happening.

Keira doesn't come to me.

I don't know if it is because she no longer wants to or if she is being held back. Perhaps both. I crave her gentle touch more now than I ever have in my life.

The panels of the temple roof slide across my vision. I am being dragged, roughly. Pain rips through me anew with each tug, as the arrowheads protruding from my back catch on the floorboards. I cry out. Klara's face hovers above mine and she says something as she frantically works over me, but it is all so far away and none of it matters anymore.

I lost Keira.

She will never forgive me and I will never have an opportunity to show her I am not the monster they believe me to be. Everything, absolutely everything, has been taken away from me.

The sounds of battle fill my ears and the static of magic crackles all around me. I recognize familiar voices in the fray, yelling orders at each other, but I can't remember why we are fighting. Where we are.

A deep black void tugs at my consciousness, pulling me down and down into a numbing peace where there is no pain. Claws of nothingness close over my mind and as they take me, the agony lessens until it is a distant memory.

~

I swim in that complete oblivion for the longest time, floating on the tide of a dark ocean.

When I peel my eyes open again, the entire world spins so violently I have to shut them immediately. The throbbing in my chest is a dull ache. I try to raise my hand to it, but my limbs are too leaden to move.

I drift off again, and rouse sometime later. My throat is painfully dry and my mouth feels like it is stuffed with cotton.

I sit up ever so slowly, my arms weak and trembling. There is a heavy weight on them. A tinkling sound reaches my ears, but it makes no sense. I squint in the dimness and turn my head to take in my surroundings, but the darkness of oblivion creeps back in and I almost pass out again.

I push my back against the wall and hold completely still, taking stock of my situation. The pain in my chest is almost gone, which means I have been here for long enough to recover from a severe wound by a weapon that inhibits my healing.

My mind is slow, and I constantly lose the strands of my thoughts. I sit on a basic pallet bed, but it is clean. This room is small, with stone walls and floors. A high, barred window lets in the moonlight and shows a slice of the night sky. There are no other furnishings.

My clothes have been changed, and my moonstone pendant is gone. I have no way to speak to Keira, if she would even hear me.

It takes a long time to muster up the courage to look down and acknowledge the weight in my lap. A chain stretches from the manacles on my wrists to the wall behind me.

I reach for air magic to move the pins and levers inside the tumbler of the lock and find exactly what I suspected. My power is blocked. I am utterly vulnerable. Helpless, in a realm that hates my kind.

I am in the lord protector's dungeon, drugged, with my magic stolen from me. I don't know if the rest of my people are dead or imprisoned like myself. They followed me into oblivion itself, because I couldn't let the woman I love go. I never deserved their unyielding loyalty.

Keira will not save me.

Not after that look on her face as she backed away from me. I lay my head down against the rough stone wall and wait for my sentence. I am done fighting. I have nothing left to lose.

THE END

# LOVED THE FORBIDDEN FAE KING?

DOWNLOAD THE FREE PREQUEL

A
## HEART
OF
## TWO REALMS

..................................................

~

..................................................

GET YOUR COPY OF BOOK TWO

A
## WAR
OF
## THREE KINGS

# A HEART OF TWO REALMS

## A DYING LANDS PREQUEL

## ROSA HEART

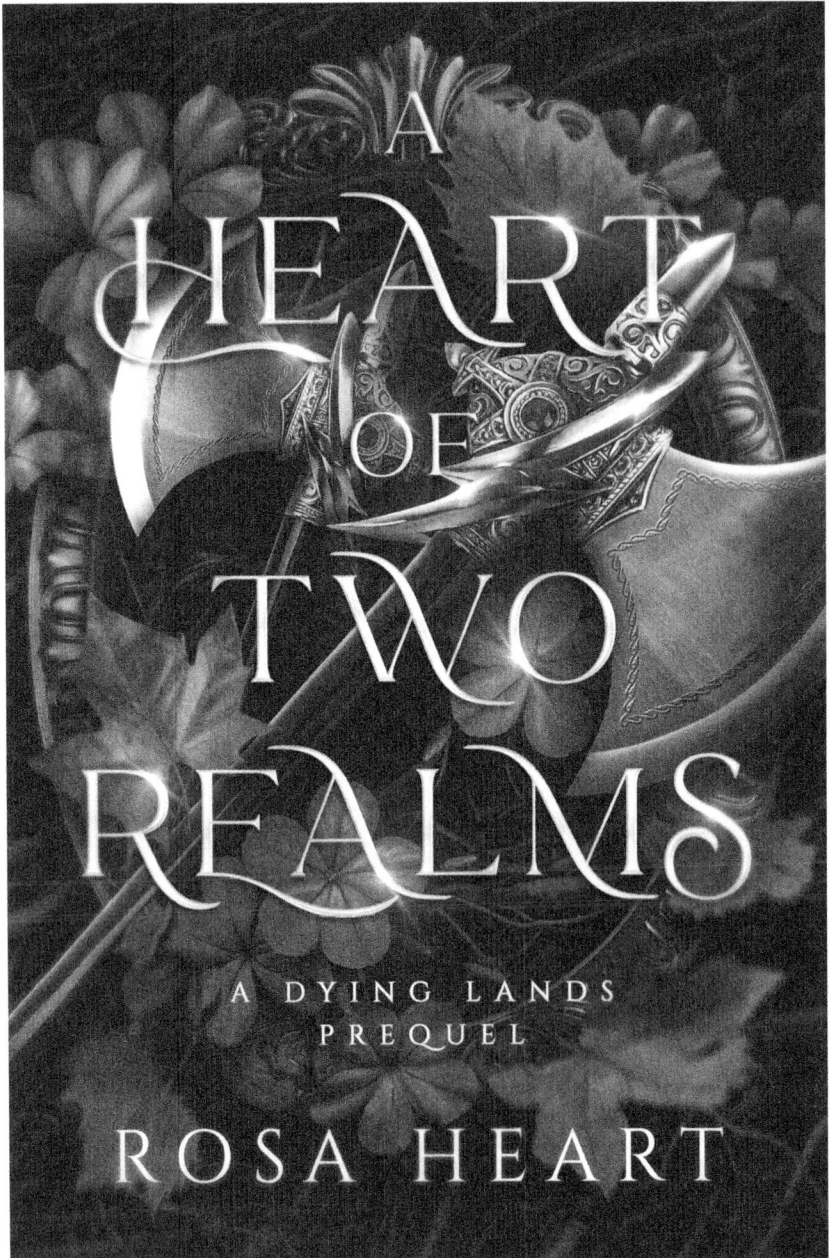

DOWNLOAD FOR FREE AT

www.rosaheart.com

# A Heart of Two Realms

## A DYING LANDS PREQUEL - FREE EBOOK

Go back in time to read the story of Keira's grandmother's pilgrimage. It is a tale of forbidden love between a young Naomi, a poor huntress, and Ronan, the Lord Protector's heir.

### DOWNLOAD FOR FREE AT

www.rosaheart.com

**A powerful lord. A dangerous fae. Both want Naomi, a lowborn huntress, but neither will share her, even if it means fighting to the death.**

The human and fae realms collide every seven years, and monsters slip through the tears between worlds. When a horde of goblins attack Naomi's hometown, she prepares to fight. The last thing she expects is Lord Ronan and his elite band of fae hunters to arrive on the eve of battle.

**Lords use and abuse peasants like Naomi. They don't risk their lives for them.**

But Lord Ronan is different. Charming. Compassionate. Beautifully lethal with a blade. And he can't seem to keep his hands off her.

When he offers her a life-changing opportunity to join his personal guard, she finds herself falling for him. A forbidden love with a lord would be Naomi's utter ruin, unless she takes the sacred pilgrimage into the deadly fae lands and returns as a priestess.

Naomi doesn't count on meeting Nissien in the intoxicating autumn court and having her heart stolen by a second man. A fae who is vicious and passionately sensual. Whose immense power has even his friends cowering.

Naomi must choose one man and one realm, but events spiral out of her control and her two worlds collide in the most devastating way.

**Only one man can live, and Naomi must decide who will die.**

# A WAR OF THREE KINGS

## DYING LANDS
## BOOK TWO

## ROSA HEART

# A WAR OF THREE KINGS

## DYING LANDS BOOK 2

Release Date 7th Feb 2025

**He stole her heart then broke it with his lies and betrayal. She must choose between forgiveness or leaving him to rot in her father's prison.**

Aldrin was revealed to be everything Keira fears from the fae; dangerous, possessive, and toxic enough to steal a human woman. He has been hunting her for decades to keep her as his slave and consort—except, that story makes little sense to Keira. Not when he let her leave him and his realm behind forever.

Before Keira can decide if she will allow Aldrin back into her heart, her trust and her bed, war arrives at her door. The mad king Finan ravages his own kingdom to get his clutches on Keira and he will stop at no atrocity to repossess her.

**If he succeeds, it won't ruin only her life. The North will fall. Her family will be destroyed.**

Keira's only protection, the single reason the lords of the North stand with her family against their king, is because she has dedicated herself to the temple. To ravish her would be sacrilege—except, she might want Aldrin to ravish her.

**As Aldrin fights for Keira's freedom, like the feral fae he is accused of being, their passionate flame threatens to reignite. If the secret is discovered, it may very well burn them all.**

Printed in Great Britain
by Amazon

57982553R00258